"Why did you do it?" Nick asked

Without any conscious forethought, he had voiced his anger, his tone cutting. "Why did you think you had to try and save me?"

The silence was brittle and foreboding, threatening the uneasy truth. Sydney didn't even pretend to misread his sudden hostility. As she turned to face him. Anger glinted in her eyes. "What do you want from me? A declaration of guilt? An apology? My conscience on a platter? What? If there was any penitence I could do to absolve me of my sins, I would. Believe me, I would. But damn it, I can't. I'm stuck with them."

"Why did you leave me when I loved you so?" he asked softly.

She went stock-still, and she stared at him, her anger diffused by the unexpectedness of his question.

"You want to know why I left?" she ground out. "Then I'll tell you. I left because I loved you. I left because I loathed myself. But most of all, I left because I was carrying your child."

ABOUT THE AUTHOR

Novelist Judith Duncan spent almost a year researching her eighth Superromance, *Streets of Fire*. The facts she uncovered about the harsh life of the inner city often reduced her to tears. "I now have a very stark insight into why there are so many kids on the streets and what's happened to them to drive them there," she says. Married for 29 years to a telecommunications consultant with a major oil company, Judith has five children in their late teens and early twenties. A dyed-in-the-wool Western Canadian, she was born in Saskatchewan and raised in rural Alberta. In addition to being a voracious reader, Judith is also a popular lecturer when she is not hard at work writing.

Books by Judith Duncan

HARLEQUIN SUPERROMANCE
143–WHEN MORNING COMES
196–INTO THE LIGHT
251–ALL THAT MATTERS
291–BEGINNINGS

Streets of Fire

JUDITH DUNCAN

Harlequin Books

TORONTO • NEW YORK • LONDON
AMSTERDAM • PARIS • SYDNEY • HAMBURG
STOCKHOLM • ATHENS • TOKYO • MILAN

Published June 1990

ISBN 0-373-70407-0

To those individuals and organizations in Calgary who assisted with background research for *Streets of Fire*

My thanks to:
Betsy Brown, Executive Director,
Association for the Rehabilitation of the Brain Injured, for providing compassionate, informative insight;

Kaye Brock, President,
Head Injured Relearning Society, for opening doors;

Child Focus, for assisting with the psychological background on sexually abused kids.

My very special thanks to:
Randy Fowler, for sharing his story with me, and to S., for sharing hers;

Nancy Roher, editor, for her encouragement;

Grace and Ilona, for their unwavering support, and for the time and effort they dedicated to this manuscript.

CHAPTER ONE

SYDNEY FOSTER STOOD with her shoulder resting against the frame of the one-way glass, a cup of coffee in her hand, her arms folded in front of her. A hollow feeling of déjà vu washed over her as she watched the young girl in the interrogation room. It was as though she'd been dragged back into an old nightmare, and her face was taut as she experienced emotions she thought she'd put behind her forever. Seeing the girl had started a chain reaction that was stripping away years of rigidly disciplined thoughts, years of not allowing herself to think back beyond self-imposed barriers. She'd managed to seal off that part of her mind, then fate had turned her willful hand, and the past overlaid the present like a twice-exposed photograph.

She turned as her lawyer entered the room. Forcibly divorcing herself from her grim thoughts, she glanced at him, her eyes unreadable. "How did it go?"

Norm Crandall set his briefcase down on one of the wooden chairs along the back wall, then raised his head, a look of exasperation on his face. "Would you mind telling me what in hell's going on?"

Sydney took another sip of the lukewarm coffee and carefully placed her cup on the ledge along the glass, her voice impassive. "I want you to represent her."

"I did make it through law school, Sydney," he retorted, his tone edged with a mixture of irritation and sarcasm. "I more or less figured that out by myself. Now would you tell me what in hell you're doing here, and why you want me to represent some kid dragged in off the street?''

There was a determined look in her eyes as she turned to face him, her jaw set. Her voice was deceptively calm when she answered him. ''They apprehended the two men I caught stealing the stereo out of my car, so they asked me to come down to identify them.''

''And you were here when she was brought in.''

''Yes.''

He exhaled heavily and dragged his hand across his face. ''Do you know what you're doing?''

''Yes.''

''Look, I think we should talk about this. I really don't think you've thought this through.''

There was a hard edge of finality in her voice. ''This is *my* decision, Norman.''

He stared at her for several moments, then conceded with a weary sigh. ''Okay. You're the boss.''

Wry amusement softened her expression as she folded her arms and leaned back against the frame. ''It's worth every cent I pay you to hear you admit that once in a while.''

The exasperated look on Norm Crandall's face relaxed into a reluctant grin as he picked up his overcoat and slipped it on. ''Yes, and you make sure I earn every damned penny.''

Sydney's answering smile was somewhat distracted, and Norm frowned slightly as she straightened and turned, her arms still folded tightly in front of her as she stared into the interrogation room. Her voice was carefully modulated when she finally spoke. ''How old is she?''

Norm absently slapped his leather gloves against the palm of his hand as he assessed both his client and the situation. ''Her ID says she's eighteen, but I'm sure it's false. I doubt if she's a day over fifteen. She's had two prior arrests and has been working the streets for at least two years.''

A swirling sensation made Sydney's senses swim, and she caught the frame to steady herself. There was a brief silence, then she picked up her own coat and pulled it on, the deep cherry red at odds with the drab, colorless room. "What's she charged with?"

"Soliciting and possession."

There was an implacable expression on Sydney's face as she looked at her attorney. "I want her out of here, Norm. And I want her out of here as soon as possible."

The senior partner of Crandall, Crandall and Lewis leaned back against the wall, his years wearing heavily on his weathered face as he watched her with narrowed eyes. "Look, Sydney, I know you don't want to hear this, but I think you should reconsider. You have no idea what you're getting into. You donated a hunk of money toward establishing a halfway decent shelter for these kids, and that was a damned noble gesture, but you can't get involved in individual cases. That's why we've got social services, for God's sake."

She picked up her purse and scarf from the chair, then gave the older man a level look. "I'm not getting involved in individual cases. I am getting involved in this one."

"Why? Lord, woman, you're thirty-seven years old. You don't start operating on impulse at this stage in the game. You don't know anything about this kid."

She gave him a grim smile. "I know more than you think."

He exhaled sharply, then picked up his briefcase, a hint of humor underscoring his exasperation. "Have I ever told you what a pain in the ass you are when you get an idea in your head?"

There was a glimmer of amusement in her eyes as she opened the door and held it for him. "Don't whine, Norman. It doesn't become a man of your stature."

He gave a derisive snort as they turned and walked down the corridor. "I'm not whining."

"Yes, you are," she said as she pulled open the door into the main squad room. "Besides, I didn't ask you to adopt her. I asked you to get her out of the slammer."

He shot her a piercing, half-amused look. "Yes, but I know you. Unless I miss my guess, I'll be up to my high-priced neck in street kids within a matter of weeks."

"Don't be such a skeptic."

He shook his head. "I have every reason to be skeptical. Somehow or another, you've managed to involve me in all your damned schemes. Fund-raising for the shelter, sitting on the board of directors for the rehabilitation program, free legal advice for the Society for the Homeless—hell, I'm lucky if I make it home for dinner three nights a week."

Sydney gave his stocky build a thorough appraisal. "It doesn't look as if you're suffering much." She flashed him a sudden grin. "And just think how much it's enriching your life."

"While rapidly depleting my bank account."

She laughed. "With the fees you charge, you can afford it."

He paused, a gleam of amusement in his eyes. "I think I'd better quit while I'm ahead." He set his briefcase down on the counter and opened it. "So what do you want me to do with her once I spring her?"

Sydney's expression sobered and she looked away, her voice brusque. "Take her over to Major Henderson at the Legion of Charity hostel. I'll give her a call as soon as I get back to the office. She'll find a place for her until we can work something out."

Norm Crandall frowned and shook his head. "I don't like this, Sydney. You're asking for trouble when you get personally involved. The rehabilitation program is a damned good example. Hell, the time and money you've dumped into that goes beyond the realms of mere social conscience. I'd hate to see you get that involved again.''

Sydney gave him a twisted smile, not a trace of humor in her eyes. ''I already am, Norman.'' She absently pulled on her kid gloves, temporarily lost in thought. Then, inhaling sharply, she glanced at him, her voice subdued. ''Give me a call when you find out something about her, will you, Norman?''

''I wish you'd take my advice on this one, Sydney,'' he counseled sternly. ''That's what you pay me for.''

She gave him another twisted smile. ''I know that.'' She paused and fiddled with the keys she held in her hand, then glanced back up at him, her gaze level. ''I know I'm sticking my neck out over this,'' she said quietly. ''A lot of things in life depend on the luck of the draw, and maybe all this kid needs is a chance.''

Rocking back on his heels, Norm studied her through half-closed eyes, his tone contemplative. ''You know, I've never been able to figure you out. Sometimes I think you're the softest touch in the country, a con man's dream come true, then I see you in action in the boardroom, and you make Margaret Thatcher look like a puffball. I'm never quite sure if you're Attila the Hun or Mother Teresa.''

There was a provoking gleam in Sydney's eyes. ''I'll make you a deal, Norm. Sometime when I'm not paying for your time in very expensive fifteen-minute blocks, I'll explain the fundamental differences between need and greed.''

Norm chuckled. ''Tell me, where does groveling fit in the fundamental scheme of things?''

She laughed aloud. ''You'd make a rotten groveler.'' She nodded at the sharp creases in his impeccably pressed suit pants. ''You might get lint on your knees.''

He checked a smile. ''Point taken.''

She gave him a significant look. ''A giant step for mankind.'' She glanced at the clock on the wall. ''I'd better get going. I have a meeting with some developers this evening, and I have some figures to go over first. I'll expect a call from you first thing tomorrow morning.''

"You won't reconsider."

"No."

His face indicated he was not happy with her decision, but he tipped his head in acquiescence. "I'm in court in the morning. I can leave a message on your office machine to let you know what Major Henderson comes up with."

She shook her head. "Make sure you use my private line. I don't want the office staff discussing this over coffee."

He acknowledged her instructions with a barely perceptible nod, his gaze thoughtful. She looked down, an air of preoccupation about her as she selected one key from the bunch clustered in the eel skin case. When she finally raised her head, her expression was solemn, her tone unusually husky. "Thank you, Norm."

He didn't say anything for a moment, then answered, "No problem. I'll talk to you tomorrow."

"Tomorrow, then." She raised her hand in a farewell gesture, and Norm Crandall nodded as he watched her depart through the big glass doors.

Large, thick snowflakes from the freak spring flurry settled in her dark hair and clung to the red fabric of her coat as she stepped onto the sidewalk. Dusk settled around her, isolating her solitary figure in the softly falling snow, and the lawyer frowned, trying to put his finger on what was so different about her tonight.

As she turned to check for oncoming traffic, a gust of wind caught her scarf and whipped the ends around her face. She brushed them aside, her face profiled by the leaden sky, and his frown deepened. The missing piece jigsawed into place. What he saw was thinly disguised desolation.

NICK NOVAK STARED out the window of Pete's Pizza Hut, his hands wrapped around a mug of steaming coffee, his mind not focusing as he watched the traffic pile up at the corner lights. The steady snowfall was turning Calgary's streets to slush, and the passing vehicles sent a muddy spray onto the sidewalk. Pedestrians hurried by, their heads bent against the huge white flakes.

There was a squeal of tires as a white van ran the changing light, and Nick automatically checked the license plate numbers as the vehicle sped by. His mouth twitched with a flicker of dark humor. Some habits died hard.

He let his gaze sweep the dimly lighted interior, then he hunched over the table and concentrated on his coffee, a cynical expression settling around his mouth. There was a time when he could have taken one look and given an accurate description of every person in the place. Now he was lucky if he could remember what damned color socks he'd put on that morning. One of life's little practical jokes. Served him right; he had been such an arrogant, smug-ass son of a bitch.

He took a sip of coffee, then looked out the window again. He wished the weather would quit screwing around. Five months of winter was enough to fry anyone's brains.

"Hey, man. Wanna buy some dirty pictures?"

Nick looked up as Tony Martinelli slid into the seat across from him, the familiar black toque slouched low on his forehead, his down-filled vest shedding feathers through the snags in the nylon fabric. As usual, his ex-partner needed a shave, and his jeans looked as if he'd spent the afternoon crawling around on some mechanic's garage floor.

When he responded, Nick's voice was a lazy drawl. "Dressed for dinner, I see."

Tony grinned as he flipped the plastic-coated menu from between the chrome napkin holder and the bottle of catsup. "You got it. I put on clean underwear this morning."

"I'm touched."

"Figured you would be. What are you having?"

"Coffee."

Tony glanced up and gave him a long, level look, then returned his attention to the menu. "Well, I'm having baked spaghetti, an order of garlic toast and Mama's deep-dish apple pie." He dropped the menu back in its place, then leaned back in his chair, devilry snapping in his eyes. "So how did it go with the Dragon Lady today?"

Nick gave him a warped grin. "I'd like to forget today, if you don't mind."

"That bad, eh?"

"That bad."

"Want to talk about it?"

"Not particularly."

"Hell, this is stacking up to be about as much fun as a night in the drunk tank."

That made Nick smile. "How's the new partner working out?"

Tony shrugged and looked away. "He'll be okay, I guess. It'll take some getting used to."

"What's the problem?"

Tony shrugged again, then met his old partner's gaze, a wry smile lifting one corner of his mouth. "Well, for one thing, he sure in hell isn't you. Wouldn't recognize an original idea if one kicked him in the ass. This guy looks like he just graduated from nerd school." The smile broadened. "The only good thing about him is he's uglier than sin, so at least the broads know I'm alive now."

Irony glinted in Nick's eyes. "Considering you don't exactly hang out at the Waldorf, I wouldn't get too excited about the kind of broads you run into."

"Hey, man, I take it where I can get it." Tony glanced up as the waitress paused beside their table, then looked back at Nick. "You sure you don't want something to eat?"

"Yeah, I'm sure."

Tony ordered, then dug a battered pack of cigarettes out of his vest pocket, tapped one out and tossed the pack onto the table. The smell of an American blend wafted up as he lit it, the smoke screening his face as he dropped the still burning match into the ashtray. He leaned back, a shrewd expression on his face as he studied the man across the table. "You look like you've got something on your mind. Somebody kick sand in your face today?"

Nick shot him an acerbic look, then shrugged. "I don't know about sand, but I have the feeling someone's been tossing dust."

Tony draped his arm across the back of the empty chair next to him, a knowing gleam in his eyes. "The old radar's still working, I take it."

"Maybe. Maybe not."

"So give me the lowdown."

Nick frowned, concentrating on organizing his thoughts. "I overheard the director from social services briefing her new replacement. Apparently Doc Robertson moved here from the States because somebody dangled a big carrot under his nose."

"What kind of carrot?"

"Substantial private funding and free rein to develop the program."

"No kidding. I thought the program was funded by social services and other service organizations."

"So did I. But this puts a different twist on it. The program has had so much press coverage and exposure, this silent-backer angle seems out of sync, somehow. It makes me wonder who's hiding what."

"Want me to check it out?"

There was pointed humor in Nick's expression. "I could stand to find out."

Tony chuckled as he folded his arms and hunched over the Formica tabletop, the smoke from his cigarette spiraling upward. "Just remember—if I fall into a big can of worms on this one, it's my ass on the line, not yours."

Nick grinned. "Just don't go thrashing around like a bull in a china shop, Martinelli. You might trip over some very prominent toes."

"Thanks, buddy. Just what I need, to stomp on some big shot's corn."

Tony butted out his cigarette as the waitress appeared with his dinner, setting the steaming dish on the paper place mat.

The amusement faded abruptly from Nick's expression. Sometimes it all seemed like a bad dream. Sometimes there were spaces when he'd forget what had happened, forget everything. But then he'd be hit with the hard, cold reality, and panic would seize him. And of all the things he'd had to fight against, panic was the worst. It had the power to pull him under. And that scared the hell out of him.

Unconsciously tightening his hand around his mug, Nick forced himself to disconnect his mind, and he glanced out the window, his face set in rigid lines. The sullen sky had settled lower, reducing everything to a monochromatic dreariness, and he stared out, lulled by the falling snow.

As long as he didn't allow himself to think ahead, to think about the future, he could control the panic. He had become a day-to-day survivor. In the beginning he had endured the pain, minute by minute, then he'd endured the nearly suffocating sense of helplessness, hour by hour. Now he simply endured.

There were still times when he wished Tony had never found him in that damned alley. But he couldn't think about that, either, or the stark reality of the life sentence he was facing would be intolerable. One day at a time. He could only face one day at a time.

Tony's voice was quiet, with a slight hint of censure. "What are you thinking about, Nick?"

Nick met his friend's gaze, managing an almost convincing grin as he lied. "That I'm damned glad I'm not sitting some drug bust tonight."

"As if the weather ever made a damned bit of difference to you." Pushing his empty plates aside, Tony downed the last of his beer, then made a halfhearted attempt to muffle a belch as he set the emptied can back on the table. "How about a movie?"

Nick could feel the onset of fatigue beginning to affect him, and he knew better than to ignore it. "Not tonight. I think I'd better hit the sack early."

Sticking a toothpick in his mouth, Tony picked up the bill, shoved his chair back and stood up. He caught Nick's coat from the back of the chair and waited as Nick unhooked his cane from the window ledge.

Nick almost smiled as he got to his feet, aware that Tony was hovering like a mother hen and pretending he wasn't. He had to give Tony credit. There had been more than one occasion when Nick's frustration had exploded in a vile temper, but Tony never batted an eye. Sometimes his unflappable patience irritated the hell out of Nick, but on the other hand, there was something to be said for the cop's warped sense of humor. He had salvaged Nick's macho pride more than once with a smart-ass comment.

Nick braced his weight on his cane as he shifted to compensate for his nearly useless left leg, then turned. Pushing the chair out of his friend's way, Tony grinned as Nick faced him. "Hey, Myrtle, wanna dance?"

"Up yours, Martinelli." Intently focusing on making his muscles respond, Nick turned and took a step into the aisle. Stabilizing his balance, he let Tony arrange the left sleeve of the leather bomber jacket, then dispassionately allowed him to work the cuff over his left hand. If he let him, Tony would start wiping his nose.

For expediency's sake, he tolerated Tony's help with his jacket, but he dug in his heels when the cop cocked his elbow in his direction. Nick managed a warped smile. "I want to see if I can get out the door under my own steam without wiping out that goddamned big plant by the cashier."

Darkness had fallen by the time they stepped out onto the sidewalk. Nick paused to pull on his gloves and turn up the collar of his jacket, the large white flakes of snow settling in his hair and catching in his eyelashes. As he started down the street, he caught sight of his and Tony's reflection in a darkened window, and he experienced a sudden feeling of disassociation.

It sometimes surprised him that he had changed so little. He still appeared hard and physically fit, still had that intractable look about him that few people challenged. The reflection did not record the changes the past two years had wrought. Nor did it reveal that he was a little leaner, that there was a little more gray mixed in his dark hair, that there was a different kind of tension stamped into his face. What had happened had irreparably changed his life, but the reflection remained the same. Another one of life's little practical jokes.

It almost amused Nick, the way everyone referred to it as the "accident." Now everything was measured from that. Before the accident. After the accident. He wondered about their choice of terminology. If some drunk smearing himself all over a concrete abutment was a "tragedy," and if a bunch of low-life druggies overdosing on crack was a "waste of human life," he wondered how they defined what had happened to him as an accident. Some accident.

"Do you need anything—get groceries, pay bills?"

Jarred from the random tack his thoughts had taken, Nick shook his head and hunched deeper into his jacket as a gust of wind caught him. Right now, the last thing he wanted to cope with was bright lights and crowds of people. It had been one hell of a day, and he knew that he had very little reserve left. His concentration was starting to deteriorate and the telltale heaviness was beginning to affect his whole left side. He'd learned the hard way there were two things he had to avoid at all costs: exhaustion and high-stress situations. An overdose of either, and he was practically back to square one. And he'd been back there too many times already.

Tony swung out to skirt an oncoming pedestrian, then stepped back beside Nick. "Want to drop by the station for a coffee?"

Turning the corner into the full force of the wind-driven snow, Nick angled his head against the wet flakes. "I think you'd better just take me home. I've got about twenty minutes before I plant my face in the cement."

Tony grinned. "Hey, man, I'm not picking you out of the gutter again. Once was enough."

Nick managed a half smile in response, but there was no real amusement in it. Once *had* been enough. Maybe once too often. He wondered if there would ever be a day go by when he didn't ask himself why he'd fought so damned hard to stay alive. Dead was dead, but this wasn't exactly a day at the beach, either. He'd put in twenty-one years with the force, exactly half his life, and his job had been his mainstay. Now he didn't even have that. Without it, he had nothing. But then, there had been nothing for a very long time.

THE SMALL, GRAVELED parking lot was dark and deserted, the heavy shadows untouched by the muted light from the street. Illumination from the city diffused upward into the blackened sky, casting an eerie pink reflection in the falling snow and framing the streetlights in misty halos. The sound of water running down a storm sewer broke the stillness, and in spite of the wintry flurry, the promise of spring lingered in the air.

Dropping her keys into her handbag, Sydney slung the strap over her shoulder and closed the car door. She was dead tired and the dull ache at the base of her skull forewarned of a blinding headache, but she disregarded the symptoms of tension and too little sleep. She had just closed the deal on a run-down piece of commercial property in an older area of the city that was, by all indications, on the upswing. If her predictions were right, she had just made a very shrewd investment.

Unfortunately the final negotiations had been messy. The group of investors selling the property had tried to unload it without full disclosure. Not only did she discover they were aware of proposed rezoning restrictions that could limit future development, but they had also neglected to mention a long-term lease agreement with the existing tenant. It had been a stupid, arrogant move on their part, and in their arrogance, they had badly underestimated her.

Had they been straightforward right from the beginning, Sydney would have made an appropriate adjustment in her offer and let it go at that, but that kind of effrontery brought out a relentless streak in her. She could play hardball with the best of them, and underestimating her had cost them dearly.

A hint of a smile hovered around her mouth as she stepped over the low concrete curb surrounding the parking lot. Maybe Norm wasn't far off when he compared her to Attila the Hun.

A chilling wind cut through her, and she shivered as she turned onto the deserted sidewalk. She should have waited a couple of days instead of coming here tonight. But when she'd stopped by her office after closing the deal on the property, Norm's message had been waiting for her. He had managed to arrange bail, and the girl had been released. And she was here at the hostel.

The message had had a jarring effect on Sydney, and she had stood staring at her telephone console, her mind numb as the machine ran out the rest of the tape. She had experienced the same reaction she'd had at the police station, but this time there was an element of stark realization mixed with it.

She was committed. And there was no turning back.

She had developed a shrewd business sense through the years, and she had trained herself to be circumspect. She'd certainly taken her share of risks, but they had been researched, analyzed and calculated, the pros and cons carefully weighed. But she hadn't even considered the pros and cons that afternoon. The bitter disillusionment she'd seen on that girl's face was a reflection from the past, and no matter how disturbing that was, there was no way she could turn her back on it.

Not wanting to be drawn deeper into those kind of thoughts, Sydney considered the present. Until now, she hadn't had an opportunity to really think about how she was going to handle the situation. She knew Major Henderson would act as an intermediary if Sydney asked her to. And maybe that was best. The older woman had years of experience in dealing with the desperate underside of humanity, and she knew better than anyone that there was no black or white, only varying shades of gray.

Coming abreast a recessed entryway, Sydney paused, no longer able to check her apprehension. She dreaded this, dreaded seeing the girl and dreaded talking to the major. She had finally attained a certain level of comfortableness in her life. It wasn't exactly contentment but more like a reconciliation with herself. It wasn't much, but it was all she had. And she was putting that in jeopardy.

Steeling herself, she turned into the dimly lighted doorway.

The building had once been an old army surplus store and now housed a soup kitchen and a thrift shop on the ground level and a temporary men's hostel upstairs. A bell jingled above the door as Sydney entered the thrift shop, a single fluorescent light giving the store a dingy, deserted look. Garment racks displaying the used clothing stood in precise rows in the half-lighted store, and in the window an aged mannequin was stiffly posed, a green velvet dress hanging limply on her form. Sydney wondered if anything in there had ever smelled new.

"Sydney? I didn't recognize you for a minute."

Sydney turned as a plumpish, gray-haired woman in the familiar Legion of Charity uniform appeared from the back of the store, her quick, intelligent eyes alight with welcome.

"How are you, Major?"

"I'm fine, my dear. Just fine. Although I could do without this weather."

"We could all do without this weather."

Major Henderson nodded in agreement as she went over to the door and locked it, then motioned toward the back of the store. "Why don't we go into the office to talk. Jenny has fallen asleep in one of the back rooms, and it might be best if we don't disturb her."

It was clear from her manner that the major wanted to speak to her in private, and Sydney followed her, the stillness closing in behind her.

The older woman pushed aside some clutter on her desk, waving Sydney into a chair as she sat down herself. Folding her hands on the stained ink blotter, she looked at Sydney, her expression solemn. "I'm not sure I understand what's going on here, Sydney," she said, her manner kindly but direct. "Frankly, I was a little surprised when I got your call this evening."

Sydney folded her gloves into a precise square, her expression guarded. She'd known the woman for a number of years. Their first meeting had come about when she had heard a community appeal for a temporary space to house the Christmas food bank when the existing location had been gutted by fire. She had just bought a piece of commercial property that had a vacant space, and she had made it available to the Legion of Charity for the duration of the holiday season.

From that association, a strange kind of alliance had developed between the two women. Sydney donated both time and money to the legion. The major seemed to sense that involvement added a meaningful dimension to Sydney's life, and because of that, she felt very comfortable about calling on the younger woman's business acumen whenever she needed it.

Sydney knew Margaret Henderson had a special concern for the kids who ended up on the streets. Unerringly direct in her approach, the major was a kind, compassionate woman who did not confuse idealism with reality. She dealt with the harsh facts of street life: the drug abuse, the teenage prostitution, the human parasites, the brutality. She did what she could to make a difference, but she knew it was a battle that would never be won. She tried to salvage the ones that were salvageable, and she prayed for the rest.

"Sydney?"

Sydney sighed and finally met the older woman's gaze, deliberately skirting the intent behind the major's comments. "Do you have any idea how old she is?"

Margaret Henderson watched her, disquiet lining her face. "I took it upon myself to do a little digging." She gave Sydney a rueful smile. "I think at first she was trying to shock me, but then it became her unburdening. Her case history is appalling but pretty much what I've come to expect.''

The major paused, and Sydney could tell by her expression the woman was upset. As if drawing on some inner strength, she continued, her manner direct and professional. ''She's not quite fifteen, has been hooking for two years, and from the sounds of it, has a major drug dependency. Her stepfather first sexually molested her when she was nine, right after he and her mother started living together. He browbeat her into believing that it was his right to do what he wanted with her, and he convinced Jenny her mother would kick her out if she ever told her what was going on—which her mother did when she found out Jenny was pregnant with his baby. The stepfather dragged her back home, and he and her mother arranged for a back-alley abortion. Jenny's mother refused to face the truth until she caught the stepfather in Jenny's bedroom several months later. She blamed it all on Jenny and threw her out again. The girl is bitter, confused—a frightened child, eaten up with self-disgust.''

The agitation that had sustained the major evaporated, and she looked away, her voice weary. ''She's like a hundred others out there, Sydney—not one person to turn to, not a shred of hope to hang on to, with drugs providing the only avenue of escape. And there's so little we can do.''

Feeling physically ill, Sydney rested her head against the high back of the chair and stared up at the ceiling, not allowing herself to respond to the despair she heard in Margaret Henderson's voice. If she allowed herself to feel anything other than this disconnected numbness, she would be sick.

A door slammed above them, and there was the sound of someone on the stairs.

Sydney forced herself to take a deep, even breath and made her muscles relax. Finally she spoke. "I won't accept that, Major. We *can* do something."

The major sighed. "It's not that easy, my dear. We can't simply give her a home and expect her to put all this behind her. She would be suspicious of any good intentions and probably hostile to boot. There has to be an element of trust, and she's never had a reason to trust anybody. And there's the drug abuse. How can she deal with that?"

Sydney finally met Margaret Henderson's gaze, a trace of humor in her eyes. "How would *you* deal with it?"

There was a spark of incredulity in the other woman's voice. "You're serious, aren't you?"

Sydney's tone was unequivocal. "Deadly serious."

The silence stretched out as the major marshaled her thoughts. "I'd want to see her in some drug rehabilitation program, preferably one where she would be admitted as a patient, and certainly one where she could get appropriate counseling—and one far enough away so that she'd be cut off from her street friends here."

"Would she go?"

Still off balance from the unexpectedness of Sydney's intention, the major exhaled sharply. "Yes—yes, I think she would. She's on the run from her last placement, which was a group home. I think she'd be more willing to agree to a clinic rather than be sent back there. She is a juvenile and a ward of the court, so she doesn't have many options."

"What about social services?"

"I don't foresee any problems there. I happen to know her social worker fairly well. She handles most of the caseload for the group homes, and she'd support that kind of intervention."

Resting her arms on the scarred wooden arms of the chair, Sydney laced her fingers together, a solemn look in her eyes.

Several moments elapsed before she spoke. "I'd like you to do something for me, Major," she said quietly.

Margaret Henderson's gaze was direct, her tone equally quiet. "If I can."

"I want you to make whatever arrangements are necessary."

"That kind of treatment does not come cheaply, my dear."

Sydney's face was impassive as she took her checkbook out of her handbag and started to write down an amount. When she spoke, her voice was taut. "I couldn't care less about the money." She finished filling out the check, tore it out, then dropped it onto the desk. "Get her some decent clothes, make whatever flight and hotel reservations are necessary for you both and get her admitted to the best clinic available." Sydney didn't look at the other woman as she put the checkbook back in her purse and closed the flap. "Whatever financial arrangements need to be made with the clinic, I'll take care of them. Have them contact me at my office. And if that amount doesn't cover the initial expenses, let me know. Norm Crandall will handle the legalities."

The major picked up the check, then shot Sydney a startled look. "My goodness, Sydney—this is a great deal of money."

Sydney finally looked up, a small smile lifting the corner of her mouth. "Buy yourself a new desk blotter with whatever is left."

The older woman's eyes twinkled with humor. "I don't think I can find one that expensive."

Sydney flashed her a dry look as she stood up. "Let me know if there are any problems."

Major Henderson rose, a note of reservation in her voice. "Would you like to talk to her?"

Again Sydney avoided looking at her as she pulled on her gloves. "No. I don't think that would be wise."

The major studied her briefly. "No. Perhaps not." She pushed the chair aside and came around the desk. "I'll keep you posted. And if there are any problems, I'll let you know."

"I'd appreciate that."

"This is a very generous thing you did tonight, Sydney."

Sydney met her gaze briefly, then began smoothing the leather over her fingers, her tone clipped. "Money only means something to those people who don't have it, Major. And I have it." She looked up, a twisted smile adding no animation to her eyes. "It's people like you who make the difference."

There was a quiet chastisement in Margaret Henderson's tone as she gently amended Sydney's comment. "No, my dear, it's people like you who make the difference. We can only do so much—we simply don't have the resources to help someone like Jenny. You've given her hope, and there's no greater gift. Take comfort in that."

Later, as Sydney stood on her balcony, watching the gently falling snow filter down between the streetlights and the shadowed river, she considered what the major had said. *Take comfort.* Her smile was without humor as she rested her shoulder against the retaining wall, the snow muffling the sounds of the city. She wondered how the major would react to the absolute irony in her remark. Comfort? She would find no comfort in helping the girl. Disruption of her hard-won peace of mind, yes; disturbing memories, very likely. But comfort? How could there be? There was too much history tied to it, a history she would erase forever if she could. A sense of aloneness swept through her, laying bare an awful emptiness that went so deep it eroded the self-imposed barriers that had held that part of her life at bay.

She wondered if it was possible to ever recover from that kind of pain.

Turning abruptly, she reentered her brightly lighted apartment and shut the patio door.

Outside the snow continued to fall, swallowed by the black waters of the shallow river, the quiet suddenly thick and oppressive.

CHAPTER TWO

NICK COULD FEEL SWEAT trickling down his back as he made his way slowly across the floor, the concentration needed for the mechanics of each step just as taxing as the physical exertion. He was determined to get across that goddamned room under his own steam or bloody well die trying.

"Why don't you rest for a minute, Nick. You're starting to tighten up, and you need to relax."

Establishing his balance, Nick shot Beth a semidisgusted look. "If I'm so damned stiff, why do I feel like I'm going to fall flat on my face any minute?"

Obviously suppressing a smile, she caught his elbow and steadied him as he wavered slightly. "Don't get all huffy with me, Novak. I said three times across the room without your cane, and you said five, so it's your own bullheadedness that got you into this mess."

He gave her a rueful grin. "You don't give an inch, do you?"

She grinned back. "Not with you I don't. I know better." Satisfied he'd fully regained his balance, she released her hold on him and nodded to the chairs on the other side of the room. "You've got another twenty feet to go. Are you going to do it on your own, or do you want me to get your cane?"

"You know what you can do with that damned cane," he muttered as he forced his left leg to respond.

"Watch it, or I'll make you crawl the rest of the way."

Nick spoke through gritted teeth. "You must have trained under Ivan the Horrible."

"It was Ivan the Terrible, and he didn't give out degrees in physical therapy. As I recall, his specialty was burning out eyes."

"Which should be next on your list. They're the only damned things that work right."

She steadied him again, her tone amused. "That's what I like about you—your sweet disposition."

Nick's mouth twitched, then he fixed his gaze on the distant chairs. He was *not* going to quit.

Very gently, she restrained him. "Relax, Nick," she said again. "And remember to take smaller steps with your left leg."

Perspiration dampened his hair as he concentrated on every move. If relearning to walk took this much concentration and effort, it was a bloody wonder babies ever learned at all.

By the time he reached the chairs, Nick felt as though he'd run a hundred miles through wet cement. His knees wobbled as he sank into a seat, and his entire body trembled. He tipped his head back and closed his eyes, waiting for the spastic tautness in his muscles to relax. There was something to be said for being left a vegetable.

"You okay?"

He opened his eyes and met Beth's concerned gaze. He managed a weak grin. "Do you think I'd make a good turnip?"

She laughed and handed him a towel. "Tell you what. When you finally ditch the cane, I'll take it home and feed it to the pigs." Beth and her husband had a small ranch outside the city. There wasn't a pig on the place, but the idea sure as hell appealed to Nick.

His grin deepened. "I thought you fed turnips to pigs."

She gave him a narrow look, then fixed a heavy elastic around his neck and stuck the attached plastic cone in his left hand. "Work on that, Novak, and quit being cute."

He put tension on the piece of equipment. "Now what? The Dragon Lady?"

He couldn't see her face, but he could tell she was trying not to laugh. "Be nice. You know darned well you go out of your way to antagonize her."

Which was true. Olga was in her late fifties, regimented, dictatorial and probably the best speech pathologist in the country, if not all of North America. She was demanding, precise and dedicated, and every one of her patients dramatically exceeded even the most optimistic prognoses. And something about her brought out the worst in Nick.

But in spite of their clash in personalities, or maybe because of it, he had regained most of his speech dexterity. He still had major problems if he got tense or overtired, but he could wade through all her damned tongue twisters with a certain amount of ease. He didn't think she'd be content until he started earning a living as either a radio announcer or an auctioneer. At least she let him chew gum.

Pulling out a chair, Beth sat down beside him and laid a blue binder on the table. It was his case file, and Nick experienced a sudden tightness in the pit of his stomach.

She would record his unassisted five laps across the room. New history to be added to all the other accumulated history from the past two years. Details of the brutal beating: broken ribs, dislocated shoulder, a punctured lung, four gunshot wounds. The black and white of what had happened.

That history he could have put behind him without any lasting effect. It was that single bullet that entered his skull just above his right eyebrow and came out the top of his head that had altered his life forever.

The binder was the chronicle of a smashed life. The medical records of his three-month coma. The assessments of the neurological damage and resulting impairment. That was the history that was irreversible. He looked away, panic flickering in him. Life after death.

Tomorrow he'd do six laps across the damned room.

Back in his apartment, Nick was reminded of his record-breaking laps as he stared out the kitchen window, a cup of coffee in his hand. He was going to pay for that bit of bullheadedness. The muscles up the back of his left leg throbbed, and the tendon in his heel felt as if someone had used a winch on it.

He took another sip of coffee and watched a robin hop across the strip of grass between the two apartment blocks. The early afternoon sun angled between the buildings, eating at the last patch of gritty ice below a ragged lilac shrub. Three days of balmy weather had erased all traces of the storm the week before.

The robin flew onto the lilac bush, and Nick considered the shrub. In the twelve years he'd lived in the apartment block, it had never bloomed. A twist of cynicism lifted the corner of his mouth; of course, the same could be said for himself.

He turned and glanced at the clock on the stove. He still had half an hour before the handicap van picked him up for the monthly afternoon session at the hospital. He was regularly assessed on specialized equipment to grade improvements in his strength and flexibility. Another go-around. He'd be ready to collapse by the time he finished.

He glanced at the clock again. He could do some exercises or read the paper. He reached for the spring-loaded chest expander lying on the counter. He could live with the leg, if he could just get the strength and coordination back in his left arm.

The jangle of the phone cut through the silence in the apartment, and grasping the four-legged cane, he moved toward the counter where the phone was located.

"Hi, Nick. It's Tony. It took some doing, but I was finally able to dig up some information about that donation to the rehab program."

Nick rested his weight on his stronger leg, his movements deliberate and calculated as he leaned back against the cupboard. "And?"

"By the looks of it, it was a corporate donation that kicked the program into high gear—a company by the name of Unicorn Holdings. Just for the hell of it, I did some checking, and the company is a hot one. Owns commercial property in Vancouver and Toronto as well as here, and from what I turned up, the head honcho has smarts—hung on to everything during that real estate crash a few years back. I kinda wondered about his reasons for maintaining such a low profile, but he's as clean as a whistle. I ran the name through the computer. Nothing on our files, nothing with the Feds, and from what I could determine, he seemed to come out of nowhere about ten years ago."

A strange sensation started to unfold in Nick's gut, and his hand tightened around the phone. "Were you able to get a name?"

He heard Tony take a deep drag on a cigarette before he answered. "Yeah, it took some digging, but I did. The guy in the driver's seat is a Sydney Foster."

It was the same numbing sensation as when he was shot— the burst of heat in his head, then the paralyzing chill settling through his whole body. Through sheer will he fought off the weakness that spread through him and forced himself to speak. "Sydney Foster?"

"Yeah. I managed to get a home address and an unlisted phone number. His residence is in the Brisco Building—you know, that condo unit off Fourth, the one overlooking the river."

The half-forgotten rage of a lifetime ago licked through Nick's jumbled nerve circuits, filling him with a consuming anger. His face was like an iron mask, but his hand trembled as he painstakingly wrote down the address and phone number Tony gave him. Sydney Foster. Once known as Roxanne Busher. The woman who had saved his life, then shattered it. The one he'd walked away from, but the one he'd never been able to forget. She had eaten away at his insides until there was nothing left but a shell, and he knew if he didn't leave, she'd destroy him. So he'd left, and the agony had nearly destroyed him, anyway. And now she was back. His rage grew calm, cold and deadly.

His voice was brittle as he read back the address and phone number to his ex-partner. "Do you have anything else? Make of car, license number?"

"Yeah, there's a white Mercedes registered to the company, and it carries business plates. Other than the car, he seems to maintain a low-profile private life, as well. Nobody knows anything about him. I didn't want to ask too many questions in case I stirred up something, but it's pretty apparent he protects his privacy."

A bitter smile twisted Nick's mouth, and his eyes hardened. "He has his reasons, no doubt." He forced himself to take a deep breath in an attempt to eliminate the edge of sarcasm in his voice. "Thanks, Tony. I owe you one."

"You don't owe me bugger-all. Just stay outta trouble, will you?"

The hardness in Nick's eyes eased a little. The entire time he'd been in the hospital, his ex-partner had never missed a day. Not one. And it had been Tony, day after day, week after week, who had both bullied and babied him, forcing him back into the land of the living. "I'll give it my best shot."

"You do that. I'm getting too old for this shit."

Nick's mouth twitched. "I'll keep that in mind."

He hung up the phone, his movements awkward and labored as he fumbled for his cane.

With a massive effort, he made his way to the living room, the numbing weakness claiming him as he lay down on the sofa. His cane thudded unheeded to the floor as he closed his eyes and rested his arm across them. So it was Sydney who was behind the expanded rehabilitation program. For some reason, that didn't surprise him. She'd do something like that—slip back into his life whether he wanted her to or not. What did surprise him was how violently he had reacted to finding out. He'd thought he'd put that part of his life behind him, but his reaction only proved he'd done a damned good job of fooling himself.

The muscles in his jaw tensed as a viselike pain shot through his chest. Fifteen years. He hadn't laid eyes on her for fifteen years and she could still do this to him, could still twist his guts into knots. And he hated himself, hated his inability to keep from reacting. But then, no other woman had ever gotten to him the way she had. And he had paid the price. God, had he paid the price.

He'd been fresh out of the police academy—twenty-one and idealistic as hell—the first time their paths had crossed. She'd been maybe sixteen years old then, scared and alone after some pimp had beaten her and left her in an alley. But even as battered as she was, there was something about her that caught his attention. A certain wistfulness, a helplessness that touched him as she stared up at him with wide, wary eyes. He had never forgotten that. He'd seen her out working the streets a couple of times after that, late at night and alone, but then she moved to a high-priced escort service, which somehow always managed to stay one step ahead of the vice sweeps. It wasn't until five or six years later that their paths crossed again, only this time it was a collision course, and one that nearly destroyed him.

When serial killings started turning up first in Toronto, then Vancouver, every police force across Canada was alerted. The victims had all been young white women who worked for high-priced escort services, and when a high-class escort was brutally slain in Calgary, every available man was put on the case. It was then, as a newly promoted detective, that Nick encountered Roxanne Busher again.

She'd left the business just prior to the slayings and was trying to build a new life for herself. But when she found out that Mabel, the old madam who owned the agency where she'd worked, was dying, she had come back to look after her.

Roxanne wanted nothing more to do with the street, but the deputy chief of police needed someone who knew the inside operations. Three years before, she had come to him with invaluable information that had led to a major drug bust, and through a combination of persuasion and coercion, he talked her into working with the force again. During a period of three weeks—and two additional slayings— Nick spent nearly every waking moment with her: on the street, at the precinct, sifting through bits of information, checking out even the slimmest of leads. And with every minute he spent with her, he found himself more and more drawn to her.

It was Roxanne who finally spotted an odd quirk in the timing of the deaths that gave them their first break, and it was Roxanne who, when a lead suddenly turned hot, took it upon herself to go in as a decoy. It was also Roxanne, battered and bleeding, with broken ribs and collarbone, who threw herself in front of Nick's sprawled, unconscious body, taking a bullet in the arm that would have, without a doubt, ended his life.

If he'd had the sense to walk away then, maybe he would have been left with only a haunting memory of eyes that could see into his very soul, a touch that hypnotized him, a sensuality that left him powerless. But he hadn't, and in all honesty, he wasn't sure he even could have. Because by then, he was so damned much in love with her he couldn't see straight.

And during the next few months he dug himself in deeper and deeper, recklessly living one day at a time, blocking out the past and refusing to acknowledge the future. And she had made it easy for him. Through the years she had taken Mabel's advice and plowed every available cent into joint real estate ventures with the woman, so by then she had enough income from those investments to support herself.

She again severed all ties with the street, moved to a different part of town with him and enrolled in a business management course. During that time he carefully eradicated every trace of her assumed identity. Roxanne Busher disappeared and Sydney Foster reemerged. But in reality he was only playing an elaborate game with himself, and he was forced to realize it when the precinct Christmas party rolled around.

He had tried first to coax, then bully her into going, but she wouldn't even talk to him about it. He'd kept at her, and she finally hauled him back to the real world. She had stood in the doorway of their bedroom, her arms clasped tightly around her as she forced him to face hard, cold reality. He was a cop. She had been on the other side of the law. She might have had a different name, but the face was the same, and no amount of subterfuge or game playing would ever change that. And Sydney saw what he had not; his open involvement with her could ruin his credibility within the force.

Nick's jaw flexed again, and he shifted his arm and opened his eyes, his gaze riveting on the ceiling. He owed her

that at least, for yanking his head out of the sand. But, by
God, it had nearly killed him, accepting her for what she
was, and eventually his jealousy controlled him, driving him
into fits of uncontainable rage, to depths of suspicion that
shredded all rationality, until he reached a point where he
knew he had to get out or go under.

Anger churned in him, scrambling his thoughts. Why did
she have to turn up now, when he was trying to piece his life
back together one more time? Why now? Why not fifteen
years ago when he had finally broken after two weeks and
gone back to the apartment they'd shared, only to find her
gone? That was when his rage found a new foothold. It was
as though she'd known he didn't have the strength to stay
away, and she'd disappeared without a trace, leaving him to
face the pain alone. He had been ready to turn in his badge,
move to a different city, try to build some kind of life with
her. But she'd left him nothing. So he had turned to the
bottle, and then to Sara, trying to block out the pain. And
to this day, he wasn't sure which had been the worst addiction: alcohol or Sydney Foster. They had both nearly destroyed him.

With an unrelenting concentration, he fumbled for his
cane and heaved himself into a sitting position. The effort
it took to make his legs respond brought beads of perspiration to his forehead, and he fought down the distanced
feeling that made his head swim.

His only conscious thought was that he had to get out of
the apartment before the van arrived to take him to a physical evaluation—part of the rehabilitation program she was
paying for. Driven by sheer animal instinct and an indomi-
table will to survive, he took one step after another until he
reached the door.

SYDNEY FROWNED in concentration and absently hooked
her hair behind her ear as she studied the computer print-

out lying on her desk. It was a financial breakdown she was working on for the major; the project, a proposed women's shelter. The printout detailed projected capital costs and operating expenses for one fiscal year, and the bottom line indicated a serious shortfall. Her frown deepened as she considered the options. From a business point of view, there were only two: they had to either cut back on facility costs or raise more money. But maybe there was another way. If she could come up with a plan, some scheme whereby the shelter was at least partially self-supporting, that would make the difference.

The phone rang, and with a preoccupied look on her face, she reached for it. "Yes, Marg."

Her private secretary's voice echoed in the earpiece. "Dr. Robertson's on line two. Do you want to take it, or shall I tell him you're unavailable?"

The preoccupied expression disappeared, and Sydney instantly focused. "No, I'll take it." Taking off her glasses and tossing them onto the desk, she pressed the flashing button on her telephone console. "Good afternoon, Doctor."

"At last. The right voice. Do you know you're a very hard woman to track down?"

Sydney grinned and shifted the phone to the other ear. Peter Robertson was an ex-football player in his late thirties who had a broad boyish grin and curly gray hair that looked like a Brillo pad. He had the most relaxed personality she'd ever come across, and he was miles ahead of anyone else in the field of rehabilitation for the brain injured. He was hardly ever in one place more than ten minutes, and he absolutely loathed leaving messages.

She reminded him of that. "If you'd leave messages, I'd get back to you, you know."

"Yeah, well. Catching me in my office is about as hopeless as catching you in yours."

Swiveling the large, executive-style chair, Sydney turned toward the window and rocked back. "So what's up?"

"We received that new piece of hydraulic exercise equipment you ordered for the program, but we're having some problems with it. I wondered if you wanted to get in touch with the distributor or if we should."

"You have the information there?"

"Yeah, we have it on file."

"Go ahead and call them. They'll have to talk to you, anyway."

"Will do."

"How's everything going?"

There was a long pause, then the doctor spoke. "Our star pupil didn't show up for his evaluation on Friday."

Her movements stilled. "What happened?"

"I don't really know. When the driver went to pick him up at his apartment, he wasn't there. He wasn't there again today, so he had the caretaker check. There was no sign of him."

Leaning back in her chair, Sydney rubbed her temple. "Do you have anyone to contact in case of an emergency?"

"Yeah, his old partner, Tony Martinelli—he volunteers at the center whenever he can. I tried to call him at work, but they told me he was unavailable for the next couple of days."

"I see."

The doctor's tone was reassuring. "It's not a big deal. The last assessment we did on him was very thorough, and he's quite capable of managing on an outpatient program. Nick's very touchy about his independence. Maybe he just decided he needed to take off for a couple of days. I thought if I hadn't heard anything by the end of the week, I'd try to get in touch with Tony again."

She hesitated, not liking the feeling that unfurled through her. Finally she took a deep breath and spoke. "That sounds reasonable. Would you mind keeping me posted?"

"No problem. I've left a message on his answering machine, so if I should hear from him, I'll give you a call."

She forced her tone to remain businesslike. "Thanks. I'd appreciate that."

"Fine. I'll be in touch."

As she turned and replaced the receiver in the console cradle, she tried to ignore the flutter in her abdomen. Nick was a big boy and quite capable of making his own decisions. He had managed on his own for six months now, she rationalized, and nothing had happened to him in that time. But the thought of him alone, struggling with his disability, made her throat ache.

She had seen the videotapes of his progress, and she was aware of all the obstacles he faced. Flights of stairs, elevator doors that closed too quickly, the nearly impossible task of getting in and out of a vehicle on his own. And that was just dealing with the physical handicap. It had been an agony to see the early tapes of him in speech therapy, his exhausting struggle to form even the simplest words, especially when she could do nothing but sit there and watch.

In an attempt to ease the ache in her chest, Sydney forced herself to relax, then she swiveled around and stood up. She went to the window and rested her shoulder against the frame, wrapping her arms around herself as she stared down at the street. It had been a mistake, getting personally involved in his rehabilitation. She should have simply provided the means to set the wheels in motion and left the rest to the professionals. She should have avoided any exposure to his long, slow recovery, but she knew she could no more have done that than stopped breathing. She had created her own hell; now she had no other choice but to live it.

Exhaling heavily, she turned back to her desk and the computer spreadsheet lying on the dark walnut surface. But the figures blurred together in an indecipherable mass as old memories turned on her. By the time she finally left her office, she was so exhausted she could barely put one foot in front of the other. All she wanted to do was go home and fall into bed and pretend that Nick Novak didn't exist.

The automatic door of her apartment building's underground parkade lumbered shut behind her as she pulled off the ramp and wheeled into her private parking stall. The small, grimy overhead fixtures emitted strips of inadequate light that barely penetrated the gloom of the bunkerlike structure, leaving the shadows heavy and impenetrable. The silence had an eerie ring to it as she climbed out of her car, the slam of the door echoing hollowly in the nearly empty garage. Turning toward the orange exit door, Sydney slipped the strap of her handbag over her shoulder, then selected the key to unlock the security door, the sound of her footsteps reverberating in the stillness.

As she stepped into the thin illumination from the light fixture arched above the door, the weak halo framed her against the shadows. There was a sound behind her, barely discernible in the silence. Her heart lurched and she whirled, her reaction sharpened by the frantic pounding in her chest.

A form disengaged itself from the murky shadows surrounding a massive concrete pillar, and a gaunt, unshaved face took shape in the dim light. For one awful split second, Sydney thought her knees were going to buckle. She stared at him, as though he were an aberration of her mind, then her pulse started to pound in a heavy, foreboding rhythm when she finally separated fact from fantasy.

Her face went white and she stood rooted to the spot, shock paralyzing her. He leaned heavily on his walking cane and dragged one leg forward, then his body twisted in a grotesque half turn as the cane clattered to the ground.

On sheer instinct Sydney reacted, and she somehow
managed to catch him before he hit the concrete. The full
impact of his body collapsing against hers nearly dragged
her down, and she staggered once before she managed to
brace herself beneath his deadweight. She locked her arms
around his chest, panic welling up inside her. "Nick. For
God's sake, Nick," she whispered, alarm gripping her.
Fighting to catch her breath, she turned her head toward the
intercom by the door, praying that the building's caretaker
was in his tiny suite at the bottom of the stairs. "Malcolm,
help! Come quick!"

Nick's head slumped against her shoulder, and her panic
escalated. God, what would she do if Malcolm wasn't there?
She was about to call out again when the door burst open
and the burly black came hurtling out, a hammer clutched
in his hand.

Realizing he thought she was in trouble, she frantically
shook her head, her voice breaking. "No! He's collapsed
and I need you to help me."

Malcolm dropped the hammer and sprinted toward her.
Cursing softly, he shoved his arm between her and Nick,
taking the full weight of the semiconscious man. "I've got
him, Ms Foster. I've got him." With a powerful shrug, he
looped one of Nick's arms around his shoulders and lifted
him free of her hold. "Here now. I have him."

Relieved of the weight, Sydney stumbled, suddenly so
weak she could barely stand. "I'll call an ambulance."

Nick lifted his head and started to struggle, trying to
break free of the caretaker's iron grip. His speech was thick.
"No! Goddamn it, no!"

His eyes were glazed and unfocused, but there was a
frightening look of determination on his face, and Sydney
frantically searched for another alternative. She looked up
at Malcolm. "Do you think you can get him upstairs to my
apartment?"

Malcolm grinned, the flash of white standing out like a beacon of reassurance against the ebony of his skin. "No problem, Ms Foster." He repositioned his hold on Nick, then nodded toward the door. "You just get that open, and I can take him anywhere you want."

Sydney grabbed her keys and purse from the floor, her hand trembling as she fit the key into the lock.

The elevator trip was an agony of slowness, and she tried to collect herself. But a mixture of shock and fear blocked her ability to think, and she could do nothing but pray.

Once inside her apartment, she motioned to the guest room door on her right. "Take him in there and I'll call his doctor."

The caretaker gave her another reassuring smile. "No problem."

Uttering another silent prayer, she dashed to the study, flipped through the Rolodex on her desk, then punched out the numbers printed on the bottom of the card.

The phone was picked up on the third ring, and a woman's voice answered. "Dr. Robertson's residence."

Sydney tried to keep her voice steady. "This is Sydney Foster calling. I need to speak to the doctor immediately. There's an emergency concerning Nick Novak."

"One moment, please."

Closing her eyes, Sydney sagged against the wall, her legs trembling beneath her. *Please hurry,* she pleaded silently. *Please, please hurry.*

"Dr. Robertson here."

She made herself take a deep breath, then as coherently as possible, she told him where Nick was and what had happened.

"I'll be there in five minutes. What's your apartment number?"

Her voice suddenly shaky, she gave him the information, then, unable to say another word, she hung up. She remained motionless for a moment, then straightened and turned.

Malcolm glanced up as she entered the bedroom, Nick's shoes in his hand. "Were you able to get ahold of the doc?"

Her voice was barely above a whisper. "Yes. He'll be here in a few minutes."

He tipped his head toward Nick's still form. "Then maybe I should strip him down. He'll likely want to check him over."

Her pulse echoed in her head as she nodded.

Malcolm's voice was comforting. "Don't worry, Ms Foster. He's going to be okay."

She managed a weak smile. "I hope so." Knowing if she stayed in the room she would come apart, Sydney turned and left.

By the time the doctor arrived, she was able to mask her anxiety, but inside she felt as though her bones were disconnected. Malcolm had disappeared when the physician arrived, and Sydney was leaning against the wall by the closed bedroom door when he reentered the apartment.

He had Nick's cane in his hand. "I figured I'd better go fetch this," he said softly. Slipping the huge ring with the building's passkeys on it into his pocket, he laid Nick's cane on the small table in the entryway.

She smiled lopsidedly at him, her eyes dark against her pallor. "Thank you, Malcolm. I don't know what I would have done if you hadn't been here tonight."

He gave her a little shrug, then grinned. "I'm always here if you need me. You know that." He pushed the cane farther back on the table, then gave her a scrutinizing look. "Is there somebody you should call?"

She blinked against the sudden sting in her eyes, then shook her head.

His soft voice carried a touch of the Deep South as he said quietly, "Would you like me to stick around for a while?"

She swallowed hard and met his gaze. His presence lent her the kind of quiet reassurance she needed right then. "Yes," she whispered unevenly. "I would."

He tipped his head in acknowledgment, then glanced at the closed door. "Do you want to go in?"

Unable to answer him, she simply shook her head.

He inclined his head again and placed his huge hand on his hip. "How about if I see how things are going?"

Locking her arms tightly around her, she nodded.

From her vantage point just outside the room, Sydney could see Dr. Robertson remove the blood pressure cuff from Nick's arm as Malcolm entered. "How is he, Doc?"

The physician's expression was noncommittal as he motioned toward the hall. Once outside the room, he shut the door behind them, then met Sydney's anxious gaze. "I don't know what's kicked this off, but whatever it was, it had to be something very traumatic."

His movements were methodical as he rolled up his stethoscope and stuffed it into the pocket of his tracksuit. "Any severe trauma can have a very debilitating effect on someone with this kind of neurological handicap, and Nick has driven himself to the absolute limit, both mentally and physically." He paused, assessing the situation. "I can certainly admit him, but Nick's going to fight that. He has a real aversion to hospitals."

Sydney took a deep breath. "Would it be all right to leave him here?"

Dr. Robertson shot her a quick glance, then pursed his lips and stared at the floor as he considered her question. "I can't see why not. I can give him something before I leave to ensure he'll have a quiet night, and I can stop by in the morning and check him before I go to the hospital." He glanced at Malcolm, then back at Sydney. "Providing, of course, that you can handle it."

Sydney didn't know if she could handle it or not. The thought of Nick's being there unearthed such a feeling of dread she felt almost paralyzed by it; the thought of his being taken out on a stretcher was even worse.

Her voice was far more steady than she felt. "Malcolm has offered to stay. Between the two of us, we can manage."

The doctor studied her, a quizzical expression in his eyes, but he said nothing, reluctant to infringe on what was obviously a very personal matter. His tone was neutral when he spoke. "I'll give him something now, and I'll leave some medication in case he gets restless later on. It's going to take about half an hour for the medication to work, but it should knock him out for a few hours. He'll likely still be fairly groggy tomorrow."

After the doctor left, Sydney went out onto the balcony, her mind dulled by shock. She couldn't face Nick while he was still awake. She couldn't face the disgust and loathing she'd see in his eyes. Hugging herself against the aftermath of fear and the chill of the wind, she stared at the sparkling waters of the shallow river across the road. Part of her desperately wanted Nick there, where she could watch over him, another part realized it was a big mistake. But no matter what she did, she would never walk away unscathed.

She waited forty-five minutes before she went back inside.

Malcolm had moved one of the wing chairs beside the bed and was sitting hunched over, his arms resting across his thighs, his fingers laced loosely together. He looked up as she entered the room. Rising slowly, he kept his gaze fixed on her, his voice quiet. "He's out like a light, Ms Foster. Hasn't moved a muscle for a good ten minutes." He motioned her toward the chair. "You sit down, and I'm going to fix you something hot to drink. You look half-froze."

Malcolm eased past as she stood transfixed in the doorway, the years dissolving in an agonizing rush. She hadn't seen Nick face-to-face since she'd gone to the hospital when he was in ICU. He had been in a coma then and was so battered she wouldn't have recognized him. Later she had watched him on video, but that wasn't the same as seeing him in the flesh. This was Nick, alive and breathing, and real. So real.

Her face scored with a wrenching despair, she numbly moved to the side of the bed. Drawn by a longing too strong to resist, she sat down, her gaze never leaving Nick's haggard, unshaved face as she gently drew the covers over his naked torso.

His dark stubble of beard shadowed the lean, hard lines of his jaw, obscuring the creases that bracketed his mouth. It was a face that carried a hint of his Slavic ancestry—the wide, defined cheekbones, the dark, heavy brows. But it was his eyes that had been her downfall—deep set, thickly lashed, so brown they appeared almost black. Eyes that were dark and unfathomable when he was angry, hypnotic when he laughed.

Nick could never really be classed as handsome. But he had been born with a smoldering male virility that was as potent as it was indefinable. He had that look—that heavy-lidded, slumberous look that aroused images of satin sheets and hot, damp skin, and when he smiled that slow, intimate smile of his, nothing else registered.

He had changed so little, yet he had changed so much. Fifteen years of hard living were indelibly etched into his face, and there was more gray at his temples than there was dark. The laugh lines radiating from the corners of his eyes were more defined, more weathered, but there were still traces of the younger man—the man who had touched her like no other, the one she could never forget. Her vision blurred and her fingers trembled as she lightly touched the scar on his forehead, then smoothed back his tousled hair.

"That's a mighty lovin' touch," Malcolm said quietly from the doorway.

She gave him an unsteady smile and shrugged, unable to speak.

The big black man handed her a steaming mug, then stretched out on the floor, his back braced against the bed. He took a sip from his own cup, then crossed his ankles as he glanced up at her. "Want to talk about it?" he asked softly.

Sydney started to shake her head, but something overrode her usual reticence. "It was a long time ago, Malcolm," she said quietly. "And there was no happy ending."

"Why not?"

She drew her thumb along the rim of her cup, her face reflective. "Because there was an insurmountable problem between us, something that neither of us knew how to deal with."

"Nothing is insurmountable, Ms Foster," came the quiet response from the semidarkness. "Not if you want it bad enough."

Sydney's vision blurred, and she tried to focus on the group of sketches hanging above the bed. "This was." She gazed at the man in the bed for a moment, then reluctantly straightened and took a sip from the mug. She shot the caretaker a surprised look. "This is excellent hot chocolate."

He grinned and raised his cup toward her in a silent salute. "Yes, ma'am, it surely is. A hefty shot of Kahlúa and Grand Marnier puts a little muscle in it."

A smile relaxed the tension in her face as she drew up her feet, looping her arms around her knees. "It'd better not be too hefty, or I'll pass out cold."

His grin broadened and he shook his head. "There's just enough in there to take the edge off things." Drawing up one knee, he rested his arm across it as he studied the toe of his worn jogger, then he looked up at her. His voice had that same quiet tone. "What happened to your friend there?"

Sydney sighed and wrapped her cold hands around the warm earthen mug. There was a brief hesitation before she spoke, her manner controlled and detached. "He was a detective on the police force. They knew a major drug deal was being set up by a local bike gang, something very significant—a regular pipeline from South America to Canada, with distribution into the States. Nick was sent in undercover, and just before the deal came down, someone in the police force leaked information to a member of the bike gang. Nick's cover was blown. He was wearing a wire when it happened, and he couldn't talk his way out of it. His partner found him in an alley."

Her voice broke and she looked away, swallowing hard to relax the awful tightness in her throat. When she finally continued, her voice was raw and uneven. "He had extensive injuries, but the most crucial one was the bullet wound in his head. It was touch and go for a long time, but he finally stabilized. There was brain damage, though. That was two years ago, and he's had to relearn everything—how to walk, how to speak."

"Is that the scar on his forehead?"

"Yes, it is."

Malcolm frowned. "If he got shot on the right side of his head, how come it's his left side he has trouble with?"

"The left and right hemispheres of the brain control the opposite sides of the body. In that respect, he was lucky. He's right-handed, so he still has that." Her voice became unsteady. "But it's been a very painful, uphill battle for him."

"I don't imagine it's been particularly easy on you, either."

She shot him a quick glance, then looked away. "No, it hasn't."

"I take it he hasn't seen you in a while."

"No."

"How long?"

"Fifteen years."

Malcolm let out a low whistle and shook his head. "Sorta makes you wonder why he showed up now."

Sydney didn't have to wonder. There was only one possible reason. Knowing that Nick had somehow discovered her involvement in his rehabilitation program made her sick inside. He would hate her for that. More than he already did.

"Sometimes we have to put our faith in the good Lord, Ms Foster, whether we want to or not. It can see us through some dark days." He drained his cup and rolled to his feet with athletic ease. "It's eleven o'clock so I have to check the security alarms, but it won't take me long."

Sydney turned her wrist to look at her watch. "I didn't realize it was so late." She stood up. "I think I can manage alone, Malcolm."

The caretaker's gaze softened with a knowing look. "In other words, you'd just like some quiet time alone with him."

She studied him for a long moment, then finally spoke. "Do you know you're a very perceptive man?" she said quietly.

He shrugged and bent his head as he fumbled with his mug. "I can understand needing somebody."

Touched by his simple honesty, Sydney found it hard to speak. "Thank you for being here for me tonight. I don't know what I would have done without you."

He looked at her, his gaze serious. "Anytime, ma'am. You know that." He turned to go. "I'll check in on you later, but if you need me before then, you call down, and I'll be up in a flash."

"I will."

He nodded and motioned to the chair. "You stay here. I'll let myself out." He paused at the door. "You take care now, you hear?"

She smiled back. "I hear."

The only sound she heard when he left was the soft closing of the door, and she found herself wondering how such a big man could move so soundlessly. She pulled an extra blanket out of the closet and curled up in the chair, then turned the bedside light down a notch. Resting her head against the wide wing of the chair, she pulled the cover up over her shoulder and studied the man asleep in her bed. How many hours had she watched him sleep during their brief time together? Dozens? Hundreds? Too many to count?

Even back then, she had known their time together was ill-fated, so she'd made the most of every minute she'd had with him. But Nick had had blinders on. His defense had been to pretend that her past didn't exist. He'd never acknowledged it, never talked about it; he'd just tried to erase it from his mind the same way he'd methodically erased Roxanne Busher from existence. But she had known the day of reckoning would come, and it had—with devastating force.

She huddled down in the chair, her solemn expression easing a little. God, but she'd loved him. Half-forgotten feelings rose up in her, filling her with such a penetrating ache she could hardly breathe. Some things never changed.

Nick uttered a low, indistinct sound and rolled his head as though he were struggling to move. Sydney brushed off her blanket and stood up. He was trembling. She wondered if it was from cold or a reaction to severe physical stress. She pulled up the quilted spread before turning on the electric blanket.

He hadn't been at his apartment for at least two days. She didn't even want to think about where he might have spent the night. The thought of him alone, struggling with his disability in some dark, cold alley was almost too much for her. With infinite care, she tucked the blankets more snugly around him, her throat contracting painfully as she smoothed back his hair.

His lips moved, then with no warning he opened his eyes and stared up at her. There was nothing to indicate he recognized her before his eyes drifted shut, and she saw him laboriously try to swallow. Sick at heart, she wondered when he'd eaten last or had something to drink.

"How's he doing?"

She started at Malcolm's soundless reappearance, and it took her a second to marshal her thoughts. "He's shivering and he keeps trying to swallow." Her voice caught. "He likely hasn't had anything to eat or drink for the better part of two days."

"How about fixing him some broth and seeing if we can get it into him."

She studied Nick a moment longer, then nodded. "All right, let's give it a try."

The aroma of beef broth rose from the earthen mug Sydney was holding when she returned from the kitchen. She tested it, then glanced at Malcolm, who was standing on the opposite side of the bed.

The caretaker nodded, and bracing one knee on the bed beside Nick, he effortlessly raised his shoulders.

Cupping her hand behind Nick's head, Sydney pressed the mug against his lips. His eyes fluttered open then drifted shut as he drank thirstily, and the ache in Sydney's chest intensified. The cup was almost empty when he made a weak

movement with his head, and she pulled it away. She
watched him for a moment, looking for some sign from
him, but there was nothing.

Malcolm carefully lowered him back onto the bed. "That
should hold him for a bit, Ms Foster. He should rest easy
now."

With her gaze fixed on Nick's face, Sydney slid the mug
onto the bedside table, then carefully tucked the blankets
around him again. She smoothed her hand across the covers before she glanced at Malcolm who was seated on the
opposite side of the bed. "I wish I knew what else I should
be doing for him."

Malcolm's soft voice was reassuring. "You're already
doin' it. You're already doin' it." He glanced at his watch
and stood up. "I'll be back in a couple of hours to take him
to the bathroom."

Sydney pulled her hair back from her face in a tired gesture and exhaled heavily. "That would probably be a good
idea."

Malcolm nodded toward the chair. "Why don't you curl
up and try to get some sleep. You look tuckered."

Sydney only nodded. How could she explain that the
tiredness she was experiencing had nothing to do with the
lack of sleep? How could she explain how she dreaded
morning? Dreaded facing Nick. She didn't think she could
endure one final confrontation with him. But she wouldn't
think about that now. She had a few more hours. She had
him for tonight. One night against the rest of her life.

CHAPTER THREE

SYDNEY STOOD STARING out the patio door, her arms folded tightly in front of her, waiting for Dr. Robertson to come out of the bedroom. He'd been in there for twenty minutes, but it seemed like an hour, and she had to force herself to keep from pacing.

Nick had rested quietly for most of the night, and it wasn't until about six o'clock that he showed any signs of waking. Malcolm had taken him to the bathroom then, and after the caretaker put him back to bed, she had the feeling Nick was far more alert than he let on. It had left her hollow, knowing he was avoiding her. It made her wonder just how deep his anger ran.

Closing her eyes, she tipped her head back, trying to release the tension in her neck and shoulders. She was so tired—tired from the lack of sleep, tired from the nearly unbearable strain, tired from the disturbing memories that had played hell with her mind most of the night.

"Hey, are you okay?"

Sighing heavily, Sydney opened her eyes and turned. Dr. Robertson was standing in the hall watching her, his friendly face touched with concern.

She gave him a weak smile as she crossed the expanse of living room. "I'm fine. How's Nick?"

"He's lucid this morning and seems to have weathered his ordeal fairly well. The trauma of the past couple of days has certainly had an effect, though."

"In what way?"

"Well, as I said last night, extreme fatigue and stress really affects him, and the medication knocked him for a loop. Sedatives tend to depress the central nervous system, so he was hit with a double whammy. His motor control is affected, and he's having trouble with his speech. He'll sleep most of the day, but I definitely want him back in therapy tomorrow. Inactivity is the worst thing after something like this."

Sydney removed the physician's squall jacket from the closet and helped him into it. "What if he wants to go home?"

The doctor shot her a penetrating look. "If he's really adamant about it, take him home. Pressuring Nick only aggravates the situation." He stuck his hands in the pockets of his jacket, his expression intent as he stared at her. "I'd feel better if he stayed here, where there's someone around to check on him once in a while. He's pretty out of it right now."

She gave him a crooked smile. "I doubt if Nick will see it that way."

The doctor opened his mouth to query her remark, then decided against it. Realizing there were things going on here he knew nothing about, he wisely changed the subject. "Don't be too alarmed by his speech. When he's tense or upset, he tends to have trouble, and that irritates the hell out of him. So he compensates by speaking as little as possible. And watch him with that cane. He always uses a quad—one of those four-legged rigs—when he's on his own. He doesn't like anyone helping him, so be aware he's going to be a little wobbly." He reached for the door. "I'll be at the hospital this morning and at the rehab center the rest of the day. Let me know if he does go home, and I'll have someone on staff stop by and check on him."

Sydney held the door as he stepped out into the hall. "I will. And thank you."

"No problem." The doctor yanked up his collar and turned toward the elevator. "Give me a call if there's any change."

"I will." She waited until the elevator door closed, then went back into the apartment, weariness washing over her. She closed her eyes and leaned back against the door, not wanting to face the long day ahead of her. Finally, with a tired sigh, she forced herself to move.

She hesitated at the guest room door, then gathered her courage and pushed it open. Nick was lying on his back, staring at the ceiling, his right arm draped across his forehead, his left lying stiffly across his chest. As she entered, he turned his head to look at her. His face was expressionless as he stared at her, then he rolled away and closed his eyes.

Hurt by his cold rebuff, she turned and left the room, closing the door soundlessly behind her. She went into the kitchen and opened the blinds, then filled the coffee maker. Picking up a heavy cardigan hanging on the knob of the pantry door, she wrapped it around her shoulders, then sank into the chair at the end of the table. An indescribable coldness encompassed her, and she shivered. Sydney had known she'd be leaving herself wide open for more agony when she got involved in Nick's life again, but she wasn't prepared for the renewed guilt. That was one feeling she thought she had conquered.

"You don't look so good."

Accustomed to Malcolm's silent arrivals, she glanced up and gave him a halfhearted smile. "I don't feel so good."

"Why don't you hit the sack for a couple of hours, and I'll watch him."

She stared at him for a moment, then sighed and shook her head. "I can't, Malcolm. I have an important meeting in—" she turned her wrist to look at her watch "—two hours. And it's one I can't postpone. I've been trying to set something up with these people for weeks."

Malcolm made a disapproving sound as he turned a chair around and straddled it. "You need some rest."

She managed another smile. "Maybe this afternoon."

"My time's pretty loose this morning," he told her. "Would you like me to keep an eye on him?"

Drained by exhaustion and emotional overload, Sydney had to struggle against the sudden sting of tears. "Could you? I don't feel right about leaving him, even for a couple of hours."

Malcolm lowered his head and stroked his bottom lip with his thumb. When he raised his eyes again, his gaze was solemn. "For your sake, I'm not sure he should be here at all."

Sydney looked away, not wanting to confront the sympathy she saw in the big man's eyes. It was too late to undo the damage. Years too late.

It was midafternoon before she was able to get away from her office, and by then Sydney had gone beyond tired and was driven by a kind of disconnected wakefulness that exaggerated every sensation. Lights were piercing, sounds were harsh, and movement aroused a sickening feeling of vertigo in her. By the time she got off the elevator in her building, she had the makings of a first-class headache.

Entering the silent apartment, she set her briefcase on the table and was in the process of hanging up her coat when Malcolm appeared in the hallway.

With his hands planted on his hips, he watched her for a minute, then released the air in his lungs. "We got a problem."

Sydney tucked her scarf in the pocket of her coat and turned, prepared for the worst. "What's wrong?"

Malcolm shrugged. "I dunno. After I fed him breakfast, he slept off and on for most of the morning, then about an hour ago he started to get pretty agitated. Said he wanted to go home. He's still pretty spaced-out, so I didn't feel right about sticking him in a cab. I told him we had to wait for you."

Sydney didn't say anything as she considered the situation, then she exhaled tiredly. "Is he dressed?"

"Yeah. He did that himself, but it tuckered him right out. I told him as soon as you got home, we'd take him back. I phoned the doc and got the address."

"How is he otherwise?"

"He's havin' trouble with his coordination, and he's not saying much, but he knows what he's doing, that's for sure."

She pulled her coat off the hanger. "I'll bring the car around to the front entrance if you can get him down to the lobby."

"No problem." He paused at the bedroom door, his hand resting on the doorknob. "Maybe this is best, Ms Foster."

"Yes," she said, her voice quiet. "Maybe it is."

Once downstairs, Nick acted as though Sydney didn't exist. Without protest he let Malcolm help him into the passenger seat and pull the seat belt around him. His expression was haggard and his eyes had a queer, unfocused look, and it was clearly evident he was operating on sheer grit. Sydney sat unmoving, her knuckles white as she grasped the wheel, rigidly refraining from doing anything to help. From the look on his face, she knew Nick did not want her to even look at him, much less touch him, and she kept her eyes averted.

With a final check, Malcolm handed Nick his cane and closed the door, then climbed into the back seat. As if reading her mind, he pulled a slip of paper from his pocket and read out the address.

Sydney nodded, and with the silence stretching into intolerable tension, she pulled onto the main street. Once the car was in motion, Nick tipped his head back against the padded headrest and closed his eyes, as though he didn't have an ounce of energy left. She cast him a quick glance, then looked away, her throat tightening as she tried to steel herself against the awful pain in her chest.

It took a little less than fifteen minutes to get to Nick's apartment, but to Sydney it felt like an eternity, and with shaky relief, she parked the car in front.

The plain, boxlike structure was an old gray stuccoed walk-up, the faded white paint peeling off the trim. The yard had large bald spots in it, and grass had crept into the flower beds, overlaying the unkempt edges. There was an air of neglect about the place, but Sydney tried to dismiss it. Peeling paint and neat flower beds had never been one of Nick's priorities.

There was a taut set to her mouth as she dropped her keys into her handbag, opened the door and climbed out. She waited on the sidewalk as Malcolm helped Nick out of the car, trying to ignore the pain that throbbed in her head.

She fell into step with Malcolm, who was watching Nick's every move as he made his way up the walk. "Does he have his keys?"

Malcolm shrugged, then addressed Nick. "We'll need your keys, Nick."

Leaning heavily on his cane, Nick fumbled with the pocket of his jacket, then slowly shook his head. "Inside."

Malcolm and Sydney exchanged a quick look, and the caretaker shrugged again. They paused at the single cement step leading into the building, and with a steadying hand from the man at his side, Nick navigated it. Sydney held open the door as the two men slowly entered, the smells of mildew, curry and cooked cabbage assailing her. Experiencing the first flutters of nausea from her headache, she had to swallow hard to keep it under control.

Swaying slightly, his face drawn with exhaustion, Nick indicated the fire alarm that housed a coiled hose. "On top. A key."

Reaching up, Sydney swept her hand along the metal frame and located a small magnetic holder. She pried it free, removed a single key, then replaced the case. Nick motioned down the long, poorly lighted hallway. "This way."

Sydney unlocked the door, dread welling up inside her. She closed her eyes and braced herself, then followed the two men inside. The place was sparsely furnished, but it was equipped with the necessary apparatus for a handicapped tenant. She was even more relieved when she saw that, although it needed a fresh coat of paint, the apartment was spotlessly clean.

Malcolm stepped toward the door. "I need to pick up a couple of things, Ms Foster, so I'll run down to the convenience store I saw on the corner. I'll wait for you in the car."

Sydney realized he was trying to be tactful, but the thought of being left alone with Nick, even for a few moments, filled her with more dread than she liked to admit. She experienced a twist of apprehension as the door closed behind him.

Avoiding looking at Nick, she opened her purse, her fingers trembling as she searched for her keys. She tried to think of something to say that would get her out of there with her composure intact, but her mind kept drawing blanks. Her heart was in her throat as she finally grasped the keys, the sharp metal biting into her clammy palm.

"Sydney." His tone was harsh, and there was an undercurrent of barely contained anger that chilled her. It took every ounce of courage she had to make herself turn to face him.

His eyes were cold and remote, and a muscle in his jaw twitched as he watched her. There was a taut silence, then he spoke again. "Why?"

She tried to dodge the confrontation. "Why what?"

He continued to stare at her with the same look of distaste she'd witnessed earlier. "Why the program?"

Her heart skipped a beat, and she tried to evade the full brunt of his anger. "How did you find out?"

"I have—my ways." She made no response, and his eyes narrowed ominously. It took a concentrated effort for him to form the next words. "Did paying for my treatment—salve your conscience?"

Sydney held his gaze for a moment, then she turned toward the door, her movements unnatural. "Nothing can ever salve my conscience," she whispered, her voice breaking. And before Nick could move across the room to stop her, she left the apartment, the slam of the door leaving a reverberating silence behind.

Sydney's headache had developed into a full-blown migraine, and it was all she could do to maneuver through the heavy rush-hour traffic without being sick. By the time she pulled into her parking stall, her eyes were glazed, the pain nearly blinding her. It took every bit of energy she had to climb out of the car and walk to the security door.

She waited as her companion unlocked it, afraid to move for fear nausea would strike before she got to her apartment.

Malcolm gave her a worried look. "I'll come up with you. You look like you ain't goin' to make it on your own."

"I'll be fine," she said, her lips colorless. "I just have a bad headache, that's all."

"Are you sure?"

She managed a wan smile. "Yes, I'm sure. I'm going to take something for it and go straight to bed."

The caretaker held the elevator door open for her as she entered. "If you need anything, you call, you hear?"

"I will."

He gave her another worried look, then let the door slide shut. "You go right to bed."

She forced another smile. "I promise."

The movement of the elevator only intensified her queasiness. Through sheer will, she managed to get into her apartment, her face white as she dashed to the bathroom in the guest room. She was violently ill, her head feeling as though it were going to explode with every heave. Knowing she would never keep any medication down now, she crept back into the bedroom, shaking so badly she could barely undo the buttons on her blouse. She was so cold. Clamping her teeth together to keep from shivering, she shed her clothes and crawled into the same bed Nick had deserted a short time before. The smell of him still clung to the linen, and she turned her face into the pillow, wanting nothing more than to sink into oblivion. She wanted to escape from the pain in her head, from the pain around her heart, from absolutely everything.

IT WAS MUCH LATER that evening when Nick Novak was finally forced to face his own set of demons. Never had he experienced such helplessness, such a boiling frustration with his disability as he had when she'd left that afternoon. He hadn't been able to go after her; he hadn't been able to vent his rage on her; he hadn't been able to tell her how much he despised her. He hadn't been able to do a damned thing but stand there and tremble, his own body betraying him with its inability to function. When the door had closed behind her, he'd almost been driven to the point of violence by feelings he didn't even try to understand.

But it was worse now. Not only had his disabled body rendered his fury impotent, but as he lay on his bed in his darkened room, his disabled mind turned on him, as well. He could no longer regiment his thoughts the way he once could, and half-forgotten memories rolled in to torment him. He was as helpless under their onslaught as he had been under the onslaught of his consuming rage. But the rage was gone now, and he had no defenses left as the pain

ripped through him. Lord, he wished he had never laid eyes
on her again. He should never have gone to see her.

He remembered nothing of how he had got to her apartment. It was all just a blur, disjointed images and sensations. But that first glimpse of her, framed in the overhead
light of the underground garage, would be forever im-
printed on his mind. All he had to do was close his eyes, and
she was there in his head, every detail, every color, distinct
and sharp.

With a massive effort he tried to shut her out. But she
hovered there in the dark channels of his mind, and the
emotions he had battled against for so long consumed him.

At some point during the previous night, he had struggled through the fog of the drug-induced sleep and, for one
awful moment, didn't know where he was. But then he had
seen her asleep in the chair, her breathing deep and even, the
muted light casting her face in soft shadows. For one brief
instant he thought that the past fifteen years had been
nothing more than a bad dream, and relief had swept
through him. He had gone back to find her, and she'd been
there.

But then recollections filtered through the fog, and he remembered why he'd come. He remembered everything except the fury that had driven him to her. That one fierce,
overriding emotion had deserted him, and he was left defenseless. And he could not, for the love of God, drag his
eyes away from her face.

It had been so long, so damned long, and a familiar ache
had grown in his chest. She was so goddamned lovely, like
an exquisitely crafted porcelain figurine, the sheen of her
thick, dark hair like mink against her skin. His gaze had
locked on to the sweep of her long lashes, the high cheekbones, the soft fullness of her mouth, and the ache had intensified. He had wanted to touch her then. Not to wake her,
but simply to reach out and touch her. But his muscles re-

fused to respond, and he'd lain there, imprisoned in his disabled body, frustration mixed with longing. The emotional upheaval had been so overwhelming that his vision had blurred, and he had closed his eyes, ashamed of his weakness. By God, he would have willingly stopped breathing if he could only have reached out and touched her.

Nick struggled against the feelings that one memory aroused. He had wanted her fifteen years ago, he had wanted her countless times since, and he wanted her now. An excruciating loneliness rose up in him, and a low sound escaped into the protective darkness of his room.

THE FOLLOWING DAY was dull and overcast, but it wasn't until early evening that it finally started to rain. The drops fell in a gentle drizzle as Sydney studied the papers spread on her desk.

The file was from Major Henderson and was Jenny Cord's case history. It made Sydney sick to read it. First sexually assaulted by her stepfather at the age of nine, repeated frequent abuse, pregnant at twelve, forcefully given the equivalent of a back-alley abortion, a prostitute by thirteen, a heavy drug user by fourteen. And the smug, untouched, unsoiled segment of society recoiled in their ivory towers, appalled by what she'd become. As if a nine-year-old—terrified, alone, waiting for the sound outside her bedroom door, helpless to stop what was about to happen—had any control over her ultimate fate.

If the untouched, unsoiled segment of society really knew the ugly facts about the frightening numbers of kids on the street who had been sexually molested as small children, kids whose trust had been brutally betrayed by someone in a parental role, they would never dare be so self-righteous, so condemning.

Clamping down on the deep, scouring anger that churned in her, Sydney made herself focus on the other document in the folder. It was only slightly less disturbing.

Jenny's welfare worker had somehow managed to clear her through the system with lightning speed, and the girl had been admitted to a clinic in the States. An initial assessment had been faxed to Sydney. The girl was withdrawn and uncommunicative, but she was cooperating at a basic level. At this point, that was all anybody could hope for.

Unable to concentrate any longer, Sydney took off her glasses and rested her head against the back of her chair. She was still feeling the effects of her sleepless night and the ensuing migraine, and she wearily massaged her neck, trying to ease the tension. She sighed and closed her eyes, knowing she was going to have to scrape up her courage to face Nick sooner or later. She wished it could be later, but for Nick's sake, she couldn't put it off any longer.

Peter Robertson had called earlier that afternoon to inform her that Nick had not showed up for therapy again. Concerned about the ex-cop's continued absence, the head of the rehabilitation program had contacted him. Nick had made it very clear that he had no intentions of going back. He'd told the doctor that he felt it was a waste of time, he wasn't progressing, and he was fed up. Sydney knew those weren't the real reasons. The real reason was her involvement.

She knew enough about brain injury to know that without consistent therapy, Nick's condition would soon begin to regress. The last thing she wanted was for him to turn his back on everything he had worked so hard to attain.

She swiveled her chair to stare out the rain-spattered window, her expression pensive. She didn't want to risk alienating him from the program completely. Maybe if she was able to convince him it was a desperately needed service in the community, maybe then he would relent. But at the same time, she knew she was going to have to be honest with him, honest about her reasons for funding the program in the first place. She hoped she had the finesse to pull it off.

She absorbed the soothing, gentle sound of the rain against the window for a few moments, then she sighed and stood up. She could never remember wanting to avoid anything more than she wanted to avoid facing Nick one more time.

The apartment building looked even dingier in the rain and the deepening dusk, and she shivered as she turned up the broken walk. She huddled deeper into her trench coat as a gust of wind whipped around the corner of the building, sending bits and pieces of loose garbage rattling along the wet, empty street.

The same smells assailed her as she entered the building, and she tried to block them out, a new wave of apprehension leaving her mouth dry. That feeling mounted as she went down the dimly lighted hall toward Nick's suite. She paused at the door, then steeled herself and knocked.

"It's open."

Her heart did a crazy little flip-flop, and she hesitated again before she grasped the knob and turned it.

Nick was just coming out of the kitchen, his weight supported by the quad cane. His expression froze when he saw who it was.

Sydney struggled to maintain her composure as she stepped into the room and closed the door, hoping that he couldn't see how unnerved she really was. "Hello, Nick."

He stared at her a moment, then looked away, the muscles in his face hardening. "What do you want?"

She tried to swallow but couldn't, and her voice was unsteady. "I think it's time we had a talk."

He cast a scathing glance at her, then looked away again. "About what?"

"About the program."

He faced her, his tone cutting. "You can stuff your god-damned program, lady. And you can get the hell out of my apartment."

Sensing she was certain to come out the loser no matter what, she gathered her resolve. "I'm going to say what I came to say, then I'll leave. But you owe it to others like yourself to hear me out."

The muscles in his jaw twitched as he turned to stare rigidly out the window.

Carefully laying her purse on the arm of an old easy chair, Sydney stuck her hands in her pockets, praying her voice would be steadier than her hands. "Yes, I provided the initial funding for the rehab program. I won't even pretend otherwise. But in the past few months, I've come to realize how important this program really is."

She paused, searching for the right words, desperate to make him understand. "Most of the work done with brain-damaged patients has been accomplished with just volunteers up till now. And it's been so frustrating for everyone involved—the patients, the medical staff, the families, the volunteers. But because of you, things are starting to happen. Dr. Robertson has developed an aggressive and innovative treatment program that's getting results. And because of him, the program's managed to acquire some decent research funding."

She hesitated, her voice breaking as she whispered, "And they have you." She had to wait a moment for the knot in her throat to ease. "Dr. Robertson says they couldn't have had a better patient than you. That you've given it all you have, that you've struggled through nearly insurmountable odds on sheer determination." She turned away, battling to hold back the tears that were threatening. It took her a moment before she could continue. "Don't throw it all away because of me. Don't let everyone down because of that."

Her throat so tight she could no longer speak, she wiped her eyes with the side of her hand, then picked up her purse and turned toward the door.

She was reaching for the handle when he spoke, his tone rough. "Sydney."

She stopped, her back to him, too uncertain to turn around.

There was a strained silence, and he spoke again. "Why?"

Visibly bracing herself, she turned, her eyes shimmering with unshed tears. "Because," she whispered brokenly. "Because I couldn't stand to see you trapped like that. I couldn't stand to see you fighting so hard, without the right equipment, without enough adequately trained staff, without enough of the right kind of therapy." She dashed away the tears again, an undercurrent of vehemence in her tone. "I just couldn't stand it, Nick." Desperate to get out, she turned toward the door.

He called her name, but she didn't look back as she opened the door, her only thought of escape. Then there was a loud crash behind her, and she whirled around.

Nick was sprawled on the floor, his cane lying beside him, and she knew he had tried to come after her.

"Nick, God—" Her reaction was swift. She slipped her arms around him as he struggled to get up, her alarm growing when she felt how violently he was trembling. Unaware of how badly her own hands were shaking, she hooked his arm around her shoulders as he laboriously dragged his knees under him. "Lean on me, Nick. Just lean on me and let me help you."

It nearly killed her to watch him struggle with every movement, his spastic muscles rigid and uncoordinated, and it hurt her even more when he made a feeble motion toward the cane. His arm tightened convulsively around her shoulders as he spoke through gritted teeth. "The cane. I need it."

His hold on her didn't slacken, and she realized he was going to need both her and the cane to stand. She slid her arm around his back, trying to balance his weight against her as she reached out, just barely grasping one leg of the appliance with her free hand. She dragged it closer, then stood it beside him. She could feel him gather his strength as he grabbed it, then with an awkward twist of his body, he fought to lever himself up. Dredging up her own strength, she carried as much of his weight as she could as she rose with him. He wavered for a moment, then clenching his teeth, he forced himself upright, beads of perspiration appearing on his forehead as he finally straightened his legs. Sydney watched as he positioned his feet to get his balance, then she glanced up at him. She had never seen such fierce determination before, and she tightened her hold on him, compassion nearly suffocating her. She gave him a moment, then spoke again. "Do you think you can make it to the bedroom?"

He closed his eyes and nodded, and with a massive effort took a step. He paused, leaning heavily on Sydney as he released his hold on the cane. And her eyes filled again as she recognized the significance of that one small gesture.

By the time she got him into the bedroom, the tremors in his body had intensified. She caught the light switch as they passed through the door, and the lamp on the bedside table came on. She was relieved to discover he had an oversized hospital bed equipped with an overhead frame that supported a trapeze-shaped handhold as well as exercise pulleys and rings.

Afraid he would collapse if she let go, she continued to support him as he grasped the frame. She could barely understand him as he whispered roughly, "I can do it now."

Apprehension filled her as she withdrew her support, and with her heart in her throat, she watched him as he maneuvered closer. It happened so fast, it startled her. The best way she could describe the movement was a calculated, controlled fall, and very effective. She managed a shaky smile. "That was slick. Scary, but slick."

His eyes were closed but she caught it, the barest twitch of a smile. And she wanted to cry.

Lifting his legs over on the bed, she removed his shoes, then pulled the tumble of covers free. He kept his eyes shut as she covered him, and he didn't open them until she smoothed her hand across his chest. "Tell me what to do," she said quietly.

He held her gaze for a moment, his eyes unreadable, then he glanced toward the bedside table. "Pills." She straightened and picked up a vial of white-and-brown capsules. He shook his head. "No. The blue ones."

She quickly scanned the directions on the vial. "How many?"

It took a massive effort for him to speak. "Two."

Taking off the lid, she dumped two into her palm, replaced the lid, then set the bottle down. She picked up the glass of water sitting by the lamp and turned back to the bed. Giving him the pills, she slipped her arm under his shoulders, a surge of protectiveness filling her as she pressed the glass against his lips.

He closed his eyes and drank thirstily, then made a weak motion with his head. Loath to sever the physical contact, Sydney slid the glass back onto the table and reluctantly eased her arm from under him. Her eyes were dark with concern. "Will the medication stop the shaking?"

He tipped his head in assent.

Bracing her arm on the other side of him, she sat on the edge of the bed and gazed down at him. Gently brushing back his hair, she let her hand curve against the side of his head as she slowly stroked his forehead. She didn't speak as she watched over him, continuing the soothing, slow caress as she waited for the medication to take effect.

Slowly the tremors abated, and his breathing became deep and even. For a moment she thought he had fallen asleep, but she felt him try to move his disabled left arm. She pressed her hand against his face. "What is it?" she murmured.

He opened his eyes and met her gaze, the tautness in his face easing. There was something in his expression that held her, and she began to stroke his temple again, her touch slow and hypnotic. But he didn't close his eyes. He just kept watching her, his gaze never leaving her face, and she sensed agitation growing in him. He tried to raise his arm again, and this time she saw the flash of frustration in his expression.

"What, Nick? What do you want?" she asked softly.

"Your hair," he mumbled hoarsely.

She stared at him for a moment, confused by what he'd said, but finally she comprehended what he wanted, and she lifted his hand and held his palm against her face. Hauling in a ragged breath, she closed her eyes, submitting to his touch.

Nothing could have prepared her for the overpowering feelings that washed through her as she felt his fingers against her scalp. Emotion caught in her throat when his hand moved to her face, awkwardly caressing her brows, her eyes, her mouth, as though he were relearning every line, every detail, by touch alone.

There was such tenderness, so much longing in each lingering touch that it broke her final hold, and a sob escaped. She pressed his hand against her mouth, trying to physically contain the unbearable pressure, but it could no longer be held in check. The tears slipped relentlessly down as she tried to draw a breath past the fierce pain in her chest.

He drew his thumb along her trembling bottom lip, then his hand tightened against her jaw as he whispered her name.

She fought to swallow as she opened her eyes, the anguish in his voice compelling her.

His face was drawn, his gaze dark and tormented as he tried unsuccessfully to speak. There was pain and anguish and a desperate longing in his voice when he finally managed to choke out, "Stay."

She stared at him, her insides contracting in an agony of hope.

He closed his eyes. "Please—don't go."

With a low sound, she slipped her arms around him, everything within her breaking loose as she cradled his head against her.

Energized by his own overpowering emotions, he managed to drag his arms up her back. Another tremor coursed through him as he tightened his arms around her with all the strength he possessed.

Overcome by feelings so raw, so profound she could barely speak, she whispered brokenly, "I'll stay."

She could feel the incapacitating tension in him as he struggled for control, then he hauled in a deep, shuddering breath and roughly turned his head into her neck, his face wet against her skin. "I need—I want—" His voice was hoarse and ragged as he tried to pull her closer. "Please, Sydney."

Responding to his unspoken need, she turned in his arms, their bodies finally connecting. He gathered her close, his weakened arm powered by a new strength as the pain, the hurt, the loneliness that once separated them now bound them together.

THUNDER RUMBLED OVERHEAD and the rain pounded down with a wind-driven force, but Sydney was only vaguely aware of the storm outside. The past half hour had stripped away every protective barrier she had, and she felt raw, battered and exhausted, as though she had been through a violent physical struggle. But she also felt emptied, as if the accumulated anguish had been vented, at least temporarily.

Slowly she combed her fingers through Nick's hair, tightening her embrace as she cradled his head closer. Her voice was very soft. "Nick?"

He stirred against her, his movements slow and awkward as he shifted his weight.

Pressing her cheek against the top of his head, she closed her eyes, reluctant to break the silence, but she knew if she didn't get up now, she never would. And she had to leave a message for Marg on the office recorder. Resting her hand against his jaw, she slowly caressed his ear. "Nick?"

"What?" His voice was thick, as though he were heavily drugged and struggling against sleep.

"I have to make a phone call, and I should lock your door. I'm just going to get up for a minute, okay?"

For a moment he didn't move, then he inhaled heavily. As if it cost him an enormous physical effort, he rolled onto his back. As she pulled away from him, she glanced down. He had dragged one arm across his eyes, and the muscles in his face were rigid. Uncertainty stirred in her. He looked so remote lying there, as if he had withdrawn into himself.

She hesitated for a moment, then slipped off the bed, her legs unsteady as she left the room. She locked the door, made her phone call, then turned out all the lights before entering the bathroom, across from the bedroom. As she was about to leave, she glanced into the linen closet behind the door and spotted a stack of freshly laundered sweat suits. She picked out the lightest set, shed her clothes and put it on.

Nick hadn't moved, and as she crossed the dimly lighted room, her uncertainty stirred again. She tried to ignore the sensation as she hung her blouse on the back of a chair, then draped her skirt and sweater over the chrome frame above his bed. What if he regretted asking her to stay?

A nervous flutter unfolded in her middle and she pressed her palms against her thighs as she turned to face him, hesitant about how to handle his withdrawal. As she raised her eyes to look at him, the flutter intensified.

He had moved his arm so it was resting across his forehead, and he was watching her with an unreadable look. She clenched her hands, anxiety tightening her chest, then he slowly reached out with his good arm.

For an instant she couldn't move, then, as her eyes filled with tears, she grasped his hand and laced her fingers through his. His grip tightened, and with a gentle tug he pulled her toward him. Sydney felt as though she were going to start shaking all over again as she braced one knee on the bed and shut off the light, then slipped into his unsteady embrace, her body molding against his as he turned on his side. Cradling his head on her shoulder, she eased onto her back, and Nick inhaled raggedly, the weight of his body pressing them together.

He shifted his arm and rested his hand along her jaw, his fingers tangling in her hair. On a jagged sigh, she heard him whisper her name.

Sydney's vision blurred again and she tightened her arms around him as she closed her eyes, the warmth from him surrounding her.

CHAPTER FOUR

DAWN CREPT INTO THE ROOM stealthily, without a blaze of color, the eastern sky still heavily shrouded with dark clouds. A soft rain spattered against the window, muffling the sounds of the city and blanketing the room in an early morning stillness.

Nick moved, fighting the effects of a drugged sleep, an elusive fragrance stirring his senses. With a start of recollection, he opened his eyes and stared at the ceiling, his pulse skipping a beat. He didn't move a muscle, then slowly he released his breath as something akin to relief washed through him. For one awful moment he thought he'd been dreaming.

She was lying with her head nestled against his rib cage, her arm across his hips, and he could tell by the regular rise and fall of her chest that she was still soundly asleep. Carefully pulling the pillow up under his shoulders, he eased his weakened left arm around her and rested his hand against her back, his expression somber. It had been a long time since he'd slept like that—a deep, undisturbed sleep, as though the past fifteen years had been reduced to nothing. He had forgotten how damned good it felt to wake up with her soft and warm beside him.

He stared into space, his eyes darkening as he reflected on what had happened the night before. He had panicked when he realized she was leaving, and he didn't know what he would have done if she hadn't looked back, if she'd just kept going. He didn't know what kind of shape he'd be in by now. A goddamned mess, no doubt.

He exhaled heavily and absently stroked her shoulder, her fragrance encompassing him. He frowned slightly; that was something different. Now she had the elusive scent of a very expensive perfume, yet it was strangely familiar. But there were other changes. The fine lines around her eyes that hadn't been there before, a few extra pounds, but what was most noticeable was the new and, he suspected, hard-won air of assurance. It surprised him how proud he was of her success. On the other hand, it didn't surprise him at all to discover he had never really gotten over her. She had been that one loose end in his life.

Sydney stirred against him, and Nick experienced a twist of panic. How in hell was he going to deal with this now? He had been in such an emotional upheaval for the past three days and so drugged up he'd been practically unconscious. Now he had to face her stone-cold sober. And that was going to be bloody hard.

"Nick?"

For an instant he considered letting her think he was still asleep, but he knew he was going to have to deal with this first conscious encounter sooner or later. "What?"

Her voice was soft, with an undercurrent of hesitancy in it. "I wasn't sure if you were awake or not."

"Yeah, I'm awake." Hell, he thought, that was a really brilliant answer.

"How are you feeling?"

He heard the anxious catch in her voice, and he felt like a complete bastard. "I'm fine." He tightened his arm around her, wishing he had the guts to say what he felt. "How about you?"

She nodded, and Nick sensed she didn't speak because she couldn't, and he closed his eyes, hating himself, hating this wall of constraint between them. They had just spent the night together, yet they were acting as if they were strangers.

"Shall I fix breakfast?"

The way he was feeling, he couldn't swallow a damned bite. "Sure, if you want."

She eased away from him and sat up, and he opened his eyes, his gaze disquieted as he stared at her rigid back. He sensed a kind of wariness in her, as if one wrong move might upset the tenuous balance. They were both walking a tight-rope, and he knew it. And that scared the hell out of him.

By the time he had his shower and got dressed, he was feeling pretty shaky, but he knew he was going to have to face her, no matter how much he dreaded it. Last night had been his mistake, not hers. He didn't feel any better when he opened the bathroom door and found his quad cane wait-ing for him. With an uncompromising set to his jaw, he grasped it and headed toward the kitchen.

Sydney had obviously heard him coming and had a plas-tic smile glued on her face when he entered. She couldn't quite meet his gaze as she fussed with a bowl of batter, her voice a little too bright. "I thought you might like some pancakes."

He watched her, experiencing a twist of guilt when he re-alized how badly her hands were shaking. Trying to ignore the feelings her vulnerability aroused in him, he started across the room, his tone impersonal. "Pancakes are fine."

He set his cane aside when he reached the sink, then dragged the coffee maker closer. An uncomfortable silence stretched between them as he filled the pot and scooped fresh grounds into the basket, his mouth set in a hard line. He hadn't wanted to get involved with her, but he had. And now he was left with the awkward aftermath, and he didn't know what to do with it.

Steeling himself for a face-to-face confrontation, he turned just as Sydney straightened, the frying pan in her hand. He saw the glimmer of tears in her eyes, and his determination faltered. In all the time he'd known her, he had never seen her cry. Not until last night.

He saw her quickly wipe her eyes, and Nick's expression became even more strained as he tried not to react. But his mind turned on him, and he remembered the first time he'd seen her, battered and alone and with no one to turn to. An awful emptiness rose up in him, and he experienced a wrenching sense of loss. And right then he would have sold his soul to have made things different.

As if sensing his thoughts, Sydney spoke, her voice laden with unhappiness and regret. "I'm so sorry, Nick. So sorry."

He closed his eyes, the ache in his throat intense. He understood the utter anguish in her voice. And he understood it wasn't just her tears she was apologizing for. She was sorry about the awkwardness between them, the lost years, the pain—but most of all, she was sorry she couldn't change the past.

He swallowed hard, his voice gruff when he finally spoke. "So am I."

And that was all. Nothing more, because there was nothing more that could be said.

Little by little, he could see her tension ease, and for a brief space of time there was a kind of unspoken understanding between them. Then she turned away.

It was odd how he could feel their common withdrawal, as though they both knew they were treading on dangerous ground. But at least the constraint was gone, and he knew that he could look her in the eye, that they had established a temporary neutral zone.

As if bracing herself, she took a deep breath. "Could we talk about the program?"

Nick made a quarter turn, the muscles in his jaw tightening. Staring at the drizzle slanting across the window, he relented with a sigh. "Yeah, I guess we could."

Sydney looked at him, her voice beseeching. "Please don't quit, Nick. I understand why you feel the way you do, but there's more at stake than just..." She looked away, uncertainty overriding her.

He studied her profile for a moment, then finished her unspoken thought. "There's more at stake than just my pride."

She faced him, her gaze unwavering. "Yes, there is. Because of the success they've had with you, there's a new line of funding coming on stream. And that means everybody in the program is going to benefit."

Nick's expression hardened slightly as he turned away, trying not to let his bloody pride get the upper hand. When he finally spoke, his tone had a cutting edge to it. "Just out of curiosity, how much did it cost you to salvage me?"

She avoided his gaze, and Nick leaned back against the counter. "How much, Sydney?" he demanded.

She went back to the stove, her body unnaturally stiff. "I didn't do it alone. I simply funneled some money into an existing program to provide quality care, then the volunteer association did the rest."

He wasn't about to be sidetracked. "What was your share?"

"It isn't relevant."

Nick didn't respond for a moment, an unrelenting expression thinning his mouth as he fixed his gaze on her. When he finally spoke there was an unmistakable steeliness in his voice. "Just answer the question, damn it. I want to know how much."

There was a taut silence, then she turned to look at him. Realizing he wasn't going to let it go until she told him, she finally caved in. "Two hundred thousand over two years."

"My God!" He stared at her, speechless. He knew it had cost. You didn't get somebody like Dr. Robertson and three other staff, plus new equipment, for a bag of peanuts. Something clicked in his mind, a half-forgotten bit of conversation, something about the program being guaranteed. "And how long did you guarantee it for?"

There was an undercurrent of weariness in her voice. "That isn't relevant, either. The association was able to raise solid funding. They didn't need to draw on that."

His tone was implacable. "That's not good enough, Sydney. What, exactly, did you guarantee?"

There was another silent battle of wills, then she finally met his gaze, a resigned expression in her eyes. "I guaranteed it for four years."

Four years. Four bloody years. How could she have possibly raised that amount? He felt as if his brain had been short-circuited by shock.

When he made no response, she went on, her voice expressionless. "If it makes any difference, I never expected to get in so deep. But when I started checking out facilities and programs, I found out how little help there was for someone with a brain injury. From what I was able to determine, I knew you'd need an intense, aggressive program. And there just wasn't one around. It made me so damned mad that I decided to do something about it." She finally looked at him, a wry expression hovering around her mouth. "It just seemed like a good idea at the time."

There was something about the way she said it, something in that self-deprecating tone that got to him, and he found himself almost amused. Almost. "You call dumping two hundred grand a good idea?"

She shot him a quick look, a glimmer of humor in her eyes. "I've had worse."

He studied her closely. "Are you implying that the continuation of the program depends on me?"

She turned back to the stove and switched on the burner. "Dr. Robertson has had several medical papers published that have drawn considerable attention. One particular paper focused on your rehabilitation. He used the neurologists' original prognosis, then detailed how an aggressive program took you beyond that in a matter of weeks. You're living proof his program is effective.

"He's also presented a paper on medical costs to the government. He compared what the projected expenses would be to maintain a patient indefinitely in an extended-care facility with the cost of rehabilitation. Initially the rehab is very expensive, but in the long run, that cost is nothing compared to the cost of long-term or permanent care."

Nick played a hunch. "That was your idea, wasn't it?"

Her back was still to him, but he could tell by the set of her shoulders he was right.

There was a pause, then she answered in a flat tone, "One thing I've learned during the past few years is that the bottom line rings a lot of bells."

"Yes," he said quietly, "I'm sure you have."

She cast him a sharp look and turned back to the stove. "Will you go back to therapy?"

He stared at her, trying to align this woman with the one he remembered from the past. He turned and looked out the window, his face heavy with resignation. In reality, he had little choice. "Yes, I'll go back."

Raindrops clung to the pane, and he watched them slide one into the other as he tried to fight the familiar flickering of panic. He was trapped in a disabled body, where every step was a struggle, every movement an effort of concentration. And there was no way out. None. He would spend the rest of his life fighting to regain a fraction of what he'd lost. The lines around his mouth were carved by bitter resentment, a resentment that was suddenly and irrationally aimed at her.

Without conscious thought, he voiced his anger, his tone cutting. "Why did you do it?"

The silence was brittle and foreboding, threatening the uneasy truce. Sydney didn't even pretend to misread his sudden hostility, her voice deceptively even. "I told you why."

He turned to face her, his body rigid. "Did you? I don't think you did. I think there was more to it than that."

She didn't look at him as she spoke, her tone sharp with rebuke. "It's a little late for analysis, Nick."

"Don't play corporate head games with me, Sydney. What really made you decide to salvage me?"

She slammed the pancake turner down and turned to face him, anger glinting in her eyes. "What do you want from me? A declaration of guilt? My conscience on a platter? What? If there was any penitence I could do to absolve me of my sins, I would. Believe me, I would. But damn it, I can't. I'm stuck with them."

"Why did you leave?"

She went stock still, her anger defused by the unexpectedness of his question.

His own anger flared. He had never planned on asking her that, but now that he had, now that he had moved onto forbidden ground, he wanted some answers. "You packed it in in two bloody weeks. Yes, I walked, but so in hell did you." With fury rising in him, Nick moved toward her, the muscles in his neck rigid. In a corner of his mind, in a sane, logical corner, he realized he had just tapped into the real source of his bitterness.

Even back then, he'd known the problems were his, but in spite of everything that was wrong, there was a hell of a lot that was right. And never once had he considered the possibility that she would ditch the whole relationship, but she had. She had walked away without so much as a backward glance, and that had been her final betrayal.

His anger accelerated. "You didn't even care enough to stick around to see if I came to my goddamned senses. Hell, no! Not a word, not even a damned letter. I tried to trace you for bloody weeks, but there wasn't one stinking lead— not one. You made damned sure I couldn't find you, and I finally had to ask myself why. Or did that just seem like a good idea, too?"

She stared at him, every speck of color draining from her face, then she closed her eyes. Her voice was barely above a whisper, shock permeating every word. "You came back."

Consumed by rage, he swept the pancake turner off the counter and sent it clattering against the wall, his eyes blazing. "Yes, I went back. If I wasn't worth salvaging then, what in hell possessed you to run a major salvage operation for me now?"

She opened her eyes and looked at him with an eerie, vacant expression. There wasn't a flicker of emotion, no indication that she'd even heard him.

It was as though she had suffered a sharp physical blow, and she started to turn away, but Nick's unleashed fury overrode his sudden start of intuition, and he yanked her around, his tone savage. "Give me an answer, damn it! Why did you drop out of sight the way you did? You owe me that, at least."

She tried to pull free from his grasp, her voice shaking. "Let me go."

Seething with anger, he forced her arm to one side. "Don't play games with me, damn it. I want to know why you left."

She ceased her struggle and he was vaguely aware of the trembling in her body. She hauled in a deep, shuddering breath, then looked up at him, her eyes ablaze. "You want to know why I left?" she ground out. "Then I'll tell you. I left because I loved you. I left because I loathed myself." She wrenched her arm free from his grasp, her fury fueling her strength. "But most of all I left because I was pregnant." She twisted away and fled from the room.

Nick stood rooted to the spot, immobilized by unbelief. Pregnant. She had been pregnant.

The sound of the door slamming snapped him out of his daze, and he fumbled for his cane. Knowing he was physically incapable of going after her, he rammed his fist against the cupboard, frustration boiling up in him with an incapacitating force. Closing his eyes, he clenched his teeth, his face contorting with sick realization. God, she had been carrying his child.

THE CAB PULLED AWAY from the curb, and Nick slowly made his way up the cobbled sidewalk of the luxury apartment building. He was still reeling from the bomb she'd dropped on him that morning, but the shock was beginning to wear off, and anger moved in to replace it.

What infuriated him more than anything else was knowing she had never intended to tell him. She had used it in unthinking retaliation; that had been clear from the look in her eyes. And she had no right to keep that from him. The kid was his, and he should have been told.

Reaching the doors, he stopped and forced himself to get a grip on his resentment, knowing full well if he faced her with all guns blazing, she would simply clam up and tell him nothing. And he was going to find out about the kid, one way or another.

Bracing his weight on his cane, he opened the outer door, then made his way into the security entryway, the heavy door hissing shut behind him. He checked the list of names, then buzzed her suite. As he waited for her to answer, he stared into the posh lobby through the second set of doors.

The man who had tended him the night he had been flat out in her bed was vacuuming the carpet, and he looked up as Nick rang the buzzer a second time.

He switched off the machine, and tucking in his shirttail, he crossed the carpeted area and opened the door. He gave Nick a welcoming smile. "You looking for Ms Foster?"

Nick resurrected his "good cop" expression and grinned back. "Yeah. I am. But she's not answering the buzzer."

The caretaker checked his watch. "It's only five. She's hardly ever home before seven."

Nick held his irritation in check and kept his tone easy. "I guess I should have called first." He motioned inside. "Is there a pay phone in the lobby I can use? I'll have to call a cab."

The other man opened the door wider. "No. But there's one in the office. Come in and wait inside. With rush hour and all, it might take a while."

Nick tried to dredge up a name, but nothing came. He extended his hand, a glimmer of wry humor in his eyes. "I don't think we ever got around to introducing ourselves the other night. I'm Nick Novak."

The caretaker grasped his hand in a strong grip. "Malcolm Jefferson. I'm the caretaker here." Malcolm indicated a door tucked into a nook by the two elevators. "There's a couple of chairs in there. If we leave the door open, we can see the cab when it pulls up in front. I'll call one for you." He unlocked the door and waited for Nick to enter, then he went behind the desk and picked up the phone.

Nick lowered himself into one of the chairs, then glanced around the small room. It was a janitorial storeroom, with a desk, a file cabinet and a wall of shelving filled with cleaning supplies. It was neat, well organized and immaculately clean, and he could tell from that alone what kind of employee this man was.

Nick considered the role the caretaker had played the night he'd collapsed in the garage. A flickering of intuition turned in his gut, and he narrowed his eyes. Sydney had been unguarded around the man—not familiar, but un-guarded. And she did not develop that kind of trust over-night. Which meant she had known the man for a long time. Which also meant Malcolm Jefferson was an unexpected source of information.

Stretching out his bad leg, Nick kept his manner relaxed. If there was one thing he'd been good at in an investiga-tion, it was picking up a thread and unraveling it. And he was going to do some unraveling now. Rarely were his hunches wrong.

Nick waited until the caretaker hung up the phone. "I take it you've known Sydney for quite a while. Have you worked here long?"

Malcolm sat in the chair behind the metal desk and rocked back, linking his hands behind his head. "Eight years. I came to work for Ms Foster just after she bought the place."

Evaluating the tone and content of the answer, Nick gazed at the man across from him. So Sydney owned the build-ing. He hadn't considered that. According to the directory at the front door, there were six apartments, and if Syd-ney's was an example, the complex was worth big bucks. He assembled that information and put some other facts to-gether, then followed the thread. "That must have been about the time that the economy crashed here."

Malcolm nodded. "Yeah. That's how come she got it— the developers went into receivership, and there was a big mess. The units were all supposed to be sold, and two or three people had made big down payments."

"So some of the units are privately owned?"

"Three are. The rest are leased."

Nick leaned back in his chair. "In other words, she put together a deal that had everyone smiling."

The caretaker grinned. "Including herself." He shook his head, his smile softening. "I tell you, I don't think I'd ever play poker with the lady."

Nick shot him an amused look. "I wouldn't advise it." His expression intensified as he again studied the man. There was something in the caretaker's tone that was very significant. It was clear he liked his boss, but underneath there was a near reverent respect. Nick kept his voice deliberately subdued, a tone that invited openness. "You've been with her a long time."

Letting his chair rock forward, Malcolm's expression altered as he rested his arms on the top of his desk, his eyes suddenly solemn. "Yeah, I have." There was a long pause, then he lifted his head and met Nick's gaze. "She's something special."

The caretaker's words were rift with feeling, and Nick instinctively knew there was a specific reason for Malcolm's loyalty. His tone was quiet. "I figured you went back a long way."

The big man stared at him for a minute, then looked down at his hands. "Yeah, a long way."

Nick read the gruffness in the other man's tone, and he sensed a kind of subtle indebtedness in it. He shifted tactics, leading without appearing to. "I know what you mean. If it wasn't for her, I'd likely still be stuck in a wheelchair."

The caretaker glanced up at him, a hint of surprise in his eyes. "How's that?"

Nick shrugged. "She was instrumental in getting a good rehabilitation program going. Without it, I wouldn't be walking."

Malcolm held his gaze for a moment, then looked back down. When he finally spoke, his voice was edged with emotion. "I owe her big time, too. If it wasn't for her, I sometimes wonder where I'd be right now."

Nick knew that if you wanted someone to talk, you had to let them know you were prepared to listen. He waited quietly for the caretaker to continue.

There was a long pause before Malcolm started talking, his tone low and subdued. "I did time down east. When I got paroled, jobs were pretty scarce. Ms Foster had just bought the apartment building and the contractor she'd hired to finish the work was looking for a night watchman. She happened to be at the building the day I was sent to see about the job. When the contractor found out what I did time for, he was ready to boot me off the place. Ms Foster looked at me with that steady look she has, and she told him she was hiring the night watchman, and she gave me the job on the spot. I've been with her ever since."

"What did you do time for?"

Malcolm looked up, his gaze level. "Attempted murder."

Nick scrutinized him, his voice quiet. "That's what it says on your rap sheet, but you're no thug, Malcolm."

Malcolm answered with a shrug.

The intentness in Nick's eyes eased. "What happened?"

Clasping his hands together on the desk, Malcolm stared at them, pain etched in his face. "I was raised in the U.S. I got a football scholarship, but the second year of college I got a chance to play pro ball here in Canada. I married a girl from my hometown just before moving up here—the prettiest, sweetest little thing you ever saw. Caroline loved it here, so I got my Canadian citizenship and we planned on starting a family. We had a good life—the best." His hands tightened and it was a few moments before he continued, his voice raw. "One of the owners' sons was always trying to put the moves on Caroline, one of those dudes who always had a string of women—hid behind Daddy's big money. Anyway, the team had been outta town on a road trip, and the owners were having a big party for us when we got back. They'd arranged for limos to pick up the wives, only this guy picked up Caroline—told her his old man sent him. He was drunk and he clipped another car on the freeway. They flipped end for end and skidded a few hundred feet on the roof. Caroline was killed instantly.''

Nick watched him, feeling the pain that engulfed the man across the desk. "So you went after him."

Malcolm raised his head, his eyes haunted by grief. He looked away, the muscles in his neck convulsing as he tried to swallow. "No. Not then. I wanted to but I didn't. The bastard got off with a suspended sentence. It wasn't until a few months later that I went after him. He started bragging one night when he was all drunked up again." Malcolm dragged his hand across his face, a shudder rippling through his big body. "He told one of the other players that he'd made it with Caroline. Jack said he didn't believe him, that Caroline would never do a thing like that. He got a smirk on his face and said she tried to fight him, but he knew she wanted it, so he cornered her in the car and gave her a good time."

Nick's face went rigid. "Good God."

"I went to see him when Jack told me. He laughed in my face and told me she was 'a sweet piece,' and that's when I went after him. I made damned sure he'd never touch another woman again."

As hardened as he was to the twisted, sick minds loose on society, Nick was not hardened enough. There was a long, heavy silence, then he looked at the other man. "How much time did you do?"

"Four years in Kingston, a year in a halfway house. I was in the halfway house when Ms Foster gave me the job."

"And you've been friends ever since."

Malcolm frowned as he sorted through his thoughts. "Not exactly. It's hard to explain. We're just *there* for each other. We hardly ever see each other, hardly ever talk. I just know she's upstairs if I get down, and she knows I'm here if she needs me. It keeps us from feeling alone."

Nick fixed his gaze on Malcolm, a sharp look in his eyes. The answer he wanted was only a question away. "Isn't there anyone special in Sydney's life?" Like a fourteen-year-old kid? he thought with a twist of bitterness.

"No. I have family in the States. Ms Foster has nobody."

Nick stared at him, a chill of awareness settling in his gut. The second question loomed. So what had she done with the baby? That was one question Sydney was going to have to answer.

THE OFFICE WAS HEAVY with shadows, the only illumination coming from the desk lamp and the computer monitor, the stillness adding weight to the darkness.

With her chair swiveled to face the computer terminal, Sydney sat with the keyboard across her lap, staring at the amber screen. The calculations were off by several thousand dollars, and for the third time she scanned the figures, trying to find out where she had made the mistake. But one set of numbers kept sliding into the next, and she finally gave up. Taking off her glasses and tossing them beside the terminal, she rubbed her eyes, fatigue fogging her concentration. She had spent two hours working on this, and she was no further ahead now than she was when she started.

Sliding the keyboard onto the desk, she closed her eyes and rested her head against the padded back of the chair, trying not to think about anything. Through sheer determination, she had blocked out everything that had happened during the past few days, but the emotional backlash had left her physically drained. She had once believed that getting older would make a difference, that she'd reach a point where age would compensate for the vulnerability of youth. But since Nick had reappeared in her life, she had discovered she could hurt just as much at thirty-seven as she had at twenty-two—nothing changed.

She opened her eyes and stared into the shadows, analyzing why she had driven herself so hard during the past fifteen years. She had amassed a small fortune in real estate and personal assets, but money had never been the motivating force. Her business had been a proving ground more than anything. She'd had to prove to herself that she had the brains and ability to do it, that she could outthink any man, that she could play ball with the big boys. And that she had proved, and in the process had regained a sense of self-worth.

In spite of how her financial success might be viewed by others, she knew, *really knew*, it had nothing to do with luck. Other than the investments Mabel had left her, she had done it on her own. She had taken courses, learned the business, worked sixteen hours a day, seven days a week. She had, through sheer hard work and determination, verified her intelligence, her ability, her motivation.

But what she'd really been trying to do was verify herself as a worthwhile human being. It hadn't been until after her confrontation yesterday with Nick that she'd fully grasped that. Her success had been indirectly motivated by him. She had remolded herself into someone he could have respected.

Wearily dragging her hand across her face, she deliberately redirected her thoughts. She was accomplishing nothing here tonight. She might as well go home and try to get some sleep, but she didn't think she could dredge up enough energy to move. She recognized the sounds in the outer office as those of the cleaning staff, and she glanced at her watch. It was even later than she thought. Heaving another sigh, she reached for the keyboard.

There was a sound at the door, the light from the outer office spilling in, and she glanced up, expecting to see one of the cleaning women standing there. But it wasn't. It was Nick.

Her stomach contracted into a hard knot as she stared at him, not quite believing what she was seeing.

Leaning heavily on his cane, he closed the door, then looked at her, his expression veiled, his eyes black and fathomless. "I think we'd better have a little talk."

Sydney could feel the blood drain from her face, and a sick feeling of dread welled up inside her. She had made a grave tactical error in telling him what she had. She had known it then, but something dark and vengeful had driven her to do it. She wished to God she had kept the truth to herself.

Trying to give herself some time to collect her thoughts, Sydney closed down the file on the computer and shut off the machine, grateful for the semidarkness that cloaked the room. Without meeting his gaze, she motioned to one of the leather chairs adjacent to the desk. "Sit down."

"I'll stand."

His terseness intensified her dread. Feeling trapped behind her desk, Sydney rolled her chair back and stood up, her back stiff as she turned toward the window. Her voice was low and impassive. "Say what you've come to say."

"And what do you think I've come to say?" he said with lethal softness. "Do you think I'm here to chat about the weather?"

She glanced at him, then rested her shoulder against the window frame as she stared down at the street. "No, I don't."

There was an edge of angry accusation in his voice. "You deliberately kept something from me that I had every right to know."

"I should have never told you at all."

There was a tense silence, then he spoke again, his anger underscored by some other emotion. "So what happened, Sydney? Have you got a fourteen-year-old kid stashed somewhere? Did you give it up for adoption? Did you have an abortion? What? Or don't you think I have a right to know that, either?"

Sydney continued to stare down at the street, remembering, a half-forgotten ache starting in her chest and working up her throat. Such tiny little fingers, so fragile and perfect.... She swallowed hard and forced the image from her mind.

"There were problems," she said, her monotone voice ringing hollowly in her ears. "There was a congenital heart defect. She died six hours after she was born."

There was a long silence before Nick's shocked voice cut through the stillness. "The baby died?"

"Yes."

"Was there nothing they could do?"

"No. Nothing." Nothing.

She heard him move, the sound of leather slipping against leather as he lowered himself into one of the chairs. Unable to disguise the pain of remembering, Sydney continued to stare out the window, her eyes unseeing. Six hours. She'd had her only six hours. But that tiny little thing had left an emptiness so big it would last a lifetime.

"Would you mind telling me about it?"

She turned her head to look at him, her arms folded tightly in front of her. In the dim light, he looked pale and dazed by shock, the darkness of his eyes standing out against the pallor of his haggard, unshaved face.

There was a soft catch in her voice. "What do you want to know?"

He studied her for a moment, then rested his head against the rolled back of the chair, his profile set as he stared off into space. There was a rough edge to his voice when he finally spoke. "I said things—" He winced slightly, then clenched his jaw in frustration. Finally he looked at her, his eyes bleak. "Of all the things I know about you, I know you'd fight to the death before you'd abandon a baby." He turned away, his voice husky. "I had no right to say what I did."

The pressure in Sydney's chest became almost unbearable as she watched him, heard the self-contempt in his voice, knowing she could never stop loving him no matter how hard she tried. As fierce as the pain was, her mouth lifted with a semblance of a smile. Nick was fighting with himself again.

He didn't know how to handle the emotional responsiveness that was so much a part of him—the part he saw as a flaw—or the feelings that his sensitivity aroused. But they were there in him, fierce and passionate, simmering just below the surface. And that, she realized, was what set him apart—his capacity to feel.

She understood why he had tried to hurt her. It was because he was hurting, and he didn't know how to avenge that pain. Her throat was so tight she could barely speak, but she managed an unsteady smile as she softly requalified his words. "I would have never abandoned *our* baby, Nick."

His gaze riveted on her, his expression even more haggard, then he shut his eyes, his voice hoarse. "God, Sydney."

Her vision blurring, Sydney turned back to the window, her fingernails biting into her forearms. She wouldn't think about it. She wouldn't think about anything.

The drone of a vacuum in the outer office penetrated the quiet, and she heard Nick move. His speech was slightly slurred. "Can we get out of here?"

She nodded, her tone lifeless. "I'll drive you home."

There was the sound of him getting to his feet, then a brief silence. "Sydney?"

Dragging up what little reserve she had left, she turned to face him.

He was watching her, his face so drawn he looked ill. "Would you mind telling me about her?"

There was a carefulness in him, as though he were uncertain how she was going to respond. Sydney realized how very important her answer was to him. Her voice caught. "No, I don't mind."

They spoke little on the ride to his apartment, and Nick was noticeably unsteady as he unlocked his door.

Waiting for him to precede her, Sydney closed the door behind them, feeling as though she had no strength left, either. Her mind felt separated from her body, and she experienced a strange floating sensation.

The sound of Nick's voice dispelled the fog. "I'm going to have to lie down."

She turned, alarmed by how gray he was. Without looking at her, he started down the hallway with dogged determination, his body warped by taut, unresponsive muscles, and she could tell that every step demanded superhuman concentration. Sydney knew if she watched him, she wouldn't be able to handle the feelings his struggle aroused. She took off her coat and laid it over the back of the chair, wondering bleakly why she kept setting herself up for more heartbreak.

The sound of the bathroom door closing interrupted her thoughts, and releasing a sigh, she turned toward the bedroom.

Nick had taken off his jacket and tossed it onto the bed, and Sydney picked it up to fold down the covers. She closed the blinds, then went to the closet to hang up the jacket. A strange sensation unfolded in her stomach when she slid open the door. The clothes she had left behind when she had bolted that morning were hanging just inside the closet. What unsettled her more than anything was how they had been hung on the hanger. They weren't bunched up, as though he had put them there just to get rid of them, but were carefully arranged, as though he had taken great care with them. Trying to ignore the sudden knot in her throat, she grasped an empty hanger and blindly placed his jacket on it, her movements jerky. It would be so much more bearable if his anger was constant.

She had just shut the closet door and was turning around when Nick entered the bedroom. He had on a pair of sweatpants, the jersey clutched in his hand. He set his cane beside the bed, the muscles across his back bunched as he laboriously positioned himself on the mattress. He rolled onto his stomach, his exhaustion evident in every movement.

Trying to will away the tightness in her throat, she approached the bed. "Is there anything you need?"

He turned his head away from her, his voice muffled. "No."

She gazed down at him, not knowing how to deal with this, with him, with the internal rawness she was experiencing. "Would you rather we leave this for another time?"

He didn't answer for several moments, then he slowly turned onto his back, the white lines around his mouth making his face appear more angular. "No. I don't want to leave it." His dark gaze was riveted on her. "It wasn't an accident, was it?"

She held his gaze, wishing she could avoid answering. Finally she looked away. "No, it wasn't."

"Are you going to tell me why?"

Knowing the answer would launch them back into dangerous, uncharted waters, Sydney steeled herself, her tone detached. "I wanted to have something to hold on to after."

"After what?"

She looked at him, her gaze unflinching. "I knew right from the beginning it wouldn't work."

There was a hard edge to his voice. "In other words, you knew I was going to bail out."

"I wasn't blind, Nick," she said unevenly. "You weren't the kind of man to simply dump your moral values because it was convenient. I wouldn't have liked you much if you were."

Some of the edge had gone from his tone. "Even though you saw everything coming apart, you still decided to get pregnant."

"Yes."

"When?"

There was a long silence as Sydney tried to ease the tension that went right through her. He had been the one piece of rightness in her life.

She forced herself to speak. "After what happened over the Christmas party." The beginning of the end. That was when she'd had to face the fact that Nick could not go on playing games with himself. Nor could she.

His gruff voice broke through her isolation. "I wish you had told me, Sydney."

She recognized the dark, solemn look in his eyes, and she covered her face with her hand, all the agony from the past fifteen years washing over her. She had thought she was going to die when she left, knowing she would never see him again. The only thing that sustained her was the knowledge that she was carrying something of his within her. Then she had lost that, too. Tiny and precious. She had wanted that baby so much. So much.

She didn't hear him move, wasn't aware that he had levered himself off the bed until his fingers encircled her wrist and pulled her hand away. Catching her by the back of the neck, he pulled her face against his naked chest, his voice hoarse. "Don't. Sydney. For God's sake, don't." His hold was achingly gentle as he tightened his arms around her and rested his head against hers, sheltering her within his embrace. For an instant Sydney resisted, then Nick whispered against her cheek, his voice rough with emotion, "I'm so sorry, Sydney. So very sorry."

Her resistance crumbled and she huddled deeper in his arms, desperately fighting to hold back the strangling pressure of unshed tears. She couldn't do that to him. She could not make him feel any more powerless than he already did.

His hold on her never slackened as he slowly stroked her hair, and Sydney blocked out everything except the solace he offered her. And little by little, the awful pain around her heart eased. Neither of them spoke, the silence like a protective shield between them and the outside world. Combing her hair back from her face, Nick hooked his knuckles under her chin and with infinite gentleness turned her head. He gazed down at her, his expression solemn as he slowly smoothed his thumb across her bottom lip. Tilting her head back, he closed his eyes and brushed his mouth against hers.

Sydney's breath caught, and she involuntarily gripped his arm as a fluttery weakness radiated through her. There was so much tenderness, so much need in his kiss that it overwhelmed her. It seemed to reach out from his very soul, and she wanted to cry from the sheer intensity of it.

With a low sound, Nick tore his mouth away and crushed her against him, his hold almost savage as he pressed his face against her neck. Hauling in a deep, jagged breath, Sydney shut her eyes, the swell of emotion so fierce she felt as if she were being torn in two. God, how she loved him.

It wasn't until she felt him sway that she realized he was on the verge of collapse. Hugging him closer, her voice breaking, she whispered unevenly, "Let me help you into bed."

He made no response, and she tightened her hold, her feelings for him making it nearly impossible to speak. "Please, Nick," she murmured softly.

A tremor coursed through him, then slowly he loosened his grip, his face like granite as he pulled away. He didn't look at her as he straightened, and Sydney knew he was fighting an emotional battle of his own. Her throat so cramped she couldn't even swallow, she slipped her arm around his waist, supporting him while he eased himself onto the bed. Sydney relaxed her hold, but before she could withdraw her arm, Nick grasped her wrist with his good hand, his jaw set. As if every movement taxed him to the limit, he closed his eyes and repositioned himself on the bed, his hold on her never slackening. Exhaling sharply, he studied her, his eyes dark and unfathomable, then pulled her toward him.

Sydney's voice was barely above a whisper. "Let me take off my jacket."

He watched her, his gaze black and intense. He started to say something, then swallowed hard and closed his eyes, his grip on her arm tightening.

She realized he wasn't going to let her go. Sydney shrugged her jacket off her shoulder, then slipped out her free arm. Unable to see him through the blur of tears, she grasped his weakened left hand, her mouth trembling as he tightened his fingers around hers. Easing her other arm from his grip, she dropped her jacket onto the floor. Nick's face twisted with anguish as he pulled her down beside him. He hoarsely whispered her name as he crushed her against him, fusing their bodies together in a desperate embrace. "Hold me. God, Sydney, hold me."

And she did, with all the strength she could muster, her face wet against his.

CHAPTER FIVE

HIS EXPRESSION SOLEMN, Nick stared at the ceiling as he slowly stroked Sydney's back, vitally aware of her weight against him. He felt as though he'd been put through an emotional wringer, but he also felt a kind of peace he hadn't known for a very long time. When she had come into his arms last night, he had been so choked up he couldn't have said one damned word if his life had depended on it. But there had been no need to talk. It was as if the physical closeness had been the start of a healing process, draining away the rage he had nurtured ever since she'd disappeared. He realized now that it was not knowing why she'd gone that had driven him over the edge. Now that he knew, he was able to let the anger go.

He glanced down at her, a smile lifting the corner of his mouth. Who would have thought either of them would have fallen asleep? He sure in hell hadn't expected to, and he probably wouldn't have if they had talked. But he hadn't wanted to, not then. Just being able to hold her, being released from that burden of rage, had been enough. And he'd sensed that Sydney had needed that physical comforting as much as he had. He had to admit, he had been a little miffed when he realized she had fallen asleep, but one look at her pale face, at the dark circles under her eyes, and he knew she was emotionally spent, as well.

Tightening his arm around her, he rested his cheek against her silken hair, more than content to hold her as she slept. A predawn breeze rattled the venetian blinds, sending a cool draft across them, and Sydney sighed and snuggled closer. Very careful not to disturb her, Nick reached down with his right hand and managed to grasp the corner of the comforter. He drew it up over them, tucking it around her shoulders.

His expression grew somber. He reflected on whether she might have wondered, when they had been on such an emotional edge why he had done nothing more than hold her. He dreaded telling her why. Closing down that unsettling thought, he glanced at the clock. Five-thirty. He had two and a half hours before he had to get up. Gently smoothing back her tousled hair, he cradled her head more snugly against him, savoring the feel of her in his arms. Two and a half hours—it wasn't nearly long enough.

Almost an hour went by before Sydney stirred. She didn't draw away from the restriction of his embrace but moved closer, as if she wanted to sink deeper into the warmth and security of his arms. Knowing that it was unconscious, an instinctive move, created pure havoc in Nick, and he had to grit his teeth against the feelings she created in him. His fingers tangled in her hair, and he brushed the top of her head with a light, lingering kiss.

She stirred again, her breath warm against his neck, then she went dead still, and he knew she had come fully awake. He tightened his arms around her, his voice gruff with emotion. "Good morning."

She raised her head, an appalled look on her face. "Oh, no," she whispered. "It's morning."

He smiled at her. "Yes, it is." He could tell from the stricken expression in her eyes what was going through her mind. "It isn't a big deal, Sydney," he said, gently chastising her. He brushed his thumb across the red mark on her cheek. "Falling asleep is not a federal offense, you know."

She managed a weak smile, but the look in her eyes remained. He caught her around the shoulders and pulled her back down, tucking her head firmly against his neck. "Besides, I fell asleep, too."

Her long eyelashes brushed his skin as she closed her eyes, a discernible tension in her body. Resting his head against hers, he stared into space as he stroked her shoulder.

Several minutes passed before she spoke. "Would you like a coffee?"

He smiled, realizing she was providing an out. "No, I don't want a coffee." She tried to raise her head, but he held it firmly against him. "I don't want a coffee, I want to hold you. Is that all right?"

He felt her smile and finally she relaxed against him. "I can live with it."

The laugh lines around his mouth deepened. "That's damned noble of you."

She laughed softly and gave his ear a little twist. He caught her hand and held it firmly against his bare chest.

"Did you go to rehab yesterday?"

"Yes, Mother, I went to rehab yesterday."

His patronizing tone got a reaction out of her, and she pulled free of his hold and propped herself on one elbow, a warning gleam in her eyes. "You're being obnoxious, Novak."

He grinned, the comforter slipping from him as he rolled onto his side.

She went to give him a playful smack on the ribs, but a look of horror flashed across her face, and she went deathly white. He knew that in the early morning light she had seen the scars. He grasped her wrist and forced her hand down so her palm covered the marks. "It's okay," he said gently. "It's only the scars from the chest tubes."

She closed her eyes, a shudder coursing through her, and he pulled her back into his arms. It was clearly evident from the look on her face that she'd thought they were bullet wounds, and his expression turned grave. If she reacted that strongly to the scars on his chest, he could never let her see the ones on his legs.

He caressed her back, trying to reassure her. "It's okay, babe. Really."

"Oh God, Nick—"

She slipped her arms around him and held him, and for the first time he realized the hell she must have gone through when he'd been hurt. He hesitated, wondering how wise it was to probe too deeply. But for some reason it was imperative that he know. "How did you find out about the shooting?"

She went very still and he could feel her body tense, then she pulled away from him. Her tone was dispassionate and tightly controlled. "I read about it in the morning newspaper, before they released your name."

He nudged her chin with his knuckles, but she refused to look at him. Nick could tell from the set of her profile that his question had disturbed her. Spanning her jaw with his hand, he forced her to look at him. The pain of remembering was etched in her face. When he spoke, his voice was quiet and nonthreatening. "And how did you find out it was me?"

She stared at him a moment, then looked past him, her tone abrupt. "That night on the evening news."

Watching her, seeing the starkness in her eyes, made Nick realize what a shock it must have been for her. He couldn't even imagine how he would have felt if he'd been in her shoes, if it had been her picture plastered all over the paper and on TV, if it had been her hovering on the edge of death. She may have damned near destroyed him once, but there had never been any doubt that he loved her. And even when he'd been eaten up with jealousy and rage, he still knew she loved him. It would have been bloody awful finding out the way she did, and if nothing else, he could relate to the utter desperation she must have felt. And for the first time, he truly understood what had driven her to get involved with his rehabilitation.

His throat constricted, and he caressed her face, waiting for the contraction to ease. His tone was gruff when he finally spoke. "You went to the hospital, didn't you?"

"Yes."

"When?"

She bent her head so he couldn't see her face, her own voice unsteady. "I stuck it out for three days, then I couldn't stand it any longer. I knew they only let family members into ICU, so I told them I was your sister-in-law."

Nick exhaled sharply and pulled her down against him. "I'm so sorry, Sydney," he whispered unsteadily. "I never would have wanted to put you through that."

She tightened her arms around him. "It doesn't matter now."

But it did. It mattered to him. God, but it mattered to him. Closing his eyes, he nestled her closer, his chest so full he couldn't take a deep breath. And he knew, as strange as it seemed, that this was the right time to ask about the baby. "What was she like?"

Sydney didn't answer for the longest time, then she shifted her position so she could look down at him. Her eyes were brimming with tears, her mouth trembling. "She was beautiful, Nick. So beautiful."

Feeling more a part of her life than he ever had, he brushed away a tear with his thumb, his touch unsteady but immeasurably gentle. There was a husky catch in his voice. "So tell me."

Drawing in a shaky breath, she managed a tremulous smile. "I named her Nichole...."

THE SOUNDS FROM OUTSIDE had the undertones of early morning traffic when Nick finally looked at the clock again. He hugged Sydney against him. "I'm going to have to get

up if I'm going to be ready when the Handi-Bus gets here,"
he said quietly, loathing to relinquish the simple pleasure of
holding her. For the past half hour, neither of them had
spoken; there hadn't been any need. She had told him all
there was to tell about their small daughter, and he had
provided what comfort he could. He would have gladly
given up his right arm if he could have only seen the baby he
and Sydney had created....

She shifted her head on his shoulder. "I can drive you."

He smoothed down her hair as he dropped a light kiss on
her brow. "I have a better idea. Why don't you come with
me?"

Sydney went very still, then she raised her head and
looked at him. "Are you serious?"

He gave her a slightly warped smile. "Yes."

Nick almost felt guilty when he saw how her eyes lighted
up. "Oh, Nick. I'd love to go."

He grinned. "Then you'd better haul ass, lady. I don't
exactly break any speed records these days."

She was off the bed so fast Nick didn't even have a chance
to react. She threw up her hands in a gesture of despair as
she glanced down at herself. Even Nick had to admit she was
a mess. Her hair was tangled, there were still sleep marks on
her face, and her clothes looked like—well, they looked as
if she'd slept in them. Frankly he thought she was appealing as hell. He watched her, his amusement showing. "Your
other clothes are hanging in the closet, there's a new tooth-
brush in the drawer in the bathroom, and the coffee's in the
canister on the cupboard."

He had to admit she looked a hell of a lot better by the
time she was ready to go. She'd put on the light gray skirt
and white silk blouse she had left, and there was a kind of
careless elegance about them that was a subtle extension of
her. She was, he decided, a very classy lady.

And obviously he wasn't the only one who thought so. Her arrival at the center turned a few heads, and he thought Beth's eyes were going to pop out of her head when he introduced them. Even the Dragon Lady was speechless.

Nick expected the three hours of therapy to be absolute hell, especially considering the emotional stress he'd been under the past week, but he felt as though he'd just tapped into a new source of strength. Beth had gone pretty easy on him the day before, but today she showed no mercy at all. She worked him until the sweat rolled off him, and his arms were shaking so badly when he finished with one piece of equipment that he felt as if he had palsy. But he got through it all and still did his six laps across the gym area without a cane.

As he came out of the locker room after showering and changing, he found Sydney in the corridor talking on a pay phone. She glanced up as he came into view and raised her eyes in an expression of frustration, then bent her head, her face intent.

Nick leaned heavily on his cane as he watched her, his legs unsteady from the strenuous workout. From the bits and pieces he overheard, it was obviously a business call. His gaze was thoughtful as he made his way slowly toward the lounge. Knowing Sydney, she probably had eight balls in the air at once, and he suddenly realized he had done a damned good job of screwing up her timetable during the past few days. That realization bothered him. He didn't want her having to make those kinds of choices.

She caught up to him, her trench coat swinging open as she fell into step with him.

He draped his arm around her shoulders and smiled down at her. "You looked very intent. Has everything fallen apart at the seams?"

She grinned and slipped her arm around his waist. "Something is *always* falling apart at the seams."

He liked the feel of her there beside him, her body offering that extra support he needed right then. But he couldn't keep her there indefinitely. His tone was solemn, his voice oddly husky. "You're cutting things close because of me, aren't you?"

She cast him a sharp look, then glanced away. "No, everything's under—"

Hooking his walking cane on his thumb, he caught her under the chin and forced her to look at him. "Don't," he said quietly. "Don't prevaricate about it." He gave her a crooked smile to take the sting out of his words. "I usually need a couple of hours' rest after a workout like that, so why don't you drop me off and do what you have to do? You can call me later, and we can set something up." He could see the reluctance in her eyes, and that made it a whole lot easier for him to stick to his guns. "Or I could take the Handi-Bus home."

"No!" she interjected sharply. She stared at him a moment, her expression unreadable, then she sighed, her tone laced with reluctance. "No, at least let me take you home."

He squeezed her shoulder as he got his balance and started walking toward the doors. "You know I'm right," he said in an offhand manner. "You've postponed important appointments and God knows what else, and there's no need."

They paused, waiting for the electronic door to open, and she glanced up at him, a glimmer of humor in her eyes. "I hate it when you're right."

He stood gazing down at her, his insides turning to jelly as he gently tucked a loose strand of hair behind her ear. He must be some kind of moron. He'd spend the rest of the afternoon alone in his bed, wishing like hell she was there, remembering how damned good it felt to hold her. He slowly caressed her cheek, wanting to say, *Come home with me.* His eyes darkened as he murmured gruffly, "Go to work, Sydney."

An hour later, he was still questioning his sanity as he lay on his bed with his hands behind his head, watching Sydney fix a scarf at the throat of her blouse. But as much as he wanted her to stay, he knew this was best. Somehow they had to get back on track, or everything would get twisted out of shape. And he didn't want that to happen.

Sydney's hair came alive with static as she pulled her gray cashmere sweater over her head, and she absently smoothed it down before adjusting her sleeves. Straightening the cuffs on her blouse, she came over to the bed and put her make-up bag in her purse.

Nick gave her a lopsided smile as he caught her wrist. "You look great," he said drowsily.

There was a gleam in her eyes as she let him pull her down beside him. "I wish I could say the same for you. You look like you've been run over by a tank."

He gave her a lazy grin. "I feel like it."

Bracing her arm beside his head, she gazed down at him, her eyes concerned. "Does therapy always do this to you?"

"Usually. I'm pretty whacked-out for a couple of hours after."

Her touch was filled with tenderness as she caressed his jaw with the back of her hand, her voice low. "Then get some sleep, and I'll talk to you later."

There was no way he could resist the look of regret in her eyes, and with a deep sigh, he slipped his arms up her back and pulled her down against his chest. He heard her breath catch, and he closed his eyes, trying to stifle the feelings that stirred in him. God, but it did feel so damned good to hold her. A poignant silence enveloped them, and he tightened his embrace, wanting to absorb every sensation she aroused. He had held her all night, but that wasn't enough. Not nearly enough. He wished like hell he could simply stop the clock.

Finally she sighed and eased away from him, her voice not quite steady. "If I don't leave now, I won't go at all."

Reluctantly he let his hands slip down her back. "I know."

She leaned over and dropped a light kiss on his jaw, then slowly pulled away. "I'll call you later."

He silently watched her cross the room, feeling as though she had left an enormous hole in his chest. She paused at the door, then she drew in a deep breath before disappearing down the hall. His heartbeat echoing in his head, Nick closed his eyes, struggling with the onslaught of feelings. God, was this all an enormous mistake, or was it the best thing that ever happened to him?

That question chased around and around in his head for most of the afternoon. He hadn't expected to sleep a wink after she'd gone, but he did. For three solid hours. But when he awoke, he didn't have her presence to sustain him, and some grim facts rose up to haunt him. He had to accept that nothing had changed. Not really. Not when it came to all the unresolved problems of their past.

He also had to face the fact that what was happening between him and Sydney was, at best, a tenuous thing, fragile and easily broken. The only thing that had changed was that they had arrived at some middle ground. He understood why she had disappeared, and he also understood why she'd felt compelled to get involved in his rehabilitation. His bitterness and resentment about both had been neutralized last night. And then there was the baby—that was a bond that could never be broken. But that gave them very limited safe ground, and that in itself was sobering.

There was also the factor of unknowns. The things he still didn't know about her—and the things she didn't know about him. The thought of leveling with her scared the hell out of him. Yet the thought of her telling him something he didn't want to hear scared him even more.

And on top of all that was his disability. Though in all honesty, he knew it was only a problem if he made it one.

What it all boiled down to, he discovered, was that there were some things he could deal with, and there were others he couldn't. One of the things he couldn't handle was Sydney's past. He didn't even want to think about that. And maybe that was the solution. If he'd learned one thing during the past few months, it was how to take one day at a time. Maybe that's how he would deal with it, one day at a time, step-by-step. Just as he had dealt with his disability.

By that evening, every bone in his body ached. His hands were so sore he could barely close them, and he was on a mental downer that was nothing short of grim. Why in hell did he do that to himself? The last thing he needed was another cloud of gloom and doom hanging over his head. He'd had enough of that when he was in the hospital.

And he wondered if Sydney was ever going to call. He'd picked up the phone half a dozen times to call her but had hung it back up, disgusted with himself. If she said she'd call, she'd call.

By six o'clock, he was beginning to wonder. All kinds of doubts were starting to settle in, and he knew if he had the physical strength to get to her office under his own steam, he'd be on his way now, but he doubted if he could make it to the front door, let alone downtown. He wished to hell he didn't feel quite so desperate.

By seven, he'd nearly convinced himself that she, too, had looked at their situation realistically and had decided there were just too many hurdles. He sprawled on the sofa, considering his options, trying to decide what to do if she didn't call, when the phone finally rang. He snatched it up, prepared to hear someone else's voice.

But it was hers—husky, soft and touched with weariness. "Hi. I'm sorry I'm so late, but I just got out of a board meeting."

He had to wait for his insides to settle before he could answer her. "You sound beat."

He heard her sigh. "A little. But I'm more hungry than anything else. How would you like to go out for dinner?"

Nick hadn't eaten in a restaurant since the shooting. Learning how to feed himself had been a frustrating, arduous task, and he still had a long way to go. He couldn't cut his own meat yet, and if he started shaking, anything could happen. And it was always worse when he was tired. Making a spectacle of himself in a restaurant full of people didn't appeal to him at the best of times, but the thought of making a spectacle of himself in front of Sydney was even worse. "Why don't you come over here and we'll order in."

"You wouldn't mind?"

The relief in her voice made him smile a little, and it was suddenly imperative that he be honest with her. "Frankly, I'd prefer it. My eating skills are barely past the Neanderthal stage."

She laughed softly. "Sounds like you could do with a little help from a friend."

The way she said it sapped what little strength he had, and he found it hard to breathe past the sudden gripping sensation in his chest. His voice was gruff when he finally spoke. "I'll have to think about that."

She laughed again, low, soft and so provocative. Nick closed his eyes, wanting to hold her so damned much his mind wouldn't focus on anything else. "You do that. And I'll see you shortly."

Feeling as though someone had just knocked the wind out of him, Nick grasped the phone, his tone gruff. "Sydney?"

"What?"

"Don't be long."

There was an electric silence, then he heard her draw in a deep, uneven breath. "I won't."

Nick placed the phone back in the cradle. How long would it take her to get there? Twenty minutes? Half an hour? He clenched his jaw, the anticipation nearly unbear-able. God, he didn't think he could last that long.

It seemed like a lifetime before he heard a car door slam outside, and he struggled into a sitting position, only vaguely aware of how badly his hands were shaking. Real-izing he would never make it to the door before she came in, he sank back down, unable to think of anything except how much he wanted to feel her against him right then.

She came breezing in, full of vitality, but she stopped short, her expression changing to one of alarm when she took a good look at him. "What's wrong?"

He shook his head, his jaw clenched against the roil of emotions that were churning in his chest.

Dropping the parcels she held, she shed her coat in one swift movement, her expression carved by anxiety as she crossed the room and knelt beside him. She took his face in her hands, a touch of fear in her eyes as she gazed down at him. "What's wrong?" she repeated urgently. "You're shaking like a leaf—"

Nick closed his eyes as he locked his arms around her, pulling her against him with every ounce of strength he had. The feel of her was almost his undoing, and he buried his face in the curve of her neck, struggling to contain the feel-ings that pumped through him.

Sydney resisted for a split second, then she yielded to the pressure of his embrace and slipped her arms around him. Her voice was soft and tinged with concern as she whis-pered against his temple. "Tell me what's the matter. Please, Nick."

It took him a while before he could answer her, and when he did, his speech was thick and hoarse. "It's been one hell of a long afternoon."

Drawing in an uneven breath, she tightened her hold. "I'm sorry I'm so late. I never expected the meeting to drag on so long."

Still struggling to get a grip on the sensations she set off in him, Nick swallowed hard and smoothed down her hair, his hand unsteady as he slowly brushed back the thick, silky curls. "It doesn't matter now." He shifted onto his side, easing her alongside him so the full length of their bodies molded together. His heart pounding in his chest, he tightened his hold, drawing her head snugly into the curve of his shoulder. A tremor coursed through him as he closed his eyes, intent on how good it felt to finally have her lying next to him. He'd been desperate for this all afternoon. Like an addict needing his fix. He wanted to draw her inside himself, to absorb her warmth, her softness, her vitality. And he wondered how he had ever endured the past few hours.

Her voice had a funny catch in it as she whispered, "I brought us something to eat."

He smoothed his hand across her hips and up her back, aware of every curve, every hollow. Reluctant to let her go, he tightened his arm around her rib cage, his tone gruff. "Could we leave it for a while?"

"If you don't mind lukewarm hamburgers."

Right then he would rather starve than let her go, and he inhaled her fragrance, his hold unrelenting. "Why don't we go the whole distance and leave them until they're stone cold."

Sydney laughed and nestled her face against his neck, her breath warm against his skin. "Stone cold it is."

As he savored the feel of her lying there beside him, he wondered how in hell he had managed to survive the past fifteen years. She *was* like an addiction; one shot and he was hooked all over again. Only now there was even more between them than before. But he wasn't going to think about that—at least not yet. He was going to stretch this moment out for as long as he could.

Slowly his feelings eased, and Nick was aware of a strange kind of peace unfolding in him. He sensed the same feeling in Sydney, and the last thing he wanted to do was destroy that. So he remained silent as he held her for long, quiet moments, so tuned in to every breath, every heartbeat, it was almost as though they were physically one.

It wasn't until he heard her stomach rumble that he remembered she'd said she was starving an hour ago. With great reluctance, he loosened his hold and eased away from her, a smile in his eyes he couldn't have disguised if he'd wanted to.

Nick brushed his knuckles slowly along her jaw. "By the sounds of it, you're running on empty."

She gave that throaty little laugh of hers as she raised up on one elbow and swept her hair back, the movement stirring her subtle fragrance. "I've been running on empty all afternoon."

Nick gazed at her, feelings he didn't want to acknowledge stirring in him. He knew what she meant; he'd been running on empty for goddamned years. But the sustenance she gave him had nothing to do with food. She fed something much deeper in him than that. There was a knot in his throat, and his voice was uneven. "Then we'd better feed you before you power-out completely."

She sighed, a flash of reluctance in her expression. "Yes, I guess we'd better."

Unwilling to sever the physical contact, he let his hands slide down her back as she sat up, and she glanced down at him, her eyes smoky as she murmured softly, "I'm not sure I really want to do this."

He knew she wasn't referring to the cold hamburgers, and for some reason it made it easier for him to let her go, knowing she was as reluctant to move away from him as he was to let her. He managed a lopsided grin as he slowly stroked the base of her spine. "I'm not sure I do, either. But you're making some pretty strange noises, lady."

She grimaced. "You aren't supposed to notice things like that."

The laugh lines around his eyes crinkled as he gave her a little push. "How could I not notice? You sound like very old plumbing."

She made a face at him, then turned, rolling her shoulders wearily as she rose. Nick watched her, realizing how exhausted she looked. The past two days had taken their toll on her, too.

As she collected the bags she'd dropped on the chair, he pulled himself into a sitting position, then twisted, trying to reach his cane. Sydney spoke, her voice soft, "Don't get up, Nick. Let's just eat in here."

He glanced at her, a wry expression hovering around his mouth. "You may have just saved me from falling flat on my face."

Crossing the room, she knelt by the sofa, the aroma of hamburgers wafting up from the bags as she set them down. She gave him a rueful smile. "If anyone's going to fall flat on their face, it's going to be me."

Nick hoisted himself up and stuffed two cushions behind his back, then took the foil-wrapped package she handed him. He looked at her, his tone a little gruff. "A bad day?"

She sighed. "Not so much bad as long and complicated."

"Do you want to talk about it?"

She looked up, a hint of a smile softening her expression. "I'd rather just forget about it."

Their gazes held, and Nick felt himself slipping back to a time when they'd been able to communicate without saying a word. He rubbed his thumb against her ear, his touch lingering as he said huskily, "Then eat, and we'll talk about something else."

She cast him another amused look, then leaned back against the sofa as she unwrapped her hamburger and took a bite. Nick watched her, his own expression tinged with amusement. He wouldn't have to worry about any conversation for the next few minutes, at least. When Sydney was hungry, all she wanted to do was eat. There was no idle chitchat, no lingering over her meal. All she wanted was silence and food. But then, that was something he'd always appreciated in her, her ease with silence.

Nick finished his hamburger and wadded up the foil wrap, then glanced at her, about to ask for a packet of catsup for his fries. But the sight of her sitting on the floor, so close beside him, arrested him. The light from the lamp at the end of the sofa caught in the sheen of her hair, highlighting the deep mink shade, and Nick experienced a familiar stirring in his abdomen. He had never been able to figure out why, but her hair had always held a deep fascination for him. It was thick and lustrous and had the texture and sheen of satin, yet it would curl around his fingers like a living thing. And he could still remember how it felt to have it spread against his naked flesh, against his chest, against his thighs, the silky thickness sensitizing his skin every time she moved her head. It used to drive him crazy.

Images and galvanizing sensations flooded Nick's mind, and he clenched his teeth and closed his eyes, his heartbeat suddenly so wild he could barely draw air into his lungs. God, he didn't want to remember. Not now. Not after so many years. Not when he was trapped inside this malfunctioning body.

His fries had spilled from the cardboard container, and he inhaled deeply, trying to steady himself. He made himself focus on the scattered food, his hands unsteady as he started picking up the pieces. "Damn," he said, more to himself than anyone.

Sydney glanced at him, and setting down her own container, she turned to help him, a teasing gleam in her eyes.

"Just out of curiosity, how do you manage something like spaghetti?"

He gave her a rueful grin. "With both hands."

She laughed as she brushed the remaining crumbs from his shirt. "I'll have to get you a big bib."

He watched her, the feelings he'd been trying to suppress stirring again. "You do that."

Laughter lightened her eyes as she reached up to wipe away a trace of mustard from the corner of his mouth, and hell broke loose inside him. He caught her hand and held it against his face, unable to handle even the most insignificant caress. The sparkle disappeared from her eyes and was replaced with a look that created even more havoc within him. Lord, she was so close, and he needed her so badly. He swallowed hard, his voice raw and ragged as he whispered unevenly, "We have to talk, Sydney."

Her breath caught and she closed her eyes, as if she, too, were struggling with some very intense feelings. When she opened them, they were dark and smoky, and her voice was husky as she answered, "I know we do."

Unable to tolerate the space that separated them, he pulled her into his arms, needing her weight against him to stop the ache. He buried his hand in her hair as he pressed her head against his chest, his jaw clenched against the emotional swell rising in him. Her mouth brushed against his throat as Sydney slipped her arms around him, molding herself even closer, and Nick shut his eyes, holding her with all the strength he could muster. It was different from before. Before, he had simply needed her. Now there was this desperation, this urgency mixed in with it, and the only time he felt complete was when he was holding her.

Inhaling unevenly, he knew he couldn't put off telling her any longer. She was going to start wondering—when it was obvious that he still wanted her, that he could still get so damned lost in her he could think of nothing else—why he wasn't acting on it. He had been obsessed with her, and he could have stopped breathing easier than he could have denied himself the physical gratification he'd experienced with her. She had denied him nothing, not ever, and because of that, he couldn't leave her hanging now. It was going to be so damned hard to tell her. But he had no choice—and he had to tell her now, before she started expecting something he couldn't deliver.

"There's something I have to tell you, Sydney."

She raised her head and looked at him, a hint of fear in her eyes. There was an unsteady catch in her voice. "What?"

He met her gaze, then looked away, his hand shaking slightly as he carefully brushed back her hair. He didn't know how in hell he was going to get the words out.

There was an edge of anxiety in her voice. "Tell me, Nick."

Nick looked back at her, self-loathing rising up in him like bile, then he turned away again, afraid of what he might see in her eyes. "I've been impotent since the accident."

Her silence cut through him, and he could not make himself look at her. She shifted and he almost expected her to get up, but instead she took hold of his face and turned his head so he had to look at her. "Nick, I'm so sorry," she whispered, her eyes filled with dismay.

He clenched his jaw and tried to turn away, but she wouldn't let him. Her voice was gentle. "Do you think that really matters to me?"

An irrational anger swept through him. How could she understand how damned emasculated he felt because of his inadequacy? How trapped he felt by it? He wanted to push her away, to put some distance between them, but there was something that kept him from reacting. He didn't say anything, he just stared at her, his gaze remote and unfathomable.

As if sensing his cold withdrawal, Sydney tightened her hold, her gaze compelling him to listen to her, her tone vehement. "I understand how you feel. I really do. But I'm so grateful you're alive, nothing else is important. Please, Nick, don't think that's going to make a difference in how I feel."

The earnestness on her face got to him, and he closed his eyes, his arms tightening convulsively around her. She was so vital to him, in ways he didn't even understand.

Her hold gentle and protective, she cradled his head against her. "Don't ever think you're cheating me," she whispered unevenly. "I'll take whatever you can give."

Nick turned his head, his voice breaking on a ragged sound. "God, Sydney...."

Her hand cupped against his jaw, she brushed his mouth with a soft, searching kiss that went on and on, wringing every ounce of breath out of him. Lost in her gentleness, he could do nothing but respond. Catching her by the back of the head, Nick moved his mouth against hers, her hair slipping like satin beneath his hand. He felt as though he had been to eternity and back when she finally eased away.

Her voice was very husky. "Do you want me to stop?"

He drew her head down, his breath against her lips. "No."

Nick felt as if he were on the verge of heart failure when she eased away the second time. "Are you sure?"

He raised her chin so he could see her eyes, then drew in a deep and very shaky breath. His voice was decidedly unsteady as he exerted gentle pressure on the back of her head until her mouth grazed his. "You are staying the night, aren't you?"

CHAPTER SIX

WITH THE HEADSET CLAMPED over his toque, Tony boogied down the hallway to the beat of a Whitney Houston tune, the appetizing aroma of a loaded double-cheese pizza and the smell of hot cardboard coming from the flat box he carried. Unlocking the apartment door, he rapped out his signature knock, opened it and walked in, snapping his fingers in time to the music.

The scene before him stopped him like a brick wall. He stood in the entryway, his mouth hanging open as a female form—a real, honest-to-God woman—pulled free of Nick Novak's arms.

Nick? A woman?

Rooted to the spot, he could do nothing but stare as she sat on the floor beside the sofa. As she curled her legs under her, she looked up at Nick, who remained stretched out on the couch, his hand resting on her shoulder. Tony caught just a glimpse of her profile as she turned, and he managed to suppress a low whistle. This was not some dog Nick had picked up at the local pound. This lady was pure twenty-four-carat gold.

There was a look in Nick's eyes that any man under the age of ninety would have recognized. And when Nick trailed his knuckles along her jaw, his touch possessive and intimate, there was enough static in the air to power all of Las Vegas. As a male of the species, and an Italian to boot, Tony got the picture—in 3-D living color.

Shaking himself from his stupor, Tony pulled off the headset and threw out the first thing that popped into his shell-shocked brain. "Sorry, man. Wrong apartment."

There was a glint in Nick's eyes as he met his ex-partner's stupefied gaze, his tone an amused drawl. "Nice try, Martinelli." He glanced down at his companion, his hand resting against her neck. "Tony, I'd like you to meet a friend of mine."

The way Nick was stroking her neck gave "friend" a whole new definition. Tony finally managed to get his brain out of park. "Hey, any friend of yours is a friend of mine."

Nick's amusement intensified. "Not this friend." He slowly brushed back a curl clinging to her face, his hand lingering briefly before he encircled her with his arm. "Syd, this is Tony Martinelli, my ex-partner."

She turned to face Tony, and he was confronted with the bluest, most direct eyes he'd ever seen. This was some woman, all right. And by the acquiescent way she sat in Nick's proprietary embrace, it was also crystal clear that she was Nick Novak's woman.

"Tony—Sydney Foster."

For the second time in less than five minutes, Tony couldn't think of a damned thing to say. Sydney Foster? *The* Sydney Foster?

As if amused by his speechlessness, she watched him, a tiny dimple appearing at the corner of her mouth, then she smiled, the effect packing enough high voltage to turn any man's knees to glop. "I'm pleased to meet you, Tony."

Her voice had a low, satiny texture to it, and a silly grin split Tony's face. Where in hell had Nick had her stashed? He'd worked night and day with the man for six years, and he had no idea this walking dream existed. His boyish grin broadened. So, Nicky had been holding out on him, had he? "I'm pleased, too, and I'm pleased you're pleased."

Leveling a look at him, Nick cocked an eyebrow in a warning expression. Indicating the box he held in his hand, Tony finally acknowledged him and approached the couch. "Pete's Pizza had a special on, so I picked up one with enough cholesterol to clog your arteries overnight. You know, three kinds of cheese, fatty salami and pepperoni. Of course, if I'd known you were entertaining . . ."

Nick ignored the way that Tony deliberately left the sentence hanging. He pulled himself up into a sitting position, his arm tightening around Sydney's shoulders. "I thought you were undercover all this week."

Tony's tone was barbed. "So I gather." He flipped open the lid and offered Sydney a piece of pizza and a paper napkin. "Help yourself, Sydney. It's the best pizza in town."

Nick watched as Sydney accepted Tony's offer, a smile tugging at his mouth. He knew damned well she didn't want anything more to eat but had accepted out of consideration for Tony and to smooth an awkward situation. The lady had polish.

"Nick?"

Nick glanced up as Tony passed the box to him. He shook his head. "No thanks. Sydney brought me a burger."

Tony barely managed to hold back a smirk. "With bacon and onions, no doubt."

It was Tony's way of establishing the obvious, that Sydney was familiar with Nick's preferences, but Nick neither confirmed nor disconfirmed. Which was an answer as far as Tony was concerned.

There was more than a little humor in Nick's eyes as he watched his friend stretch out on the floor, his back propped against the easy chair. Tony might be able to fool most people into thinking he was a mental featherweight, but Nick knew from experience there was an astute mind and an even more astute intuition behind that bland expression.

And he was willing to bet Tony Martinelli had put more pieces together in the first three seconds than someone else would have in half an hour.

As he mulled over the implications arising from his ex-partner's unexpected arrival, Nick stroked Sydney's arm, semiaware of the soft texture of cashmere against the silk of her blouse. He hadn't expected to see Tony at all this week, and even if he had, he still wouldn't have been prepared. He'd been thrown into such a tailspin over Sydney's turning up in his life again, he'd never once thought about the possible consequences her sudden appearance would create. And there were consequences. Especially when it was Tony who'd tracked her down in the first place. He knew damned well his ex-partner was sitting there right now, assembling the facts. And that made him just a little uneasy.

Sydney's voice broke through his thoughts. "Are you sure you don't want a bite?"

He looked at her, his gaze softening. "No."

She countered his refusal with an amused, resolute look. "Yes you do."

He tried to outstare her, but she didn't back off, and he finally relented with a wry grin. "I guess I do." He caught her wrist and held her hand steady as he took a bite of the pizza she offered him.

As if compelled by some force, her gaze slid to his mouth, and the pulse in her neck became suddenly erratic. That awareness sent Nick's own pulse rate into a frenzy, and he felt as if every speck of air had been driven out of his lungs. Disregarding the gleam of interest in Tony's eyes, he caught her by the back of the neck and pressed her head against his chest, her hair tangled between his fingers. He wanted to say to hell with propriety, but he knew he had to defuse this emotional time bomb or Tony would have a damned sight more to go on than sheer speculation.

He hugged her closer, a tinge of humor in his gruff tone. "I told you I didn't want the damned pizza."

That wrung a shaky laugh out of her, and he could see in a glance how deeply affected she was, but there was a glimmer of amusement in her expression.

The gleam in Tony's eyes intensified as he watched the two of them. "So tell me, Novak, what *do* you want?"

The laugh lines around Nick's mouth deepened. "I want you to mind your own business."

Tony chuckled. "I figured you would." He helped himself to another piece of pizza, then glanced at Nick. "Is there any beer left in the fridge?"

Nick nodded and Tony got up and headed for the kitchen. Catching her under the chin, Nick lifted Sydney's face. Her eyes were still glazed with emotion, and he sensed a real vulnerability in her. She tried to smile, and her voice was unsteady when she spoke. "I think it would be a good idea if I left for a while."

His expression grew solemn. "Why?"

She swallowed hard and closed her eyes, her pulse frantic beneath his fingertips. She took a deep breath and looked at him, finally managing a wobbly smile. "I think it's pretty obvious, don't you?"

He drew his knuckles along her chin, his own voice gruff. "Yeah, I guess it is."

She swallowed again and covered his hand with her own, her eyes drifting shut as she kissed the sensitive hollow of his palm. Her caress sent a jolt of ice and fire sizzling through him, and Nick felt the effect right down to his toes. Clamping down on his instant response, he kissed her softly on the forehead, then lifted her face so that she would look at him. Her voice was low and uneven. "He's the one who found out about me, isn't he?"

Nick gave her a sharp look, then carefully laced his fingers through hers. "Yes, he is."

Sydney shifted her gaze, her fingers trembling as she straightened the cuff of his sweatshirt. There was an odd edge to her voice. "What does he know?"

"Nothing."

"He's bound to start asking questions, and I think it would be less awkward if I weren't here."

Nick sighed and rested his head back against the cushion.

"And there really are some things I should take care of tonight."

He turned to look at her. He was not thrilled with the idea.

Tony stuck his head around the kitchen arch. "Hey, Sydney, want a beer?"

She smiled. "No thanks. I should be going. I have to stop by my office, and I don't want to leave it too late." She glanced back at Nick, her eyes soft and a little anxious. "You understand, don't you?"

He reluctantly gave in. "Just don't be long."

Sydney's voice was uneven. "I'll be back in an hour."

He held her gaze. "For sure?"

"For sure."

He eased his hold on her, hating like hell to let her go, but Sydney was right. He owed Tony an explanation, and he did not want her around when he gave it to him. This thing with her was too damned unsettled. He could handle Tony's questions on his own, but if she were there, it would create one hell of a strain. And that was something they could both do without.

Sobered by those thoughts, he kept his gaze fixed on her as she slipped out of his loose embrace and stood up. He wondered if he'd ever be able to watch her walk out that door without feeling a certain amount of dread. He caught her hand, giving it a squeeze. "Don't be long."

He sensed her own reluctance as she bent over and kissed him softly on the corner of his mouth. "I won't."

Nick slid his hand through her hair as he murmured softly, "And plan on staying. There's a spare house key on a hook beside the fridge."

Her hand tightened around his. Visibly collecting herself, she straightened and turned to face Tony, a residue of emotion giving her voice a husky pitch. "It was nice meeting you, Tony, and thanks for the pizza. Next time it's my treat."

Tony chuckled and gave her a mock salute. "I'm in there. Nick has no appreciation for junk food cuisine."

"Yes," she said. "I know." She glanced back at Nick, her smile softening as she gave his hand another squeeze. "I'll see you later."

The apartment seemed empty as hell after she left, and Nick experienced the predictable flicker of dread. Maybe if he was physically able to go after her, to bring her back if he had to, it wouldn't be so bad.

"So. Sydney Foster wasn't a guy, after all."

The ironic tone in Tony's voice made Nick smile, and he turned his head to meet his ex-partner's gaze.

"You noticed."

Tony grinned and sat down on the floor. "Hey, man, you'd have to be dead not to."

Nick didn't bother to respond. Resting his arm across his chest, he stared into space, aware of her lingering fragrance.

"By the looks of things, I'd say you know her pretty well."

"You could say that."

Tony stared at his buddy. "Give me a break, will you? Have you known her a long time, or did she pop out of your Cheerios box this morning?"

"A long time."

Tony heaved an exaggerated sigh. "Look, Novak, I've been freezing my ass off in a stinking hole of a stakeout, I'm forty hours short on sleep, and I haven't changed my socks in three days. I'm in no mood for this."

That dragged a smile out of Nick, and he turned his head to look at his ex-partner. "I can see that."

Tony fixed him with a narrow look. "So *when*, Novak?"

Nick stared at Tony a moment, then turned away, his expression shuttered. "It was a long time ago."

"Before or after Sara?"

There was a long pause. "Before."

Tony stared at him as he assembled the facts. "So that makes it about fifteen years ago."

"Yes."

"I take it it was pretty major."

Nick's voice was quiet when he finally answered. "Very major."

"Just how well did you know her, Nick?"

Nick exhaled heavily. "We lived together for a few months."

"What happened?"

"There were major problems and I walked out on her. When I finally came to my senses and went back, she was gone. I didn't know she was still around until a few days ago."

"Until I told you about Unicorn Holdings."

Nick confirmed his statement with a barely perceptible nod.

"And?"

"I went to see her."

Tony knew Nick, knew how he kept things to himself. And his gut was telling him that this was something that was absolutely off limits. It was time to back off. He grinned and took a different tack. "And you haven't let her out of your sight since."

Nick managed a wry smile. "That's stretching it a little, Cinderella."

Tony chuckled, took a long swig from the can of beer, then reached for another piece of pizza. "You're missing some main marbles if you let that one get away, Novak. That lady is a class act." He indicated the box on the floor. "Are you sure you don't want a piece?"

Nick shook his head. As he watched Tony devour the piece of pizza, he wondered how long it had been since his ex-partner had had a day off. Tony was beginning to develop that hollow-eyed look that came from long hours, lousy food and extended exposure to a side of life that preyed on the weak and exploited the helpless. After years of dealing with the lowlifes, with the slime, even the best cop could get tainted by it. And the boundaries between the right side of the law and the wrong side got very blurred.

"She left so you could talk to me, you know."

Nick exhaled sharply. "I know."

"Does she know about Sara?"

"No."

Tony's expression sobered. "You'd better think that one through, buddy."

Nick didn't respond. He knew the point Tony was trying to make. There had been a time during his recovery when he had been unable to apply any kind of rationale or logic to even the simplest decision, a time when his moods and responses had been unpredictable. And it had taken hours and hours of structured, intensive therapy to relearn that discipline. But as far as Sydney was concerned, his judgment was still scrambled.

It wasn't as though Sara was something he could shovel under the rug and forget about. Sydney was bound to find out about her sooner or later, and he knew he had to be the one to tell her.

"I have to hit the road, man. We have a tail on this sleazy drug dealer, and it looks like he's got something coming down."

"That shipment of coke?"

"Yeah. It could be a big one. I hope we can nail the bastard tonight. I sure in hell could do with the weekend off." Tony slapped his thighs in a gesture of finality, then picked up the pizza box and got to his feet. "I'll stick this in the fridge, and you can have it for breakfast."

Nick shot the other man a look of barely disguised distaste. "No thanks."

"Hey, what's wrong with cold pizza for breakfast?"

"It loses something in transition."

Tony grinned and tucked the box under his arm. "Then I'll take it with me. I can eat anything at four in the morning."

"I remember."

Tony started toward the door, then stopped. Finally he turned, his expression serious. "Think about it, Nick," Tony counseled quietly. "If she means anything to you at all, you'd better level with her. It's going to get harder to tell her the longer you put it off."

It was the only time Tony had ever come close to interfering, and even though it bugged his ass that his ex-partner was acting like a mother hen again, Nick knew he was right. But he still didn't like it.

NICK WAS IN THE KITCHEN unloading the dishwasher when Sydney returned, a bag of groceries in her arms. He gave her a dubious look. "You went grocery shopping at ten o'clock at night?"

She set the bag on the counter, then grinned at him. "I was afraid if I didn't we'd be stuck with cold pizza for breakfast." She stripped off her trench coat and started putting things away in the fridge. She had changed into a pair of casual slacks and a deep cherry-red sweater, and Nick experienced a sudden hollowness in his chest. Red had always been her favorite color, and he remembered buying her a red velvet robe for the one Christmas they had been together. Shaken by the memory, he turned back to the clean dishes sitting on the counter and started putting them away.

He heard the fridge door shut, then the sound of Sydney folding the paper bag. Her voice was underscored with humor and a touch of awe. "This kitchen is so organized, it's almost frightening."

The expression in Nick's eyes eased. "That bothers you?"

"I'm not sure. Neatness is one thing, but this is ridiculous."

He shrugged and gave her a warped smile. "One of the little fallouts from the accident."

Folding her arms in front of her, Sydney braced her hip against the cupboard. "Explain."

Nick continued putting the dishes away. "Nearly everyone ends up with a few new personality quirks after a serious head injury, especially if they've been in a coma for any length of time. I ended up with this compulsion for order, but I could have gone the other way and ended up a total slob." He looked at her, a wry expression around his mouth. "It's more or less a crapshoot how you turn out."

The twinkle in her eyes intensified. "Just out of curiosity, what happened to your temper? Better or worse?"

He grinned and closed the cupboard door. "Just more erratic."

She laughed. "That's even more frightening than your regimented cupboards."

He didn't answer right away, his eyes narrowed in speculation as he scrutinized her. His tone was quiet when he finally spoke. "But you already knew all this, didn't you?"

She shot him a startled look, her eyes suddenly guarded.

He played out his hunch. "You know all about the personality changes, about the memory loss, about the period of inappropriate behavior. You probably know more about my recovery than I do."

There was an apprehensive look in her eyes as she stared at him. "Yes," she said tersely, "I probably do."

Nick's gaze was thoughtful as he studied her. All those months, when he thought he was struggling alone, she had been watching out for him. It made him feel very humble.

"Don't be angry, Nick."

"I'm not." He gave her a crooked smile. "I told you my temper was erratic. I might have been mad as hell about it an hour ago, but I'm not now."

"You don't like talking about it, do you?" she asked quietly.

His tone was clipped. "I don't even like thinking about it." He unloaded the cutlery rack, a brooding expression settling on his face as he automatically sorted the flatware. There were a lot of things he didn't like thinking about.

"Is there anything I can do?"

He placed the empty rack back in the dishwasher, closed the door, then glanced at her. "No, I don't think so." He indicated the cupboard beside the fridge. "Tony keeps some liquor there if you'd like to fix yourself a drink."

She shook her head. Nick turned out the light above the sink, then grasped his cane and headed toward the living room.

She picked up her coat and followed him, pausing at the hall closet to hang it up. "Did Tony stay long?"

Her offhand tone might have misled anyone but Nick. He sensed her unease, and his own kicked into gear. Lowering himself onto the sofa, he leaned back in a semireclining position, his shoulders braced against the arm. His voice was slightly brusque when he finally answered. "No, he left shortly after you did."

Sydney shot him a quick look, then closed the closet door, her movements just a little too precise. She turned out the light in the entryway then crossed the room. His somber gaze connected with hers as she bent over him, a soft look of concern in her eyes. She smoothed her hand up his arm and across his shoulder. "You look tired."

He caught her hand in his. "I'm fine," he said gruffly.

She knelt beside him, trying to disengage her hand. "Let me fix the cushions so you're more comfortable."

He shook his head, firming his grip on her. A tightness banded his chest as he caressed her face, his eyes becoming more intent as he smoothed his hand up her jaw until his fingers were deep in her hair. Whispering her name, he exerted pressure on the back of her head until her lips brushed his in a light, searching kiss. Her mouth moved softly against his, the infinite tenderness slaking one hunger, the moist sensuality creating yet another.

He finally dragged his mouth away, inhaling raggedly as he pulled her head against him, moved by the tenderness of her kiss. He wanted to haul her up beside him, to feel the full length of her body pressed against his, but he denied himself even that incomplete relief. Cradling her upper body across his chest, he caressed her scalp, her hair tangling around his hand like strands of silk. Every time he held her, it was as though he had reconnected with a part of himself that had been missing for a very long time.

His expression sobered as he slowly stroked her back. Tony was right; the longer he put off telling her about Sara, the harder it was going to get. And it was going to be bloody well hard enough as it was.

His voice was strained. "What else do you know about me?"

Sydney raised her head, a quizzical look in her eyes. "What do you mean?"

Nick felt like the worst kind of traitor as he forced himself to say the words. "Did you know I was married?"

Her expression froze into a stark stare. There was a brittle silence, then she visibly pulled herself together and withdrew, her back stiff as she moved away from him. "No, I didn't."

Nick watched her, knowing there was little he could do to stop her if she decided to leave. Giving her time to assimilate the shock, he reached out and slowly smoothed her hair behind her ear, feeling so damned inadequate.

When he finally spoke, his voice was tinged with self-loathing. "I did a pretty good job of screwing up my life after you left. I started drinking pretty heavy, and the only time I had any real focus was when I was on the pistol range, blasting the hell out of targets. I had this bloody big chip on my shoulder, and I was as bitter as hell—I hated the whole goddamned world."

Nick paused, his eyes hard with recollection, steeling himself to deliver the blow that would hurt her the most. He kept staring at the wall, not daring to look at her. "I met Sara seven months after you disappeared. I don't know why, but she thought I was worth salvaging. I was so bent out of shape, I guess I saw her as a means of getting over you. I married her two months later."

He looked at Sydney, his gut contracting into a hard, cold knot. Her pale face was rigidly controlled, the absence of emotion almost frightening. And Nick knew he had hurt her far more than he had ever anticipated. Sickened by what he'd done to her, he covered his eyes with his arm, the muscles in his jaw hardened by self-directed anger. He was such a goddamned contemptible bastard. And he didn't know what to say to stop her pain.

Exhaling wearily, he shifted his arm and looked at her. Somehow he had to break the silence. He positioned himself so he could reach her with his right hand.

As if spurred by his movement, she quickly got to her feet and turned toward the kitchen. "I think I'd like something cold to drink. How about you?"

Realizing what she was doing, Nick reacted. With a speed he didn't think he possessed anymore, he turned and grabbed her wrist, stopping her short. "No," he said roughly. "You can't walk away from this, Sydney."

She tried to pull free of his grip, her voice uneven. "It has nothing to do with me."

"It has everything to do with you. I sure in hell didn't want to tell you, but there was a chance you would have found out anyway." He eased his hold just a fraction. "I thought you should hear it from me."

She didn't look at him. She stood stiff and resistant in his grasp, and realizing the futility of trying to force her to hear him out, Nick let her go and closed his eyes. Hell, what was the use?

"Was she in love with you?"

He wasn't prepared for her question, and his attention instantly focused on her. She was sitting on the small wooden trunk he used as a coffee table, toying with a paper napkin. She wouldn't look at him, and guilt twisted in him as he glanced away. There was a hard edge to his voice. "Yeah, in the beginning. Until I destroyed that, too." He fell silent, his thoughts locked on the past. When he spoke again, his tone had mellowed just a little. "I convinced myself that if I worked at it, we could make a go of it. But I couldn't fight the shadows, and we called it quits two years later."

He didn't tell her that it took him another three years to get his act together and to get off the booze. Nor did he tell her about his attitude on the job. Without realizing what he was doing, he'd set himself up as a walking target. As far as he was concerned, his life wasn't worth a rat's ass anyway, so he didn't give a damn whether he got blown away or not.

Unconsciously, he'd dared every punk he faced to try to take him down. The creeps would take one look at his face and back away. Nobody would tangle with him. Nobody. His performance earned him a couple of commendations and a reputation as a hard-nosed cop, but the truth was, he didn't give a shit whether he lived or died.

Bone-numbing exhaustion washed over him. He looked at Sydney. She was still pleating the napkin, not a single trace of emotion on her face.

He'd forgotten how adept she was at that, at turning inward, retreating so deeply into herself it was as if she weren't even there. At one time that kind of withdrawal would have sent him into a rage. But he had done the same thing himself during his recovery. It was a way of surviving.

But knowing all that didn't make it any easier now. Reaching over, he took the napkin out of her hands and wadded it up. "Don't, Sydney," he said quietly.

She met his gaze, her eyes revealing nothing. The only indication that she was affected at all was her extreme pallor.

He watched her, his eyes never wavering from her face. "It was a mistake, and I did it for all the wrong reasons."

Nothing. Not a flicker. The look on her face scared the hell out of him. Knowing he couldn't handle the guilt about doing this to her, he allowed his anger to surface. "Damn it, don't pull that silent treatment! Talk to me."

She looked past him with a frightening detachment. "There really isn't anything to say, is there?"

He reached out and caught her chin, forcing her to look at him. "Isn't there? Or do you think by not talking about it, you can pretend it never happened?"

She tried to twist her head out of his grasp, but he tightened his hold. Knowing he had to force a response from her, he reacted out of desperation and fired a cruel accusation.

"Can't you see what you're doing? Or don't you even care?"

Every last speck of color drained from her face, and he saw the flash of pain. Tears welled up in her eyes, and her control shattered. "What do you want from me, Nick? Do you want hysterics? Do you want acceptance? Tell me what you want." She jerked away, the tears brimming over as she scrambled to her feet.

Knowing he couldn't let her leave with this still hanging between them, he grabbed her arm and yanked her around, his grip on her wrist almost brutal.

She tried to pull free, her tone low and vehement. "Let me go!"

Twisting his upper body, he used her resistance to lever himself into a sitting position, determination stamped into his face. "Not a chance, lady. You're not going to pull that disappearing act this time."

Like a cornered animal, she continued to struggle, the skin on her wrist turning white from the pressure. Never before had he used physical force on her, but this was different. This time he could not allow her to leave; this time he had to make her listen. Using all the strength he had in his right arm and shoulder, he forced her off balance, then caught her behind the knee with his leg, bringing her down on top of him. Somehow he found the coordination to roll with her, trapping her beneath him.

But the minute he let her absorb the full weight of his body, the fight went out of her and she started to cry. Unable to endure her anguish, he cradled her beneath him, nestling her head against his neck. "Don't, Sydney," he whispered gruffly. "Please don't. I should be shot for doing this to you."

Dragging her arms free, she slipped them around him in a desperate embrace. "God, don't say that," she sobbed. "Don't ever say that."

Wrenched by the horror in her voice, Nick closed his eyes, holding her with all the strength he could muster. Suddenly she was pliant and giving in his arms, and his response was instantaneous. He locked his arms around her, unable to breathe for the frantic pounding in his chest. He clenched his jaw as he tried to fight through the wild sensations she aroused in him. Burying his face in the tumble of her hair, he forced air into his laboring lungs, waiting for the storm to ease. She clung to him, her body trembling beneath his, and he cradled her even closer, wanting to shield her from the rawness he was experiencing.

He held her for a long time, until his heart stopped slamming against his ribs, until the tension slowly eased from her body. The fragrance of her hair entrapped him, and he pressed a kiss against the soft curve of her neck, her pulse wild beneath his lips.

Inhaling raggedly, he shifted his position, his strength depleted as he braced his arms on either side of her head, then cupped her face in his hands. He brushed his mouth against hers in a soft, gentling kiss, his heart lurching wildly as her lips parted beneath his. Reluctantly he drew away, his eyes dark and intense as he gazed down at her.

She looked up at him, her lashes still matted with tears. "Nick, I—"

He pressed his thumb against her mouth to silence her, then he kissed her temple, his voice catching as he whispered unevenly, "Easy, love. Easy. Just let me hold you for a little while."

Tenderness rolled over him in a great, inundating wave, and he closed his eyes. She was so defenseless right then, and his need to shelter her from her own vulnerability overrode all else. God, if he could only make this moment last a lifetime.

It was a long time before she relaxed completely in his arms, and Nick brushed another kiss across her mouth as he eased his hold on her. Bracing his weight on his elbow, he gently smoothed back a wisp of hair that was clinging to her cheek, aware that she was watching him with a kind of uncertainty that made his gut knot.

A muscle in his jaw twitched as he pulled her arm from around his neck, his eyes darkening when he saw the red mark on her wrist. "I'm sorry I hurt you," he said gruffly, "but I couldn't let you go."

She touched his face, her fingers unsteady as she trailed them down his cheek. She tried to smile but her eyes filled with tears, instead. "You didn't hurt me."

"Yes, I did." He frowned, an unreadable expression in his eyes as he covered the back of her hand with his, then very carefully and deliberately laced his fingers through hers.

Sydney's voice cut through his dark thoughts. "Did you love her?"

His voice was clipped with self-castigation. "I should have, but I couldn't. She tried her best to make me happy."

"What happened to her?"

"She remarried a couple of years later, and the last I heard, she was living in Toronto and had a couple of kids." He tightened his hold on her hand. "It was a mistake. Right from the beginning, it was a mistake."

Tears slipped down her temples as Sydney touched his mouth. "Hold me, Nick," she whispered, her voice breaking.

Nick did, with all the strength and gentleness he had in him, wishing to God he hadn't had to hurt her. But in spite of how hard it had been for her, he realized they had taken one small step forward. At least now they were dragging things out into the open.

Sydney shifted slightly, and he pressed his mouth against her hair. She drew a deep breath, and he could feel the tautness leave her body. He'd had enough upheaval for one night, and he suspected she had, too.

Having her pinned beneath him kicked off a memory, and he recalled the no-holds-barred wrestling matches they used to get into when he tried to teach her some basic self-defense.

A smile lightened his eyes as he tucked his head beside hers, his mouth against her ear. "Give up?"

He was rewarded with a shaky laugh. "Not a chance. It wasn't a fair throw."

"Yes, it was. I have a physical disability."

"Not to mention a sixty-pound weight advantage."

He couldn't let an opportunity like that slide by. "It used to be seventy."

"So you've lost ten pounds."

Nick grinned. "Nice try, Sydney." He raised his head and looked down at her, his eyes gleaming. "I may be handicapped, but I'm not blind."

She barely managed to restrain a smile. "You're not very tactful, either."

His gaze was warm and intimate, a feeling of well-being infusing every muscle and bone in his body. It felt so right, lying there with her.

Easing onto his side, he braced his head on his hand, his smile deepening. "Truce?"

Her hair clung to the rough fabric of the sofa as she turned her head to look at him, her eyes soft and evocative, glinting with just a touch of sass. "Truce does not mean surrender, Nick. Especially if you're contemplating foul play."

"I never play foul."

"You don't play by the rules, either."

"Do you know you've got a tiny freckle right here on your lip?"

She tipped her head back and laughed, the sound rich and effervescent. Nick watched her, unaccountably pleased with himself. She expelled the last of her amusement on a sigh, her eyes sparkling. "You're slick. You really are."

His expression altered, and his voice got very husky. "Are you comfortable?"

The laughter faded in her eyes and was replaced with a look that made him think of dark nights and sweat-dampened skin. "No," she whispered unsteadily. "I'm not."

NICK WAS ALREADY STRETCHED OUT on the bed, clad only in a pair of sweatpants, when she came out of the bathroom. She had on a pair of tailored silk pajamas, exactly the same shade of blue as her eyes, the outline of her body visible through the light fabric. Feeling as though everything else were out of focus, he watched her as she shut off the hall light and turned toward the bed. He caught a flicker of uncertainty as her gaze connected with his, then she came toward him. His heart beat suddenly erratic, Nick never took his eyes off her.

As she neared the bed, he reached out his good hand toward her. She slipped her own hand into his, and as his fingers closed in a firm grip, he realized that she was shaking.

She turned to switch off the small lamp by his bed, and he tightened his hold, drawing her to him. "No," he said softly. "Leave it on."

Her eyes were unfathomable and he could feel how tense she was when she yielded to his steady pressure, but the minute their bodies connected, she came apart in his arms. He hugged her close, trying to still her trembling. "It's okay, Syd. Sh, love. It's okay."

She turned her face against his neck as a tremor coursed through her, and Nick could feel her heart pounding against his ribs. He was lying on his right side, his strength encumbered by his weight. Unable to hold her as tightly as he wanted, he eased onto his back. "Lie on top of me. Let me hold you."

She inhaled raggedly, her words barely coherent. "No. I can't do that to you."

"Please, Sydney," he whispered hoarsely.

His face contorted with agonizing pleasure as she moved on top of him, her weight between his thighs such a relief it was all he could do to keep from groaning. He had been wanting to hold her like this since that night in her apartment, to feel her heavy against his groin, and it felt so good. So damned good. And for right now, it was enough.

He pressed his mouth against her forehead, his lips brushing her skin as he asked her gently, "Hey, are you all right?"

Her tone was raw with guilt. "This is so unfair to you."

Nick's expression sobered as he hooked his knuckles under her chin, tilting her head back so he could see her face. "It's unfair to you, too," he countered softly.

Her eyes were stark with remorse. "But it's different for me, Nick."

He smoothed his finger across her bottom lip. "Tell me how it's different." She gave a little shrug, distress clouding her eyes as she looked away. Nick applied gentle pressure to her jaw, his face somber. "Please, Syd. It's important."

"I don't know how to explain."

"Try."

Her reservations made her hesitate, and Nick realized that she was afraid he would misunderstand. He cradled her head against his shoulder, trying to reassure her with a quiet tone. "I want to know, Sydney."

It took her a moment to answer. "Whether we made love or we didn't was never that important to me."

"Why not?"

She turned her face against his neck. "This is so hard, Nick."

Her honesty stirred some deep feelings in him, and he held her closer, trying to make her feel secure. "I know it is."

There was a weighty pause, then she answered, her voice strained. "What was important was knowing you really wanted me."

The significance of her response hit Nick like a ton of bricks. His wanting her—that was what had been important to her. Physically she had brought him to his knees, and that had scared the hell out of him. He had become addicted to those feelings she'd aroused in him, but until now he had failed to understand that they had been sacrosanct, something she had given him, and him alone. No other man had ever touched that part of her.

But there was that other part of her life that had not been inviolate. And he knew when he was most reminded of that. It was when he was deep inside her, when she'd brought him to the verge of excruciating pleasure, that the demons would rise up to haunt him. And he would wonder how many others had paid for the pleasure. And jealousy would eat away at him until it consumed him. He didn't want it to matter, but it did. And if he hadn't needed her so damned much, it wouldn't have.

Nick closed his eyes, torment carved into every angle of his face. God, he did not want to lose her again. But jealousy was an insidious, malignant disease with him, preying on him like a cancer, and until he could put the past behind him, once and for all, he was its victim.

Sydney raised her head and looked at him, an edge of disquiet in her voice. "What's the matter?"

He slid his hand up her neck, his expression reflective. "I was never just content to hold you, was I?"

She laid her hand against his face, her eyes filled with such tenderness it made his heart contract. Her voice was low and husky, gentle censure in her tone. "You never cheated me, Nick. Never. I never felt anything but loved by you."

He knew that wasn't quite true. He had hurt her and nearly finished himself off in the process, but he grasped the deeper meaning of what she was trying to say. She loved him. For better, for worse; disabled, impotent; or if he was a jealous, unreasonable bastard. It didn't change things for her. Her love was constant—and forever. Unable to utter one damned word, he drew her head down and kissed her softly, his heart slamming into high gear when she responded. And Nick forgot the demons. Forgot everything. She was his for tonight.

CHAPTER SEVEN

THE GRAYNESS OF DAWN seeped into the room, drawing the chill and stillness of early morning with it. This was the time Nick liked best—those one or two hours when the city was suspended in a metamorphosis between night and day, when it was silent and unmoving, the streets like lifeless arteries.

Shifting slightly, he glanced at the sleeping woman nestled against him, his expression softening as he gently drew the covers over her shoulders. It was a little frightening how easily he had slipped back into the routine of sleeping with her. He had always been a light sleeper, and any movement would awaken him, but with Sydney it was different. He could remember coming home from a grueling shift, so damned exhausted he'd be beyond sleep, and the minute he had her in his arms, he'd be out like a light. He couldn't count the times he'd fallen asleep in her embrace or the times he had reached out for her in the middle of the night and dropped off the instant he felt her against him.

Pressing a soft kiss against the top of her head, he eased onto his back, his thoughts centering on what had happened the night before. Until last night, he had never really analyzed their relationship.

It took her candor to make him realize just how deep this need between them went. And if he was to be as honest as she was, he would have to admit that knowing he could arouse her to the point of mindlessness was a major power trip for him. It pumped up his male ego to know he could elicit that kind of response from her when he touched her.

What had been important to her was knowing he wanted her; what had been important to him was knowing he could arouse and satisfy her. Two sides of the same coin.

They had something very special, and after last night he realized the sexual aspect was only part of it. A part. Not the whole. And he had been so goddamned obsessed with his male pride, he had never seen that before. He had lain half the night with her, lost in the feel of her mouth against his, the weight of her body molding them together, and he discovered he didn't have to be inside her to feel so connected to her, he felt almost reborn. And for the first time since she'd walked back into his life, there was a glimmer of hope. Because of his impotency, because he couldn't have her the way other men had had her, that whole physical aspect of their relationship had been put on hold. And since he wouldn't be constantly reminded of the thing that drove him into fits of obsessive jealousy, maybe he could put it all behind him. He could endure the sexual frustration; he wasn't so sure he could endure the renewed jealousy or the emptiness if he lost her again.

Disengaging himself from those disturbing thoughts, he looked down at her, a tightness forming in his chest. She was so lovely, sleeping there beside him. He moved down in the bed, then turned on one elbow and hooked his knuckles under her jaw, gently shifting the angle of her head. Closing his eyes against the wild flurry in him, he brushed his mouth against her parted lips, his touch light and caressing.

She stirred and murmured his name, even in sleep yielding to him, and Nick experienced a rush of feelings so strong it was all he could do to keep from dragging her against him. With the languor of someone just awakening, she sighed and moved closer, responding to the gentle movement of his mouth. Nick felt as if he were on the verge of suffocation as she drowsily smoothed her hand up his naked back. He thrust his fingers into her hair, holding her head steady as he deepened the kiss. Sydney sighed again and tightened her arm around him, urging him closer, the silk of her pajamas like a caress against his skin.

Unable to breathe for the frantic hammering of his heart, Nick slowly withdrew, his expression softened with a gut-wrenching tenderness as he gazed down at her. "Good morning."

Her eyes had that just-kissed glow in them, and her tone was very husky. "Good morning."

There was something so damned appealing about her lying there in his arms—her hair tousled, her lips still moist from his kiss—and Nick's need thickened with a heavy ache. He felt he would disintegrate if he couldn't feel her flesh against his. His eyes held hers with a mesmerizing intensity, and his movements were slow and deliberate as he undid the top button of her pajamas. Sydney shivered, her eyes drifting shut, her breathing suddenly labored. The softness of her skin beneath his touch intensified his need, and he moved to the second button.

Struggling to curb her reaction, Sydney caught his hand. "Don't, Nick," she whispered raggedly. "Please don't."

He twisted his hand free, his voice gruff. "I just want to hold you. That's all."

She looked up at him, her eyes dark with uncertainty, but she didn't resist as one by one he slowly undid the buttons. Without shifting his gaze from hers, he brushed back the fabric, then slipped his right arm around her hips and drew her on top of him. The instant her weight connected with his groin a low sound was wrenched from him, and he closed his eyes, his arms locked around her in a fierce embrace. "Lord, but you feel so damned good."

Hanging on to him as if she didn't dare let go, she turned her face against his neck, and Nick held the back of her head. Sensation after sensation washed through him, and he was vividly aware of every texture of her—the silk of her hair against his hand, the softness of her naked breasts pressed against his chest, the hard weight of her against his pelvis. But through the fever in his mind, one crystal clear thought emerged. This sensual intensity they shared had never been violated—not by any man. This was his, and his alone.

And for the first time ever, he transcended the physical need. He had loved her with his body; now he loved her with his very soul.

Turning her head, he kissed her with such overwhelming tenderness it seemed to pour out of every cell in him, and he felt as though he had suddenly been set free. "I love you, Sydney," he whispered. "God, but I love you."

He could taste her tears, and he could feel her try to respond, but a ragged sound broke from her, and he held her so tight it was as if her heartbeat were his own.

Sensing how raw she was, he slipped his hand under her loosened top and caressed her bare back, soothing her with his touch. And slowly, so slowly, he felt the tension ease in her—and in him.

When he felt her totally relax against him, he kissed her ear, his voice husky. "Are you okay?"

She pressed her face more tightly against the soft skin of his neck. "Yes."

"Are you sure?"

She lifted her head and gazed down at him, her eyes shimmering with unshed tears. She managed a tremulous smile. "Yes," she whispered unevenly. "Very sure."

Watching her face for a reaction, he caught her across the hips, rocking her slowly against his pelvis. A tremor ran through her and she closed her eyes, resting her forehead against his chin. Aware of the sexual tension in her, Nick slid his hand under the waist of her pajamas as he shifted her weight, not wanting to leave her hanging on the edge of that kind of torment.

But before he had time to caress her, to feel her warmth and moistness, she caught his hand and pulled it from between them, her voice raw. "No. Please, Nick. Don't."

He pressed his face against hers. "Sydney, don't do this to yourself."

She tightened her arms around him, locking her body against his. "Just hold me," she said, her voice breaking. "I just need you to hold me."

His face taut with strain, Nick enfolded her trembling form in a secure embrace, oddly disappointed, aching for her in a way that had nothing to do with his own unsatisfied hunger. He didn't want to hurt her. He had never wanted to hurt her. But he had. Damn it, he had.

The room had lightened and a slight breeze was ruffling the blinds when she finally stirred in his arms, then slowly, so slowly, she touched his mouth with a gentle, lingering kiss. Releasing her breath on a sigh, she raised her head and looked at him, her gaze so full of love it made his throat close.

As if trying to reassure him, she took his face between her hands, her eyes locked on his with a kind of sincerity that came straight from her heart. "I don't need it all, Nick," she said softly. "I just need you."

Her face was framed with an untidy tumble of curls, and he brushed them back. "I don't like leaving you like that."

He caught the glimmer of humor in her eyes as she lowered her head and gave him another light kiss. "It passes."

There was such a dry inflection in her voice that it made him smile, and he hugged her, feeling happier than he had for a very long time. If they maintained the balance, if they didn't ignite that deep, driving hunger, they would be all right.

Catching a handful of hair, he tipped her head back, a smile in his eyes. "Are you going to make me breakfast?"

She gave him a tart look. "Not at 5:00 a.m., I'm not."

He grinned. "So what are we going to do for the next few hours?"

She barely managed to restrain a smile. "Is the word *sleep* in your vocabulary?"

He rubbed his hand against the base of her spine, knowing full well it made her go all weak and breathless. "Don't be a bore, Sydney. You had three hours of sleep already."

She grinned down at him, slowly stroking the corner of his mouth with her fingertip. "What did you have in mind?"

Cupping the back of her head, he pressed her down until her lips grazed his. "We'll think of something."

It was eight when they finally got up, and Nick couldn't remember the last time he felt so damned energized. It was a gorgeous morning, it was the weekend, and they had two whole days without any interruptions.

When he made his way into the kitchen after his shower, he felt as if he had dumped at least twenty years. One look at the counters, and it was clear his compulsion for neatness had been dumped, as well. The place was an utter disaster.

He had always been relatively tidy, but that trait had turned into a compulsion after his head injury, and he couldn't stand it if anything was out of place. At the moment, he doubted if anything was in its place. Somehow she had managed to create total chaos in less than half an hour.

He leaned on his cane and shook his head. "My God. This place looks like it's been vandalized."

She turned and flashed him a knowing grin. "And you can't stand it, can you?"

"I've seen places that have been in better shape after a major drug search."

She made a face and turned back to the counter. "Don't hyperventilate, Detective. It's only temporary."

He moved slowly across the kitchen, still amazed at the destruction. "Just out of curiosity, how did you manage all this in half an hour?"

She looked at him, a treacherous gleam in her eyes. "We're going to have a quick breakfast, and then we're going on a picnic."

"A picnic? A *picnic*?"

She came over to him, caught his face between her hands and gave him a quick, hard kiss. "Yes, a picnic." Her eyes were dancing. "Lighten up, Novak. You'll love it."

Releasing his hold on his cane, he slipped his arms around her, a grin pulling at the corners of his mouth. "Lord, woman. The snow's barely off the ground. And I'll likely plant my face in the first piece of rough ground we come across."

She chuckled and pulled his head down, giving him a kiss that nearly had him planting his face in the kitchen floor. "I'll make you a deal," she said. "Wherever you fall, that's where we'll have lunch."

Nick hugged her against him, loving her more than he thought possible. He'd have hated it if she'd gone all soft and sympathetic, if she'd tried to baby him. "It's a deal. But you have to clean up your damned mess before we go."

Sydney made two stops on the way out of town; one at a sporting goods store to pick up a roll of foam matting, and another at a corner deli. Nick relaxed in the leather bucket seat, the breeze from the open window rolling over him as he watched her drive. She handled the high-powered luxury car with the kind of offhand ease that spoke of many hours behind the wheel. There were several cassettes lying on the console, a bag of peppermints and two pens, and a thick pad of paper was wedged between the console and her seat. It wasn't much to go on, but he strongly suspected she often left the city to give herself a chance to think.

He helped himself to a peppermint, put on his sunglasses, then glanced over at her. "So, Ms Foster, where are we headed?"

"Someplace where there's a great view of the mountains, where there isn't another living soul within fifty miles, and where there are some big rocks to lean against."

"And where's that?"

She smiled. "We'll know when we get there."

Amused by her answer, he slouched down in the seat, his head against the padded headrest as he watched the scenery slip by. He hadn't been out of the city for months, and he felt as though he had just been released from jail. It was breathtaking country west of Calgary—the rolling foothills, the snowcapped Rockies in the distance, the sense of space. He inhaled deeply, savoring the freshness of crystal clean air whipping in through the open window. He almost forgot the cane lying at his feet.

They had turned onto a narrow gravel road that was lined with spruce and bare-branched aspens, the sunlight glinting through the trees and casting shadows on the dusty surface. Sydney pulled over to the side, stopped and undid her seat belt. Nick cast her a questioning look as she left the engine running and climbed out. He shrugged when she disappeared behind the car and focused his attention on a lone hawk riding the thermals over a shallow valley.

His door opened and he glanced at Sydney, who was standing there with her hand on her hip. "Out you get, Nick."

He folded his arms across his chest, giving her a perverse smile. "Why?"

"Because."

"'Because' doesn't get you bugger-all, Sydney," he retorted.

She stared at him, a resolute set to her chin. "If you get out, I'll tell you."

He studied her, challenging her with a bland expression. "What are you going to do—leave me in the ditch for the vultures?"

She bent over and retrieved his cane, then gave him a steady look. "There isn't a vulture within several hundred miles, so your body's safe. Now get out of the car."

The contrary side of him wanted to see what she'd do if he continued to defy her, but curiosity was getting the better of him, and with an exaggerated sigh, he unlatched his seat belt and levered himself out of the car. She gestured for him to follow her around to the other side of the vehicle, the same resolute look on her face as she rested her hand on the open door. She tipped her head toward the empty driver's seat. "Get in."

Nick stopped dead in his tracks. "Are you out of your mind?"

She simply looked at him, an unperturbed expression on her face.

He stared back, absolutely certain she had dropped her brain in the ditch. "I can't drive."

"Why not?"

"Why not? Good Lord, Sydney, are you for real? My coordination is practically nonexistent, my reflexes are shot, and you want me to drive a car that's worth more than I made in a damned year?"

She tipped her head to one side, and he could swear she was laughing at him behind her sunglasses. "How many cars have we seen in the past twenty minutes?"

He glared at her. "None. But that's not the bloody point."

"Yes it is," she interjected calmly. "There isn't a soul on the road, the car is an automatic, and your right leg works just fine. And in case you haven't noticed, this is hardly downtown Calgary." She watched him, the dimple at the corner of her mouth appearing. "And you know damned well you're itching to try it."

Nick couldn't think of a single rebuttal. She knew him too well. Having to face the fact that he was not competent to drive had been the hardest self-imposed restriction he'd had to accept. He would ransom his grandmother to get behind the wheel of a car.

She watched him, a knowing smile hovering around her mouth. "Get in, Nick."

He wrestled with his conscience, but the temptation was too damned strong. And for once in his life, Nick did as he was told. Sydney adjusted the electric controls on the seat and helped him with his seat belt. When he was settled in, she grinned at him. "Go get 'em, Tiger," she said, then kissed him and shut the door. Nick closed his eyes, his hands clenched around the wheel. The woman was scary.

He didn't look at her when she climbed in the other side, nerves stirring in his stomach. He'd give it a shot. He'd drive a few hundred feet down the road, let her win, then get out before he killed them both.

It was eerie how perfectly ordinary it felt. It had been two years—two damned years—and it felt like yesterday. And he felt exactly the same way he had when he'd taken his first steps unassisted. As if he wanted to bawl.

And Sydney. She sat in the seat beside him, her elbow braced in the open window, holding back her wind-whipped hair, acting as if she didn't know this was the first real taste of freedom he'd had in two years. He had to swallow hard to get past the huge knot in his throat.

He made it a little more than two miles down the road before he couldn't stand it any longer. He pulled off onto the narrow shoulder, dust rolling in the open windows. Sydney gave him a questioning look as he undid the locks on both belts, then released his seat so it slid back as far as it would go.

"Why are you stopping? You're doing fine—"

She never had a chance to finish. He took off his sunglasses, then hers, and tossed them onto the floor. Catching her by the wrist, he half dragged her across the console and into his arms, hugging her so hard he thought he might crack her ribs. She had given him a taste of freedom, and God, it felt so damned good.

Using his shoulders as an anchor, she positioned herself between him and the wheel, pulling herself fully onto his lap. She slipped her arm around his back and cradled his head against her, holding him with a comforting kind of strength that soothed the rawness in him.

Neither of them spoke for several moments, then she leaned back in his embrace, amusement glinting in her eyes. "So," she said huskily, "have you got that out of your system?"

Nick gave her a wry grin, wondering how anyone's eyes could be so blue. He kissed the corner of her mouth, his voice not quite steady. "Yeah, I think I have."

There was a hint of self-directed irony in Sydney's tone. "Has it crossed your mind that we're regressing into adolescence?"

He laughed and hugged her hard. "As a matter of fact, it just did."

She gave him an amused, assessing look. "So how does it feel to be a kid again?"

Nick smiled down at her. "It feels bloody wonderful."

She smiled back, then drew his head down and gave him a light kiss. "I think," she said unevenly, "it's time we got this show on the road."

He acceded with a sigh, knowing if she didn't put some distance between them, they could end up parked there for the rest of the day. Reluctantly he eased his hold on her, steadying her as she disengaged herself and crawled back into the other seat.

They drove for more than an hour, on narrow country roads that wound through the heavily treed high country. The land was wild and beautiful, the purple-hued granite mountains forming a jagged palisade against the western sky. It was just after one o'clock when they crossed a weathered wooden bridge that spanned a swollen mountain stream, and an open grassy space just off the road came into view. There was a sizable area that had been worn bare, indicating regular use, and Nick eased the car over the rough approach, then parked in the shade of a stand of spruce.

Switching off the ignition, he glanced at Sydney. "So what do you think?"

She shrugged and cast him a teasing look. "There's no view of the mountains."

He grinned, undid his seat belt and opened the door. "Too bad. At least I can make it from here to the creek without killing myself."

Sydney found a grassy clearing along the bank that was easily accessible for him, and by the time Nick made it there from the car, she had everything unloaded and set up. Feeling as though he had run fifty miles instead of crossing a few hundred feet of uneven ground, he lowered himself onto the foam matting she had placed beside a granite slab. He leaned back against the warm stone face of the boulder and closed his eyes, suddenly aware of how unsteady he was.

"Here. You look like you could use this."

He slowly turned his head and opened his eyes. Sydney stood before him, her form backlit by the brilliance of the sun. He reached out and took the steaming cup of coffee she offered him. "I sure in hell need something."

She contained a smile as she poured a second cup, then screwed the top back on the thermos. "You'll feel better after you eat."

The sunlight caught in the sheen of her hair, and Nick could feel the familiar flutter start deep in his belly. "I'd feel better if you came over here."

She flashed a grin at him, then started unloading the cooler. "Not a chance."

"You're a hard-hearted woman, Sydney Foster."

She grinned again. "I'm a starving woman, and if I come over there, it'll be another hour before we eat."

He watched her unpack the bag she'd got at the deli, then she started dishing up food onto paper plates. The warmth of the sun seeped into him, easing the tension in his body, and he closed his eyes again.

He heard Sydney cross the grass, then she sat down beside him. She smoothed her hand across his face as he turned to look at her. Her voice was soft with concern. "Tired?"

He managed a crooked grin. "I could do with a refueling."

She brushed back his hair, then leaned over and gave him a light kiss. "We'll start with lunch and see what happens after that."

He gave her a long look, then took the plate she handed him. "Sounds good to me."

Although the use of his right hand was practically back to normal, getting food from the plate to his mouth still took a fair amount of concentration—of which he had zip at the moment. He bypassed the other food on the plate and picked up a ham and cheese sandwich. That he could manage without dribbling food all down the front of him.

Sydney sat cross-legged on the mat beside him, the breeze ruffling her hair and sunlight framed her in a halo of light. He looked away, finding it very difficult to swallow the food in his mouth.

When he reached for his coffee, he caught Sydney watching him with an intent expression. "Aren't you going to eat your potato salad?"

"No, the sandwich is fine."

A small, wise smile appeared. Without saying anything, she selected a spoon from the pack of plastic utensils, then moved closer. She took a scoop from his plate, and with a gleam in her eyes, lifted it to his mouth. "Open."

Caught off guard, he did as he was told, and she shoveled the food in.

Of all the things Nick had hated about his recovery, bedpans and having to be fed rated one and two in the top ten. "Damn it, Sydney, don't you start treating me like some snot-nosed kid."

She grinned at him. "Don't talk with your mouth full."

Nick opened his mouth to make a heated retort, but she stopped him dead with another spoonful of salad. He swallowed in a lump. "Look, damn it, I hate being fed."

She met his irate gaze, her own perfectly calm except for a sparkle of humor. "It never bothered you before."

A memory, clear and complete, focused in his mind. They were sitting in bed, Sydney feeding him steak and baked potato while they watched an old movie on TV. And he remembered how unbelievably sensual and erotic it had been.

The gleam in her eyes intensified, as though she'd read his mind. "Still feeling huffy?"

He gave her a reluctant grin and folded his arms across his chest. "How about some of the baked beans?"

"How about 'please'?"

His eyes still alight with amusement, he let her feed him another mouthful.

His expression altered as he watched her take a bite of her own sandwich. "Tell me about your company," he said quietly.

She shrugged and helped herself to more coffee. "There's not much to tell. I buy and sell real estate, some I hang on to for a few years, some I don't."

"You've done very well."

She looked at him, her tone clearly indicating she wasn't overly impressed with herself. "Anyone can do well in this country if they have half a brain and are willing to put the effort into it. This is the first weekend I've taken off in six months, and I put in at least ten hours a day."

"It takes more than hard work, Sydney," he amended gently.

She shrugged. "I've played some lucky hunches. I bought several pieces of property in Vancouver and Toronto before the recent booms, so I did very well when I sold them. But mostly it takes knowing the market."

"What does the president of Unicorn Holdings do for fun?"

Her laugh was low and throaty. "I read multiple listing books."

Nick watched her, part of him amused by her offhand manner, part of him troubled by her response. He wondered if she had allowed anyone other than Malcolm to touch her private life since they'd split up. He doubted it. He also realized they had communicated more the past few days than they had the whole time they lived together. And he knew why. Now they had a safe arena. The baby, his accident, her business, his rehabilitation—topics distant and separate from the thing that threatened them the most.

"What are you thinking about?"

He looked at her, his gaze solemn as he tried to find the words to frame a halfway honest answer. "That we have things we can talk about now," he said quietly.

Sydney stared at him, her expression suddenly altering as she bent her head and fiddled with the bag of plastic cutlery. "Yes," she said, "we do."

He could tell by her tone that she had understood more fully than he had intended, and he experienced a surge of guilt. Reaching out, he touched her face. "I've missed you like hell. It's been a bloody long fifteen years."

Moved by his words, she slipped into his ready embrace, her voice shaky as she put her arms around him. "Do you know how much I love you?"

Nick closed his eyes and pressed his face against her temple. "Yes, I do."

A shadow fell across them as a cloud moved in front of the sun, blocking the warmth, and Nick drew her deeper into his embrace. Neither of them spoke, the quiet solitude like a balm, and Nick was more at peace with himself than he'd been for years.

"Nick?"

He glanced down at her. She was watching him with a pensive, hesitant expression, an expression that made him feel just a little wary.

"What?"

There was an uncertain silence, then she pulled out of his embrace and sat up. "Would you mind talking about your impotency?"

He stared at her, his expression suddenly cold and remote. No, he did not want to talk about it. He didn't want to drag it out into the open and have it probed and inspected like a damned broken leg. It was one more kick in the gut, and he had been eaten alive by bitterness when he had finally faced it. Not only had the sons of bitches destroyed his life, they had stripped him of his masculinity, as well.

Reaching for his coffee, Nick forced down the rage. "No. I don't mind."

There was another tense pause, then he heard her take a breath. "What do the doctors say about it?"

He took a sip, his movements controlled and deliberate as he set the cup down beside him. "They don't know."

"They don't know?"

Nick didn't look at her, his tone curt. "I didn't tell them."

There was a strange inflection in her voice. "Wouldn't they have found out from their assessments?"

He looked at her then, bitterness scoring his face. "They only know what I choose to tell them. Do you think they'd give a rat's ass about something as inconsequential as that? They treat the body, Sydney. They don't give a damn about the person or the quality of life after they've reassembled you. If I hadn't been lucky enough to have one therapist who bucked the system, the doctors would have ignored my left hand when I was in a coma, and it would have withered up. And if that had happened, they would have disregarded it with some stupid comment, like I should be grateful I even survived." He shifted his gaze, fighting to contain his rage. "It's bad enough as it is without subjecting myself to that kind of medical crap again."

"Even with Dr. Robertson?"

Nick stared across the creek, the muscles in his jaw twitching as he tried to bring his anger under control. His voice had lost some of its edge when he finally spoke. "It's not Pete I don't trust. It's the medical profession as a whole. It's not his field, so he'd want to bring in specialists, and I cannot face being put in a fishbowl again." Closing his eyes, he leaned his head back against the rock, his face suddenly haggard. His voice was taut with strain when he admitted to her what he had not wanted to admit even to himself. "My male pride couldn't handle it."

Sydney turned so she was facing him, her hips touching his. She gently bracketed his face in her hands, then leaned over and brushed her lips against his. "Then to hell with them all."

There was something in the way she said it that completely smothered his anger, and he smiled against her mouth as he caught her by the back of the head. "My feelings exactly."

"Do you want some dessert?"

Dragging his fingers through her hair, Nick closed his eyes and smoothed his tongue across her bottom lip. "No."

She tried to speak but she couldn't catch her breath, and on a tremulous sigh, she let her mouth go slack beneath his.

Nick slid his arms around her hips, carrying her down with him as he rolled to the side, her body half-trapped under his. And right then it didn't matter a damn if there were physical limitations. It didn't matter one bloody damn. He was drowning in her, surrounded by her, and he felt more complete than he had ever thought possible.

CHAPTER EIGHT

SYDNEY BARELY RECOGNIZED HER. It had been more than eight weeks since she had first seen Jenny Cord in the police station, and it was hard to believe she was the same girl. Gone was the long, stringy bleached hair, the emaciated thinness, the blotchy skin. She looked healthy and tanned, with a hint of youthful vitality that hadn't been there two months ago. Watching the fourteen-year-old, Sydney was unaccountably reminded of the tiny daughter she had lost, and a painful hollowness unfolded in her.

Trying not to acknowledge the ache, she watched the young girl in the yard below as she played with two small children, all charges who had been placed in the care of the Legion of Charity's Blairmore House. Unwanted, abused, abandoned—children of an uncaring society. Children of a lesser God.

Feeling suddenly very drained, she forced herself to speak. "How's she doing?"

Major Henderson leaned back in her chair, her kindly eyes fixed on Sydney. "She's only been back four days, so I haven't spent that much time with her. But all things considered, very well. Have you read her assessment?"

Sydney turned from the window. "Yes, I have. And I talked to the psychologist at the center."

"Then you know that they did extensive testing on her. They said there was a significant change in her attitude when she found out she'd scored extremely high on the IQ tests."

Gripping her upper arms, Sydney absently rubbed her shoe against a worn spot in the carpet, a distant expression on her face. "It was likely the first time in her life that she realized she wasn't powerless. She found out she has the resources to make something of herself, that she has the wherewithal to turn her life around."

The major cast the younger woman a long, oddly curious look, then she tipped her head in agreement. "Well, if I've learned nothing else since she's been back, I do know she's determined to make something of herself. She wants to enroll in a special summer school program that one of the high schools is offering. It will be hard for her. She's missed more school than she's attended, and it's going to be difficult for her to catch up."

Sydney looked up, her full attention focused on the major. "If she has any trouble, let me know, and we'll get her a tutor."

The older woman nodded, her movements precise as she straightened the loose papers in the girl's file. "What else did the psychologist tell you?"

"That she still needs extensive counseling and a secure environment."

"Is that why you came to see me today?"

A small smile appeared as Sydney gave the older woman a wry look. "Partly." She shifted her position slightly, then slipped her hands into her pockets. "I want to discuss the secure environment first. I was expecting them to keep her longer than they did, so I've made no other arrangements for her. I was wondering if you could keep her here at Blairmore House until I can check out some of the private group homes."

The major shrugged. "I don't see why not. It's not an ideal situation for her, but it's better than most."

Sydney pulled a piece of paper from the attaché case sitting on the chair beside her, then handed it to the major.

"There's a clinical psychologist here in town by the name of Catherine Brown. She has an excellent reputation in the community for her work with victims of sexual abuse. I've talked to her, and if you agree, I'd like Jenny to start seeing her."

A twinkle appeared in the major's eyes. "You do believe in going to the best, don't you?"

Sydney tipped her head. "Yes," she said as she stared at the older woman. "I certainly do."

The major shot her a surprised glance, then looked flustered as she grasped the meaning behind Sydney's response. With characteristic modesty, she sidestepped the compliment. "Catherine is outstanding. You won't find a better clinician."

"Fine. I'll make the necessary arrangements."

The major leaned back in her chair, watching the younger woman with an air of uneasy preoccupation as she sorted through her thoughts. Making a decision, she wearily rubbed her eyes. "I'm afraid I have some bad news, Sydney. Jenny saw her file when she was at the treatment center, and she knows about you."

Sydney shot her a quick look, then let out a sigh of annoyance. "How did that happen?"

"Carelessness, likely."

"How did she react?"

"With wariness and suspicion. She can't understand why someone she's never laid eyes on would take any interest in her or spend that kind of money on her."

"Which is understandable. She doesn't have much reason to trust anyone."

"No, she doesn't."

"Reassure her that the funding for her care is permanent and is being funneled through you. Maybe that will allay her suspicions a little. At this point, it's absolutely essential she knows she's not going to find herself back on the streets."

The major nodded, her expression thoughtful as she fiddled with a pen lying on her desk. "I wonder if it wouldn't be best if you talked to her."

Sydney pulled her hair back in a weary gesture, then turned to the window again, her face stark. She didn't want to meet the girl face-to-face. She didn't want to get directly involved in her life. The past few weeks with Nick had brought new meaning to her own life, and she was happier than she'd ever thought possible. She didn't want to risk that. If her involvement with Jenny and her involvement with Nick should ever overlap, there would be serious repercussions. She wasn't so blind as to think there wouldn't be.

As she stared down at the lawn below, a puppy came scampering around the corner of the building, chased by one of the smaller children. Thrown off balance by its own speed, it tumbled over in a bundle of fluff at the teenager's feet, and she scooped it up. As the girl straightened, Sydney caught a brief glimpse of Jenny straight on. There was something almost mystical about her, something that made Sydney think of wild Gypsy music. She was lithe and slender, with fine features and wide, dark eyes that dominated her small face, her shortly cropped dark hair giving her a solemn, waiflike appearance.

A strange feeling unfurled in Sydney as the young girl cuddled the puppy against her and buried her face in the soft fur. There was something so emotionally destitute in that one small gesture that Sydney was nearly undone by a painful swell of nostalgia. She could remember what it was like, needing something to love that would love you back. Something that belonged to you, something you could hold and talk to when you were scared and alone—something that was always there for you, no matter what. She'd had a kitten when she was on the street—small, helpless and hers, and it had nearly killed her when it disappeared after three years.

"Would you be opposed to talking to her?"

Sydney stared blindly out the window, hurting for the young girl on the lawn. She drew in a deep breath, trying to ease the awful ache around her heart. "I'm not sure that would be wise, Major," she said unevenly. "It might make her all the more wary."

Major Henderson watched Sydney with a very thoughtful expression in her wise eyes. "You're very troubled by her, aren't you, my dear?"

Turning from the window, Sydney glanced at the major, then closed her attaché case. "Lost souls trouble me," she said flatly. "No child should have had to endure what she did." Her face drawn, Sydney locked the clasp on the case and straightened, finally meeting the major's gaze. "Keep me posted, Major. If there's anything she needs, let me know."

"Perhaps what she needs most," the major said with gentle observation, "is you."

Sydney shot her a sharp, startled look, then picked up her case. "I'll let you know about the arrangements with Catherine Brown."

The major came around her desk and laid her worn hand on Sydney's arm, her kindly eyes filled with maternal warmth. "You have a good, generous heart, my dear," she said quietly. "Learn to listen to it." She gave Sydney's arm a little shake, reaching out to her with a lifetime of caring. "Whatever your burden, the good Lord will lighten it if you let him. And so will I."

Caught off guard by the compassion in the older woman's eyes, Sydney swallowed hard, her throat full. Her usual restraint breached by this loving woman, Sydney kissed her weathered cheek. "God bless you, Major."

Major Henderson patted her in a motherly gesture, her tone rich with sincerity. "He has, my dear. He's given me you."

Sydney squeezed the woman's hand, then pulled away, riddled with unexpected pain. As she opened the door, she avoided looking at Margaret Henderson. "I'll be in touch."

Alone in the upstairs hall of the old, renovated building, Sydney closed her eyes and leaned weakly against the wall. She felt afraid. So very afraid. It was as though cracks had suddenly fractured the very foundation of her life, and there was nothing she could do to stop them from spreading.

"Are you here to see Major Henderson?"

Sydney's eyes flew open, and she was confronted with the dark brown aloofness of Jenny Cord's gaze. She had been so traumatized by her own feelings, she had been unaware of the girl's presence. And she had been caught with her defenses down.

She straightened, forcing herself to speak in even tones. "No. I was just in to see her."

There was something—an assessing look in the young girl's resentful gaze—that Sydney found disturbing. Folding her arms in front of her, Jenny very deliberately appraised Sydney's clothes—the white raw-silk suit, the gold and jade chunky jewelry, the jade-colored snakeskin shoes and purse. Then, just as deliberately and coldly, she met Sydney's eyes. "I see," she said, her voice filled with contempt.

Sydney froze, her mind numbed by a sickening feeling. Before she could respond, the girl whirled around and raced down the stairs, her angry footsteps echoing in the stillness. Without a shred of doubt, Jenny knew who she was. Sydney shivered. And an awful fear gripped her.

THE AFTERNOON SUN SLANTED shadows across the entryway of Nick's apartment building, but neither the warmth nor brightness penetrated the chill of foreboding that had Sydney's pulse racing. She knew she was overreacting, but she had this nearly frantic need to assure herself that he was really there, that he was all right. She was almost certain he would be asleep, but that didn't matter. Just as long as she could see him, maybe she would be able to shake this panicky feeling. By the time she entered the cool, silent apartment, she was shivering.

His room was shuttered against the June heat, and Sydney paused in the doorway, her relief so intense it made her legs want to buckle. He was stretched out on the bed on his back, his head turned away from her, his left arm draped across his bare chest. His breathing was deep and even, and it was clear he was soundly asleep. God, but she loved him. He was everything to her, and she didn't know how she could keep going if she ever lost him again.

He stirred in his sleep and shifted his head. "Hi," he murmured thickly.

Caught by surprise, Sydney tried to smile, her throat so tight she could barely speak. "How did you know I was here?"

He opened his eyes and gave her a drowsy smile. "I just knew." He reached out his good arm toward her. "Come here."

Sydney was trembling so badly she didn't think she could make it across the room, but neither could she refuse him.

As soon as her hand closed around his, Nick became instantly awake. "What's the matter?" he asked gruffly.

She wouldn't lie to him, but neither could she tell him the whole truth. "I'm just feeling really shaky."

"You're shivering." Letting go of her hand, he braced his weight on his left arm and reached for the buttons on her jacket. "Get out of your clothes. You're coming to bed."

Trying to force her muscles to relax so she'd stop shivering, she let Nick strip her jacket from her, then she slipped out of her shoes and unzipped her skirt. As soon as it slid to the floor, he pulled her down beside him, his arms enveloping her. "Lord, woman, you're like ice." Leaning over her, he snagged the edge of the spread they were lying on and pulled it over her, then cuddled her tightly against him. "What's the matter, Syd? Are you sick? You're so damned pale."

Forcing herself to take a deep breath, she shook her head and pressed her face more tightly against the warmth of his neck.

Nick molded her closer, then began stroking her back, his touch firm and consoling. "Then tell me what's wrong?"

She somehow managed to make herself answer, her voice muffled and unsteady. "I just got really panicky all of a sudden. And I had to make sure you were all right."

With a slow, tender touch, he brushed back her hair. "Of course I'm all right," he reassured her gently. "Except that I was as lonely as hell."

Her panic held at bay by the warmth and security of his embrace, she was finally able to relax. Her voice carried an undertone of amused censure. "You were dead to the world, Nick."

He brushed his lips against the silky tumble of her hair, his voice husky. "But I can't get to sleep as well when you're not here." Tipping her head back, he covered her mouth with a soft, sensual kiss.

Sydney melted against him, the last tendrils of fear dispelled by his gentleness. Nothing could touch her when he was holding her. Absolutely nothing.

On a deep sigh, Nick slowly eased away, his eyes as black as onyx as he gazed down at her. He combed her hair back from her face, then dropped another soft kiss on the corner of her mouth. Leaning across her, he reached for the phone on the nightstand. Setting it on the bed beside Sydney, he punched out the numbers, keeping her close against him as he tucked the receiver into his shoulder.

His attention focused when his call was answered, and his gaze settled on Sydney. "Hi, Marg. It's Nick Novak. Sydney isn't feeling well so I'm keeping her here with me for the rest of the afternoon. If you have to get in touch with her, you can reach her at my number."

He moved the phone out of reach when Sydney tried to take it from him. "Fine. I'll tell her that."

Without taking his eyes off her, he dropped the receiver back in the cradle, daring her to argue with him. "Norm Crandall has to fly to Vancouver this evening, so he had to cancel his appointment with you tomorrow morning."

Her protest was nearly as weak as her voice. "Nick, I should go. Marg needs some checks signed."

He leaned across her to put the phone back, then placing his arms on either side of her, he took her face between his hands. "You're not going anywhere. You can sign the checks tomorrow, but I'm keeping you in this bed for the rest of the afternoon. You looked like hell when you came in here, and I'm going to spend the next few hours putting your fears to rest." Shifting his position, he turned her heavy necklace so he could unhook the clasp. "But first of all, we're going to get rid of the hardware." He pulled the necklace free and tucked it under the pillow, then he caught her arm and undid the clasp on the wide bracelet, slipping it off her wrist.

Sydney struggled to suppress the feelings his protectiveness aroused. "Do you ever have irrational bouts of fear?"

He lifted a wisp of hair off her cheek, uncomfortable with his own vulnerability. "Yes," he said gruffly. "Every time you walk out that door."

She shivered, another chill seeping into her, and for the first time in weeks, her past intruded on the present.

But the moment his mouth covered hers in a moist, searching kiss, the fear was extinguished by feelings so intense they overrode all else.

Without interrupting the kiss, Nick pulled her under him, his weight pressing her down as he reached out and fumbled for the phone, then let the receiver drop to the floor. With a tormenting lightness, he trailed his mouth down her neck, making her shiver all over again. "Marg," he whispered huskily against the sensitive hollow below her ear, "is just going to have to sweat it out on her own."

SYDNEY FELT SATURATED WITH love as she lay with her head on Nick's shoulder, his hand moving languidly across her back. If she had learned anything during the past few weeks with him, it was that there was a vast difference between making love and loving. And since their lives had reconnected, they had spent hours in the simple act of loving. In the beginning, she was afraid Nick would be tied in knots from frustration, but it hadn't happened. His impotency removed the most threatening aspect of their old relationship, but it also brought something very special into their existing one. She discovered layers of sensuality and tenderness in him that she hadn't even known existed, and in some ways, their relationship was far more physical now than it had been before. Granted, they were both very careful to do nothing to push the limitations. And there were times when she'd be in a cold sweat from wanting him, but she made sure she sweated it out alone. Unsatisfied desire was a small price to pay.

Shifting her head on his shoulder, she smiled as she idly trailed her fingers along his collarbone, recalling the past weekend. It had been miserable and blustery, and they had ended up spending most of it in bed at her apartment. With a mixture of amusement and dumbfounded awe, Nick had awakened Monday morning with the observation that up until then, he hadn't realized one kiss could be dragged out for two whole days. His comment had delighted her, partly because it was very nearly true, partly because she felt so thoroughly loved, and partly because he had so obviously reveled in their almost constant physical closeness.

"You're smiling, and I want to know why."

The smile deepened. "I was thinking about the crack you made Monday morning about one kiss lasting two days."

He laughed and hugged her, dropping a light kiss on her forehead. "God, I was so bloody giddy when I went to therapy, I think Beth thought I was losing it. She'd give me supreme hell, and I'd grin at her like the village idiot. She was ready to push me down a flight of stairs."

"You were probably suffering from a lack of oxygen," Sydney responded dryly.

He grinned and gave her another squeeze. "I wasn't suffering at all." Neither of them spoke for several moments, then Nick sighed and stroked her shoulder. "Sydney?"

She tipped her head back and looked at him.

Reluctance was in his eyes. "Tony phoned this morning. He has a couple of weeks of overtime coming to him, and he wants to take me to the coast to do some salmon fishing."

"So what's the problem?"

He looked at her, then slowly ran a finger through her tousled hair. "He wants to leave Monday. I hate leaving you, but he's been talking about this for months. I'm afraid if I back out, he won't go. And I know he needs the break."

Propping herself on one elbow, she gazed down at him. "Don't let me stop you, Nick. I should make a trip to Toronto, so I'll go when you're gone."

He gave her a warped grin. "I don't think I'm going to handle two weeks without you worth shit."

She smiled down at him and trailed her fingernail along his bottom lip. "Well, when you put it like that, it makes it almost tolerable. But what about your therapy?"

"Tony knows the whole regime, and we'll take some of the light equipment with us. That won't be a problem."

She grinned at him, trying to lighten his mood. "Tell you what, I'll practice holding my breath when you're gone, and we'll go for a new record when you get back."

He laughed and looped his arms around her back. "How about a trial run now?"

She glanced at the clock on his bedside table, then back at him, her voice soft with regret. "I should make you some supper and go. I'm putting a bid in on a piece of property in Vancouver, and it has to be ready to go tomorrow."

"Are you going back to the office?"

"No, I can access the data I need from home."

He pulled her down and gave her a quick kiss, then lifted her off him. "Then haul ass, lady. I'll keep you company."

On Nick's suggestion, they had dinner at her place, and as soon as they had finished eating, he banished her from the kitchen so he could clean up. Sydney found it somewhat amusing that, little by little, her cupboards were becoming nearly as organized as his. On the other hand, she worried about it, because she knew that it was his way of combating absolute boredom. He never complained, but there was a restlessness in him, especially in the evenings, that was a dead giveaway. His therapy filled his mornings, and he usually slept for a couple of hours in the afternoon, but that still left hours to fill. He'd always read a lot, but he'd been a great tinkerer when they had lived together. He had restored an old World War II motorcycle just before she moved in with him, but his real love was woodworking. She had bought several pieces of old furniture, and he had spent hours and hours refinishing them for her. In fact, they were pieces she still had.

But because of the physical limitations he had now, any activity where he needed to use power tools was out of the question. And she knew of all the things he had to struggle with, boredom was the most detrimental. He needed something to do, something to fill his time. Financially, he wasn't hurting. He was getting a substantial pension, and he had made some excellent investments through the years. Money was not an issue. Unproductive time was.

Her large study was across the hall from the guest room, and Sydney dropped her attaché case on the sofa as she turned on the light. Like the rest of her apartment, it was a comfortable mixture of traditional furniture and antiques, the exception being her state-of-the-art computer center. Without that, she would have gone out of her mind long ago.

She grinned as she heard Nick swearing in the kitchen, suspecting he was having another war with the peculiarities of her garbage disposal unit. She liked having him wandering around when she was working at home. Often he'd stretch out on the sofa in her study and read, and rather than finding his presence a distraction, she found she was able to really focus when he was there. His closeness kept her from thinking about him.

Ignoring the flashing light on her telephone console that indicated messages on the answering machine, she turned on the computer and sat down. If she had to start returning calls she would never get anything done.

It was about half an hour later that Nick wandered into the study. Scrolling through the data on the screen, she grinned. "Well, Bernice, did you get all your chores done?"

He gave the back of her head a playful push. "If you don't get that damned garbage disposal fixed, Bernice is going to take a sledgehammer and a crowbar to it."

"Bernice will be happy to know that Malcolm is installing a new one tomorrow."

"It's about time. It barely grinds up spit." He reached over her shoulder and pointed to a set of figures on the screen. "How come you have 11¼ percent there and 11½ over here?"

Sydney looked at the two columns, then with an odd feeling of expectancy, she rotated her chair and glanced up at him. "I have this funny feeling you've been holding out on me, Nicholas. What do you know about spreadsheets?"

Resting his weight on his good leg, he grinned down at her. "I've been diddling around with computers for about eight years. I kinda got hooked on them when they started using them in the department, so I got one and I took a few courses."

She narrowed her eyes at him, her response a flat statement of confirmation. "You have a computer."

"I have a computer."

"Why haven't I seen it?"

"Tony has it. I can't type with my left hand the way it is, so I lent it to him for a while."

Her eyes narrowed even more. "What courses?"

He listed them, the gleam in his eyes bordering on blatant one-upmanship. His grin deepened. "And I know you're going to end up with a bloody mess if you enter two different interest rates."

"I think," she said through clenched teeth, "I'm going to strangle you. Do you mean you've watched me slave over this night after night, and you haven't offered to help?"

He gave her a dismissive shrug. "Your business is your business."

Right then, she really did want to strangle him. "I'm not working on top-secret defense documents here, Nick. I'm trying to figure out if a piece of property is a good investment or not." She got out of the chair and pointed to it with the authority of a top-notch dog trainer. "Sit."

He gave her a surprised look. "Just a minute—"

"Sit, Nick. Or so help me, I'll stuff you down the garbage disposal." She slapped a pad of paper on the keyboard in front of him. "These are the figures I've researched, here's the current inflation rate, and I want figures based on ten, fifteen and twenty-year mortgages. Now see what you come up with."

He folded his arms and stared up at her, looking very much like a recalcitrant child. "And what are you going to do?"

"I'm going to do a rough draft of the bid, check through the messages that are no doubt jammed up on my machine, and maybe, just maybe, with the two of us working on this, we'll get to bed before midnight."

She caught a glimpse of reluctance in his expression. "I can only use my right hand...."

"Nick," she said very distinctly and very deliberately, "I don't care if you have to use a pencil stuck between your teeth. Just do it."

He stared at her for a second, then grinned. "Does this mean I get to hang up my apron?"

Loving him so much she could hardly contain it, she bent over and gave him a kiss. "If you can do this, we'll have the damned thing bronzed."

He laughed against her mouth. "To hell with the apron. I'm working on a four-day weekend."

Sydney cleared a space at the short end of the L-shaped computer work station and spread out her papers. From her vantage point, she could keep an eye on what Nick was doing, but she had a hard time concentrating on her own paperwork. The range of movement in the fingers on his left hand was very limited, but the number pad on the keyboard simplified things. She watched him, feeling much the same way she had when she saw the videos of his first steps, agonizing through every second with him. She wanted him to succeed so badly she could almost taste it. Nick had al-

ways had a mathematical bent, and if he remembered half
of what he had learned about various computer programs,
she could bury him with work.

After half an hour, she had accomplished practically
nothing, but she could see that was not the case with Nick.
His success thrilled her, but what was nearly her undoing
was the look on his face. Intent, focused, absorbed. For
him, crunching numbers was a challenge, and there wasn't
a trace of boredom in sight. She could feel her eyes fill with
tears.

"I can't read your writing. Is this a three or an eight?"

Keeping her gaze averted, she glanced at the figures on the
pad he dropped in front of her. "It's a three."

He took the pad back, and she thought her wobbly voice
had gone undetected until he reached out and caught her
hand. "Look at me, Sydney," he said very quietly.

"No."

"Yes."

"Nick—"

"Quit stalling and look at me."

Pulling free from his grasp, she quickly wiped her eyes,
then steeled herself to meet his gaze.

He leaned back in his chair and studied her thoughtfully.
"Would you mind telling me what in hell this is all about?"

She shrugged and tried to relax the ache in her throat.

His voice carried an undertone of warning. "Sydney?"

She had a hard time maintaining eye contact. "I know
having nothing to do is driving you crazy. And you looked
like you were enjoying yourself."

He didn't speak for several moments, then he gave her a
slow grin. "There have been other times," he said in a low,
husky tone, "that I have thoroughly enjoyed myself. Like
this afternoon, for example."

She gave him a dry look. "That's not what I meant."

His dark gaze never wavered, a ghost of a smile lingering around his mouth. "I know that's not what you meant."

Feeling vulnerable, she gave another little shrug. "So."

His eyes took on a very sensual gleam. "So... why don't you come over here?"

The way he said it made her laugh, and she shook her head. "Not a chance. You're up to your old tricks, and I'm not buying."

He grinned, then turned back to the computer. "I didn't think you'd go for it."

They worked in quiet harmony for the better part of an hour. Sydney plowed through a stack of paperwork, prepared the rough drafts for the bid plus several other letters and did some basic research on another piece of property she was considering. It was nine o'clock when she finally cleared her desk. Propping her chin on her hand, she waited for Nick to finish inputting the data.

He entered the commands to compile the figures, then leaned back in the chair, waiting for the computer to process the information.

Aware that she was watching him, he swiveled the chair to face her. "No wonder you get off on this number crunching." He grinned. "It's better than bingo."

Sydney was willing to bet a year's profit that Nick had never played a game of bingo in his whole life. She grinned back, then gave a dismissive little shrug. "I used to really enjoy it, but it takes so much time, I don't do it as much as I should." There was a touch of hopefulness in her rueful smile. "I don't suppose you'd like a job, would you?"

He folded his arms across his chest and stared at her, his expression hardening into something cold and unpleasant. "Is this a make-work project?"

Knowing what was going through his mind, Sydney deliberately kept her response indifferent. "Hardly. This is a fundamental part of my business. Making a decision to buy or sell is simplified once I've worked the numbers."

His tone was ominously quiet. "And just what outrageous salary were you going to offer me?"

Her chin still on her hand, Sydney fixed him with an amused look, knowing he had just cornered himself. "I wasn't going to offer you anything. I thought you might do it out of the simple goodness of your heart. And because you like me."

He continued to stare at her with the same unwavering intensity, but she caught a glimmer of humor in his eyes. "You're serious."

"I am."

He finally gave her a warped smile. "Has anyone ever told you you throw a mean curveball?"

"If the game is hardball, you play hardball, Nick."

He laughed and shook his head. "I think," he said very dryly, "that you're definitely out of my league." He turned back to the computer. "Show me how to print this off. I've never used a laser printer before."

Sydney showed him, then went to the kitchen to get them some coffee. Upon returning, she handed Nick his, giving the printout a cursory glance. Now that the messages wouldn't create a distraction for him, she turned on the playback on her answering machine.

She sat back down, jotting down notes concerning the various messages. There were several from Marg, one from Norm Crandall and one from Tony for Nick.

As the tape replayed, Nick stared at the computer screen and sipped his coffee, obviously preoccupied by his own thoughts. But the moment Sydney heard the next voice, she tensed, all her senses on alert. Had she been sitting where Nick was, she would have shut off the machine the minute she heard her name spoken. But she was trapped on the other side of him, and there was nothing she could do but sit there and listen, apprehension like a rock in her midriff.

"Sydney, this is Margaret Henderson. Could you get in touch with me at Blairmore as soon as possible? I'm afraid we have a problem with Jenny."

Trying to act as though the call were nothing unusual, Sydney made a note on the pad in front of her, her hands suddenly clammy. Calgary was a small enough city that the agencies and the professionals dealing with troubled kids knew one another. And everyone knew about the Legion of Charity's Blairmore House. And everyone knew Major Margaret Henderson. Her only hope was that Nick was so preoccupied he didn't put two and two together.

There was an unnerving silence, then Nick switched off the machine and turned to face her, his voice deadly quiet. "*Major* Margaret Henderson, I presume."

Sydney tossed the notepad on top of her other papers, trying to maintain a veneer of normalcy. "Yes," she replied, forcing herself to look at him. "I set aside a certain percentage of Unicorn profits annually for various charities. And the Legion of Charity is one."

He was watching her, his eyes glittering with a ruthless look that made her skin shrink. "And Major Henderson gets your approval on individual cases because of that, I suppose. Or is this Jenny another one of your lame ducks?"

Sydney stared back at him, dread snaking through her. She turned away, her voice strained. "She's a special case."

"How special? Is she an abandoned baby, a nine-year-old abused kid, a bag woman? Tell me, Sydney. Who is she?"

All the avenues of escape swung shut, and Sydney felt her whole world slip out from under her. He knew, and he'd never forgive her for it. Her face devoid of color, she turned back to look at him, the stark expression in her eyes revealing the truth.

He stared at her, his disgust deep and bitter. "You just can't stay away from it, can you, Sydney? And you have to keep rubbing my face in it." Swearing violently, he grabbed the phone and entered a number. There was a brief pause, then he spoke, his tone harsh. "Would you send a cab to the Brisco Building on Fourth Street. It's for Novak and I'll be waiting in the lobby." Casting her one last scathing glance, he grasped his cane and levered himself out of the chair.

Sydney braced her elbows on the desk and weakly rested her head against her clasped hands, incapacitated by the kind of pain only he could inflict.

Like a recurring nightmare, history was repeating itself. She heard the door slam behind him, and she closed her eyes, knowing there was nothing she could do or say that would change the way he felt. He could never forget. And she knew that.

CHAPTER NINE

WITH IMPASSIVE DETACHMENT, Sydney stared out the window, watching the trees bend and shudder from the force of the wind, the heavily overcast skies insulating her in the gloom of Major Henderson's office.

With a desolate smile, she realized that fate was a malevolent player. Had the sequence of events been altered, if Nick had reappeared in her life before Jenny, she wouldn't be standing here now, experiencing this terrible emptiness. But she had learned a long time ago that that kind of thinking was futile.

History had repeated itself, and Nick was gone. Only this time, she didn't have his baby to sustain her. This time, there was nothing. Nothing. Except the emptiness.

She rested her shoulder against the window frame, her profile illuminated by the grayness outside as she watched the storm roll in. It would help if she could isolate his reaction as male jealousy, but she knew it went much deeper than that. He had been raised with an old-world set of ethics, and they were as deeply ingrained in him as was his sense of right and wrong. His mother had died when he was fifteen, his father when he was twenty-five, but even after all these years, his mother was still a major influence. Even after he had become hardened and disillusioned by his job, he still maintained a quiet respect for the kind of woman she was.

Although he had drifted away from his Catholic upbringing, he maintained one single connection; every

Mother's Day he lit a candle for the woman who had shaped his life. Even this year, when Sydney had taken him to a small Catholic church, it was clear that this was not a ritual but an act of remembrance. And she knew there was one factor underlying his inability to accept her past. Subconsciously he wanted her to be the kind of woman his mother had been, untarnished and worthy of that kind of reverential respect. And Sydney wouldn't have wanted it any other way. She loved him for the very reasons he could not accept what she had been.

And now she was here, Nick was gone, and it was all over a girl who had made it plain to Major Henderson that she bitterly resented Sydney's meddling in her life. If it wasn't such a tragedy, it would almost be funny.

"Sydney."

Sydney turned, her expression coolly composed. "Hello, Major."

Margaret Henderson studied her drawn face with a look of concern, then turned to the young girl standing rigidly beside her. "Jennifer, I'd like you to meet Sydney Foster."

Jenny's eyes were cold with hostility. "We've met."

Sliding her hands into the pockets of her jacket, Sydney faced the girl. Without breaking eye contact with her, she addressed the major. "Would you mind leaving us alone, Major."

The older woman glanced from one to the other, worry lines appearing. Noting the inflexible set to Sydney's jaw, she sighed heavily. "No. Of course not. I'll be in the lounge downstairs if you need me."

As the door closed behind the departing woman, Sydney braced her hip against a worn credenza and folded her arms in front of her, a feeling of hard, cold resolve settling over her. She knew the look in Jenny's eyes; she understood it. The girl would go for the jugular if she let her. Her voice was low and impersonal. "The major said you wanted to see me."

Jenny stared at her, insolence and resentment in every line of her body. "Yeah, I did. I wanted to see one of you f——— rich bitches up close. You all think you're so f——— hot."

There was a steely glimmer in Sydney's eyes. She had left the streets before this child was even born, but a hard edge of that life was still in her, and she could play whatever game Miss Jenny wanted to play.

She gave her a brittle smile, her tone smooth and cutting. "If you want to talk like a whore, by all means, use the language of one. And if you want to continue to cultivate your trashy image from hooker stroll, that's certainly your pre-rogative. But just don't try to shock me, Jenny. It won't work."

She watched the insolence in Jenny's eyes give way to un-certainty, and she straightened, not giving the girl a chance to regroup. "Now that we've got that out of the way, these are the facts. I don't know how you found out about me, and I don't care. I suspect you insisted on this meeting so you could find out why I'm doing this. Frankly, that's none of your business.

"What is your business is this—without doing one thing to deserve it, you've been given an opportunity to turn your life around. If you want to feel hostile about what you per-ceive to be some rich snob's meddling, that, too, is your choice. Just don't try to vent your hostility on me. If you want to make something out of yourself, then do it. If you don't, you can walk out that door right now. I've got better things to do with my time and money than to try to help someone who doesn't want to be helped."

There was a dazed expression on Jenny's face. Whatever she had expected to happen at this meeting, this clearly wasn't it.

With calculated deliberateness, Sydney moved away and straightened a stack of envelopes on Major Henderson's desk. "The decision is yours. And just so there are no misconceptions, I'm telling you now that I'm prepared to follow through on this. If you want to get a Ph.D. in finger painting, that's fine. I'll do whatever I can to help you." She turned and faced the girl, her gaze unflinching. "However, there *will* be expectations. I expect you to clean up your language, I expect you to start acting like a young lady instead of something that crawled out from under a rock, and I expect you to make an honest effort. This isn't a free ride. No one can do it for you. You have to be prepared to make those changes yourself."

Sydney picked up her coat and handbag, then came to stand before the girl. The hardness went out of her voice, and for the first time she allowed herself to ease up. "You've had a rotten deal, Jenny," she said evenly. "There isn't a human being alive who deserved to get the hand you were dealt. But nothing is going to change that—not anger, not resentment, not drugs. I'll do whatever I can to give you a fresh start, but the rest is up to you. You can either let what happened drag you down, or you can fight back and surmount it. You can be whatever you want to be—or you can take the easy way out and spend the rest of your life on some flea-bitten bed in some filthy, run-down hotel."

She turned and opened the door, not wanting to acknowledge the panicky, trapped look in the girl's eyes. "Think about it, Jenny. Don't throw it all away because you resent me, because you think I've had the good life handed to me. It wasn't handed to me. I've worked damned hard to get where I am."

It was not until Sydney was back in her car that she allowed anything to register. Not the way she'd spoken to the girl, not the way she had gone on the offensive, not the harshness of her words. She had separated herself from all that, because she knew if she showed one bit of compassion, Jenny would translate it into weakness, and the game would be lost. What she tried to do now was contain the anger that had been building in her. The past had trapped her, the present was empty, and panic was moving in. Needing to outrace her feelings, she headed for the open road.

It was midafternoon when Sydney finally returned to her office. She was still tense and filled with a kind of nervy energy, but at least she felt as though she had regained some sense of balance.

Her secretary looked up and frowned as she entered the paneled outer office. "Are you all right?"

Sydney exhaled heavily. "I had a rotten morning, that's all. Did you get the bid away?"

"I faxed it twenty minutes ago." Marg picked up the pink slips lying beside her computer terminal. "Norm Crandall called. He closed the deal on the Marcus complex. And Major Henderson wants you to call her as soon as you get in."

Sydney took the pink slips and turned toward her office. She did not want to call the major. She didn't want to call anybody. She wanted to crawl into a hole and stay there for the rest of her life. She sank into the chair behind her desk and closed her eyes, not wanting to think about anything.

"Are you sure you're okay?"

Sydney opened her eyes to see Marg's worried face. "I'm fine. I had a late night and a lousy morning."

Marg set a cup of tea down on her desk. "I made you this. You looked like you could use a bracer. And be forewarned. I'm going to monitor all calls today. If it isn't death, taxes or impending financial disaster, you're not available until Monday." She started to close the door, then stopped. "Oh, one other thing. Tony Martinelli stopped by.

He said to tell you that he got today off, so they decided to leave this afternoon. He said he'd see you in two weeks."

Sydney experienced a cold, sinking sensation, and her one small flicker of hope died. There would be no phone call, no knock on the door, no Nick showing up at her office. He was gone. And he had taken any hope she might have had with him.

Without looking at her secretary, she forced herself to speak. "Thanks, Marg."

There was the sound of the door latching, and Sydney closed her eyes again. She didn't know how she could find the strength to endure losing him a second time.

Knowing she couldn't let herself think about it, she opened her eyes and reached for the phone. She might as well get all the bad news at once.

"Major. It's Sydney Foster returning your call."

There was a note of real concern in the older woman's voice. "Hello, my dear. I was wondering how you were doing. I take it things didn't go very well this morning."

Sydney's expression was stark as she stared out the window. "It's hard to say. It's going to depend on whether Jenny is a fighter or not. I wasn't easy on her. I knew she was spoiling for a fight, so I never gave her a chance."

"I suspected something like that. She spent the rest of the morning in her room. But she came to see me a few minutes ago, and I think you might have gotten through to her. She said she'll keep her appointment with Catherine Brown tomorrow morning, and that's a significant step for her."

"I hope so."

"So do I, my dear. So do I." There was a brief pause, then the major continued, her kindly voice like a balm. "I'll be praying for both of you." Sydney could hear the smile in her voice. "I like to think I have an open line."

For the first time all day, a genuine smile showed in Sydney's eyes. "I don't doubt that for a minute." Her face sobered as she fingered the telephone cord. "Let me know how it goes with Jenny."

"I will, my dear. And God bless."

Sydney hung up the phone. Unable to face the rest of the day, she pushed herself away from her desk. She was going home.

When she let herself into her apartment, the first thing she noticed was that her mail was lying on the hall table. The second thing was the sound of someone working in her kitchen. She had completely forgotten about Malcolm and the new garbage disposal unit.

Dredging up what little energy she had left, she called to him as she hung up her coat. "It's just me, Malcolm."

There was a brief pause before the caretaker answered. "In the kitchen, Ms Foster."

Picking up the mail, she leafed through it as she went down the hall. She was scanning a brochure for a new piece of computer software as she entered the kitchen, and her insides dropped when she looked up.

Nick was leaning against the cupboard, a bottle of mineral water in his hand, and he was watching her with dark, unreadable eyes.

Stunned by the unexpectedness of his being there, she scrambled to think of something to say. "So how's it going?"

Malcolm was lying on his back, his head and shoulders hidden in the cupboard under the sink. "It's a good thing you weren't around. I've used every cuss word I've ever heard."

The corner of her mouth lifted. Malcolm rarely swore. Avoiding Nick's gaze, she laid the mail on the kitchen table. "Don't restrain yourself on my account. I've used a few myself today." Squaring her shoulders, she turned to face the man at the counter, her insides in knots. "I thought you'd left."

He was watching her with a steadiness that made her want to bolt. "Tony decided to get the oil changed in the car."

"I see."

The intercom for the front door buzzed, and without taking his eyes off her, Nick reached for the phone. "That's probably him now."

Desperately needing time to collect herself, she turned to leave the kitchen. "Tell him the door will be unlocked."

Reaching the front foyer, she opened the door, then turned down the short hallway that led to the master suite. Once inside her bedroom, she shut the door, then closed her eyes and leaned back against it, so shaky she could barely stand. Never in a million years had she expected him to be there.

The master suite was a long, spacious room that ran the full length of the apartment. There was a glassed-in solarium at the far end that housed a Jacuzzi and countless plants, and beyond that was a secluded patio, which was also accessible from the kitchen. Sydney had turned this into her retreat. There was a sitting room area, with a built-in stereo unit and TV and a small fireplace. And right now she desperately needed the soothing effect this room always provided for her.

Her hands were trembling so badly she could barely undo the buttons on her jacket. She stripped off the outfit she'd worn to work, laying it on a large wicker hamper as she entered the dressing room. She put on a pair of casual slacks, then pulled a blouse off the hanger and went back into the main room. She was doing up the buttons when she sensed a presence. She looked up.

Nick was standing in the doorway leading from the solarium, his shoulder braced against the doorjamb. His eyes had that same inscrutable look, and deep lines of tension were carved around his mouth.

Attempting to appear as unaffected as possible, she tied the shirt around her waist. "Is Tony here?"

"He's helping Malcolm in the kitchen."

"I take it all is not going well."

He straightened and slowly made his way toward her. "I didn't come in here to talk about disposal units."

Her heart started beating wildly, and Sydney pressed her hands against her thighs, transfixed by the look in his eyes. Never shifting his gaze, he tossed the cane onto the bed. Without giving her time to react, he caught her by the back of the neck and covered her mouth with a kiss that broke all the rules. Hot, wet and plundering, it ignited a fever that drove the air out of her lungs and made her legs want to buckle beneath her.

Fighting for breath, she slid her arms around him and moved into his urgent embrace. Widening his stance, Nick caught her around the hips and locked them against his, his tongue plowing into the deep recesses of her mouth with a near savage hunger. And the fire that they had deliberately kept banked for so long flared into a fury, sending her senses reeling.

Nick tightened his hold on her and dragged his mouth away, his breathing raw and labored. A tremor coursed through him as he forced her head against his shoulder, his chest heaving. "God, I wasn't going to let that happen," he whispered hoarsely.

Shaken to the very core, Sydney hung on to him, trying to ignore the thick, unsatisfied ache that throbbed through her, her relief that he was even there pushing her to the verge of tears. She swallowed painfully, knowing if she tried to answer him, she would start to cry.

As if realizing she was struggling, he softened his hold on her just a little and stroked her back, his voice low and very uneven. "I couldn't leave. Not without telling you how damned sorry I am."

The husky regret in his voice took the edge off the awful pressure in her, and she tightened her hold, her whole body trembling. Whispering softly against her ear, he slid his fingers through her hair in slow, gentling strokes.

The trembling finally abated, and drawing in a deep, jagged breath, Sydney raised her head. Catching his knuckles under her chin, Nick tipped her head back and brushed her mouth with a soft, lingering kiss that drugged her with comfort. When at last he raised his head, his eyes were black with smoldering desire, guilt and regret. "I should be horsewhipped for doing this to you."

She managed a shaky smile. "I'm not complaining."

The corner of his mouth lifted a little, and there was the barest trace of humor in his eyes. "I think it's a damned good thing I'm going away for a couple of weeks." He dropped another kiss on her mouth, his lips brushing against hers as he whispered gruffly, "It's going to take me that long to calm down."

Sydney's legs went weak all over again. "Let's lie down, Nick."

Hugging her tightly against him, Nick buried his face against her neck, his voice even gruffer than before. "If I lie down on that bed, we're going to be in over our heads in about two seconds flat. And neither of us needs that right now."

Sydney could feel him steel himself as he eased away. Putting his arm around her, he led her into the solarium, his expression rigid as he lowered himself into the deep, loose-cushioned sofa. Grasping her wrist, he pulled her down so she was sitting across him, then with a deep, unsteady sigh, he cradled her tightly against him.

He didn't say anything for several moments, then he brushed back her hair and kissed her gently on the forehead. "I was a bastard last night, Sydney," he said huskily.

"I keep getting pulled back into the old garbage, and I hate myself when that happens."

"It doesn't matter—"

"It does matter," he interjected firmly. "This past couple of months have been so damned good, and I don't want to screw things up again." He met her gaze, his eyes bleak. "But I don't know how to deal with my feelings, Syd."

Sydney had to fight the sting of tears. Another step. He had taken another step, and that ignited such a wave of hope in her it almost frightened her. "Would it help if we talked about it?"

Leaning his head back against the pile of cushions, he clenched his jaw. "No, it wouldn't. I think it would make it even worse. Somehow I've got to distance myself from it before I can ever do that." He looked at her, his expression so filled with torment it was like a knife in her heart. "I know I have to make that first step, that I have to deal with it, and it scares the hell out of me." He smoothed his hand across her cheek and started to say something, then winced and looked away. His voice was ragged with strain when he finally spoke. "I've got so much anger, but last night made me realize I can't keep on letting it fester. It'll destroy us both if I do."

He met her gaze, his face scored with suffering. "I want to be able to put the past behind me. I want to be able to make love to you." A tremor coursed through him as he crushed her against him. "And I want to crawl into your arms and stay there for the rest of my life."

Struggling against the awful pressure of unspent tears, Sydney held him with all the strength she had, loving him so much it was breaking her apart. But amid the pain and anguish there was that single thread of hope, and fear was powerless against that. Drawing in a raw, tremulous breath, she buried her face in his neck and wrapped her love around him.

Nick's voice was muffled against her hair. "God, but I love you."

"I've never doubted that for a moment."

His arms tightened around her. "God, Sydney—"

She silenced him with a gentle kiss. "No more," she whispered against his mouth. "Show me."

His mouth opened hungrily beneath hers as he tightened his hold on her. The agony gave way to need, and they sank into the oblivion of loving.

It was a very long time later that Nick pulled away, fighting for air, his heart pounding frantically against his ribs as he roughly dragged her head against his neck. "Lord, woman, much more of that, you'll have to carry me out of here."

Sydney leaned against him, feeling as though every bone in her body had turned to jelly. Knowing she had to do something to defuse the situation, she tightened her arms around his neck and pressed her lips against his skin. "Your mouth," she murmured softly, "gets us into more trouble."

He managed a husky laugh. "It was yours that got us into this mess. 'Show me,' she says. Lord Almighty."

"That's not the kind of trouble I meant, and you know it."

He hugged her hard. "When I get back, we're going to crawl into a hole for four days, and so help me, I'm going to love you till you're senseless."

She smiled, her tone dry. "It won't take four days, Nick. You can do that in a heartbeat."

Easing his hold, he looked down at her, the gleam in his eyes making her breath catch. He gave her a quick kiss, then grinned at her. "Then we'll go for speed *and* distance." He brushed her ear with his thumb, his expression sobering. "Two bloody weeks—I don't know if I can hang in there that long."

She tried to ease the sudden ache in her throat, her vision blurring. "Two weeks won't last forever."

"They're going to feel like forever." He sighed and smoothed down her hair, then he eased her away from him. "I want you to do something for me, Sydney."

"Anything."

Frowning slightly, he rubbed his knuckles along her jaw, preoccupied by his own thoughts. Finally he raised his eyes and looked at her. "I've left the address of the fishing camp on your desk in the study. I want you to write me a letter about this girl. Maybe I can handle it better if I have the distance and the time to work it through." He cupped his hand around her neck. "Will you do that for me?"

"Yes."

He watched her for a minute, then he gave her a smile that made her heart lurch. "I think," he said softly, "I need to check out your mouth again." And tightening his hold on her face, he lowered his head.

It was some time later that Nick and Sydney finally made it back to the kitchen. Tony and Malcolm were sitting at the table, each nursing a beer and shooting the breeze. Sydney couldn't restrain a smile when she saw Tony. He had on a pair of white pleated pants, a stylish blue, green and white striped shirt with the cuffs folded back, and he looked as if he had just stepped off the front of some men's magazine. "Well, Mr. Martinelli. Don't you look handsome."

He leaned back in his chair and looked from her to Nick, then back to her, flashing a totally irreverent grin. "Well, Ms Foster. Don't you look well kissed."

For the first time in years, Sydney blushed, and Nick chuckled and hugged her against him. "Don't mess with him, Syd. He fights dirty."

Malcolm rested his arms on the table, his eyes twinkling. "I don't know. Maybe he just calls 'em as he seems 'em."

Tony's grin broadened and he raised his beer in a salute. "I like your style, Mal, old buddy."

Keeping Sydney close against him, Nick rested his weight on his good leg. "Are you ready to go?"

Tony made a big show of checking his watch. "Hell, I was ready an hour ago. But Nicky-boy took a waltz and stuck us with a bunch of rusty plumbing." The devil was in his eyes as he tipped his head and looked at Nick. "Tell me, Novak—what took you so long?"

Nick held back a smile. "When you're old enough to know, I'll tell you."

Tony grinned again. "Yeah. Sure." He drained the last of the beer, set down the empty bottle, then slapped the table. "Let's roll." He nodded toward Malcolm. "Come on down and take a look at my new set of wheels."

Heat and the sound of rush-hour traffic hung in the air as they stepped out of the front doors. Parked in a loading zone in front of the building was a low, hot, cherry-red Iroc, the black louvers on the back window adding a touch of sizzle. Tony gave Malcolm the grand tour, and Sydney smiled as she watched them circle the car. Like kids with a new toy.

She glanced up at Nick, about to make some comment, but she could see that behind his aviator sunglasses, his expression was very strained. She slipped her arm around his waist. "What's the matter?" she asked softly.

He tightened his hold on her shoulders as he glanced down at her, his voice gruff. "Saying goodbye is going to be a damned sight harder than I thought."

Sydney tried to smile. "Don't, Nick," she whispered unsteadily. "Or I'm going to make an awful scene."

He pulled her into a tight embrace, his breath warm against her ear. "I love you, and Lord, I'm going to miss you." His fingers beneath her chin, he covered her mouth with a kiss that was filled with such poignancy it made her weak.

He tightened his hold on her face, then forced himself to let go. Without looking at her, he turned away.

Tony was sitting in the car, the powerful engine idling, and Malcolm stood by the driver's door as Nick lowered himself into the bucket seat. His face rigid, he stowed his cane and did up his seat belt, finally meeting Sydney's gaze as she closed the door. She bent down and gave him one last kiss through the open window. Nick caught the back of her head, his mouth ravaging hers with an unleashed hunger that broke all the boundaries of the past few weeks. It was a kiss that spoke of dark nights, sweat-dampened bodies, a passion that could only be assuaged by deep, thrusting strokes. And Sydney thought she was going to suffocate from the rush of wanting him.

Roughly breaking the contact, Nick squeezed her hand hard. Without looking at her again, he released her hand and turned to Tony. "Go, damn it."

And Tony did. He laid thirty feet of rubber as he dropped the clutch, and Sydney stood there, remembering what Nick had said about the way he felt every time she walked out the door.

CHAPTER TEN

THE LONG SHADOWS of early evening were already slanted across the patio as Sydney dropped the Saturday paper onto her kitchen counter. Pushing her hair behind her ear, she answered the phone as she braced her hip against the counter. "Hello."

"Sydney, it's Margaret Henderson. I hate to trouble you so late in the day, but something's happened with Jenny, and I'm not quite sure what to do."

Sydney glanced at her watch, instantly alert. "What's the problem?"

The major's voice was wrought with anxiety. "She's missing. She disappeared sometime between five and six this afternoon."

Sydney's insides dropped. "What happened?"

There was a heavy sigh. "She went for her appointment with Catherine Brown this morning, and apparently she came back very upset. I wasn't here when she returned, but the worker told me what kind of state she was in, so I went to see her.

"When I went into her room, she was on the floor curled up into a tight ball, her arms over her head, absolutely rigid. I've seen it before in abused children, but never quite so severe. I know from experience there's not much you can do but talk them through it, but it must have taken me the better part of an hour just to get her into bed."

Sydney closed her eyes and rubbed her temples. "Did you talk to Dr. Brown?"

"Yes, I did. Catherine said that they were about twenty minutes into the session when Jenny became extremely distraught. Apparently the history of sexual abuse we saw was only the tip of the iceberg. Not only had the stepfather abused her, but there were instances when he handed her over to his friends. It was all quite horrible."

Sydney's stomach curled, and for an instant she thought she was going to be sick. Fighting down the nausea, she forced herself to focus on the sound of her own voice. "Have you any idea where she might have gone?"

"Other than back to the street, no. Josh, one of the workers here, is downtown looking for her, but something tells me that's not where she is."

"We've got to find her."

For the first time, Sydney heard an undercurrent of defeat in Major Henderson's voice. "I don't even know where to begin."

"Have you got her file handy?"

"Yes. It's right here."

"Give me the names and numbers of whatever contacts you have. Her old group home, her social worker, whatever."

"What are you going to do?"

Sydney got a pad of paper and a pen out of the drawer. "I'm going to find her."

It took Sydney more than two hours to track her down. She probably wouldn't have found her then, except one of the other girls from the group home told her about a place where Jenny often hid out. It was under the concrete abutment of one of the bridges, a small, dank crawl space with only one way in. And jammed back in the far corner, curled up in a tight ball, was the form of a girl.

The light of the long spring twilight was beginning to fade, but Sydney could tell from the girl's hair that it was Jenny, and she was almost light-headed with relief.

She crouched down and crawled into the opening. Almost able to smell the girl's panic, she kept her voice quiet and nonthreatening. "Jenny? It's Sydney Foster." She waited, giving the girl time to put everything together. She moved deeper into the concrete cave, then positioned herself a few feet away from her. Stretching out her legs, Sydney leaned back against the concrete wall, knowing if she blew this, she would never get another chance.

"Major Henderson said your session with Dr. Brown upset you very badly. Do you want to tell me about it?"

Silence.

"I know you're frightened, Jenny. And I know you don't trust me. You haven't had any reason to trust anyone, let alone a stranger. But if it's any consolation, I know what you're going through." Searching for the right words, Sydney frowned and picked up some loose pebbles from the ground, absently rolling them together in her palm. "You don't have to talk if you don't want to. And you don't have to tell me anything. I just don't want you to be alone right now, that's all."

After several minutes, Jenny slowly pushed herself into a sitting position, then huddled in the shadows. She swiped the heel of her hand across her cheeks, and it wasn't until that moment that Sydney realized she was crying. Compassion twisted inside her with a wrenching force. So young, and so much pain.

"You're going to get your slacks dirty."

The choked whisper, the simple acknowledgment of her presence, affected Sydney more than she thought possible. Battling her own intense feelings, she managed a smile. "They'll wash."

She looked at the girl, the outline of her face barely distinguishable in the failing light. There was a glimmer from the tears slipping down her cheeks, and Sydney remembered what it was like to be scared and alone. Drawing up her knees, she rested her arms across them and stared into the dusk.

Another whisper from the darkness. "You'd better go. It's getting dark."

Sydney looked down and rattled the pebbles in her hand. "I'm not leaving unless you come with me."

"I've got no place to go."

Closing her hand around the bits of granite she held, Sydney looked at her, her voice quiet. "Yes, you do. You can come home with me."

Silence. It was like total blackness, impenetrable and smothering, and Sydney waited, the sharp edges of the pebbles cutting into her palm. She could do nothing but sit there, afraid to move, afraid to break the quiet.

"Okay."

Closing her eyes, Sydney let her breath go and unclenched her hand.

All the way to the car, she waited for Jenny to bolt. She wasn't fooling herself; she knew Jenny had come with her because she had caught the girl when she was numb with emotional turmoil. And because she was terrified of being alone in the dark. Sydney had no illusions. Only a small ray of hope.

There was one tense moment, when they were walking from the car to the service door of her building, when she sensed Jenny was on the verge of running. But once she got her in the elevator, there was an element of curiosity in the girl that outweighed her mistrust.

It wasn't until after Jenny had eaten and Sydney called Major Henderson that she saw any outward sign of the girl's wariness. And when Jenny physically distanced herself, Sydney knew the clock had run out.

Her insides were wired with tension as she placed the dirty dishes in the sink, then turned toward the girl. Jenny was standing at the patio door, looking onto the terrace, nervously fingering the vertical blinds. She would have made a dancer, Sydney thought, with that natural graceful carriage, the slender neck, the slightly imperial lift to her chin. She sensed a tenor of steel buried deep beneath the damaged self-esteem—and a trace of pride. She also saw a reflection of herself at that age. If the pride was there, there was a chance.

She slid her hands into the pockets of her slacks, knowing she couldn't put the confrontation off any longer. "I think we'd better talk, Jenny."

Suspicion flared in the girl's eyes, and her fingers tightened on the blind. "About what?"

Leaning back against the cupboard, Sydney crossed her ankles. "Have you thought about what I said yesterday?"

Jenny turned, her eyes filled with angry tears, her body shaking. "What do you want from me? You said you know what I'm going through. You *don't* know what I'm going through!"

Sydney's stomach twisted, knowing she was faced with a predicament she'd never wanted to face. "You're wrong."

"Why did you go looking for me?"

"Because I was worried about you."

Jenny clenched her hands, a panic-driven rage gripping her. "Oh, sure. And because you know how I feel, right? Well, let me tell you—you with your real gold jewelry and your Mercedes—you don't have a clue. You don't know what it's like to have your mother's boyfriend come into your bedroom and start pawing you when you're nine years old. And when he gets to be your stepfather, it gets even worse.

"You don't know what it's like to be so revolted by the things he's made you do that every time you look in the mirror you heave your guts out. And when your mother finds out, she's so bloody scared he's going to walk out on her like your real father did, she won't do anything. You

don't know what it's like when some slime comes along, and
you think he's so wonderful because he's the first person
that's ever treated you like you were somebody special, and
then you find out he's nothing but a lousy pimp, and when
you won't go to bed with some creep he owes a favor to, he
starts slapping you around. And you'll do anything so he'll
stop beating on you, so he'll be nice to you again. So you
find a corner to work and you become one of his sluts, and
you stand there because you're so damned scared, but as
much as what you're doing disgusts you, you do it, because
if you don't, you know you're going to get your face kicked
in. And pretty soon you don't care anymore, so you keep
doing it so you can buy enough coke to keep you so stoned
nothing registers.

"And you sit here in your fancy apartment trying to convince me you know how I feel. You'll never know how I
feel!"

The moment of reckoning was finally upon her. Sydney
met the girl's rage and resentment with a hollow stare. "It
wasn't my mother's boyfriend."

Time stopped, and a brittle, expectant silence cut through
the room, the sudden tension like a static charge. And Sydney finally faced her ghost. "It was my father."

IT WAS LATE. Very late. Sydney sat at the kitchen table, her
hands clasped tightly in front of her, her thoughts miles
away. Unconsciously she rubbed one thumb along the other,
thankful for the numbness that blocked everything out.

Jenny sat across the table, her ashen face ravaged from
weeping, her dark eyes stark against her pallor. She brushed
away a tear, then looked at Sydney, her voice tight. "So you
were eleven when your mother died."

"Yes."

"Did you ever go to a psychologist?"

"That kind of abuse wasn't even discussed twenty-five years ago, Jenny."

"But did you go later?"

Sydney shook her head. "No."

"Why not?"

There was a long pause, then Sydney slowly raised her head and looked at her. "I was so ashamed, I could never bring myself to tell anyone. My father was so influential and so well-known in the community, I knew no one would believe me." Her face somber, she locked her fingers together and opened her palms, her attention fixed on her hands. "This is the first time I've ever told anyone the whole story."

Jenny's attention riveted on her, her expression unbelieving. "Not even that woman you worked for—Mabel? Not even Nick?"

"I told Mabel a bit. But not all. Nick couldn't deal with what he did know, let alone anything about my childhood."

The girl stared at her, nonplussed by Sydney's admission. Finally she shook off her shock, her voice dazed. "Why me?"

When Sydney finally raised her head again, her eyes were shimmering with unshed tears. "Because I wanted you to know that I really do understand. Because I can't stand to see another human being suffer through that kind of pain alone."

Jenny reached across the table and touched her hand, her voice shaking. "I'll never tell anyone," she whispered vehemently. "Never. And I won't let you down. I'm going to stay clean, and I'm never going back."

Sydney couldn't see as she tightened her fingers around Jenny's hand, so many emotions breaking over her. The girl had reached out. Maybe Major Henderson's prayers had been answered, after all.

SYDNEY LAY IN BED, listening to the wind chimes on the patio as a light breeze ruffled through them. She didn't know what had awakened her, but whatever it was, it left her feeling melancholy. She had returned from Toronto late the night before and had met with Catherine Brown early that morning. The psychologist had seen Jenny four times and felt her noticeable change in attitude was extremely positive.

However, she did caution Sydney about the tone of her association with the girl, warning her about the very real possibility of Jenny's overidentifying with her mentor. She also cautioned Sydney to keep her conversations with the teenager casual and to try to focus on anything other than what was being discussed in the sessions. Pacing of the treatment was critical.

With so much coming at Jenny at once, Dr. Brown had some concerns that the girl would be overloaded emotionally, which could set her back. Because of that, the psychologist recommended that Jenny remain at Blairmore House and that visitations between Jenny and Sydney be limited to once a week, with daily phone calls if they wanted.

There were two things Dr. Brown said that Sydney found unsettling. She told her that as far as Jenny's behavior went, there would be times when it got worse before it got any better. The other comment was that there was no cure for the kind of emotional damage Jenny had suffered. All they could do was help her cope with it more effectively.

A tight ache formed in Sydney's chest as she realized that if her daughter had lived, she would be only a few months younger than Jenny. The daughter who would have had dark hair and dark brown eyes.

The wind chimes tinkled as another soft breeze caught them, and Sydney rolled onto her side and stared into the darkness, her thoughts drifting to Nick. The loneliness was bad enough, but the uncertainty was even worse. She had written him every day, and to make sure he got her letters, she sent them by courier service to the fishing camp's base in Victoria. For the most part, they were love letters, but in every one she included some information about Jenny, keeping it as impersonal as possible. And every day she wondered how he was dealing with that information. Sometimes she felt very hopeful; other times she would experience a rush of dread that she just couldn't shake.

And there was the memory of that last kiss that had shattered the boundaries of their existing relationship. And because it had, it had opened a channel to the past. A deep and dangerous channel that led to an explosive passion that, once ignited, would rage like wildfire—hot, furious and uncontainable, with the power to destroy. And the only barrier between them and that destructive, uncontrollable hunger was Nick's impotency, and it was an uncertain barrier at best.

There had been weeks when she'd felt totally insulated from the past, but it was seeping into the present, and that frightened her more than anything else.

A gripping loneliness welled up in her. A future without Nick was simply too empty to contemplate. But the threat was there, dark and ominous, like an ever present shadow.

The next few days went from bad to worse.

The weather was overcast and dreary, there were frustrating snags at work, and Jenny had had a couple of bad sessions, which showed in her behavior. Dr. Brown assured Sydney it was a common occurrence with someone who had the abusive history Jenny had. The positive fallout was that the teenager had centered her anger, and the anger was directed at her mother. She loathed her stepfather, but she blamed her mother for not protecting her. Now that she had connected with that very basic source of her pain, she was having a hard time dealing with it. And the one visit Sydney had had with her had been alarming. If Jenny had vented her anger, Sydney could have dealt with that, but the girl had become catatonic—silent, rigid, huddled on her bed in a tight fetal position. The only thing Sydney could do was sit beside her, rubbing her back and quietly talking to her. She had never felt quite so helpless in her life.

And then there was Nick. Her letters to him were her only lifeline. She felt as though everything were washing away from under her, and her awful uncertainty about what was going to happen when he returned gave her more sleepless nights than anything else. Nick and Tony had planned on being gone for two weeks and were due to return late on Sunday. But after nine days without his presence to reassure her, the strain was beginning to take its toll.

By Thursday night, she could hardly cope. Dragged down by sheer physical exhaustion, she let herself into her apartment, shut the door, then leaned against it. She was so tired she couldn't think. It was drizzling outside, the heavily overcast skies filling her apartment with gloom and an isolating silence that was oddly comforting.

Wearily straightening, she set down her briefcase and put away her raincoat. As she shut the closet door, she noticed a light was on in the kitchen. Dredging up what energy she had left, she started down the hallway. "Malcolm?"

Partway down the hall, she caught the smell of rain carried in by a soft breeze, and she wondered why the caretaker was out on the terrace. She rounded the corner into the kitchen, her heart missing a beat. Nick was standing just outside the door, his dark hair and jacket misted with rain.

"Nick! You're home."

His head jerked up and his gaze fixed on her with determined intensity as he started toward her. His face was haggard, scored with exhaustion and strain, and as he dragged his left leg over the step, his movements were unusually awkward and unsteady. Relief, love and an agony of missing him swamped her, and Sydney was across the room in a flash.

The instant she touched him, Nick's cane clattered to the floor and he hauled her against him, locking his arms around her in a viselike grip. "Ah, Sydney, I didn't think I was going to hang together until you got home."

So overwhelmed that she didn't know if she was laughing or crying, she slipped her arms around his neck and hugged him hard, happiness filling her until she could barely speak. "Lord, but I've missed you."

A tremor coursed through him as he dragged her hips flush against his, his voice gruff and unsteady. "My God, but I needed this so bloody bad."

Quickly wiping her face with the back of her hand, Sydney tried to ease away from him so she could look at him.

Nick instantly tightened his embrace. "No," he whispered roughly, "just let me hold you."

His body was rigid with tension, and Sydney smoothed her hand across his shoulders, savoring the feel of his arms around her. He was back, and that was all that mattered.

It took a while for most of the tension to ease from him, and when it did, he relaxed his hold a little. Sydney felt him sway as he tried to align his balance, and she realized it was sheer will that was keeping him on his feet.

She tried to lift his head. "Nick?"

He wouldn't meet her gaze, his voice thick and slurred. "I'm going to have to lie down."

By the time they crossed the patio and went into her bedroom, he was shaking, and every movement was one of grim determination.

Sydney stripped back the quilted spread, then steadied him as he lowered himself to the edge of the bed. Worry lines formed around her eyes as she removed his jacket and shoes, sharply aware of his lack of protest. Using his weakened left arm as a pivot, he turned and rolled onto his side.

Expelling his breath in a shaky rush, he stretched out and closed his eyes.

Sydney kicked off her shoes and crawled over him, anxiety riddling her expression. Stretching out beside him, she slipped her arm under his shoulders and drew his head against her. "Should I get your pills?"

He shifted, pulling her under him, using his weight to hold her. "No. All I need is this."

She remembered what he'd said about needing to hold her to go to sleep, and a tightness formed in her chest. She brushed back his hair, then kissed him softly. "Your sweat suit is damp. Are you cold?"

She felt him tip his head. Holding him against her, she reached down and managed to grasp the corner of the spread, then drew it up over them. In less than ten minutes, he was asleep in her arms, and she closed her eyes, content with the pure pleasure of holding him.

It was dark when she awoke, and the city had an early morning stillness. Careful not to disturb him, she raised her head and looked at the clock on her bedside table. Twenty after two. Seven hours. She hadn't slept that much in a stretch since Nick had left.

"What time is it?"

She'd been so sure he was still asleep that his drowsy-thick voice caught her off guard. She caressed his back, drawing him closer. "Almost two-thirty."

She felt him smile. "You're good medicine, Sydney Foster."

She smiled back. "You're not so bad yourself." She kissed his brow, then ran her hand across his shoulders. "Hungry?"

"No. Are you?"

"Not enough to move."

He gave a husky laugh and rolled onto his back, pulling her with him. "My sentiments exactly."

Sydney raised herself up on one elbow. "I feel like I'm hanging myself in these clothes. Do you want anything while I'm up?"

"My cane and something cold to drink."

Without turning on the lamp, Sydney slid out of bed and headed for the solarium, the light spilling from the kitchen onto the terrace lighting her way. She got Nick's cane and took it to him. Collecting a pair of pajamas from the armoire, she returned to the kitchen. She fixed a fruit drink and added crushed ice, then went into the guest bathroom to change and brush her teeth.

When she returned to the master bedroom, the lamp was on and Nick was lying in bed, the pillows stuffed behind his shoulders, his chest bare. He turned his head as she approached.

He gave her a wry smile. "I didn't mean to die on you the minute you got home."

She grinned. "Dying's okay. It's nearly collapsing at my feet that was a little unnerving."

Nick caught her arm to steady her as she crawled over him, watching the angle of the glass she held. "If you dump all that ice on me, your life won't be worth a damn."

She made a face at him as she handed him the drink, then crawled under the covers beside him. "So tell me all your fish stories."

Nick hiked himself higher, then slid his arm around her shoulders. "The fish stories are mostly secondhand. It rained for four days."

"Is that why you came home early?"

He took a drink, then looked at her, a ghost of a smile around his mouth. "No, that's not why we came home early." There was a touch of wryness in his tone. "Tony brought me back because I was a pain in the ass."

Sydney shifted so she could look at him, a contemplative expression in her eyes as she watched him down a third of the drink. "Were you?"

He glanced at her, his eyes crinkling. "A pain in the ass?"

She nodded.

He held her gaze with a steady look. "Yeah, I was." He drained his glass and set it on the bedside table, then reached for his jacket on the floor. Pulling his arm from around her, he unzipped one of the pockets and pulled out something, then dropped the jacket back onto the floor. Catching her jaw, he turned her head and brushed a soft, lingering kiss against her mouth. "And it was your bloody fault."

Drawing away, he dropped something in her lap. Sydney glanced down, a flutter starting in her midriff when she saw her letters bundled together with an elastic band. "My fault?"

Nick pulled her against him and gave her another kiss. "Your letters," he murmured against her lips, "gave me more damned sleepless nights than I like to count."

Moving closer into his embrace, Sydney smoothed her hand up his arm and across his shoulder, the tormenting lightness of his mouth against hers throwing her off center. "I had a few of those myself."

"Every one had me in knots, lady."

Sydney felt barely coherent as he moistened her bottom lip, her train of thought completely fractured by the feelings he was arousing. "Couldn't we talk about this in the morning?"

He chuckled and kissed her hard, then reached out and shut off the lamp. "I suppose that could be arranged." Pulling two of the pillows from behind him, he snuggled down with her head cradled in the curve of his shoulder, his touch unsteady as he combed back her hair. "I couldn't get back here fast enough."

There was something in his voice, a barely perceptible edge, that caught at Sydney, and she wondered what underlying emotion had caused it. It sounded almost like fear, and that set off her own uncertainties. "Did the letters bother you that much?"

Nick kissed her forehead, his voice uneven as he whispered against her hair. "I woke up one night in a cold sweat. I had this bloody awful feeling if I didn't get back here, you'd be gone."

Disquieted by his admission of doubt, Sydney turned so she was looking down at him, his face barely discernible in the darkness. "I'll never do that again, Nick. I swear it. No matter what happens, I'll never leave."

He caught her hand and pressed it against his mouth, then sighed. "God, Sydney, I hope you mean that."

She moved on top of him, then took his face between her hands. "Believe it, Nick. I'll never make that mistake again."

Catching her by the back of the neck, he pulled her down into a rock-hard embrace. "I'm trying to work it all out, Syd. But it's so bloody hard."

Unable to endure the torment in his voice, she raised her head and covered his mouth with a gentle, searching kiss, and for an instant, he responded. Then he dragged his mouth away and forced her head back down. "Don't, Syd. I'm hanging by my fingertips, and it isn't going to take much to push me over the edge."

Realizing she wasn't the only one who had been affected by the longing that one blazing kiss had aroused, she started to ease off him. Nick held her firm. "No. Don't. I want you like this." She closed her eyes then, hurting for him, wishing there was some way she could stop the battle that was raging in him.

THE DREAM WAS HOT and erotic, filled with the heavy, throbbing sensations of a hard agony of arousal, of flesh deeply embedded in flesh, with sweat-dampened bodies moving together in an urgency of passion, driving to the ultimate release.

Nick came fully awake, his body rigid and damp with perspiration, and it took a moment to separate the dream from reality. But the arousal was real, hard and engorged in his groin, and the sweet agony of it made him grit his teeth.

Extracting himself from Sydney's arms, he made it to the bathroom. Bracing his arms on the long vanity, he bent his head and closed his eyes, his whole body shaking and damp with sweat.

He wanted her so damned bad he could kill for her, but he didn't dare follow through. The dream was a replay of one he'd had while he was away, but there had been others—dark, disturbing and filled with suppressed rage and shadows. When he had awakened from those, he had been left with a haunting feeling. He sensed there was something buried in his subconscious that ignited his irrational jealousy and rage. And until he found out what it was, he would be incapable of disarming the anger that sliced through him whenever he tried to deal with Sydney's past.

Now he was fighting himself on two fronts: Jenny, and the fact that tonight he had awakened fully aroused. Knowing he could walk back into the bedroom and perform, that he was capable of fulfilling both her needs and his, pushed him to the very limit of his control. He wanted to lose himself in that mind-bending passion they had once shared, he wanted to arouse her until she was incoherent with need, and he wanted to bury himself inside her until there was nothing but tight, wet sensation.

But he knew, as sure as hell, what would happen the minute he gave in to that need. And as much as he wanted her, he loved her more. He clenched his teeth, the muscles across his shoulders bunched with strain as he fought the agony of wanting her. Trembling from the pain of denial, he could only hope this would never happen again. This was his own private hell, and he'd endure it. Just as long as he could keep her safe from his destructive jealousy, nothing else mattered a damn.

CHAPTER ELEVEN

NICK WAS STANDING with his hip braced against the cupboard, a cup of coffee in his hand, watching the scrambled eggs simmer on the stove. Sydney's gaze softened. "You're up early."

He glanced up, giving her a wry half smile. "I woke up about five. I thought I'd better get up before I OD'd on sleep."

She slipped her arm around his waist and gave him a light kiss, then leaned into his warmth as he draped his arm around her shoulders. "Mmm. Smells good."

His voice was quiet. "You've lost weight."

"I missed your cooking."

Setting his mug on the stove, he drew her into a full embrace and hugged her against him. "I was hoping you'd missed me."

She rested her head on his shoulder, loving the feel of him. "I did. I don't think I could have lasted another three days."

She felt him smile against her temple. "Good. I'd hate to think I was the only one who was bloody miserable."

"Are you going to therapy this morning?"

"Are you nagging?"

She laughed and looked up at him. "No, I'm not nagging. If you weren't going, I'd give Marg the day off and stay home."

The corner of his mouth lifted, and an intimate gleam appeared in his eyes. "Then I'm not going." He gave her a soft kiss, his voice gruff as he trailed his mouth down her neck. "The eggs need to be stirred."

She tilted her head to give him full access. "Let's toss 'em down the garbage disposal."

He laughed and straightened. "Lord, but you're a nuisance. Get yourself a cup of coffee, phone Marg and let me salvage what's left of breakfast."

With reluctance, Sydney did as she was told. She lounged against the counter as she dialed Marg's home number, then leaned back and watched Nick. "Hi, Marg. It's me. I decided to declare today a civic holiday, so get a trashy book and go back to bed."

Nick shot her an amused look and shook his head, and Sydney made a face at him as she listened to her secretary. "As a matter of fact, he is." She glanced up at Nick and smiled. "I'll tell him." She hung up the phone and took a sip of coffee.

"So what are you supposed to tell me?"

She gave him a reluctant grin. "That I've been about as much fun as a pile of mold."

Nick chuckled as he took the toast out of the toaster and buttered it. He dished up the breakfast and poured two large glasses of juice. "Here you go. Let's see how you do on this."

As they ate, Nick told her about the fishing trip. Sydney couldn't wipe the smile off her face as she wallowed in the contentment of having him there.

"So what have you been up to since I've been gone?"

"By the sounds of it, driving Marg crazy."

Nick pushed his empty plate out of the way and rested his arms on the table, a smile in his eyes. "Don't take it personally." He looked away, his expression altering as he rubbed his thumb against the rough texture of the earthenware mug. When he looked at her again, his eyes were solemn. "We need to talk about Jenny, Sydney."

Breaking eye contact, she covered his spastic left hand, massaging the taut muscles. "Yes, I guess we do."

"I think it would be a good idea if I talked to Dr. Brown."

Sydney sighed. "She won't discuss the specifics of Jenny's case history with you."

Nick looked down at their hands. "I don't want specifics. I need to understand the psychology."

Sydney understood why he was avoiding her gaze, and she also understood that there was more than Jenny's past that he was trying to come to grips with. She squeezed his hand. "I'll set up an appointment with her as soon as possible."

He frowned as he folded her fingers around his. "I can only handle this a little at a time," he said gruffly. "I know the problem is mine, and I've got to be the one to address it."

A wave of uncertainty washed through her, and she tightened her grip. "Just don't ever doubt how I feel about you, Nick."

He looked up at her, his eyes intent. "That's never been an issue, Syd. I've never doubted that for a minute."

She managed an unsteady smile. "Just don't start now."

Letting go of her with one hand, he leaned over the corner of the table and caught her by the back of the neck, his mouth warm and tasting of coffee as he gave her a gentle, softly searching kiss. Inhaling unevenly, he slowly drew away. "Let's go lie down for a while."

They ended up on one of the sofas in the living room. Silence enfolded them as they watched the rain beyond the balcony, the odd gust of wind driving drops against the patio door. Sydney didn't want to think about anything. His warmth sedated her, and she watched the rain, soaking up the tranquility of it all.

Sliding her hand under his clean sweat suit top, she rubbed his ribs, the smell of shampoo and soap clinging to him. "I didn't see your luggage last night."

"I'd set my duffel bag in the study when I came in." There was a brief pause, the lashing of the rain against the window breaking the silence. "Sydney?"

"Hmm?"

"How would you feel about my meeting Jenny?"

The lassitude was instantly dispelled, and Sydney's hand stilled. There was an undercurrent of caution in her tone when she finally spoke. "How would *you* feel about it?"

He exhaled heavily. "Uncertain."

"Maybe it would be better if you talked to Dr. Brown first."

"Probably."

Sydney raised her head and looked down at him. "You don't have to meet Jenny, Nick. I would never expect you to do that."

"I have to start somewhere."

Sydney stared at him, knowing he was right, knowing she was afraid of the risk. "I could set something up for next weekend. Maybe have Major Henderson and Tony over for dinner. And Malcolm, if he'd come."

"Why wouldn't he?"

Sydney gave a little shrug, a warped smile appearing. "Malcolm and I have an association that's hard to define."

"He told me about it."

Sydney shot him a surprised look. "When?"

"After you dropped the bomb about being pregnant. I came over here and ended up talking to him."

His admission threw her completely off stride. "Oh."

"He's a good man, Syd. And loyal as hell to you."

Sydney shrugged again, trying to cover up her feelings. "I know. He has this ability to reach people at such a basic level. Jenny's met him, and I don't think she realizes it yet, but she instinctively trusts him. She tends to keep her distance—you can almost measure how she feels about someone by how close she gets to them."

Nick watched her, a thoughtful expression in his eyes. "You do that, too. It's very, very rare that you let anyone get close enough to touch you."

It came as a surprise that he saw that guardedness in her, and she looked down, discomfited by it. "It's part of the psychological profile," she said tautly.

Catching her under the chin, he impelled her to meet his gaze. He gave her a long, intimate look, his eyes glinting with a mixture of sensuality and humor. "As long as I'm the exception, I really don't give a damn."

That got a small smile out of her, and her eyes softened. "You've always been the exception."

"FOR GOD'S SAKE, SYDNEY, I don't know how I ever let you talk me into this."

Sydney shut the door on the eye-level oven and turned, just barely restraining a grin. Nick was standing in the middle of the kitchen, frustration crackling around him.

He shot her an irate look. "And damn it, it's not funny."

One look at his face and it was all she could do to keep from laughing. Getting him out of his sweat suits and into some decent clothes had launched a war. The new loafers he had been agreeable to; the new slacks had been begrudgingly accepted. It was the argument over the shirts that turned the battle nasty, and the tie—well, that was when all hell broke loose. Sydney knew it wasn't the clothes, it was the frustration of trying to get into them on his own that had him ready to explode.

He glared at her, the veins in the side of his neck distended. "Well?" he snapped.

"Why don't you throw yourself down on the floor and have a good temper tantrum?" she said mildly. "Maybe you'd feel better."

"It's not funny, damn it!"

She started doing up the buttons on his shirt. "No, it isn't."

"I told you I can't do up these goddamned little buttons."

"Yes, you did." She did up the last button and tucked his shirt into his pants.

"And I told you I can't get the clasp done up on these damned pants."

Sydney zipped up his fly and did up the clasp. "That's true." Deliberately avoiding looking at him, she began threading the leather belt through the loops.

"And I can't tie the bloody tie."

"I'll do it."

"Who taught you how to tie a damned tie?"

"You did."

That took some of the steam out of him. "Oh." He stood motionless as she did up the belt. "And I'm acting like a bloody two-year-old, aren't I?"

The disgust in his voice was Sydney's final undoing, and she rested her forehead against his chest, her shoulders shaking with laughter.

There was reluctant amusement in his voice. "It's still not funny, Sydney."

"Yes, it is," she managed to get out.

Grasping her shoulders, he pushed her away from him, a glimmer of humor in his eyes. "You'd better make all this damned frustration worthwhile, or so help me, I'm going to give these damned clothes to Major Henderson the minute she walks in the door."

Trying to get a grip on herself, Sydney wiped her face with the back of her hand. "You look very handsome."

The glint in his eyes intensified. "Not good enough."

Still threatened by laughter, she took his face in her hands and gave him a quick kiss.

Nick caught her by the back of the head, holding her still as he deepened it. Sliding her arms around his neck, Sydney yielded as his mouth moved against hers, a sigh escaping when he finally drew away. "That's better," he murmured huskily.

He looked down at her, the amusement in his eyes touched with wryness. "You'd better do the damned tie thing before I throw another fit."

Sydney gave him another light kiss and smiled up at him as she pulled the tie from his shoulder, deciding a little gratitude was in order. "Thank you for humoring me."

Nick looped his arms around her hips as she turned up the collar on his shirt and slid the tie around his neck. He grinned. "I guess you're welcome."

"You really do look nice, you know." And he did. The slacks were a dark brown, the shirt was a stylish plaid of various shades of brown, with the tie matching one of the lighter tones. Nick had always had good taste and wore his clothes well, and Sydney knew that even though he wouldn't admit it, the daily uniform of sweats was tiresome for him. She knew he would enjoy the change once he got over being huffy.

"I like the way you did your hair."

She tightened the knot on the tie, then looked up at him. "Thank you."

He pulled her closer as she straightened his collar. "How soon will everybody be here?"

Knowing what that smoky tone of voice meant, she smiled. "Twenty minutes."

He gave her that lazy, intimate grin that did weird things to the base of her spine. "Everything ready?"

"Yes."

"Good," he murmured as he covered her mouth again.

Sydney needed the distraction. She had worked herself into a state of nerves before Nick had come into the kitchen.

It had been more than a week since he had made the suggestion he meet Jenny, and she'd had anxiety attacks ever since. She desperately wanted the evening to go well, for both Nick and Jenny. Especially since Nick had gone to see Catherine Brown; in fact, he had gone twice. But he had said nothing to Sydney about what had happened, and she hadn't asked.

But right now, she wasn't thinking about any of that. Not when Nick was sapping her strength with his gentle loving.

By the time the doorbell rang, Sydney was so light-headed she had a hard time walking a straight line down the hall. And it didn't help knowing Nick was watching her from the kitchen doorway with amusement and male sensuality gleaming in his eyes.

She opened the door to find everyone there. Tony had offered to pick up the major and Jenny from Blairmore House, and he had buzzed Malcolm's suite when they had arrived. The commotion of having everyone arrive at once took the edge off her sudden nervousness, and it helped knowing that Nick had made his way down the hallway and was standing behind her.

Of course, Sydney thought with a twist of humor, it would be impossible for anyone to feel ill at ease with Tony around. He even had Jenny in a fit of giggles.

The young cop looked at Nick and grinned. "Well, well. If it isn't Ken doll. Color coordinated, too. I am impressed."

Nick turned to Sydney. "Did you invite him?"

Tony took the major's coat and hung it in the closet. "Hey, man. It's my salmon we're eating. I guess I'm invited."

Amusement dancing in her eyes, Sydney put up her hands. "Stop." She smiled at the major. "I hope you're made of staunch stuff, Major. You could be a little overwhelmed tonight."

Major Henderson's eyes twinkled. "I've never been opposed to a good chuckle, my dear. And I've had several already."

Sydney slanted a look at Tony. "I'm sure you have." She met Jenny's gaze. "You look very pretty, Jenny."

Jenny gave a slightly embarrassed shrug, then glanced at Malcolm. Sydney didn't miss the reassuring wink he gave the girl, and Jenny drew her hands from behind her back and handed Sydney a bouquet of flowers. "These are for you," she said softly. Sydney caught herself before she glanced at the caretaker, almost certain that he had got them for Jenny to give to her.

Sydney was deeply touched by his thoughtfulness and heartened by the conspiracy the two shared. Her voice had a husky edge to it. "Thank you, Jenny. That was really sweet of you." Her stomach tightened, wondering what the girl's reaction was going to be when she was introduced to Nick.

She took a deep breath. "Nick, I'd like you to meet Major Henderson. Major, Nick Novak."

Nick met the major's gaze directly, and because of the way he was standing with his quad cane, it was easier and safer for him to extend his left hand. There was an easy smile on his face. "I've heard a lot about you, Major. It's a pleasure."

The major firmly grasped his hand. "And I've heard a lot about you." With the poise of a diplomat, she released his hand and put her arm around Jenny. "This is Jenny Cord, one of our new residents at Blairmore."

Sydney's heart stopped as Nick turned to the girl. She felt as if she were locked in some kind of time warp with everything on the peripheral fading into a blur.

Sydney couldn't see his face as Nick extended his hand, his tone noncommittal. "Hello, Jenny."

For an instant, Jenny stared at him, wide-eyed and wary, the pulse in her neck beating like a scared rabbit's, then her gaze slid away. Her eyes changed and became guarded, but she slowly took his offered hand. Clearly absent was any aversion to his stiff and twisted fingers, and without realizing she was doing it, the girl revealed an unquestioning acceptance of his disability.

"Hi," she said shortly.

Feeling almost faint with relief, Sydney released her breath. She loved Nick and she cared about Jenny. And more than anything, she wanted this to work. And it had to start with acceptance, at any level.

Sydney had been concerned that there might be times during the evening when a certain amount of strain would surface, but she had not taken into consideration Tony's straight-from-the-hip humor or Malcolm's subtle wit. She couldn't remember laughing so much or enjoying a group of people more.

She also had a chance to observe, and she realized, with a bit of a shock, that she had never had the opportunity to watch Nick in a strictly social setting before. After dinner he had settled himself at the end of the sofa closest to the chair where Major Henderson sat knitting, and with a deftness stemming from genuine interest, he drew her into the conversation. In half an hour he knew more about the woman than Sydney did after a nine-year association. And Sydney saw firsthand why he had been so damned good at his job.

He was also very good at plain old group dynamics. Not only had he drawn the major into the general conversation, he managed Tony's humor and energy with a finesse that made her smile, and at some level she couldn't even detect, he and Malcolm were connecting.

But what was most heartening of all was Jenny. Sydney knew the teenager had arrived feeling very much out of her depth and more than a little nervous. It was for that very reason Sydney had decided to have a casual buffet, knowing the teenager would freeze up completely if faced with a full place setting, white linen and crystal.

And it was for that very reason she had her help with the final preparations of the meal while the others relaxed in the living room. She knew Jenny needed some time to get her feet under her, and little by little, Sydney could see the girl relax. There were even two occasions when she really laughed out loud, and that was the first time Sydney had ever heard her do that.

It was also significant how she related to Malcolm.

Sydney wasn't the only one aware of that subtle alignment. When she went into the kitchen to put on a fresh pot of coffee, Major Henderson followed her, her teacup in her hand. "I do believe Mr. Jefferson has taken our young lady under his wing."

Sydney locked the basket into place and turned on the coffee maker. "He's a very empathetic person, Major. He's completely nonjudgmental, and I suspect Jenny senses that. Even the first time she met him, she seemed to be at ease with him."

The major indicated the can of mixed nuts and the wooden bowl on the counter, and when Sydney nodded, she started filling the dish. "He's offered to do some volunteer work at one of the group homes. He's just the kind of person we're looking for."

Sydney refilled the cream pitcher, then placed the container in the fridge. "He has a prison record—if that means anything."

The major gave Sydney a sharp look, her eyes twinkling. "With some of those young hellions, it will be a plus."

Sydney grinned. "I suppose there's that side to it."

"I very much like your young man, my dear. One senses a deep moral strength in him. I admire that."

Her expression clouding, Sydney looked away. "So do I."

The major patted Sydney's hand, her tone bolstering. "Don't be downhearted because Jenny is giving him a wide berth, my dear. I suspect she feels a little envious because he obviously means something to you. And he has that air of authority about him, and that's very intimidating for someone like Jenny."

Sydney followed the major into the living room, carrying a tray with a plate of cookies, cheese and grapes and a stack of napkins. As she set it on the coffee table, she glanced at Nick. He was slouched down in the sofa watching Malcolm and Tony try to outdo each other with card tricks. Only it wasn't really them he was watching. It was Jenny.

The girl was sitting cross-legged on the floor just a couple of feet from Malcolm, her eyes sparkling, and it struck Sydney how very pretty she was. And how very young.

She managed to keep her voice even. "There are goodies on the table if anyone wants anything." She glanced at the girl. "There's some canned pop in the fridge if you want one, Jenny."

The teenager nodded and scrambled to her feet.

Tony glanced up at her and grinned. "Hey, muffin, would you bring us back a beer?"

She gave him a shy smile. "Sure."

When she returned, she handed Tony the two cans of beer, then crossed her legs and sat back down, popping the snap top on her cola as she did. For some reason the carbonated drink fizzed, and foam spewed out and puddled on the carpet. Acute embarrassment stained her cheeks, and she looked at Sydney as though she expected her to be angry. But before Sydney had a chance to say anything, Nick was holding out a stack of paper napkins to her. "Here, use these to blot it up with, Jenny," he said quietly.

She stared at him, her mortification so intense she was almost paralyzed from it.

Nick gave her a small smile. "Believe me, if anyone knows about slopping, it's me." Deliberately directing the attention away from the girl, he looked at Tony. "Have you shown Malcolm your four-quarters-and-a-dime trick?"

Tony grinned. "Hey, man. It's a week until payday. I don't have four quarters and a dime."

Her hand not quite steady, Jenny set her can of pop on the coffee table and started to clean up the spill. Sydney picked up some more napkins and crouched beside her. "It's not a big deal, Jenny," she said softly. "Things like this happen all the time." Jenny looked up at her and gave her a pathetic little shrug, tears just a blink away.

Sydney smiled at her and wiped the droplets of pop off her cheek. "Remind me to tell you sometime what I did at the official opening of a very classy hotel in Vancouver." That got a small smile out of the girl, and Sydney wadded up the damp napkins and handed them to her. "Throw these in the garbage and bring out the box of chocolates beside the fridge. They'll make you feel better."

Sydney watched her go, hoping that in time Jenny would acquire some insulation against her feelings of inadequacy. As she stood up, her gaze connected with Nick's. His expression was dark and unreadable. He held her gaze for just an instant, then he looked away. And Sydney experienced a sudden twist of doubt.

It was nearly midnight when she shut off the light in the kitchen and crossed the patio to the solarium. Nick had been very quiet after everyone left. Sydney knew that part of his silence was due to weariness. Since the brain injury, it was hard for him to deal with more than one conversation at a time. But there was more to it than that. Undoing the cuff of her dress, she switched off the light in the solarium as she entered the bedroom, her gaze turning immediately to the bed.

Nick was lying on his stomach with his arms under the pillows, his head turned away from her. "Tired?" she asked.

"Yeah."

"Your leg's bothering you tonight, isn't it?"

"A little."

"Take off your sweats and I'll massage it for you."

No answer. A hint of a smile appeared at the corner of Sydney's mouth. He could be so damned stubborn. He didn't like her seeing his legs, and because of that he always wore the lightweight sweatpants to bed.

Granted, the first time she'd seen the scars, she had been badly shaken. Besides the gunshot wounds he had suffered a compound fracture in one leg and two in the other, and the doctors had had to pin the breaks in his left leg. Most of the time it didn't bother him, but there were other times it did. And she could tell that tonight was one of them.

"If you don't take off your sweats, I'll do it for you, and I won't be nice about it."

She could tell he was smiling when he gave his muffled reply. "Fine."

Amusement glinted in her eyes as she crossed to the bathroom. When she came back, she had changed into a big T-shirt nightie and carried a tube of cream in her hands. Nick was still lying on his stomach, but the sweats were on the pillow beside him. Climbing onto the bed, she knelt between his knees and squeezed a liberal amount of cream onto both legs. She started on his foot, working the muscles in deep, kneading motions.

He groaned. "God, you have no idea how good that feels."

The corner of her mouth lifted. "I have some idea."

"You're better than Beth."

She smiled. "Just generally or specifically?"

"Overall performance."

"Sure." She worked up his ankle to the tight muscles in his calf. Nick pushed the pillows aside and rested his head on his folded arms, and Sydney saw the look of pure gratification in his expression. Neither spoke as she massaged her way up both legs. She could tell he didn't have the energy to roll over, so she straddled his hips and started on his back and shoulders.

"She could pass for your daughter," he said quietly.

Caught from behind by his comment, Sydney froze for a moment, then she began kneading his muscles again. Her own voice was uneven when she finally spoke. "Is that what you were thinking when you were watching us?"

"Yes."

There was another long silence, then he spoke again. "Our kid would have been about her age if she'd lived."

A sudden lump formed in Sydney's throat. "Yes, she would have."

"Do you ever wonder what she would have been like?"

The lump grew more painful. "Yes."

He turned his head so his forehead was resting on his arms. "So do I."

Sydney swallowed to ease the ache as she started working on his shoulder. Drawing his arms out from under his head, Nick shifted, turning his face toward the light. She worked her way down his left arm, paying particular attention to the pressure points in his hand and the spastic muscles in his fingers.

He exhaled heavily, his hand knotting into a fist around her fingers. "I want to make it work this time, Syd."

Feeling the torment in him, Sydney moved so she was no longer straddling his body. Rolling onto his side, Nick pulled her down beside him, locking her in a tight embrace. An embrace that was fueled with desperation rather than reassurance, an embrace that filled Sydney with desolation.

He was trying to come to terms with himself, with her past, with her involvement with Jenny, but it was a tough struggle for him. Nick was not the type of man who could talk about his feelings—he never had been. And even if he could—if by some miracle he was comfortable enough with Dr. Brown to try to work through his feelings with her—Sydney knew he would never do it. Because to do that, he would have to expose Sydney's life on the street, and he would never do that to her. He would never betray her secret.

And for the same reason, they could never work through it together. His feelings were too intense, too raw, too uncontrollable, and because he didn't trust himself when he was in a full-blown rage, he would never confront her with them. In the past, he had smashed a cabinet he was working on to smithereens, spent hours hammering out his frustrations at the gym or, on a couple of occasions, picked a fight with someone else, but never once had he turned the full force of his fury on her.

Nor would he now. If that kind of rage was ever ignited again, he would leave. That was a hard, cold fact. And that scared her to death.

CHAPTER TWELVE

JULY ROLLED IN on a heat wave. The first week was bearable, the second was not, and that weekend, Sydney and Nick never left the air-conditioned comfort of her apartment. On the Sunday, the Elbow River across the street suffered a major traffic jam from senior citizens drifting sedately down in canoes, to teenagers on makeshift floats of several inner tubes lashed together, to whole families on rubber rafts.

Nick stood on the balcony off the living room, a glass of lemonade in his hand, his expression unreadable as he watched the activity on the river.

He had been an avid canoeist before the shooting, and Sydney wondered if he was thinking how he had been deprived of that enjoyment, too, or if there was something else that was bothering him. She suspected it was a bit of both.

Ever since the dinner party in June, there had been a change in him. He was quieter, more introspective, and there were times when he was uncommunicative and moody. When he was like that, he avoided being around her, yet she never had the feeling it was *her* he was avoiding. In fact, in many ways, he was more warm and giving than he'd ever been. Thoughtful, tender, gently loving. It should have reassured her, but it didn't.

She couldn't remember the last time she'd heard him laugh, and a real smile was so rare it almost depressed her when she got one. And there had been three days when she hadn't seen him at all. He had talked to her on the phone and done some cost estimates for her, and he had sent her a beautiful bouquet of gladioli, but he'd stayed away from her. The day she came home from work and found him in the kitchen preparing dinner, she was so relieved she'd had to fight back tears.

He was to have spent the previous Sunday afternoon with her and Jenny, but he left after an hour, and since then, Sydney never mentioned the girl unless he brought her name up.

Standing just inside the patio door, she watched the man on the balcony, wishing she knew how to reach out to him. She leaned against the doorjamb, her eyes solemn with concern. He had been standing out there for more than an hour, and the back of his tank top was damp with sweat. "Would you like me to fix you some dinner?"

Shifting his cane, he turned to look at her, perspiration trickling down his temples. "It's too hot to eat."

"Why don't you come in, Nick," she said softly. "It's so hot out there. I'll fix us a fruit salad."

He set the glass down on the small table on the balcony, avoiding her gaze. "I think I'll have a shower."

Sydney watched him cross the living room, feeling such compassion for him it made her chest hurt. He was fighting, and he was doing it alone. And that made her hurt even more.

She closed the patio door and turned toward the kitchen. She and Nick needed some time on their own right now, but that was impossible. Jenny had started her summer school right after the Canada Day weekend, and every day was an anxiety attack for the teenager. And on top of that, Sydney was in the middle of two business transactions she could not walk away from right then.

She had made arrangements for time off in August, though. For the first time since she had started Unicorn Holdings, she was closing the office for an entire month.

But that didn't help. They needed the time now, not two weeks down the road.

She fixed the fruit salad and placed it in the fridge to chill, tidied the living room and loaded the dishwasher, but Nick still hadn't reappeared. Thinking he had lain down, she went into the bedroom through the solarium.

He was sitting in one of the chairs in front of the TV, and it wasn't until she was through the door that she realized he had a video playing in the VCR. He glanced up as she entered the room, switching off the machine with the remote control. His eyes were cold. "You left the top drawer in the armoire open." Sydney's stomach twisted as he went on. "And being the compulsive I am, I went to shut it."

Her gaze stark with horror, Sydney stared at him, then she closed her eyes, a sick feeling washing through her. She had forgotten all about the two videos. They had been sitting in that drawer for nearly a year and a half.

The tapes had been made when he first started his rehabilitation program with Peter Robertson. He had been helpless then; he couldn't walk, he could barely speak, and every movement was an agony to watch. And he would hate it, knowing she'd seen him in that condition.

She heard him get up, and she looked at him, her heart constricting when she saw the rigid set to his jaw. He ejected the tape and angrily tossed it onto one of the shelves of the unit. "You must be some kind of bloody masochist to watch that crap," he snapped. "It even makes me sick." He snatched up a clean T-shirt from the arm of the chair. "Forget dinner. I'm going home."

Without giving any explanation, without saying anything at all, Sydney turned and left the room. He knew why she'd done it. But there was nothing she could say that would discharge his pent-up resentment and humiliation over his own utter helplessness at that point in his recovery.

Sick at heart, Sydney went into the living room and sank into one of the sofas. Raking her hair back off her face, she rested her head against the back cushions and stared at the ceiling, waiting for the slam of the door in the front hall. She likely wouldn't see him for a week after this.

"Sydney?"

She jerked around, her heart suddenly lodged in her throat. He was watching her from the archway, his gaze fixed on her with an enigmatic expression, his mouth compressed into a hard line. "If you tell me to take a damned hike, I won't blame you."

Through the frantic flutter in her chest, she found her voice. "Did it ever occur to you that I might understand how you feel?"

He stared at her, then he looked away, the muscles in his jaw tensing. Gripping his cane with a white-knuckled hold, he started across the room. He sat down beside her, not moving for a moment, then he took her hand and carefully laced his fingers through hers. "I don't know why you put up with me lately."

She tightened her fingers around his, a hint of a smile in her eyes. "Because the alternative stinks, Nick."

The corner of his mouth lifted a little. "The reason that video shook me so damned bad was because I don't remember much about those first few weeks when I came out of the coma. There are some things that stick in my mind, but I've never seen that tape before—I refused to watch it."

"I want you to know something, Nick," she said softly. "Of all the things I respect about you, your determination and courage are high on the list. I could have never fought back the way you did. Never. And I know you hated it, but maybe seeing that tape was a good thing. You can see for yourself how far you've come in a year and a half."

He sighed again, then tipped his head back against the cushions. "There are days I get really fed up, but it's not the disability that got to me today." He hesitated, then he turned his head to look at her. "It was you seeing me like that."

She smiled, fighting the sudden lump in her throat. "I know that," she whispered.

Not wanting to drag either of them into emotional overload, Sydney said nothing more. Several moments passed before she gave his hand a reassuring squeeze. "Does this mean you're staying for dinner?"

There was a glint of humor in his eyes as he looked at her. "If the invitation includes breakfast tomorrow morning, as well."

They were just finishing their light dinner when Malcolm stopped by. "Have some fruit salad," Nick offered. "Sydney thought she was feeding a horde again."

Malcolm straddled the chair at the end of the kitchen table and shot Sydney a grin. "I've eaten, but I could still manage a helping."

Sydney got a bowl out of the cupboard, then glanced back at him. "Were you out today?"

Malcolm rested his massive arms on the table, his expression altering as he fingered the place mat. "Yeah. I went to church with Major Henderson, and she asked me to stay for supper."

Sydney and Nick exchanged glances, then Nick leaned back in his chair, waiting for the caretaker to speak.

When he did, it was almost as though he were thinking out loud. "I haven't been to church in years. It felt good to be back, and she's got me working with those kids.... It's like she's pulling me back into the fold." Malcolm's face was unusually solemn. "And it's the first time in years I've felt like I've got a reason for being here."

Nick had been watching the other man, a thoughtful expression in his eyes. "I think Major Henderson knew exactly what she was doing when she matched you up with those kids in the group home."

Malcolm gave him a lopsided grin. "I don't know. There's a couple in there that test a man's mettle."

Nick chuckled. "I can imagine."

Sydney placed a dessert spoon and a serving of fruit salad in front of the caretaker. "Would you like ice cream on it?"

"No, thanks. This is fine." He looked at Sydney as she sat down beside Nick. "I think it'd be a good idea if you had a talk with Jenny, Ms Foster. She came to church with us, but I could tell something was bothering her."

Sydney didn't look at Nick. "Did she say anything?"

Malcolm took a spoonful of salad, then tipped his head in a gesture of uncertainty. "Sort of. I take it she's having problems at school."

"Has it to do with a girl—Tiffany, I think?"

"Yeah. That's the one. I got a feeling it's something Jen's havin' big trouble with." He looked up and met Sydney's gaze. "The major says she's got her teeth into the school thing, though. Does four or five hours of homework a night."

Pride stirred in Sydney. "She's doing very well."

Malcolm continued to watch her, obviously bothered by something. Finally he spoke. "I don't know why this is sitting so heavy with me—maybe it's because she acts like she's got nobody to turn to."

Sydney's expression became very somber. "I'll call her."

"There's something else you should know," he said quietly. "I don't know how she did it, but she's registered as Jenny Foster. I asked her why, but she said I wouldn't understand."

Sydney's gaze involuntarily swung to Nick. He looked at her, nothing registering on his face. She didn't know what she expected to see in his eyes—anger, maybe, or a look of distaste, but there was nothing except a strange steadiness.

As soon as Sydney had tidied up the kitchen, and while Nick and Malcolm were watching a ball game on TV, she slipped into the study and called Jenny. Sydney didn't bring up Jenny's falsifying her name. What she did ask about was what was happening at school. Jenny wouldn't say much, but Sydney did find out that Tiffany's boyfriend spent considerable time hanging around Jenny, and Tiffany didn't like it. The only thing Sydney could do was reassure Jenny, telling the girl that if she ever needed her, no matter what, she was only a phone call away.

She hung up, heartsick for the girl. Jenny was alone in a new environment with no friends and no experience in dealing with that sort of thing. She had to feel isolated. Sydney only hoped the whole thing would blow over soon.

She thought it had until two days later. It was just after lunch and she was in her office when Marg flung open the door. "Get on line two. Jenny's on the phone and she's crying so hard I can't understand her."

Sydney tossed her glasses onto the desk and snapped up the receiver, her tone clipped. "What's wrong, Jenny?"

The girl was sobbing, panic making her almost incoherent. "The school cop did a locker inspection today. And they found hash in mine. I told them it wasn't mine, but they're going to expel me anyway."

Sydney's face went white, but there was a sudden crisp edge in her voice. "Where are you? In the main office?"

Jenny sobbed out her answer. "Yes."

Sydney was on her feet, her tone curt, calm and businesslike. "You stay there. Don't say anything. Don't do anything. Is the principal there?"

"No, but my guidance counselor is."

"Put him on the phone."

There was the sound of conversation, then a woman's voice came on the line. "Connie Brooks, Ms Foster."

Anger was flaming through Sydney, but she clamped it down, the tone of her voice brooking no argument. "I'll be at the school in twenty minutes. I want a meeting with you, the principal and the police officer. And I want a full and detailed explanation."

"Yes, but—"

"No buts, Ms Brooks. Twenty minutes."

Sydney slammed down the phone. If Jenny was charged
with possession, her whole program would be put in jeopardy. Closing her eyes, she tried to think. Norm. Maybe she
should call Norm. No.

She picked up the phone and punched in Nick's number.
He answered on the third ring.

As quickly and as calmly as possible, she told him what
had happened. There was a pause, then his voice came back
to her, sharp and decisive. "Pick me up at the corner by the
fitness center. That'll only take you a few blocks out of your
way."

"Nick, I don't expect you—"

He cut her off, his tone commanding. "Just do it, damn
it. Ten minutes."

"But you can't be there in ten—"

"Beth stopped by on her way home. She'll drop me off.
Now move it. Ten minutes."

Sydney had no idea how she made it from her office to the
designated corner in the allotted time. She was shaking, the
beginning of panic twisting her insides into knots. She
pulled over to the curb, and Nick had the door open before
she was at a full stop. She closed her eyes and forced herself to take a deep, steadying breath. God, this couldn't be
happening.

Nick slammed the door. "Let's go."

Sydney pulled into traffic, her voice shaking. "Nick, if
she's charged, she could end up in juvenile detention—"

"I know that." He checked the back view, that same edge
of command in his voice. "Get in the other lane."

Sydney made the lane change, her hands white knuckled
around the wheel. "She was so scared."

Nick did up his seat belt. "How long has she been clean?"

Sydney shot him a confused look. "About three
months."

"Is there a chance she's lying?"

His question threw her. She had the awful feeling he believed the worst. It was as though Nick read her mind. "I
can't go in there cold," he pointed out bluntly. "If it isn't
hers, somebody's planted it, which means someone has it in
for her. I need to know what in hell is going on."

Taking another deep breath, Sydney forced herself to relax. "I don't think she's lying. And yes, someone has it in
for her." As briefly as possible, she told him about Tiffany.

As they turned onto the tree-lined street where the high
school was located, he shot her a stern look. "Let me handle it, Syd," he said flatly. "If she's lying, she deserves to be
caught. If she isn't, we'll get to the bottom of this."

Swallowing hard, Sydney nodded. She parked in the re-
stricted zone in front of the school, and Nick pulled the blue
handicap symbol from the glove compartment and stuck it
in the window. "The cops won't tow it with this in the window."

Sydney was desperate to get into the school. At the front
doors, Nick caught her arm and stopped her. "Get a grip,
Syd," he said firmly. "You won't do her any good if you go
in there ready to unravel."

Knowing he was right, Sydney closed her eyes, willing
herself into at least a semblance of composure. As she
straightened, she heard a car squeal to a halt on the road. It
was a squad car, and at first she thought they were stopping because of her parking infraction. But the passenger
door opened and Tony climbed out. For no earthly reason,
Sydney found herself suddenly fighting tears. Nick gave her
a ghost of a grin. "I called in the big guns. And a detective
from vice is something they won't be expecting."

Tony jogged up the sidewalk, a big grin on his face.
"Well, well. Nicky's running a sting. This should be good."

Nick gave him a dry look. "Just don't blow it, Martinelli, or Syd will chop you off at the knees."

They entered the front foyer, then Nick paused and filled
Tony in. There was a cool, determined look on the detec-

tive's face as they turned toward the main office. "Okay. Let's do it."

They were ushered into the principal's office by a small woman who looked as if she were expecting them to eat her. And Sydney felt like doing exactly that the minute she stepped into the office. There were several adults and one terrified, white-faced Jennifer, and Sydney's agitation over a child being so badly outnumbered turned into hard, cold resolve. She gave Jenny a reassuring smile, then turned and faced the balding man seated behind the desk, his name plate identifying him as Mr. Finch. She leveled a withering look at him. "Mr. Finch, I'm Sydney Foster. And I'd like to know what's going on here."

Rising slowly to his feet, the principal looked decidedly uncomfortable. "Yes, of course." Not quite sure what to expect, he made the introductions. The police resource officer, two counselors and a vice principal. Nick introduced himself, and a hint of dark humor glinted in Sydney's eyes when he deliberately neglected to introduce Tony. The resource officer, a member of the city police force involved in community service, did a double take when he recognized Nick's name, then he frowned and looked at Tony. Tony had gone directly to Jenny, knelt down and whispered something to her, then moved to the far corner, putting himself out of the field of view.

With obvious discomfort, the principal motioned to two empty chairs in front of his desk. Nick ignored him and crossed the room. He crouched in front of the trembling girl, and Sydney had to swallow hard. She knew how difficult it was for him to do that, and how hard it was for him to get back up.

His face was without a trace of emotion. "This is serious, Jenny. And I need the truth, and I need it now. Is the stuff yours?"

A sob escaped and she wiped away the steady trickle of tears, but she held his gaze. She shook her head.

Like a shadow, Tony picked up an empty chair in the corner and placed it beside Jenny's, then nodded to Sydney. She sat down and put her arm around the girl. "Don't worry, Jen. Nick and Tony are going to get to the bottom of this."

Nick positioned himself in front of the desk, a look on his face that could cow anyone. "I'd like to see the evidence," he said quietly. Too quietly.

Glancing at the resource officer, the principal took a small plastic bag out of his drawer, laying it very carefully on his desk. Nick turned to Jenny. "Did you touch this, Jenny?"

"It's not mine—"

"I'm asking you if you touched it."

Confused, she shook her head.

"Who's handled it?"

It was the constable who spoke. "Since it was discovered in the locker, myself and Mr. Finch."

Nick nailed him with a look. "Would I be wrong in assuming that you checked Jenny's locker because of a tip?"

The constable fidgeted. "No, sir. You wouldn't be wrong."

"I see."

Tony's voice came from the shadows. "What do you have, Nick?"

Nick picked up a pen and moved the package closer. "Four two-chips of hash, foil wrapped and in a plastic bag. The two-chips are slightly under two grams, and there's a red seal on the foil. Street price—probably fifty bucks."

The principal noticeably paled and glanced at his vice principal. Nick turned to the resource officer, his tone relaxed. "Would you agree, Constable?"

"Yes, sir."

Nick looked down at the principal. "The gentleman in the corner is Detective Tony Martinelli of the Calgary Police Vice Squad. Ms Foster asked him to be here."

Upon Tony's introduction, the resource officer rolled his eyes and exhaled sharply. Obviously he recognized the name, and Sydney realized that Tony was, indeed, a big gun.

Tony patted Jenny on the shoulder as he moved toward Nick. His tone was easy, almost casual. "Now, Mr. Finch, this can go two ways. I can take the evidence downtown and have it lasered for fingerprints, or we can try to sort it out here."

Mr. Finch wiped the perspiration off his brow. "We didn't want to make an incident out of this, Detective."

A cold smile appeared on Nick's face. "I was under the impression you did just that when you told Jenny you were going to expel her. Is that correct?"

"Well, yes, but—"

"Well, sir," Tony said easily, "I suspect this whole mess can be sorted out if we could talk to the person or persons who reported the drugs in Jenny's locker. If we investigate, the witnesses would be asked to come downtown for questioning, and possibly fingerprinting, and they might like to know that."

Sydney had the nearly uncontrollable urge to laugh. She had the feeling that this was a ruse, but a ruse that had been used before and had worked.

The vice principal, Mr. Roscal, leaned over and said something to Mr. Finch, then he straightened and met Nick's gaze with a directness that was strictly man-to-man. For some reason, Sydney had the feeling he was not at all unhappy about the direction the meeting was taking. There was the barest hint of a smile around his mouth as he looked at Tony. "Let me clarify this in my own mind, Detective. You simply want to talk to the person or persons and make it clear to them that you're prepared to move this downtown."

Tony grinned. "You've got it."

"Yes," he said. "I believe I do."

When the vice principal returned, he had a young girl with him—blond, pertly pretty, expensively dressed, with the insolent air of a child who was used to getting her own way. Sydney disliked her on sight.

"This is Tiffany Cross. She's the student who reported seeing Jenny place the drugs in her locker."

With a glance at Nick that had an entire dialogue in it, Tony crouched in front of the seated girl and turned on all his charm. "I'm Detective Martinelli from the city vice squad, Tiffany. We have a bit of a problem. Jenny claims the drugs aren't hers, that she's never seen them, and she says she didn't even touch the package. Now, I can take the package the constable found in her locker downtown, and we can lift fingerprints from it. If Jenny's prints don't turn up, you and your parents would be asked to come downtown, since you're the only witness. In a drug investigation, we check everyone's stories very carefully, and if Jenny's prints aren't on the package, then we try to find out whose are."

There was a moment of incomprehension, then the girl's face went deathly white, and a stricken look appeared in her eyes. Tony looked at Nick, and again, the unspoken communication was there. Tony stood up. "It's only a suggestion, of course, but I wonder if there's any place where I could talk with Tiffany alone, along with you, Mr. Finch, and Mr. Roscal—and whoever else should be there."

Mr. Finch looked absolutely fractured. He glanced at Jenny's counselor. "Miss Brooks, would you mind showing Ms Foster, Mr. Novak and Jenny to the outer office."

As Sydney rose, she saw a hand signal from Nick to Tony, and she realized how solid their partnership was. And for the first time she realized what a loss Tony had suffered—losing Nick as a partner must have been like losing his other half.

Once out of the principal's office, Nick made sure Jenny was between him and Sydney, and there was a set to his face that radiated barely controlled anger. He turned to face the counselor, the look in his eyes chilling. "This fiasco," he said very quietly, "was inexcusable."

Connie Brooks met his gaze. "I couldn't agree more. It was very clear to me that Jenny was telling the truth right from the beginning." She looked at Sydney. "You have a very forthright daughter, Ms Foster. And an outstanding student. You must be very proud of her."

Sydney didn't miss a beat, her chin lifting a fraction as she tightened her arm around Jenny's shoulders. "I am."

Both Jenny and Nick shot quick looks at her; Jenny with astonishment, Nick with something that closely resembled amusement.

The counselor touched Jenny on the shoulder, her voice gentle. "I'm sorry about this, Jenny."

Nick braced his weight on his cane as he gave the woman one of his cool, leveling looks. "I suspect it's common knowledge that drugs were found in Jenny's locker. I would hope the outcome of this meeting will be made public to the rest of the students."

Connie Brooks met his gaze. "You have my word on it."

A very agitated and disturbed Mr. Finch came rushing out of his office, closely followed by Tony, who grinned and flashed Nick a thumbs-up signal. Nick tipped his head in acknowledgment, and Sydney could see him visibly relax.

The principal, red faced and sweating, stammered out his apologies. It was clear the drugs had been planted, and the culprit, whom he left unnamed, would be severely dealt with. Nick watched him with a steadiness that would have made a rock squirm. There wasn't a shred of forgiveness in Sydney's expression, either. If she so chose, she could shred the man, and he knew it. Tony watched the whole scene, his hands rammed in the back pockets of his jeans, obviously enjoying himself to no end. Catching Jenny's eye, he gave her a broad wink, and for the first time, she smiled.

Mr. Finch addressed Sydney. "And I can assure you this will be dealt with, Ms Foster." When she said nothing, he blustered on, trying to extract himself from an increasingly difficult situation. "But while you're here, perhaps we could straighten out the problem of Jenny's transcripts."

Sydney stared him down. "Transcripts?"

"Um, well, yes. We need Jenny's academic records from her last school, and we haven't received them yet."

Transcripts. School records. Her expression impassive, Sydney stalled. "Is there a problem with Jenny's grades, Mr. Finch?"

"No, no. My, no. She's doing very well." He gave Jenny a condescending smile. "She's an excellent student, but we must have her transcripts from the last school she attended."

Nick's voice was brusque as he interjected, "We'll see to it." He glanced at Tony, and Tony imperceptibly tipped his head and held up one hand, his five fingers splayed. Nick looked back at the principal. "They'll be on your desk in five days."

He beamed and mopped his head. "Fine, fine." But he looked decidedly ill when he tried to smile again. "We hope you understand that this sort of thing doesn't happen often."

Nick stared at him. "I should hope not."

Sydney looked at the counselor. "I think Jenny has had about enough for today."

Connie Brooks nodded. "I think so, too." She smiled at Jenny. "You come to see me tomorrow morning—first thing, okay?"

Jenny managed a weak smile. "I will."

Nick turned toward the door. "Let's get out of here."

It wasn't until they were in Sydney's car, with Tony grinning behind the wheel, that they got the whole story. Tiffany, realizing she was in major trouble, had confessed in hysterical weeping. When Tony had left the office, the vice principal was on the phone to Tiffany's parents.

Tony met Sydney's gaze in the rearview mirror. "I got the distinct impression that Roscal was not unhappy that the kid ended up with egg on her face. He suspected something was cooking when he found out she'd gone directly to the principal—got the impression that Finch is scared to death of her old man." His grin broadened. "I also got the impression that Tiff-baby is also scared to death of her old man."

Sydney glanced at Jenny, who was sitting in the back seat with her. The kid was so pale, her face was the color of chalk. Sydney reached over and took her hand in hers. "It's over, Jen. And by tomorrow, everyone's going to know the truth."

Jenny looked at her, then promptly burst into tears. "But what about my school records? I didn't even finish grade eight."

"You let us take care of that," Nick interjected.

"But they want my grade nine transcripts," she sobbed out. "And there aren't any. I can't go back to junior high. I'd feel so dumb with all those little kids."

Tony glanced over the seat at her. "Don't sweat it, kid. Nick told Finch they'd have a transcript in five days—and, sweetheart, he's going to have a transcript in five days."

"But how...?"

"Hey, have a little faith, muffin. For you, we can move mountains."

Jenny wiped her face with the back of her hand. The tears kept coming, but there was relief and hope and a glimmer of gladness mixed with them. It had sunk in that these people were rallying around her. Through the tears came a very shaky laugh. "So help me," she said vehemently, "I'm going to get straight A's or die trying."

There wasn't a person in the car who doubted her sincerity.

THE STREET LAY TRAPPED in purple, hazy twilight—still, quiet, the hush broken by the twitter of robins and the soft chit-chit-chit counterpoint of a symphony of lawn sprinklers.

Sydney got out of the air-conditioned comfort of her car, the afternoon heat still embedded in the concrete of the city, the night breezes yet to move in from the mountains. She had a weird weightlessness in the pit of her stomach. Nerves, maybe. Or uncertainty.

After the episode at the school, her day had taken on a dreamlike quality. Tony had dropped himself off at work, then Nick had asked to be taken back to his apartment. Not wanting Jenny to have time to sit around and think, Sydney had taken her to the office and put her to work filing. There had been two phone calls from the school, one from the counselor and one from the vice principal, both assuring her the mess had been straightened out. Sensing Jenny needed the reassurance of a steady presence, Sydney had taken her home with her, partly so the girl had constant company, partly so Sydney could take her to school in the morning.

But what disturbed her most of all was Nick. Torn between her concern for the girl and her uneasy concern for him, she had left the teenager and Malcolm eating pizza and working on a jigsaw puzzle. She had a feeling the other concern wouldn't be quite so simple to deal with.

She had tried to call him just before she left the office, but there was no answer, only his answering machine. She had tried to call him again at eight o'clock, and still nothing. But what kicked her apprehension into gear was that the second time, she didn't even get the answering machine. Nick, without fail, turned it on when he left the apartment. Which meant, she suspected, that he was at home. It was after nine-thirty; there was nowhere else he could be.

Before, she had not infringed on his privacy when he'd shut himself off, but this time his isolation made her feel shaky inside. There had been something different about him when she had dropped him off, something in the expression in his eyes and the set of his jaw that bothered her. And it wasn't until much later that she was able to identify it. It was, she realized, an expression of finality. Nick had made a decision.

The inside of the apartment building was lighted, sharp and silent, at odds with the soft twilight outside. She paused at his door, selected the proper key from the case and inserted it in the lock.

It was as though she had stepped back outside. Dusk and the twilight stillness had settled heavily into the room, the twitter of robins and the chit-chit-chit of the sprinklers distinct through the open windows. Soundlessly she closed the door, a flutter starting just below her ribs. The apartment was in total darkness.

Lowering her canvas bag onto the chair, she started down the hallway.

Nick was standing at the open window of the bedroom, his shoulder resting against the frame, a glass in his hand. From his vantage point, he had a view of a small park behind the apartment building, but he was so immersed in his own thoughts he wasn't even aware of her presence, let alone the view. He was alone in the shadows.

Leaning back against the doorjamb, Sydney watched him, hesitant about trespassing on his solitude, even more hesitant about making her presence known.

"It's eerie," he said softly, as though he were thinking out loud, "how things appear so clear at this time of night."

Her heart stopped, then started again. "How did you know I was here?"

He didn't look at her. "A sixth sense I've developed over the years." He took a drink, then turned toward her, his face indistinct in the dusk. "It's just stronger with you."

The flutter had moved higher into her chest, and she drew a deep breath. "Do you want me to go?"

He looked out the window again. "No."

Feeling suddenly shaky, Sydney shoved her hands into the pockets of her cotton skirt. "I take it you have something to tell me."

He didn't say anything for a space, then he started to speak, his voice very quiet. "It's taken me a long time to see it, but I finally realized I had some very unrealistic expectations about life. Especially about you. I was pretty god-damned self-righteous. I blamed you for not being what I wanted you to be. I can't hide behind that crap anymore. I have to come to terms with it. It's not going to be easy, and I don't even know if I can do it, but I have to quit backing away from it. I have to face it dead-on."

Sydney didn't know what to say. He had said the words before and meant them, but this time they didn't come from his conscience; this time they came straight from his gut. He had decided to risk the tenuous balance, and that scared her.

The silence was like a chasm between them.

Finally he turned from the window, facing her across the twilight-filled room. "I'm tired of the tightrope act, Syd," he said softly. "And I'm tired of the constant guilt about what I'm doing to you."

An awful ache of compassion welled up in her, and her voice broke beneath the weight of it. "I love you, Nick. I'll take whatever you can give."

He shook his head, his expression somber. "That's not good enough anymore. You deserve more than bits and pieces. I realized this morning how much I'm screwing up things for you and Jenny. She needs you. She needs to be living with you. She needs to have the permanence of a home and someone who cares about her. You can give her that. She's lived half her life with nobody to turn to, nobody to look out for her."

He paused, a twist of emotion scoring his features. "You made it bloody clear this afternoon that if anyone was going to get to her, they had to get through you first. And the look on her face when you cruised into that office—God, it was like a kick in the gut.

"It hit me today how very much like you she is. She could have been ours. Don't put her life, and yours, on hold because of me. Go after legal custody. Give her a home, buy her a kitten, teach her to cook—do the things you would have done if she were yours."

Hit with the full implication behind his words, Sydney stared at him. Her knees wanted to fold under her, and dread settled in her stomach. "What are you trying to say?"

He shifted so his back was to her, his face profiled against the fading light. When he finally spoke, his voice was low and husky. "You can't go on like this, walking on eggshells around me, trying to protect my feelings. Either I learn to deal with it or I let you get on with your life."

There was an edge of panic in her voice. "I don't want to get on with my life. I'd rather be dead than lose you again."

"What I want," he said quietly, "is to be able to look you square in the eye and know I've put the past to rest. I want to be able to make love to you without thinking about the other men who were there before me, and I want to stop harboring this goddamned jealousy. I hate myself, Sydney, and I want to stop. And above all else, I want to stop hurting you."

He turned to face her, his expression haggard. "I need you so damned much it scares the hell out of me, but I know if I don't do this now, I'm going to end up drinking again."

Sydney's chest was so tight she could barely speak. "Does this mean I'm not going to see you?"

He stared at her across the room, his jaw rigid, but there was so much love and pain in his voice. "No, that's not what it means. But if I stay away for a couple of days, understand why."

Torn to shreds by the torment in his voice, Sydney started to go to him, blinded by tears. But the minute she moved, the expression in Nick's eyes stopped her. "No, don't," he commanded sharply. "For God's sake, don't. If I even so much as touch you now, all this will go out the window. And if I ever needed anything, I need you to help me now." His voice caved in on him, and he looked away. "I need you to walk out that door, Sydney. Give me tonight to work on this."

She stared at him, wanting to go to him so badly, hurting for him so much she could barely stand it. But right now, she would have stopped breathing if he'd asked her.

With one last glance, she turned and walked out the door.

Nick closed his eyes, clenching his jaw to keep from calling her back. He wanted her. God, as he had never wanted her before. He wanted to have her naked beneath him, to feel her hot, slick sheath around him, to drive into her until he exploded. And he knew if he touched her, that's exactly what would happen. He wouldn't be able to stop himself.

It had happened again that afternoon—the hard arousal, the pulsating ache that wouldn't go away. How he had found the strength to send her away, he'd never know. But he would cut off his right arm before he'd hurt her the way he had in the past. Somehow he had to work through all the garbage alone.

And somehow he had to get through the night.

CHAPTER THIRTEEN

SYDNEY WONDERED how four weeks could change her life so much. Her once ordered existence was now cluttered with jars of peanut butter, a kitten, rock music and teenage clothes. She stood in the doorway of what once had been her guest room, boggled by the rummage sale mess. It looked as though a clothing store had exploded in there.

"So what do you think, Sydney? What should I take? Should I take four pairs of jeans and these sweaters?"

Sydney gave Jenny a wry look. "Why don't we just call a moving van and you can take everything, including the furniture."

Jenny giggled and made a face. "I'm taking too much, huh?"

"Let's see the list you got from the camp counselor."

Jenny had finished her summer school and was going to summer camp with the major and a group of older kids from Blairmore House. Excited didn't even come close to describing how the teen was reacting. She had finished classes two days before and had made A's in the three courses she'd completed. And she'd been coming off the walls ever since.

Sydney scanned the list, then looked at the pile of clothes stacked on Jenny's bed, most of them with price tags still attached. She handed the list back to the girl, trying her best to restrain a grin. "I think you have to make some critical decisions here, Jen. By the looks of it, you're over the recommended items by at least seventy-five percent."

A flash of reluctance darkened the girl's eyes. "It's just that I've never had such nice clothes before, and I can't wait to wear them all."

"Why don't you see what Malcolm says?"

A bundle of calico fluff tumbled through the pile of socks, and Jenny swept the kitten up and cuddled her under her chin. "Come on, Lint. Let's go talk to Malcolm." There had been great agonies of indecision about what to name the cat when Sydney brought her home for Jenny. The poor beast would likely still be running around nameless if it hadn't been for Tony. He had taken one look at it when it tried to climb up his pant leg, and he had picked it up, wanting to know where this big piece of lint had come from. Jenny thought it was so funny, she'd named the cat Lint on the spot. Sydney personally thought the cat looked more like a Muffy or a Fluffy, but what did she know?

She watched the girl talking baby talk to the tiny bundle of fur. "I'm still not sure it's a good idea to take her to camp with you, Jen. She's apt to get lost."

Jenny smiled and shook her head. "Malcolm says there's a pen there that he can fix up for her, and Major Henderson told me she'd keep her in her cabin."

The caretaker was taking his holidays and was going to camp as one of the group leaders. Sydney felt better knowing he was going to be there. She had discovered she had a terrible streak of maternal protectiveness in her. Clear-headed logic told her that if Jenny could survive on the streets for two years, she could certainly survive a seven-day camp. The new mother in Sydney, however, was feeling a little anxious.

The girl kissed the cat on the nose and turned toward the door. "I won't be long."

Sydney leaned against the doorjamb, her hands in her pockets, a tolerant smile on her face. She sincerely hoped the cat wouldn't mess on Malcolm's carpet again.

As Jenny dashed into the corridor, Sydney heard her speak to someone, then there was the sound of the elevator door closing. Nick came through the doorway, and Sydney realized he must have come straight from the rehab center.

Her pleasure shone in her eyes. "Well, hi. This is a surprise."

He closed the door and gave her a hint of a smile. "Hi, yourself."

She tipped her head to one side, a speculative gleam in her eyes. "How come an afternoon visit? Is the cleaning lady loose in your apartment again?"

He gave her a tart look. "No, she's not loose in my apartment again." A sudden tension radiated from him as he carefully leaned his cane against the wall, then turned toward her. There was an expression in his eyes that made it impossible for her to think, and Sydney's pulse went into a frenzy as he caught her by the shoulders and backed her into Jenny's room. Shutting the door behind them, he roughly gathered her into his arms, his embrace deep and urgent with need. "God, Syd, I wanted to hold you so damned bad, I couldn't stand it any longer."

The rough timbre of his voice made her go weak all over, and she hung on to him, the rush of love so intense she was swamped by it. The past four weeks had been completely unpredictable as far as Nick was concerned, and the few times he'd risked physical contact, he'd held her as if there were no tomorrow.

Trying to steady her reeling senses, she pressed a kiss against his neck, her voice husky. "I missed you yesterday."

"I miss you constantly." He tightened his hold, molding them together from shoulder to thigh. "Ah, God, Syd," he whispered hoarsely. "If I could just drag you inside me, maybe all this would stop."

She tried to pull away so she could see his face, but he held her fast. Disturbed by the almost frightening restraint she felt in him, she caressed his back, her voice soft. "What's the matter, Nick? It's as though you've been fighting yourself for days."

His breath was hot against her skin as he kissed her shoulder. "It's been one hell of a week, that's all."

Catching his head between her hands, she pulled away, forcing him to look at her. "Let's take Norm up on his offer. Jenny leaves for camp tomorrow, so we have seven days to ourselves. We can go out to his cabin and have some time alone."

He wouldn't meet her gaze. "No."

Feeling as though he were pulling back and she didn't even know why, Sydney applied pressure, her eyes pleading with him. "Please, Nick. I want some time alone with you."

His hand was shaking as he brushed back her hair and hooked it behind her ear. "I'd miss too much therapy."

She knew he was using that as an excuse, and suddenly it was imperative that they have that time, imperative that they were someplace where he couldn't call a cab and go home. "We can leave Thursday and come back Sunday. Four days. All I'm asking for is four days."

He finally looked at her, his eyes boring into her with a drilling intensity. "It's not a good idea," he said flatly. "Believe me."

Annoyance and fear made her react, and she pulled free of his hold, her chin set. "Not a good idea from your point of view, perhaps. I'm not asking for much, Nick. Just four days."

He stared at her for the longest time, then finally he spoke. "If that's how you feel about it," he said quietly, "then you've got your four days."

HE HAD SAID IT WASN'T a good idea, but she hadn't believed him. After two days, she realized he was right.

Sydney lay in bed, the gray light of early dawn filtering into the room as she listened to the breeze in the stand of spruce just outside her window.

As far as locations went, this one was picture perfect. Norm's log house was on the outskirts of a small tourist town an hour's drive from Calgary, and although it had all the amenities of urban living, it was secluded, tucked away in a heavily treed acreage that bordered the Bow River. But other than the pure, rugged beauty of the setting, the break from the city had not been what she had expected. Nick had been quiet and guarded yet oddly watchful, and she'd had the uncomfortable feeling he was waiting for some reaction from her.

There had been a constant undercurrent of strain, but last night had brought it to a head. They had gone for a walk along the bike path behind the cottage, and Sydney had taken a pocketful of peanuts for the squirrels. She had been on her knees, laughing at a particularly sassy fat one. Delighted with its antics, she had glanced up, expecting Nick to be amused. But he wasn't amused. He was watching her with black, smoldering eyes, tension like a force field around him. He stared at her for a moment, then he turned abruptly and headed for the cabin.

She had watched him go, knowing what she'd seen in his eyes was a grinding, unrelenting sexual frustration, and guilt washed through her with a debilitating force. She had pushed him, he had given in to please her, and now he was paying for it. She had felt cheap before in her life, but never quite so cheap as she did right then.

When she had finally returned to the cabin, Nick was in the other bedroom, the door closed, and she couldn't have felt worse if she'd been the one who had shot him.

Knowing she would never go back to sleep, Sydney got up, hugging the warmth of the old-fashioned flannel night-shirt around her. The early morning chill caressed her bare thighs, and she shivered as she quietly opened her door, preserving the silence.

Rounding the corner into the living area, she stopped, her insides flip-flopping when she saw Nick at the window overlooking the river. His arm braced against the frame, he stood unmoving, his profile uncompromising against the gray light of dawn. The only sign that he was aware of her was a tightening in his jaw.

Feeling very ill at ease, she wrapped her arms around herself, chilled from within. "Good morning."

He didn't look at her. "Good morning."

There was a rigid silence, and Sydney's stomach tightened into a hard knot. Collecting what little nerve she had, she forced herself to speak. "I'm sorry I was so insensitive, Nick. I should have never pushed the issue."

His voice was harsh, cutting and underscored with anger. "Just drop it, Sydney."

"But it's my fault and—"

"Yes it is," he interjected curtly, "but not in the way you think."

Shaken by his answer, she moved toward him. Nick shot her a quelling look, his tone icy quiet. "I said, drop it."

"Nick—"

Without giving her a chance to finish, he used his cane as a pivot and limped into the other bedroom. The slam of the door reverberated right through her.

She didn't know how long it took her to scrape up the courage to face him again, but the room was perceptibly lighter when she finally opened his door. He had showered and shaved, and he was standing in the bathroom doorway in a pair of old cutoffs, towel drying his hair.

He tossed the towel onto a chair and rammed his hands on his hips, his eyes glinting dangerously.

She met his gaze dead-on. "Do you want to go home?"

He stared at her. When he finally spoke, his voice was brittle. "How far are you going to push this, Syd? Don't you have enough sense to leave it alone?"

She raised her hands in a gesture of confusion. "I know what's bothering you—"

"Do you?" he said a little too softly as he moved toward her. "Do you really?"

"Yes, I—"

"No," he said in that same deadly quiet tone. "You don't."

She went to touch him and he caught her wrist, his grip like iron as he muttered through gritted teeth, "You have about ten seconds to clear out of here before all hell breaks loose."

"I can't do that, Nick," she whispered, her eyes suddenly brimming with tears. "I can't walk out and leave you like this."

The steely control held for another split second, then he closed his eyes, torment etched into every line of his face. "Just get out of here, Syd," he whispered raggedly. "Just go."

She touched the white lines around his mouth, and it was as if something shattered in him. Swearing hoarsely, he pulled her into his arms. It was instant, total contact, his mouth hot, wet and frantic on hers, their hips jammed together, and the fire that he had held banked for so long flamed instantly out of control.

As she moved into him, he groaned against her mouth, the agony of wanting her so intense there was no way out except through the flames. The only thing that registered was the instant she became aware of the hard, pulsating ridge beneath his zipper, and she tried to draw her mouth away. But Nick caught her head, holding it in a viselike grip as he went completely over the edge, his mouth moving in a frenzy of feeding against hers, driven by a hunger he could no longer control. Like a starving man, he sought the sustenance within, tremors coursing through him as she drew him deeper into her moistness, sucking the strength out of him.

A spasm shuddered through him when she forced her hands between them, and a low, agonized sound was wrenched from him as she undid the zipper and protectively cradled him, dragging the cutoffs down his hips with her other hand. Driven out of his mind from wanting her, Nick tore his mouth away, holding her against him as he pulled her down onto the bed.

Her senses spiraling and splintering, aware of nothing except his unleashed need, she moved beneath him, feeling his desperation, urging him into her. The muscles in his lower back bunched and he thrust forward, burying himself deep inside her, his whole body taut and urgent.

He twisted against her, frantically searching for the rhythm, and it was at that instant that his disabled body betrayed him. His muscles refused to respond as tremor after tremor slammed through him, leaving him helpless.

His arms locked around her in a convulsion of need, and he buried his face in her hair, his voice raw with agony. "Sydney. God, help me."

Dragged back from the heat of his passion by the desperation in his voice, Sydney fought for control. She realized what was wrong, that he was helpless against the delirium raging through him. Holding him with all the love and strength she had, she forced him onto his back, whispering to him as she straddled him, slowly sheathing the full, hard length of him deep inside her again. His body damp with sweat and painfully tensed, she withdrew, and Nick ground out her name. Caring about nothing but him, she murmured what she was going to do, then she covered his mouth with her own, his thrusting tongue setting the pace, her body giving him the cadence. Crushing her against him, a ragged groan was wrung from him as he shuddered violently, his heat pulsating into her. And Sydney held him with all the tenderness and compassion she had.

Nick hung on to her for a long time, as if there were nothing else solid in his reeling world. But as the morning sun lightened the room, there was a noticeable change in him. There were no gentling caresses. No soft murmurings. Sydney could feel him withdraw, and when he eased away from her, he wouldn't look at her. And once again, the past overlaid the present.

Rather than see his expression, she moved onto her back and rested her arm across her eyes, tears slipping down her temples into her hair. Something was wrong, very wrong, and she didn't know how to approach him. When the door closed softly behind him, she went to the bathroom and splashed cold water on her face, dread, uncertainty and an awful feeling of foreboding slithering through her. Drying her face, she avoided looking at herself in the mirror, and meticulously hanging up the towel, she left the room.

Nick was in one of the easy chairs by the fireplace, his head tipped against the rolled back, his profile cast in shadows.

Sydney sat on the hassock facing him, her hands clamped between her thighs, knowing that the confrontation they had avoided years ago, the one they had avoided up until now, was about to unfold. She forced herself to meet his gaze. "I take it we're back to square one."

"And why do you think that?"

She gave him a twisted smile. "I can guess what's going through your mind right now."

"Can you?"

She looked down at her hands, determined not to let him see how much he'd hurt her. "Why didn't you tell me?"

He didn't even pretend to misunderstand. "Where would it have gotten us if I had?" His tone took on a rough edge. "If I had told you weeks ago I'd had an erection, we would have played out this little scene then instead of now. That would have been the only difference."

Hurt by his tone, hurt by his rejection, she had a sudden need to hurt him back. "So, Nick. How was it? Did it bring back old memories? Did I completely disgust you?"

With the aid of his cane, he rose and moved away from her. Staring out the window, he rested his hand on his hip. "Don't start something you're not prepared to finish, Syd," he said, his tone underscored with a quiet warning.

She bolted to her feet, hurt, frightened and suddenly angry. "Well let's finish it, Nick. Let's quit playing games, shall we? Let's drag the whole seamy mess out into the open."

His voice was soft, but there was a hard edge to it. "You're pushing it, Sydney."

She slammed the footstool out of her way, her anger building as unnoticed tears spilled over. "So what does it matter? You've sat as judge and jury on me from day one. You're never going to forgive me no matter what I do, so what's the point? You wanted a woman who was sweet and innocent—I think the term for me is 'decidedly shopworn.' You wanted someone who was above reproach, someone as worthy as your mother was, but I hardly fit the bill, do I? You can never accept me for who I am!"

He turned to face her, meeting her gaze with a directness that went right through her. "Maybe," he said in the same soft, hard tone, "I could accept it if you could."

She stared at him, not believing that something like that could have come out of his mouth. "That's garbage. *I've* put it behind me. I've built a new life and made something of myself."

There was the first flicker of anger in his eyes as he leveled his finger at her. "You brought it into our goddamned bedroom every night. And you did it again today."

A fury like she'd never known was building in her, and her voice seethed with it. "I wasn't the one who walked out today. And I wasn't the one who used to smash things in fits of rage. How can you stand there and accuse me of something like that?"

"Because it's true."

Shaking from the force of her resentment and anger, she circled, her eyes blazing. "Don't dump the problem back on me, Nick. Are you going to stand there and tell me that you didn't go into a blind rage every time you thought about how many men I'd serviced? Are you going to try to deny that subconsciously you thought I got some kind of perverse pleasure out of doing what I did? Come on, Nick. For once in your life, have the guts to be honest!"

Grasping his cane, he came across the room toward her, her taunts goading him into a full-blown anger. "If we're leveling accusations here, let me get a few shots in. You refuse to face things, Sydney. You always have. You knew I was going to see Dr. Brown. The problem was mine, so I should be dealing with it. Fine! I can accept that. But there's one hell of a lot more to it than just me, lady. I tried to sort through all that goddamned garbage. I was never proud of how I acted. And I hated what I was doing to you, but at least I tried to work it through. You did bugger-all to put this relationship on solid ground."

Clenching her hand to keep from slapping him, she shouted, "What the hell was I supposed to do? Amputate my past? I can't change that! You can't alter the truth."

He stared at her, the muscles in his jaw twitching, a cold expression settling on his face. "Do you want the truth, Syd? Do you really want the truth? Or have you got the guts to face it?"

"You can't tell me anything I don't already know."

He came closer, his voice grating with an icy fury. "No? You think not? Well how about you try this on for size. Do you want to know what the absolute bottom line is to all this? It took some bloody grim soul-searching and too damned many sleepless nights to count to figure it out. I said you brought the problem into our bedroom every god-damned night, and that, lady, *is* the truth. And I'll tell you what the problem is, Sydney. What happened this morning is a damned good example. You used the word 'serviced.' Well, you serviced me in there. And you've been doing it ever since I met you.''

Her face wet with tears, she stared at him, an awful, cold, sick feeling twisting inside her.

Tipping his head back, Nick closed his eyes and exhaled sharply. When he looked at her again, he had managed to rein in some of his fury. ''You're not some concubine in a harem, Sydney. But subconsciously you think it's your duty to provide sexual satisfaction, regardless of how you feel.''

She backed away from him, her eyes wide with shock. She couldn't believe what he was saying.

He stared down at the floor, knowing he had lost it all, hoping he could salvage some of her pride. Inhaling heavily, he finally looked at her. ''We've both been at fault. But the biggest mistake we made was trying to stuff it all under the rug. I played games, you played games, but we didn't deal with it. But in working through all this, there are some things I've learned about you. You have a distorted view of sex, and I can only assume you were abused as a kid. But I don't even know that—we stuffed that under the rug, too.''

Clamping his hands on his hips, he braced his weight on his good leg as he tried to frame his thoughts. When he looked at her again, all the anger was gone. ''When I was lying awake night after night, I kept going back, trying to figure out what it was that kept bothering me. It came as quite a revelation when I realized there was not once I could ever remember when *you* verbalized your needs. It was as though you didn't count. You have never asked me to touch you, to do anything for your pleasure. You provided for mine this morning, but it would have never entered your head that you deserved the same consideration back. You're not just a vessel to service a man's appetites. But that's how

you think of yourself. I suspect you were brought up to believe that, that providing sex was your duty as a woman.

"It's not your duty, Syd. It's your right. There must have
been a dozen times during the past few weeks when you were
ready to climb the wall, but you would have felt cheap asking me to satisfy you. You gave me satisfaction this morning, and if you had just asked for the same loving back, I
would have been so goddamned happy. You told me once
that what mattered the most to you was knowing I wanted
you. But I want you whole, Sydney. You're a passionate,
responsive woman. You aren't just an object for my satisfaction."

Unable to level the final blow face-to-face, he moved to
the window and stared out, his voice weary. "My jealousy
and fits of rage were only a manifestation of the real problem. And the real problem has always been that, unconsciously, I've always felt I was nothing more than one of
your johns. The fact that you were a prostitute is not the issue. The fact that you continue to prostitute yourself is."

There was a chilling silence, then Nick heard Sydney leave
the room. A few minutes later the back door slammed, and
he closed his eyes, knowing it was the final exit.

TONY STOOD with his legs locked, his hands in his pockets,
a somber expression in his eyes as he stared at his ex-partner.
"So when did you start hitting the booze again?"

There was a hint of indifference in the way Nick swirled
the amber liquid in the glass. "I've got news for you, Martinelli. You are neither my wife nor my mother."

"If I was your mother, I'd paddle your ass. That stuff is
poison for you, especially now. And you know damned well
that Doc Robertson would skin you alive if he knew you
were pouring back the Scotch." Tony sprawled on the sofa
and put his feet up on the old wooden trunk Nick used as a
coffee table, then folded his arms across his chest. "So spill

it, Nick. Why are you sitting here looking like somebody died?"

Nick took another drink, then sidestepped the question. "So how was your trip?"

Tony shrugged. "A three-week course in high-tech electronic surveillance is hardly my idea of a good time. The Feds know how to put on a good show, though. And Toronto is a swinging city." He paused, assessing the situation. He decided to launch a frontal attack. "I stopped by Sydney's when I rolled into town last night. It got awful quiet when I asked where you were."

There was a caustic bite in Nick's tone. "I'm sure it did."

"So what happened?"

Nick shrugged. "I said some things I shouldn't have."

"She walked out on you?"

"Something like that."

Tony watched him. "You aren't going to be worth squat if you start drinking again, Nick," he said flatly. "You've got enough problems without loading your brain down with booze."

Nick rested his head against the back of the chair. "If you want to lecture, adopt a kid."

"Who needs a kid? I've got you. I stopped by rehab this morning. I thought we could go for coffee when you were finished. And Beth cornered me. You've missed a whack of sessions in the past three weeks, and she's having anxiety attacks over you. You're going to be back to needing two canes if you keep this up."

Nick didn't respond, and Tony stared at him. It didn't take a detective to see where Nick was headed unless he got turned around. "Can't you talk to her?"

Nick lifted his glass and downed a third of it. There was no reaction on his face at all. "No. I blew it big time."

"Do you want to tell me about it?"

Nick twisted the glass back and forth on the upholstered arm of the chair. He took another drink, his tone impassive. "I can't."

"You mean you won't."

Nick looked at him, his expression intractable. "It's between Syd and me."

Tony studied him, a keen, intuitive look in his eyes. "In other words, there's some deep, dark secret involved."

Nick drained the glass, then set it on the floor. "Are you working tonight?"

"No, and quit directing traffic. When was the last time you had something decent to eat?"

There was a faint gleam of humor in Nick's eyes. "Why don't you get married, Martinelli, and give me a break?"

Tony read the signals and backed off. He grinned as he stood up. "That's a hell of an idea. I think I'll go out and do exactly that." He dug his car keys out of the pocket of his jeans, his expression altering as he shifted the keys around the ring. "I'm sorry as hell about you and Sydney, Nick."

Nick glanced at him, then his gaze slid away. "So am I."

SYDNEY WAS FIGHTING the onset of another headache, and the amber figures on the computer screen wavered as she tried to focus. Taking off her glasses, she rubbed the bridge of her nose, then reached over and turned off the machine. She got up and closed the vertical blinds on the window, shutting out the midafternoon sun.

There was a light tap at the door, and Jenny poked her head in. "Hi. I'm here. Where's Marg?"

"She had to slip out to the bank. How was your day?"

"Great. I got a neat math teacher. I did like you said and told him I had a tutor, so he sent home a course outline." She grinned and made a face. "Now I know what I don't know."

There was a touch of humor in Sydney's eyes. "Some people go through their whole life not knowing what they don't know."

"Profound, Sydney. Really profound." The girl let go of the doorknob, her tone serious. "Is that basket on the corner of Marg's desk the stuff you want me to file?"

"Yes, please. And would you mind watering the plants?"

"Sure." The phone in the outer office rang, and Jenny turned. "I'll get it. Are you taking calls?"

"Just take a message. I've had about all the phone calls I can handle for one day."

"Gotcha."

Sydney watched her, a sudden tightness in her throat. There were good days and there were bad, but bit by bit, Jenny was putting her life together. Norm had started custody proceedings, and providing the natural mother didn't contest the suit, Sydney would be Jenny's legal guardian in a matter of weeks.

Then, Sydney thought with a wry smile, they could legally change her name to Foster. She had to admit, she'd suffered a niggling guilt over having aided and abetted in that fabrication. And it gave her a funny feeling when anyone referred to Jenny as Jenny Foster, but when she found out Cord was the stepfather's name, the justification far outweighed her guilt.

Closing the door, Sydney turned back to her desk, the dull ache behind her eyes intensifying. It was ironic. Jenny's life was coming together, and hers had fallen apart. That final scene with Nick had stripped away so many layers of scar tissue, raw flesh was laid bare. He had hurt her as he had never hurt her before, and he made her feel cheap and used. When she'd returned to the cabin and found him gone, she had shivered for an hour, relieved that she had been spared the humiliation of having to face him.

But what unnerved her more than anything was how exposed she felt. After she left the street, she had started con-

structing emotional barricades, dividing her new life from
the old. She had walled off the abused, exploited, manipu-
lated adolescent and had spent years turning herself into a
confident, polished businesswoman.

Nick's accusations had changed all that. He had stripped
away those protective layers, and she'd had to face that part
of herself that she had spent half her life pretending didn't
exist. But what hurt most of all was his accusation that she
had done nothing to put the relationship back together. And
that hurt because it was true.

She hadn't wanted to make public her history of prostitution, so she had used that as an excuse not to talk to Dr.
Brown; the truth was she didn't want to deal with the horror that had set her on that path in the first place. She had
used Nick's jealousy and rage as something to hide behind,
an excuse to remain silent. She had allowed him to assume
the full blame for the collapse of their relationship, when
she'd been just as much at fault.

But what had been the final, shattering stroke was his
brutal honesty about her sexuality. It was true; she didn't
think she was worthy of any consideration when it came to
that. If she was asked to call up a visual definition of inter-
course, it would be of her as an adolescent lying naked on a
bed in a pitch-black room, being commanded not to move,
not to speak, told that it was her duty as a daughter to provide for her father's male needs. And it sickened her to think
she had allowed that subverted image to taint what she and
Nick shared. He had stripped away all her defenses and uncovered her deepest shame, and she could never face him
because of that.

"Sydney, Tony's here."

Sydney didn't want to talk to Tony. She was so raw and
so emotionally naked she didn't want to talk to anybody.
She heaved a sigh and looked at Jenny. "Send him in."

There was a murmur of voices, and she heard Jenny
laugh, then Tony strolled into the office, a small gift-

wrapped package in his hand. "Hi, Sydney. How's it going?"

She forced a smile. "It's going. Have you recovered from your trip?"

He grinned. "Well, I got my suitcase unpacked, if that means anything." He handed her the gift. "I found this buried in the bottom with my dirty socks, and it has your name on it."

For the first time in days, Sydney experienced a twist of genuine amusement. "Do you always travel with dirty socks?"

He chuckled as he stretched out in one of the leather chairs. "It's an occupational hazard." He clasped his hands behind his head and nodded at the parcel. "I saw it in a pawn shop and I thought of you."

His thoughtfulness hit her hard. "That was really sweet of you."

He grinned again. "I thought so, too. Open it."

With unsteady fingers, Sydney unwrapped the gift and opened the box. Folding back the tissue packing, she lifted out an animal figurine. It was an alabaster unicorn about five inches high mounted on an ebony base, and it was evident from the workmanship that it was very old. The beast was a stallion challenging, its head arched in defiance, its nostrils flaring, and there was such an element of power and movement in the lunging form it seemed almost real. The workmanship was exquisite, capturing a raw physical strength, an untamed fury that brought the cool, white calcite to life. It made her think of Nick.

"It's beautiful, Tony."

Pleased by her response, Tony studied the sculpture. "I'm glad you like it. I thought it had a touch of class."

She set it on the polished wood surface of her desk, caressing the powerful lines. "Thank you so much."

"You're mighty welcome." He slouched farther down in the chair, his gaze sobering as he watched her. "Nick can be a jerk sometimes, but if it's any consolation, he's hurting like hell right now."

Sydney jerked her hand away from the alabaster form and turned, folding her arms tightly in front of her. An awful pain developed around her heart, and she drew her arms tighter in an attempt to ease it. Her voice was taut and hurting. "Don't, Tony. Please. I don't want to talk about it."

"I didn't think you would. I don't know what happened. All he told me was that he'd screwed up good and proper, that it was his fault." Tony levered himself out the chair and came over to her, stuffing his hands into his pockets as he solemnly studied her face. "He needs you, Sydney. I know Nick. He's got this strong Catholic conscience, and he's going to stay away from you because he's hurt you. And he can never forgive himself for that." He stared at the floor. "He's a hard man on himself."

She turned, her touch lingering as she rubbed her thumb along the arch on the unicorn's neck. Her voice was laced with pain. "He has nothing to feel guilty about. He was honest."

Tony chewed on his bottom lip, not sure of how much to say or how far to go. "I hope you can find it in yourself to forgive him, Sydney. Because he's never going to forgive himself. He's heading down a dead-end road right now, and if he doesn't get turned around, there won't be many pieces to pick up this time."

Sydney's head came up, her gaze riveting on his face. "What do you mean?"

Tony stared at her with unnerving directness. "Nick had a problem with booze a few years back. He beat it, and he's never touched the stuff since. He's back on it, and if he keeps it up, we may as well shoot him now and put him out of his misery."

The color drained from her face and Sydney shivered, his choice of phrasing chilling her to the bone.

"Sydney, I'm not laying a guilt trip on you. I care about the dumb bastard. But if it's over, it's over. I just wish there was some way you both could put it behind you so he could stop hating himself."

Sydney didn't answer. She couldn't. The pain was simply too intense. For her, the chasm was unbridgeable. There was too much self-disgust and shame in between. And she did what she did best; she shut it out.

But it was the phone call that night from Catherine Brown that made Sydney realize she was making the same mistake with Jenny that she had made with Nick; she was avoiding issues rather than talking about them, and Jenny had picked up all the wrong signals. The psychologist had contacted Sydney because she was concerned about the girl's acute agitation over Nick. Jen felt she was directly responsible for his prolonged absence, but when Dr. Brown tried to get her to talk about why she felt that way, she would become evasive and belligerent. The focus of her sessions had shifted drastically because of it, and Catherine wondered if there was a major problem between Nick and Jenny.

What upset Sydney more than anything was that she should have seen it coming. But she hadn't. And she was going to have to talk to the girl. She just didn't know how she was going to find the courage to do it.

The teenager was lying on her bed doing homework. She looked up when Sydney entered her room. "Hi. Did you ever read *To Kill a Mockingbird*?"

"Yes, I did."

"Neat story. I thought it would be boring, but it's not."

Sydney leaned against the door frame, her expression solemn as she studied the girl. The very real love she felt for her amazed her sometimes. She'd never thought she could feel that way about someone else's child.

She steeled herself for a confrontation. "That was Dr. Brown who called. She tells me you've been very preoccupied with Nick's and my breakup."

Jenny's expression lost its animation, and with a touch of rebellion, she focused on the book lying on the bed.

"The problem was between us, Jenny. It had nothing to do with you."

There was a lengthy silence, then Jenny closed the book with a snap and tossed it aside. "Come on, Sydney. Who are you kidding? If I hadn't come to live with you, he'd still be here."

Sydney couldn't honestly deny that. If Jenny hadn't come, Nick wouldn't have been forced to deal with his feelings, but the teenager couldn't assume responsibility for that. Sydney looked up at the ceiling, trying to will away the sudden blur of tears. If she hadn't been such a coward, none of this would have ever happened. She swallowed hard. "Nick left because I refuse to deal with certain issues. I keep hiding from things—pretending they don't exist. He forced me to see that, and he said some things that hurt me, and I left. It wasn't Nick who walked out. I did."

Jenny rolled over onto her back and stared at Sydney, her face set in a mutinous expression. "What kind of things?"

Sydney looked away. "Personal things."

"You mean sex, don't you?"

"Yes."

"And he made you feel like slime, didn't he?"

Exhaling heavily, Sydney met her gaze. "It's not what you think, Jen. I spent years pretending my adolescence didn't exist, that it was not a part of who I am today. But he made me realize that that part of my life still affects me as an adult."

Jenny stared at her, resentment snapping in her eyes. "Come on, Sydney. Quit defending him. He's got to be some kind of jerk. If he'd put it together like that, why isn't he here?"

With horrifying clarity, Sydney realized what was happening. Tony had assumed Nick was to blame, and so had Jenny. They had judged him guilty, and that was wrong. So terribly wrong. She had accused him of doing the same thing to her. Unable to handle that reality, she blindly left the teenager's room. She made it to her own room before her emotions completely overwhelmed her, and she heard nothing but the sounds of her own uncontrolled weeping.

She didn't hear the footsteps outside her door, she didn't hear them depart, and she never heard the sound of Jenny leaving the apartment.

CHAPTER FOURTEEN

NICK'S HAND SHOOK as he poured the bottle of Scotch down the kitchen sink, the smell of the amber liquid making his stomach clench. The evening breeze from the open window cooled his sweat-dampened skin as he waited for a spell of dizziness to pass before tossing the bottle into the garbage. He'd been on a suicide mission and it had taken a swift kick in the ass to make him realize it. That morning he had been unable to do an exercise that he had mastered weeks ago. Tony was right; if he didn't get his act together, he'd be back to using two canes in a matter of weeks. And that was too high a price to pay for numbness.

Turning on the tap, he splashed cold water on his face and rinsed out his mouth, disgusted with himself. He was such a weak-minded bastard. But he'd survive in spite of himself. Somehow, he'd learn to live without her. He braced his hands on the counter and closed his eyes, an overwhelming sense of loss swamping him. If only he'd hung on to his damned temper. If only he'd handled things differently. But he hadn't, and now he had nothing except a lifetime of emptiness.

Straightening, he let his breath go. He'd live. If he could get through the next forty years, he'd have it made.

A knock on his door punctured the silence, and he heaved an exasperated sigh. The last thing he needed right now was contact with another human being. Grasping his cane, he turned toward the entry, hoping whoever it was would get tired of waiting and leave before he got there. Steeling himself to be semicivil, he unlocked the door and opened it.

He didn't know who he expected to see there, but it certainly wasn't Jenny. She looked up at him, open contempt in her eyes. He was in no mood for contempt. He had more than enough of his own. "What do you want?"

She gave him a belligerent look. "What do you care?" She brushed past him, slinging her tote bag onto the chair, then turned to face him, her eyes filled with disgust. "I think you're an absolute jerk."

Nick almost smiled. At least the vote was unanimous. He shoved the door shut, ignoring her as he crossed the room. He needed this as much as he needed another hole in his head. Not having the strength or energy to do anything else, he stretched out on the sofa, his back braced against the wide arm. "So what's on your mind?"

She jammed her hands on her hips and glared at him, anger radiating from her. "Where do you get off, Nick? It must be nice to have such a high opinion of yourself that you can pass judgment on the rest of us slime."

Feeling another rush of dizziness from too little to eat and too much booze, he leaned his head back, fixing his gaze on the girl across the room. There was a hard edge to his voice. "You don't know what I think, Jenny. You think you do, but you don't."

"Who are you kidding? I'm not stupid. I know you think Sydney and I ended up on the streets for kicks. But that's not how it was. For your information, it wasn't fun and games out there."

"I spent twenty years on the force—I know what goes on out there."

"Is that so?"

"Yes, that's so. You accused me of passing judgments. It sounds to me like you're passing a few of your own."

She stared at him, some of the fight knocked out of her. She shoved her hands into the pockets of her jeans, but not before he saw how badly they were shaking. For several moments she didn't say anything, and when she started to speak, her voice was thick with unshed tears. "You might know the conditions, but you don't know what it feels like. No one does unless they've been there. On the street you have nothing, and you know it. Nobody cares if you live or die, and you know that, too. And it gets so bad you can't stand to look at yourself. And you keep hoping for a miracle, that somebody's going to come along who'll love you, really love you, somebody who'll take you away from all the filth, somebody who'll make you feel clean again. But deep down you know that's never going to happen. And there isn't a day goes by that you don't wish you were somebody else."

She looked at him with old, disillusioned eyes, tears slipping down her face. "You feel like a slab of meat. You pretend it's not happening to you when you're under some sweaty, grunting john who gets off because he likes making it with kids. You learn to shut it out, to pretend you aren't even there. But down deep, the awfulness never really goes away. You're just so revolted by what you're doing, you can't stand yourself. And your mind gets so messed up, but you don't know it's messed up because everything you live with is so sick and warped. You're brainwashed into believing you have no say over your own body, that it's just there to be used by anyone bigger and stronger than you are."

Nick had to look away from the emotional pain he saw in the girl's eyes. But what made his gut churn was knowing that it was victims like Jenny who carried the scars; scars that went soul-deep. It was the victims who were the ones who were handed out life sentences, not the abusers, not the bastards like her stepfather.

Silence hung between them like a thick pall. There was nothing he could say to change the facts, nothing he could say to ease the revulsion that Jenny, and hundreds like her, had lived through. It was a horror of endless dimensions.

Jenny's tense, quavering voice cut through the silence. "Did Sydney tell you about me?"

He forced himself to meet her gaze. "Yes."

"But she didn't tell you about herself, did she?"

His voice was very quiet. "No."

The trembling had hit her legs, and Jenny sat down in the chair, wiped her face, then clamped her hands between her thighs. "She's never told anyone. She told me because she knew I would never believe her when she said she understood."

His eyes fixed on her, Nick hesitated. He wasn't sure he could handle having his suspicions confirmed. There was a tightness in his gut when he finally spoke. "Was Sydney sexually abused as a kid?"

Jenny nodded. "Yes. It was her father, which makes it even worse."

This time the twist of nausea in Nick's stomach had nothing to do with booze. He waited for the feeling to pass, then he spoke, his voice gruff. "I'd like to know what she told you, Jenny."

She stared at him, caught between loyalty and candor, then took a deep breath and looked down. "She grew up in Winnipeg. Her father was a commodities broker, whatever that is, and he was on the Chamber of Commerce and a whole bunch of other things. They had a big house, lots of money—Sydney went to a private school and wore uniforms and everything. Her mother died when she was eleven, from a brain hemorrhage or something. That's when it started for her."

Closing his eyes, Nick clenched his jaw. He didn't know if he had the fortitude to hear the rest. "Go on."

"That's all I know." There was a long pause before Jenny spoke again, her voice uneven. "She said she never told anybody because she knew they wouldn't believe her."

Twenty-six years ago—who would have believed her? Especially coming from a background like that. If she had told him fifteen years ago, he probably wouldn't have believed her, either.

"Nick?"

His face haggard, Nick looked at her, catching the hesitancy in her tone. He waited for her to speak.

She huddled on the edge of the chair, staring down at the floor, her hands still jammed between her thighs. "What really happened between you and Sydney?"

He read between the lines of her hesitancy. "It had nothing to do with you, Jenny. It was strictly between Syd and myself."

There was an undertone of remorse in her voice. "But if it hadn't been for me, it wouldn't have happened."

Releasing his breath on a sigh, he rested his head against the back of the sofa. "It would've happened, Jen. It had happened before. And it was bound to happen again."

She didn't say anything for a moment, then she spoke, her voice taut with anxiety. "Are you ever coming back?"

"I don't think so."

She lifted her head, her eyes shimmering. "Why not?"

"Because she doesn't want to see me."

"But she does. She's so unhappy and she looks awful."

He looked at her, a flicker of pain darkening his eyes. "But she doesn't want to see me. She doesn't want to face a lot of things, Jenny, and I'm one. You've decided to face your past, to deal with it, but Sydney won't. And until she does, nothing's going to change."

She wiped her face, her eyes filled with misery. "I feel so stupid."

Nick's gaze softened. "Why?"

"Because I thought it was your fault that she was so miserable. And I wanted to blame somebody. I blamed myself. I thought it was because of me that you were staying away."

He studied her, a glint of compassion in his eyes. "Why don't you tell me what's really bothering you?"

More tears spilled over and she wiped them away, then clamped her hands between her thighs again. "I was really jealous of you at first. I wished you'd fall in the river. I didn't like it when Sydney was with you."

The corner of Nick's mouth twitched, and there was a trace of humor in his eyes. "You might have done everyone a favor if you had shoved me in."

That got a shaky smile out of her, but her eyes overflowed again. "Then you got me out of that mess at school, and I felt really guilty about being so selfish."

"You're not selfish, Jenny. Just mixed-up. And that's no big crime. Being mixed-up is part of growing up."

As though she hadn't heard him, she hunched forward, her voice uneven as she whispered, "Then Sydney told me you said I should have a kitten, and Malcolm said it was your idea that I go live with her. And I started thinking maybe we could be like a real family."

A lump lodged in Nick's throat, and he had to look away. A real family. The sudden contraction of pain was so deep and hard and biting he couldn't see. The losses kept mounting.

Darkness settled more heavily into the room, and Nick finally stirred. Feeling almost too drained to move, he reached out and turned on the table lamp at the end of the sofa. He studied the girl across the room. "I don't want you blaming yourself, Jenny," he said quietly. "What went wrong between Sydney and me started a long time ago— before you were even born."

She heaved a tired sigh and lifted her head. "Then why do I feel so awful?"

He managed a wry half smile. "Teenagers are supposed to feel awful. It's their lot in life."

Her smile was fleeting. "Yeah, well."

Nick folded his arms across his chest and stared at her. "Does Sydney know you're here?"

"No."

He glanced at his watch. "Then I'd better call a cab and get you home. It's getting late."

Looking far too world-weary for her age, she sighed again. "I can take a bus."

Nick grasped his cane and got to his feet. "You, young lady, are taking a cab."

It wasn't until the taxi arrived and the teenager was at the door that Nick faced the absolute finality of what her leaving meant. He met her gaze, his eyes steady. "Take good care of her, Jen. She's really going to need you now."

She swallowed hard. "I know." Jenny looked away, her eyes suddenly shimmering with tears. "I wish you'd come back."

Bracing his arms on the doorjamb, Nick stared down the corridor, his voice rough. "I can't."

SYDNEY STOOD IN THE STUDY, trying to control the desperation that was building in her. It was ten-thirty and Jenny was gone. She closed her eyes, forcing herself to think rationally. It had been an hour since she had discovered Jen wasn't in her room. She wasn't with Malcolm, she wasn't at Blairmore House. She didn't have a clue where she was.

Clear reason told her Jen could take care of herself. She was streetwise and knew how to survive. But every time Sydney tried to convince herself the girl was all right, the recollection of that concrete cave beneath the bridge cropped up in her mind, and her anxiety rose.

She should never have tried to explain to Jenny about Nick. Not when she was feeling the way she was. She couldn't even think about him without coming apart inside.

She glanced at her watch for the hundredth time. She would give Jenny another half hour, then she would phone Tony. How she was going to get through another half hour without coming unglued was something else altogether.

Something soft and warm brushed her ankles, and Sydney looked down, a ghost of a smile appearing as she picked up the kitten. She nestled it on her shoulder, her anxiety easing just a little. The cat was still here, and that was a sure sign Jenny would be back.

Pressing her cheek against the comforting warmth, Sydney stroked the silky fur. "Where is she, Lint? I don't even know where to begin looking for her this time."

She crossed the living room and went out onto the balcony to check the street below. Maybe Jen had gone for a walk along the bike path by the river. Maybe she was sitting huddled in the shadows somewhere, trying to work things out. Holding the kitten with a maternal need, Sydney paced the living room, the hands on her watch marking out the agonizing seconds.

It was exactly quarter to eleven when she finally heard a key in the lock. Letting the kitten jump from her arms, she started toward the sound, her heart in her throat.

She had just reached the hall when Jenny came through the door. The teenager glanced at her, her expression shuttered as she closed the door. She swung her tote bag to the floor, then looked at Sydney. There was an undercurrent of defiance in her voice. "Aren't you going to ask me where I was?"

Sydney was so relieved to see her she felt light-headed. Knowing she was on shaky ground as far as Jenny was concerned, she kept her tone even. "I was hoping you'd tell me."

Jenny folded her arms in front of her and tipped her head to one side, her chin set, a look of unmitigated determination in her eyes. Sydney got a funny feeling when she recognized the stance; it was her own, one that she adopted when she was annoyed.

Jenny's chin came up a notch. "I went to see Nick."

Sydney stared at her, shock driving the remaining color out of her face. "You did what?"

Jenny stared back at her. "I went to see Nick."

"What for?"

The teenager shifted her weight onto one hip, her tone accusing. "I thought he was to blame for everything. I thought it was all his fault."

Sydney abruptly turned away. Scooping up the kitten, Jenny followed her into the darkened living room. "But it's not just his fault, is it, Sydney?"

Sydney stood at the open patio door, her arms clutched in front of her. The last of her barriers was being attacked and fear moved in, and she remembered the first time her father had come to her, and afterward she had huddled in the closet in a state of shock, crying for her dead mother.

"I thought I wanted to be like you," came a tear-filled voice from behind her. "But I don't, Sydney. You're afraid to talk about things. It's like being scared of the dark when you're little—you think something awful is hiding in there. But that's not really why you're scared. You're scared because you know you're all alone. Do you really want to spend the rest of your life alone in the dark, Sydney? Or do you want to reach out and find somebody there?"

The words were like a razor, shredding the last veil obscuring the truth. And Sydney closed her eyes, realizing how badly she had misplayed her life. She had huddled in the dark, afraid of the shadows, afraid to reach out for fear of what she might find. But if she had reached out, Nick would have been there. There would have been anger and pain and times when she'd have been shattered by the revulsion of what had happened to her. But he would never have abandoned her. He would have been her warmth, her strength, her safe haven. All she would have had to do was reach out. But she hadn't; she had shut him out, too.

NICK PAUSED INSIDE the entryway of his apartment building, so damned exhausted he could barely stand up. He fished the keys out of his pocket, trying to ignore the pain in his leg. He knew he was going to regret the bout of self-punishment he'd put himself through at therapy. But if he had a dollar for every regret he had, especially where Sydney was concerned, he'd need a damned vault to keep them in.

And the regrets had come thick and fast after Jenny's visit the night before. He had lain awake most of the night, thinking about Sydney and the abuse that had shaped her life and the scars she had suffered because of it. And of all the things he regretted, her burden of shame was number one. She should never have had to carry it alone.

Grasping his cane, Nick made his way down the hallway to his apartment, his limp more pronounced than usual. He was going to pay dearly for overworking his leg. But it wasn't the pain that had his insides balled up in a wad. It was images of Sydney as a terrified eleven-year-old that tore him to shreds. And knowing he had hurt her made it even worse. He had created an unbridgeable chasm. He couldn't go to her, and she wouldn't come to him. That left him with an empty ache that was eating him up inside.

Ignoring the muscle spasms, Nick rested his cane against his thigh as he unlocked his apartment door, dreading the afternoon. He had nothing to do but think.

The hum of the refrigerator was the only sound that permeated the silence of his apartment. Nick closed the door and dropped his gym bag onto the floor, so damned drained he could barely drag one foot behind the other.

Just as he reached the bedroom door, he sensed a presence, and his gut twisted into a hard ball of recognition. He closed his eyes, the frantic pounding in his chest so intense it knocked the wind out of him, and he tried to argue away the sensation. It couldn't be. She would never come to him.

But she had.

She was standing at the window, her pale, drawn face etched with the kind of uncertainty that bordered on fear.

Nick stared at her, every muscle in his body instinctively tensing.

"Hello, Nick."

The clamor beneath his ribs was so paralyzing he couldn't even answer her. Feeling as though he had just been blindsided, he crossed to the bed, needing something more substantial than his cane to support him. Her unexpected presence had shaken him as nothing else ever had, and he didn't know what in hell to make of it. He grasped the exercise frame above the bed, then looked at her, his face so tense it felt like granite.

He could tell she had been crying, and there was such anguish in her eyes it made him wince. She opened her mouth to speak, but a low sob escaped and she looked away, her hand trembling as she quickly wiped away the tears. Compassion crippled him as he watched her struggle, wanting to go to her so damned bad it was killing him, afraid if he made a move she would leave. He waited, tension mounting until he felt as if he would come apart.

She hauled in a shaky breath and met his gaze, tears slipping relentlessly down her face. "Nick, if I—" Her voice broke on a jagged sob, and she turned away, struggling for composure, struggling for the words. She took another deep breath and looked at him, her eyes swimming with anguish. "If I made an appointment with Dr. Brown, would you come with me?"

Emotion slammed into him and he took a step toward her, his voice so choked he could barely get the words out. "Come here, Sydney." He reached for her, his control shattering as she came into his arms. Burying his face in her neck, he crushed her against him, his voice breaking as he whispered hoarsely, "Yes. God, yes. Whenever you want."

She clung to him, her body racked with violent weeping, and Nick closed his eyes in a grimace of pain, absorbing her anguish, finding relief for his own. She had come to him. That was all that mattered. She was back.

Sydney hung on to him as she finally let go of all the guilt, the shame, the fear she had kept locked up inside her for so long. Wanting to give her all the solace he could, Nick caught her around the hips and drew her even closer into his embrace.

But the instant their bodies fully connected, she caught fire in his arms. It was as though her emotional rawness freed a desperate need, and a low, tormented sound was wrung from her. Pulling her head free of his hold, she found his mouth, her kiss hot, deep and desperate, and Nick's response was electric. His control shot by the feel of her hips against his, he groaned her name and locked his arms around her, desire like a flash fire in him.

Feeling as though his legs were going to cave in beneath him, he dragged his mouth away, his breathing labored. "Syd—Lord. I have to lie down."

With a low sound of desperation, she tightened her hold on him, her voice breaking with urgency. "No. Don't let go. Hold me, Nick. Please."

Realizing how absolutely defenseless she was, his protective instincts took over. With his heart pounding erratically, Nick tightened his arms around her, his voice husky with tenderness. "I will, sweetheart. I will." He never knew where he found the strength to do it, but somehow he was able to pull her down onto the bed with him, his hold on her never slackening.

She was trembling, shaken and helpless, tears streaming down her face, and he molded her against him, trying to soothe her. But Sydney didn't want soothing. She wanted a fire storm. Her nails bit into his back, and she clutched him to her, her need consuming her. "Love me," she sobbed out. "Please love me."

Nick closed his eyes and exhaled sharply, aware of what she was asking, joy and relief and anticipation surging through him. She'd asked him to love her. And he would, until she was so high on wanting she wouldn't be able to think about anything else. Choked with emotion, he whispered her name and pulled her under him.

His fingers tangled in her hair as he grasped her face and slanted his mouth across hers. For an instant she was immobilized, then suddenly she came alive. Dragging her arms free, she slid her hands up his back, urging him closer with frantic desperation. Her mouth slackened beneath his, her response fueling a fever in him. Like a starving man, he sought the sustenance within, tremors coursing through him as her hot, liquid kiss pulled him deeper and deeper into the delirium of wanting her. The taste of her, the softness of her breasts against his chest, the feel of their hot bodies fused together ignited an escalating hunger in him, and Nick was launched into a fire from which there was only one escape.

But as she moved beneath him, a sliver of rationality penetrated his fevered mind, and he realized what he was doing. She had asked. She had given him that trust. Now he had to give it back. This time was for her, and her alone.

Ignoring the demands of his own body, he focused on her. She was past asking, past speaking, raw with sensation, and he took her mouth again, giving her everything he had to give. With infinite care he loosened the waistband of her slacks and undid her blouse, then he closed his eyes, losing himself in the feel of her skin beneath his touch. And he loved her with his mouth, with his hands, with every caress, carrying her higher and higher until she cried out, her body arching against the pressure of his hand, convulsions shuddering through her with a devastating force.

Experiencing a rending emotional release of his own, Nick gathered her against him, heedless of the throbbing ache in his groin.

Swallowing hard, he smoothed her hair back from er face, then kissed her softly, tenderness filling him. He loved her; he had never stopped. But now his love was unconditional, and he felt as though something dark and heavy had been lifted from him.

Trying to ease the awful tightness in his chest, he cupped her face and looked down at her. Her eyes were swimming with tears, but the anguish was gone, replaced by a look that made his throat ache even more. He brushed his thumb against her wet lashes, his mouth lifting with the gentlest of smiles. "God—how I love you."

She tried to answer him, but her mouth trembled and the tears spilled over. He kissed her again, then gently tucked her head against his neck, his voice tender. "Shh, sweetheart. Just let me hold you."

A soft sob escaped as she moved deeper into his embrace, her arms tightening around his neck. "Nick, I'm so scared."

"Don't be. There's nothing you can ever tell me that's going to change how I feel. Nothing. We'll deal with it together."

He could feel her fighting the tears, and he stroked her back, trying to ease the tension in her. "Don't, love. You're exhausted and you've had about all you can take today. And we've got the rest of our lives to talk."

"I need you so much."

Knowing what she needed to hear, he caressed her jaw with his knuckles. "I know you do," he said softly. He kissed her eyes, then cuddled her firmly against him. She needed gentle comforting now, and he was more than content to give it to her. He knew she loved him. And by deciding to face her past, she showed how very much.

She stirred and tried to lift her head.

He restrained her. "Shh, Syd. Just close your eyes and relax. Let me enjoy holding you. We've got all the time in the world."

Nick slowly rubbed her back, whispering soft, soothing words against her hair as he maintained the tranquilizing pressure. He needed this time, too, time to feel protective, to savor the pleasure of having her safe in his arms.

He felt her finally relax a few moments later, her breathing deep and even. A wry smile appeared. He hadn't expected to sedate her quite that much. He brushed the top of her head with a light kiss, then slipped his arm around her waist. For some reason, having her asleep in his arms made him feel even more protective.

The scent from her hair encompassed him, and he tried to ignore the unsatisfied ache from wanting her. He could wait. He wanted to give her time to catch her balance, to be confident enough to want their lovemaking for herself, not just to provide gratification for him. A glint of amusement appeared in his eyes. He just hoped like hell his endurance held out.

The rays of sunlight streaming in the window slowly moved across the bedroom as Nick continued to hold her, a deep sense of contentment building in him. For the first time since she'd come back into his life, he considered a future with her. And he remembered Jenny's comment about them being a real family. He liked the idea.

He sighed and kissed Sydney's head very lightly, then glanced at the clock. Two hours. He had been holding her for two hours. It seemed like a matter of minutes. He shifted, a painful cramp shooting up the back of his leg. He flexed his foot, trying to ease it, but he could tell it was going to get worse if he didn't walk it out. Watching closely for any sign of her waking, he slowly withdrew his arm, then edged away from her and reached for his cane. The muscles in his calf knotted painfully as he put his full weight on the leg, and he swore under his breath. Served him right for being such a stupid bastard.

He glanced back at the bed. The last thing he wanted was for her to wake up alone, but neither did he want to disturb her. He opted for a trip to the kitchen to leave a message for Jenny.

He was on his way back to the bedroom when he noticed a plastic bag from a convenience store sitting just inside the apartment door. The only ones who had keys were Tony and Sydney, and one body was certainly accounted for. He wasn't so sure about the other. He picked up the bag and opened it. Inside was a can of apple juice and a package of not very fresh looking doughnuts. There was also a note written on a brown paper bag.

Nick,
I stopped by to harass you, but damned if there wasn't a white Mercedes parked in the back parking lot. Being the hotshot detective I am, I put two and two together and came up with four. (I *won't* be a happy camper if I find out I screwed up on my math.) Anyway, I won't set you on the road to perdition by supplying you with champagne, and I can't afford caviar. But the occasion called for something. So eat, drink and be merry. Don't get crumbs in the bed, and I'll see you in church. I'll be the guy standing on your right with a pink carnation.

T.

Nick found it a little hard to swallow. There had been too many times to count when Tony had been there, right beside him. Affected more than he liked to admit, he dropped the note back into the bag and turned toward the bedroom. At least, he thought wryly, it wasn't a cold double-cheese pizza and two warm colas.

Entering the bedroom, he set the bag on the bedside table, then glanced down at the sleeping woman. There was something about her that aroused fiercely protective instincts in him. Her tousled hair, her parted lips, the bruised look around her eyes, the absolute vulnerability about how she was lying. He knew she was facing a hell of an ordeal, but even if he had to crawl, he was going to be beside her every step of the way. And God willing, she'd eventually learn how to forgive herself.

Loving her so much and needing to touch her in the worst way, he gently brushed back a few wisps of hair clinging to her cheek. Lord, she was everything to him. Whether she realized it or not, she was the sum total of the rest of his life.

She sighed and rolled onto her back, her unbuttoned blouse falling open, exposing the swell of her breasts. And the desire he had denied earlier instantly knotted in his gut. They had been so careful to maintain the balance that he hadn't seen her in anything more revealing than a pair of silk pajamas. And it was all he could do to keep from brushing the fabric back even more. He wanted her naked in his bed, he wanted her hot and desperate under him, but most of all, he wanted to give her time. Clamping down the pulsating heaviness that settled thickly in his groin, he tenderly caressed her cheek with the back of his hand. Sighing again, she turned her face toward the warmth of his touch, then her eyes fluttered open.

She gave him a drowsy smile, covering his hand with hers. "Hi."

He leaned over and kissed her forehead. "Hi, yourself."

With the languid movements of someone just waking, she slipped her hand up his neck. "How come you're up?"

He had no intention of telling her about his leg. "I left a message for Jenny with Marg."

She kissed his jaw, the warmth of her breath feathering along his skin like a caress, and Nick struggled against his instant response. "What time is it?" she asked.

Nick's voice was unnaturally husky. "A little after three."

She moved like a cat wanting to be stroked as she pulled his head down and murmured against his ear, "Come back to bed."

Nick closed his eyes, knowing he should resist, knowing he couldn't. Letting his cane slide to the floor, he slipped his arm under her shoulders and stretched out beside her. Before he could gather her against him, Sydney smoothed her hand up his thigh, and Nick stopped breathing altogether, every muscle in his body tensing as the heel of her hand brushed the hard ridge beneath his fly. Sydney's hand hesitated and she drew in a deep breath. "You've been holding out on me, Nick."

He covered her hand with his own, holding it still, his flesh so sensitized he felt as if he were on fire. "Sydney, it's okay—"

She shifted her hand beneath his and caressed him, sending a shudder coursing through him. "Shut up, Nick."

The way she said it wrung a shaky laugh out of him, and he rolled onto his side, pulling her against him. "God, you've got a mouth on you."

She rose up on one elbow, her lips brushing his. "Yes, and I intend on using it."

He exhaled sharply to keep from groaning. "Syd—I don't want you doing this for me."

She continued to brush her mouth slowly back and forth across his, her hand cupping his chin. "I want it all, Nick," she whispered unevenly. "I want to spend the next hour in this bed with you." She drew her mouth along his jaw, her tongue leaving a moist trail on his skin, then she kissed his ear, the warmth of her breath sensitizing him even more. "I want you to make love to me until I can't think anymore. I want you to..."

By the time she finished telling him what she wanted him to do to her and what she wanted to do to him, Nick was so far gone a whole army could have marched into the bedroom and he wouldn't have noticed. Pulling her under him, he wedged his thigh between hers, a sound somewhere between a groan and a laugh coming from deep in his chest as he found her mouth. "Shut up, woman," he murmured, moistening her lips with his tongue, "and put some effort into this kiss, will you?"

IT WAS MUCH, MUCH LATER when Nick finally came back down. He was lying with his arms around her, the weight of her body on top of him the only thing that was holding him together. It had been wild and beautiful and so damned intense. He had gone to pieces at the end, and she'd had to take over the way she had before, but this time it didn't matter. This time she had gone over the edge with him, and she hadn't held back. Not once had she held back.

Letting his breath go on a contented sigh, he caressed her bare back, loving the feel of her on him, loving the erotic intimacy of still being inside her. He could spend the next twenty years like this.

Realizing she was even more drained than he was, he shifted his head and kissed the side of her face. "Are you okay?" he asked.

He felt her smile against his neck. "I may never walk again."

He grinned and rested his head against hers. "Well, don't expect me to carry you."

"You already did. To unbelievable highs—and so many times I lost count."

Her words touched him, and he tightened his arm around her, his hand tangled in her hair as he cradled her head closer against him. "I love you, Syd."

And she gave back to him what he wanted to hear. "I know you do."

Neither of them spoke for the next several minutes, then Sydney raised her head, a hint of hesitancy in her eyes. "About seeing Dr. Brown—would you consider moving in with me for a while?"

He smiled up at her with a wealth of tenderness. "I hate to be the one to tell you this, but husbands and wives usually do live together."

She stared at him, then she swallowed hard. "Nick, you don't have to—"

He pressed his thumb against her mouth. "Oh, yes I do. I won't settle for anything less." He smoothed her hair behind her ear, his touch gentle and lingering. "I know you're uncertain, Syd. But believe me, I've put it all behind me. Now we have to get it behind you, and I'm going to be there, through every damned nightmare. We're going to face this together, and I'll stick to you like glue if you want me to."

Tears welled up in her eyes, and her mouth started to tremble. Nick wiped them away and grinned up at her. "And I'll make you a deal. I'll do your cost estimates if you promise to do up all my damned buttons."

She gave him a shaky laugh. "It's a deal."

He drew her head down and kissed her. "And just so you know it's official, Tony left us an engagement present."

Sydney lifted her head and looked down at him. "When?"

A smoky gleam appeared in his eyes as he slowly caressed her bottom lip. "Sometime this afternoon."

That jarred her out of her tears, and she stared at him, then a blush crept up her cheeks and she closed her eyes. "Oh, no."

Nick grinned. "What's the matter, Syd? Does that shake you up a little?"

She let out an embarrassed groan and rolled off him. "I'll kill him."

Nick shifted so he was lying on his side, his head propped on his hand. "It's in the bag on the table."

Sydney gave him a dubious look, then pulled the sheet around her. His eyes softened as he watched her. Before, he had thought that she was very reserved about letting him see her naked, but now he realized it was because she was subconsciously ashamed of her body. And that was something else he was damned well going to change.

His eyes glinting with amusement, he waited for her to open the bag. She frowned and glanced back at him. "Doughnuts and a can of apple juice?"

Nick reached out and straightened the sheet across her back. "There's a note inside." He watched her read it, expecting to see a smile appear. But when she looked at him, her eyes were shimmering with tears again. He caught her and pulled her back down into his embrace. "Don't cry, Syd. He's probably sitting at Pete's Pizza right now, smug as hell."

She smiled at him through her tears and touched his mouth with unsteady fingers. "We're really going to make it this time, aren't we?"

He smoothed his hand along her jaw, framing her face with infinite gentleness as he grazed her lips with his. "Yes," he said with husky assurance, "we are." He tightened his arms around her as he deepened the kiss, wanting to lose himself in her, wanting her to get lost in him. The shadows could no longer haunt them. They had passed through streets of fire. And they had a lifetime beyond.

dressed. And he was so damned proud of her. His lady had come a long way.

It had been rough for her in the beginning, when she first started going to Dr. Brown. There had been countless nights when she had wept in his arms, times when she was so moody she wasn't fit to be around, but with the psychologist's help, she had crossed some major bridges. She was healing. Slowly but surely she was healing.

And then there was sweet Jenny. The hard edges were gone, her confidence was up, and she was sailing into life with the zest of a kid who had just been turned loose in a games arcade with a pocketful of quarters. She was a breath of fresh air. But what was so special about her was how damned protective she was about Syd, especially when Syd hit the down times. Jenny would fight with her, but when the chips were down, the kid was like a rock. And as young as she was, she faced things dead-on, and she made Sydney face them, too.

He watched her play the board, amusement glinting in his eyes. And she had a mind like a steel trap. He could tell by the look on Malcolm's face that she had totally screwed up his next move with a complicated shuffle of the numbered tiles.

Major Henderson's voice broke through his musings. "Our Jenny is something, isn't she?"

Nick met the older woman's gaze. "She keeps us on our toes, that's for sure."

The major's eyes twinkled as she nodded knowingly. "I'm sure she does." She adjusted her knitting on the needle, then looked at Nick again. "Sydney started to tell me something in the kitchen, but Jenny came in so she wasn't able to finish. Just what did she tell everyone at school about you?"

Nick grinned again, his eyes gleaming with recollection. "We didn't find out about that until last week. We went to a parent-teacher interview at the school, and one teacher

EPILOGUE

THE FRAGRANCE of an April Sunday wafted in through the open patio door, the air flavored with sunshine and damp earth, layered with a taste of dust from a long winter.

Nick sat slouched on the sofa facing the balcony, his fingers laced loosely across his chest, humor ripe in his eyes as he watched the four people on the floor argue their way through a game of tile rummy. He grinned to himself. He felt like a benevolent uncle.

It was a year since Sydney had come back into his life, a year of painful discovery, of checks and balances, a year of so many ups and downs he had lost track of them all. But in spite of everything, he was happier than he'd ever thought possible.

He and Sydney had been married for seven months now, Jenny's adoption had been finalized two weeks ago, and little by little, he was getting more involved in Sydney's business and she was getting less. And through it all they were knitting together as a family unit. It was as though his existence had been a scattered jigsaw, and the pieces had finally been assembled into a whole. And it felt damned good. In fact, he couldn't believe how damned good.

His expression softened as he watched Tony ruffle his wife's hair and Sydney retaliate with a light shove. He couldn't believe how much she'd changed. A year ago that kind of casual contact would have never happened. She was so much more at ease with herself, and it showed—in the way she talked, the way she acted, and even the way she acted really flustered. We didn't know what was going on, so we quizzed Jen about it later. As it turned out, he'd made a big production out of her missing class the day we got married. He assumed she'd cut classes and he was in a lather about it. She told him she'd been absent because her mother and father had got married. She didn't explain the situation, just left it at that.''

Major Henderson chuckled. ''Good for Jenny.''

Nick rested his head back against the sofa, watching his adopted daughter with warm affection. ''She does keep life interesting. She had a couple of her friends over last night, and we heard one of the girls ask her how come she called us Sydney and Nick. Jenny lifted her chin and gave her that leveling look she's perfected. She told her not to be ridiculous—could she imagine anyone calling us Mommy and Daddy? Sydney had to fight so hard to keep from laughing I thought she was going to blow a valve.''

The major smiled, her voice taking on a gentle, understanding tone. ''Having a family is so important to her. She told me her school counselor made the comment that she really looked like her mother, but she certainly had her father's eyes. It really meant a lot to her that the physical similarity was there. I suppose it makes her feel more a part of you both.''

Nick's voice was filled with emotion. ''Well, she's pretty damned special to us, I can tell you. Having a kid to think about gives your life a different perspective.''

''And Sydney is so happy.''

''Yes, she is.''

There was a howl from the floor as Jenny went out, and Malcolm and Tony pelted her with tiles. She covered her head with her arms, laughing as she ducked the flying pieces. ''Jeez, you guys are rotten losers.''

Tony gave her a hard push and rolled her over. ''You must have cheated, brat. Nobody can win three games in a row without cheating.''

Jenny grinned impishly as she sat back up. "Hey, I'm just a superior player, that's all. And it serves you right for sitting on both jokers."

Sydney got up and left the three of them on the floor bickering, her eyes sparkling with laughter as she gave Nick a little grimace. "Now that war has broken out, I think it's a strategic time for me to check the roast."

Major Henderson put her knitting down and stood up. "I'll do it for you, dear. I was going to put the kettle on for a cup of tea, anyway."

Sydney paused in front of Nick. Her tone was soft and sensual as she braced her arm on the back of the sofa, then leaned over and gave him a light kiss. "You're looking very smug, Mr. Novak."

He grinned as he caught her by the back of the neck, holding her head down as he kissed her back. "Do you have any idea how sexy you look right now, Mrs. Novak?" he murmured against her mouth.

He felt her shiver, and he closed his eyes. Sliding his hand up the back of her head, he deepened the kiss, the taste of her mouth doing unbelievable things to his pulse rate. Sydney went along for a moment, then she took a deep breath and eased away. There was an edge of humor in her voice as she kissed the corner of his mouth. "You're as bad as your daughter. You don't play fair, either."

"You started it."

With a low laugh, Sydney rested her forehead against his. "This had better not be a teaser, Nick."

Nick tightened his hold on her head, his tone gruff. "Rest assured, it is not a teaser."

Taking another deep breath, she pulled free from his hold. "I think," she said unsteadily, "it would be a very good idea if I did go check the roast."

Reluctantly he let her go, trying to suppress the fevered feelings pumping through him. Seven months and he still hadn't had enough of her. But he'd just have to sit on it until later. When everyone was gone and they were alone in their bedroom—then they could finish what she'd started. All he had to do was keep a lid on it until then. *All.* Hell, who was he kidding? By then he would be practically incoherent.

IT WAS NEARLY MIDNIGHT when Sydney finally came into the bedroom. Nick was already in bed, lying with one arm under his head and the other draped across his chest. He watched her as she went into the bathroom, every nerve in his body primed for her. He hoped like hell she didn't take all night in there.

He smiled to himself. There had been changes for him, too, changes in his physical condition. He used the cane less and less, and his concentration and coordination were much better. His left hand had improved to the point where he was almost able to type, and the strength in his left arm had increased dramatically. There was, however, still a problem with his impotency. It was improving, but a full arousal was still unpredictable and erratic. The unpredictability, he admitted ruefully, added a certain edge of anticipation to their love life. And as Sydney had put it, tongue in cheek, they'd simply make the most of it when the occasion arose.

Nick's attention riveted on her the moment she came out of the bathroom, and his heart started pumping in a thick, heavy beat. She had taken to wearing his old shirts to bed at night, and there was something decidedly erotic about the starched, tailored look and her long, long legs.

He waited until she was at the side of the bed before he spoke, his voice low and commanding. "Lose the shirt, Syd."

She looked at him, her movements arrested, then a hint of mischief glinted in her eyes. "No."

He watched her, his gaze hooded and smoldering. "If you don't dump the shirt," he warned softly, "I'm going to rip it off. And the supply is dwindling."

She stared at him a moment, a provoking gleam in her eyes, then with deliberate slowness, she undid the top button. Nick watched her, so intent on each lazy movement he stopped breathing altogether. God, the woman did know how to torment the hell out of him. Her eyes never wavered from his as she dragged out the act of disrobing, knowing damned well she was slowly driving him up the wall. His pulse kicked into high gear when she languidly let the fabric droop down her shoulders, and it was all he could do to keep from reacting. Slowly, so slowly, she let the shirt slip down her arms, inch by inch revealing a little more flesh. Nick felt as though he were on the verge of asphyxiation when the garment finally slithered down over Sydney's breasts and puddled on the floor at her feet.

Released from the agony of waiting, Nick inhaled air like a drowning man. Grabbing her wrist, he pulled her down on top of him. "What are you trying to do, finish me off for good?"

Bracing her arms on either side of his head, she eased her thighs between his, then brushed her mouth along his neck with tormenting lightness. "I just wanted to make sure I had your attention."

That wrung a low, shaky laugh out of him, and he pressed her tighter against the thick ache in his groin. "God, woman. You've had my full attention all day." He shifted his legs, adjusting to the width of her hips, then he grasped her head and held it steady as he ran his tongue along her bottom lip. "The forecast is for a long, hard, wet night, so be prepared."

A tremor coursed through her as he moved beneath her, his movement slow, specific and erotic as he tormented her in return. Her voice was unsteady. "Can we expect a little urgency in there?"

Her hair slipped between his fingers as he drew her head down, his mouth grazing hers. "Whatever you want. Just help me, Syd. Help me make it through the night." She shuddered again, and all coherent thought fragmented in his mind. He loved her. He would love her until the day he died, and even beyond that. She was his. The night was theirs. And the shadows were gone.

Harlequin Superromance.

COMING NEXT MONTH

#410 JENNY KISSED ME • Cara West
Sam Grant was flabbergasted when kennel owner Jenny
Hunter transformed his rambunctious fox terrier into an
obedient pet within a few short weeks. Jenny seemed to
have a special relationship with the animals she trained.
Sam sensed depths beneath Jenny's professional
exterior that he wanted to explore, but Jenny didn't
even seem willing to test the waters!

#411 CHOICE OF A LIFETIME • Barbara Kaye
Matt Logan, one of three contenders for the coveted
presidency of the Hamilton House restaurant
conglomerate, finds himself faced with the most
difficult choice of his life: achieving a lifetime goal, or
sacrificing his ambition for the woman he loves....

#412 BLESSING IN DISGUISE • Lorna Michaels
In an attempt to find out who was behind a series of
kidnappings in Houston, investigative reporter Greg
Allen went undercover—as a priest! But his new role as
"Father Gregory" became a frustrating one when social
worker Julie Whitaker insisted on keeping her distance
from a man who was definitely off-limits!

#413 SILVER GIFTS, GOLDEN DREAMS
• Megan Alexander
Brad wanted a condo. Erica wanted a house. Then he let
his mother move in with them, and she wanted their
privacy back. But worst of all, he seemed attracted to
the shapely phys-ed instructor down the block. Erica's
golden dreams lay in tatters. She loved Brad. But would
their silver anniversary be their last?

Praise for Rose Pressey
and
If You've Got It, Haunt It

"Rose Pressey's books are fun!"
—Janet Evanovich

"A delightful protagonist, intriguing twists, and a fashionista ghost combine in a hauntingly fun tale."
—Carolyn Hart

"If you're a fan of vintage clothing and quirky ghosts, *If You've Got It, Haunt It* will pique your interest."
—Denise Swanson

"Chic and quirky heroine Cookie Chanel and a supporting cast of small-town Southern characters are sure to charm lovers of high fashion and murderous hi-jinks alike."
—Jennie Bentley

"A delightful mystery full of Southern charm, vintage fashion tips, a ghostly presence, and a puzzler of a mystery."
—Jenn McKinlay

"Fun, fast-paced, and fashionable . . . a sheer delight."
—Kate Carlisle

Also by Rose Pressey

The Bayou Series
Lost on the Bayou

The Hadley Wilds Series
Dead Girl's Guide to Style

Maggie, P.I. Mystery Series
Crime Wave
Murder Is a Beach

The Halloween LaVeau Series
Forever Charmed
Charmed Again
Third Time's a Charm

The Rylie Cruz Series
How to Date a Werewolf
How to Date a Vampire
How to Date a Demon

The Larue Donovan Series
Me and My Ghoulfriends
Ghouls Night Out
The Ghoul Next Door

The Mystic Café Series
No Shoes, No Shirt, No Spells
Pies and Potions

The Veronica Mason Series
Rock 'n' Roll Is Undead

A Trash to Treasure Crafting Mystery
Murder at Honeysuckle Hotel
Honeysuckle Homicide

The Haunted Renovation Mystery Series
Flip That Haunted House
The Haunted Fixer Upper